Set Fire to Sicily

'We'll be a republic by Whitsuntide,' said Blasio. His wrestler's face was glowing with hope. 'No more King, Charles or Pere. Government for the people.'

The others were all nodding and murmuring with eagerness, but I was puzzled by the timing. Did they mean to rise against the French, or didn't they? 'Whitsuntide?' I said. 'That could be too late. All the French in the island will have gone to attack Constantinople.'

Andrea looked at me with narrow eyes. 'If you want to help us kill Frenchmen,' he said slowly, 'I promise you you'll have your chance. Before the Angevin fleet sails for Corfu we will attack. They won't know what's hit them.'

SET FIRE TO SICILY

A MARCELLO D'ESTARI STORY

Jane Heritage

First published in 1997 by
Virgin Publishing Ltd
332 Ladbroke Grove
London W10 5AH

Jacket illustration by Mike Posen

Typeset by TW Typesetting, Plymouth, Devon

Printed and bound by
Mackays of Chatham PLC, Lordswood, Chatham, Kent

ISBN 1 852 27614 2

CONTENTS

Dedication
Edessa, where it began

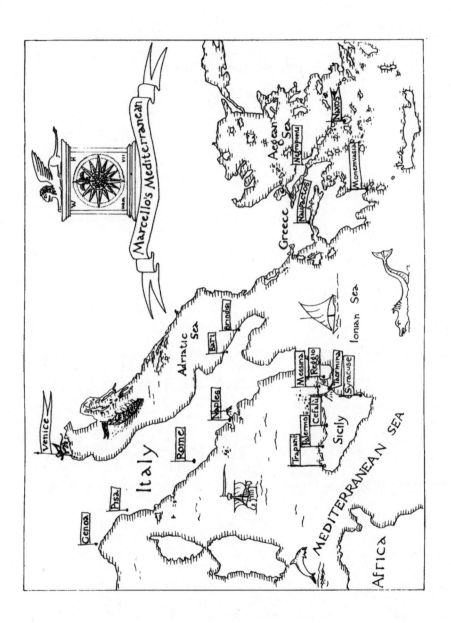

SET FIRE TO SICILY

DECEMBER 1281

ONE

Our orders would be waiting in Naxos. If we ever got there.

The Aegean was getting its breath together for a real winter storm, and there was nowhere on the Greek mainland where our galley could take refuge. The ports and castles were back under Byzantine control, and the Byzantines have no love for Venice. We had to make the Cyclades, or risk ending up on a Greek gallows. The crew looked askance at me. It was my fault that they were in this mess.

The wind came straight down from the Steppes. The snow it carried turned to sleet and stung our faces, and the seas were choppy and dangerous. The rowers stood by their shipped oars, wincing every time a wave struck us. A big enough wave could break every oar. We shouldn't even have left port in such heavy weather.

We scudded before the wind under a storm sail. The galley cleaved through the waves, shipping so much water that the master set the rowers to bailing out through the rowing-ports. The three long scarlet standards, embroidered with the golden Lion of St Mark, snapped and rattled above our heads. The sky looked murderous.

At last our lookout screeched, 'Naxos, sir! Port beam!'

'Port beam? By God –' The captain hurried to the rail and stared out through the gloom. There was Naxos, to the north, with Paros beside it. The wind had driven us almost past the channel that led to the harbour.

For three breaths the captain stared in silence. I knew what he was thinking. If we passed Naxos there was no safe harbour for leagues, and the rising sea would swamp us. But if he used the oars in this heavy sea to try to row us into the channel, he risked snapping every blade, killing the rowers, leaving the ship helpless.

He turned from the rail, his jaw set, and roared, 'Oars!' After a beat of unbelieving silence the master below deck shouted the orders and the oars rattled down from the rowing-ports. I could have stayed with the captain, but I hate having nothing to do when there's trouble. I ran below deck and found an unmanned oar. It made the wound on my arm open up again, but it was better than waiting to drown.

The rowing-master nodded approvingly when he saw me keeping the stroke. I knew what I was about. I was a rower myself once, when I was eighteen and wanted to see the world and forget how miserable I was.

I needed all the experience I had got. The ship was heeling so violently that sometimes our blades missed the sea entirely, and there was water around our ankles. But we were rowing for our lives. We heaved and sweated and at last we turned her in the teeth of the wind and just managed to crawl in to the channel between Paros and Naxos. It was a little calmer there, and in less than an hour we brought her in behind the safety of the big new mole protecting Naxos harbour. We rested on the oars and coasted across the still water and everyone on board sighed, officers, sailors, rowers and me.

I left the rowers congratulating each other and walked up to join the captain under the awning on the stern. The exercise had made me sticky, but I slung my fur-lined cloak around my shoulders to keep off the cold blowing rain. I jerked my head at the town before us and said, 'Looks good.'

Naxos town was a fine sight, and not just because we had barely reached it. The renegade Venetian Dukes of Naxos were great builders, and there was a good modern harbour sheltered behind the mole, complete with wharves, berths, splendid brick-built warehouses and a small arsenal. Beyond the harbour the town spread up the hillside, a close-packed huddle of buildings studded with the dark green of citrus trees. The lower half was old Greek, with little square houses washed in white and a domed Orthodox church. The upper town clustered around the castle, sheltered by its heavy walls, and it looked distinctly Venetian. There were seven tall stone towers belonging to the most important families on the island, a new cathedral with a campanile and brightly-polished bells, and a few big mansions with round-headed doorways and shuttered windows. In the summer the whole town would smell of myrtle, and even in cold winter rain it was attractive.

The captain was a surly devil. He didn't think much of putting his ship at risk to rescue a spy, and he didn't deign to answer me.

We examined the other shipping in silence. There were Naxian and Venetian merchantmen warped into the quay and the usual covey of fishing smacks pulled up on the beach. And in one quiet corner there was a lean, small, fit-looking galley, as different from the round-bellied merchantmen as a greyhound from a lapdog, heeled over against the harbour wall and apparently refitting after a rough passage.

'That galley's Genoese,' said the captain pensively. I had already noticed the Genoese badge on her pennon. 'And she doesn't look exactly ship-shape.'

The sight of a Genoese galley unable to fend for itself was bound to bring out his most piratical instincts, but he was being undiplomatic. 'We aren't at war with Genoa,' I reminded him, 'and Venice's writ doesn't run here. Don't even think about it. I'm in enough trouble already.'

He looked at me as if I was adding insult to injury. 'If the Doge had the brains he was born with, he'd ban the sons of whores from all our ports.'

'I'm sure that he'd love to. But the Duke of Naxos doesn't take orders from the Doge.' Which is ironic, when you consider that the original Duke of Naxos, Marco Sanudo, was given the Duchy eighty years back because he was the then Doge's nephew. That particular piece of nepotism miscarried. Sanudo promptly developed delusions of grandeur and declared the Cyclades independent. So while we might feel irritated to see our deadly rivals the Genoese brazenly refitting in Naxos town, there wasn't much we could do about it. And if you ask me, this proves that whenever a man sees the chance to grab individual power, he forgets his loyalties, his principles and his friends. Kings, dukes, emperors, they're all the same.

We berthed without incident and the captain announced his intention of going straight up to the Venetian residency by the Castello for his orders. That was fine by me. One of the advantages of operating undercover is that somebody else gets to do the dull administration. We agreed a rendezvous and I sauntered off along the harbour front to find a bite to eat. I had left a débâcle behind me in Monemvasia on the mainland, my arm was aching with the cold, and I wanted comforting.

I like Naxos. The Sanudi keep it clean and tidy, and because it isn't Venetian it is not a main trading station, so it doesn't stink of pigs and cargoes the way the great bases of Modon and Coron do. If the weather had been fair I would have enjoyed a stroll along the harbour front, but it was windy and threatening rain. Like a homing pigeon, I headed straight for my favourite tavern.

I have travelled around the Mediterranean for the last ten years, and in all my regular ports I know where to turn for company. Naxos is fairly small, so as far as I'm concerned it's a one-girl town. Two would have been bound to find out about each other, which is a recipe for aggravation. The current girl worked at the Golden Lion tavern, which was situated conveniently close to the harbour and served Venetian specialities fit to make a sailor homesick.

The tavern was busy, like all places with a roof when it rains. It was full of fishermen and sailors, with a fair sprinkling of landsmen and even a couple of Greek priests in black robes. Their tall hats almost brushed against the smoky roof-beams. I managed to find an unoccupied seat in a warm corner by the fire. The place smelled of fish stew and the customers. There were cats everywhere, and a lean silver tabby with eyes like almonds came and wreathed itself around my ankles on the off chance that I might order something to eat. The landlord emerged from behind a barrel of Cyprus wine, looking harassed. I asked for a plate of fish stew and a jug of red.

A boy brought the wine at once with half a loaf of bread. I was hungry, and I dipped the bread in the wine while I waited for my meal. The smell of the stew was making my mouth water. One of the Orthodox priests was absorbing a large bowl of it, filtering it noisily through his beard. Disgusting.

A round, dirty hand put a loaded plate in front of me and soft lips brushed my ear. I looked up smiling into Gratiosa's face. She looked like one of the cats, furry and almond-eyed. There was a cooking smut next to her snub nose. She said in a voice that was throaty with welcome, 'Welcome, Marcello.'

'Gratiosa!' A roar from behind the barrel of Cyprus wine. The landlord was her father, of course. He never liked me. I turned up from time to time, spent thinly and devalued his daughter. She glanced over her shoulder and then said quickly, 'Come round the back when you're done.'

The stew was good. I took my time over it. I've always found that anticipation enhances satisfaction. When I had finished I gave the bones to the cat, tossed a Venetian coin onto the table and went out the front door. Then I circled purposefully around the low dingy building and went in again at the back.

Gratiosa was waiting for me. She put her finger to her lips and caught hold of my hand, towing me back out of the door and across the little frowsty courtyard to the storehouse. We'd been there before. I kissed her eagerly as the door closed. She tasted of steam and cooking, a comforting taste.

I eased her down onto a heap of flour sacks and lowered my body onto her. She was as warm as new bread and had more curves than the plump bags of flour. I was already hard for her. It was cold in the storehouse, but she begged me to take my damp tunic off and told me that she would keep me warm. When I obliged she saw the bandage on my arm and fussed over it for a while, but I hadn't come to her for medical advice. I kissed her again and put my hand inside her coarse dress and she decided not to worry about my wound.

Her thighs opened to admit me, soft and white and welcoming. As she had promised, I didn't notice the cold. Warmth distilled from her plump body underneath me and her silken flesh around me, and soon I was panting and sweating with effort. She liked me to be fierce. I bit her neck like a mating tom cat and she wailed and dug her dirty nails into my labouring buttocks. I snarled with pleasure and pounded into her so hard that ripples flowed up her dimpled body every time I lunged. When I dragged myself out of her, only just in time, I roared like a bull.

Afterwards I lay on her, breathless and dripping. She held on to me and said, 'Are you staying this time?'

She always asked me, though the answer was always the same. I pulled back from her and pushed my damp hair out of my eyes. 'Just passing through, *mia cara*.'

Her round breasts lifted and fell with a sigh. 'You don't care about me.'

'Of course I do.' No word of a lie. I've never had a woman I wasn't fond of. Well, that's not strictly true. Not for ten years, anyway. 'But my business keeps me travelling, sweetheart. You know I come here when I can.'

'My father wants me to get wed.' That was a common threat, too.

'Luck to the bride, then. What shall I give you as a bride-gift?'

'Oh, Marcellino, I hate you.' She caught hold of me and pulled me down on top of her to prove how much she hated me.

I emerged a little later, combing my hair with my fingers and tugging down my tunic. I felt pleasantly weary and much, much better. There's nothing like a vigorous bout of uncomplicated, earthy fornication to take your mind from a brush with death.

Gratiosa's future husband would have his work cut out if he was going to keep up with her. I could see him having more horns than a snail.

The captain and I were due to meet at a harbourside tavern as the bells rang for Vespers. It was coming on to dark now and I went back towards the harbour, lifting the hood of my cloak against the strengthening rain. Thanks to Gratiosa I wasn't feeling the cold. I emerged onto the harbour front near the little Genoese galley and stood in the shadows under a chandler's awning to watch them working on her.

'Well met. Or maybe not,' said a voice in Genoese dialect. I concealed a start and turned to look into a face I knew well.

'Daniele,' I said, not smiling. I can speak Genoese, but I replied in Venetian. 'Small sea, isn't it?'

'Were you on the galley that came in today?' We must have looked like colleagues as much as rivals. We were both dressed in quiet, unremarkable clothes, long hooded cloaks and dark tunics of sober-coloured cloth and soft short boots. Agents don't often get the chance to wear silk and their best jewels. We were even about the same age, just the right side of thirty, though I am dark and Daniele was tall and fair and craggy with smallpox scars. It was a shame, he should have been handsome. There but for the grace of God –

I nodded. 'And you're refitting,' I said, with a jerk of my head towards the Genoese galley. 'Had a rough trip?'

'Coming back from the Black Sea we hit a squall. Do you want a drink?'

'I've got an appointment.' We stood for a moment in silence. Daniele was a Genoese agent, working for them as I worked for Venice. We had encountered each other often enough to know that if our cities were not enemies we would have been friends. But we kept our distance. Venice and Genoa wavered between armed peace and open war, and at any time we might be called upon to try to kill each other. Our conversation was symptomatic. He spoke in his dialect, I spoke in mine.

Presently Daniele said, 'The word is out that Venice and King Charles of Anjou are planning to invade the Byzantine Empire.'

'Everybody knows it,' I agreed, 'since we signed the treaty.'

'You really think that Venice can win back a half and a quarter of the Empire?' He shook his head. 'It won't happen.'

'Why not? Charles of Anjou and Venice make a strong combination. And the Emperor has troubles all over the East. He's a sitting duck.'

'Even if you beat the Emperor, Charles will make sure that he gets the lion's share, the wily French fox.'

Now Daniele might have something there. I would personally have preferred the Republic to win back its possessions without the help of a king, and especially the cold, ambitious, unprincipled Charles of Anjou. But the Council of Forty believed that Charles would make a good ally, and who was I to disagree? 'We can manage him,' I said, with more conviction than I felt.

'I bet you ten florins it all comes to nothing by this time next year.'

That made me suspicious. I looked hard into Daniele's narrow blue eyes. 'You know something I don't? Are you betting on a certainty?'

'Oh, come on, Marcello.' He opened his big bony hands, the picture of innocence. 'That wouldn't be honourable, would it? I swear I have no information you couldn't get.'

I didn't really think he would lie to me, not on a wager at least, but ten florins is a lot of money. I hesitated, and Daniele grinned. 'Are you a man or a mouse?' he demanded. 'Any patriotic Venetian would jump at the chance of a quick profit.'

'Done, you dog.' I spat on my hand and held it out and he took it. We had never shaken hands before. It felt strange.

Behind us the bells began to ring for Vespers. I glanced over my shoulder and detached myself from Daniele. 'I have to go. See you around the Mediterranean.'

'If I win my bet, I'll be in touch,' he called after me. 'This time next year, Marcello. Remember it.'

He sounded hellishly confident. I felt uncomfortable, as if there was a hole in my purse and I was leaving a trail of lost coins behind me in the muddy street.

Two

January rain and a high tide do not make the best of Venice. However, the miserable weather suited my mood. The Security Committee had summoned me and I wasn't looking forward to it. It is never pleasant to give an explanation of failure.

There weren't any boats about, so I walked from my house through the narrow submerged streets, jumping from doorway to doorway to try to keep the water from my boots. I had been summoned to appear before the second bell, and my route should have been full of the bustle of one of the great trading and manufacturing centres of the world: weavers, carpenters, smiths of every sort, ivory carvers, intarsia-makers and mosaicists all busily at work in their workshops, apprentices and messenger boys running to and fro, women doing the shopping or snatching an opportunity to gossip between one window and the next. But everywhere was deathly quiet. When I emerged onto the Piazzetta, the small square that links the Piazza San Marco to the Lagoon, I understood why.

The crowds had to be seen to be believed. People stood shoulder to shoulder in six inches of water. The rain was thickened with a veil of sweaty steam. The west side of the Piazzetta, opposite the Doge's Palace and next to the Campanile, is lined with three-storey brick buildings with handsome arcades, and people of the better sort were hanging out of the windows and dangling from walls and balconies, wherever they could get a grip. I glanced up and saw that every window of the palace was occupied too, filled by those patricians influential enough to command a view from the Doge's rooms. The white stone arches framed noblemen and women smothered in silk damask and fur, with gold and gems glittering on their velvet-gloved hands.

I stood for a moment, running my eyes over the faces. I didn't find who I was looking for, but I did see my father, in a good position as befitted his station as one of Venice's council of Forty

10

patrician rulers, with his wife Isabella beside him. She was wrapped warmly in a cloak and hood lined with sable, but her cheeks were still flushed with cold. She nursed a tiny white lapdog in her fur-lined silk sleeve, while my father drank from a chased silver cup, no doubt enjoying warm spiced wine to keep the cold at bay.

He didn't see me, but I was used to that. I returned my attention to the crowd. I had missed the big Christmas procession and it wasn't Epiphany yet, so why all the excitement?

All soon became clear. Between the two marble pillars which stand on the waterfront – spoils of a war with Genoa, by the way – there was a tall scaffold erected with a stake in the centre, surrounded by piles of brushwood. An execution by burning, not common at all, and as popular a diversion as the biggest religious procession. I hadn't heard about it, but then when I arrived last night I had delivered my report to the Committee secretary and gone straight home to the luxury of a meal cooked by Lucia, a visit to the local bath house, and my own bed.

'What's going on?' I asked the man in front of me.

'Burning a bugger,' he said succinctly, without even turning round.

The penalty for proven sodomy in Venice is death at the stake. Giving them a taste in this life of what they can expect in the next, if you ask me. I would set light to the wood myself if the executioner was taken sick.

But I have never been a great execution watcher, especially when it is raining. I pushed and waded my way through the crowd towards the far side of the Piazzetta, beside the Campanile, where the Security Committee met. They used a room in a big building otherwise completely occupied by tax collectors and customs officials, boring, subfusc people. If anyone saw you going in they assumed you were off to complain about your latest tax demand. That would certainly have suited my expression.

Of course the whole of the Committee was out with the other noble judges watching justice done, so I had to wait outside the anteroom for them to come back, tapping my toe with anxiety and impatience. I had a good view: one of the tall windows outside the Committee chamber directly overlooked the Piazzetta. I found myself a warm spot near a brazier and stood among a crowd of well-dressed tax collectors, shrinking my wet cloak in the heat.

From the great Campanile the bell began to toll. It was the

second chime of the *marangona*, the bell that marks the Venetian working day. It should have signalled the time for workmen to take their morning break, but they had better entertainment today. Today the bell rang for a man's death.

The last stroke of the bell was drowned in a great fierce roar of glee from the crowd. They were bringing the criminal out. He was a grizzled middle-aged man, dressed just in his shirt. He looked as any middle-aged man would look dressed in just a shirt on a wet winter day, huddled and shivering and cheese-coloured with cold.

Some priest shrived him and then they pushed him up towards the stake. He began to fight and cry out, and the crowd shouted encouragement to the men dragging him up the ladder. He struggled like a mad dog, but they got him up there and tied his hands around the stake. His shirt was stained with the shit of fear.

The wood was wet and hard to light. When they finally persuaded it to catch it smoked. The crowd were disappointed, because smoke kills a man fast and you can't see anything. The criminal screamed and started to cough, at which point I turned away and said to one of the tax collectors beside me, 'What did he do?'

'Sodomy on a minor,' said the tax collector, a big jolly-looking man with a splendid paunch under his worsted and fur robe. He flipped self-consciously at the heavy gold and enamel chain he wore around his neck, showing off his substance. 'His page. The boy complained to his older brother. The investigators found physical evidence when they examined the page, and he,' he waved a fat beringed hand towards the stake, now invisible behind a pall of smoke, 'confessed.'

'Under torture?'

'Oh, yes.'

'Serve him right,' I said, turned my back on the window and folded my arms.

Presently the show was over and people began to trickle back into the building. My fat friend went off to massage another set of tax assessments. The secretary of the Committee opened the anteroom door, saw me and summoned me with a polite jerk of his narrow chin.

'You're not popular,' he said as we crossed the anteroom. I shed my wet cloak and slung it over a chest in a corner. My boots were beyond help. 'I hope you have a good excuse for what happened at Monemvasia.'

He didn't deserve a reply. He opened the door to the Committee chamber and announced me. I walked in, swept off my hat and bowed elegantly low. I like to look urbane.

'Marcello D'Estari.' The Chairman of the Security Committee sat in the centre of a long narrow table, dressed from head to foot in scarlet. He answered only to the Doge, Giovanni Dandolo, which made him a very powerful man. Plenty of people expected him to be elected to succeed Dandolo in due course, which would be nothing but good for Venice. There were four other men flanking him, two on either side, which was more than usual. I had seen two of them on the Committee before: two were new. They were dressed in patrician's robes, with the wide red capes over their shoulders which were the badge of their office. The secretary sat at the end, dressed in rusty black and hunched among his mountains of papers. I stood, my hands hitched in my belt, uncomfortably aware that the heat from the great fireplace was making my wet tunic steam.

The Chairman said, 'Ser D'Estari, this is Signor Pirano dela Mota, a new member of the Committee. And this is Signor Vallerio Dolfin, co-opted for this meeting alone.'

I bowed again. Both of the new members looked at me with blank faces. They were middle-aged noblemen, the same age and rank as my father, with the level, haughty expressions of men accustomed to influence. Dela Mota I did not know, but ten years ago I had known quite a lot about Signor Dolfin. He had not changed much: a handsome, sturdily built man with heavy features and thick grey curls under his white linen coif and his expensive beaver-fur hat. He had seen me before, but he did not remember. It made me uncomfortable to have him sitting there. Co-opted for one meeting? Why?

'My lord,' the Chairman said to dela Mota, 'I believe that you had some questions for Ser D'Estari.'

Was this the inquisition on Monemvasia? Dela Mota hitched forward the folds of his heavy scarlet robe and folded his hands on the table in front of him. He was wearing velvet gloves embroidered with gold thread and lined with ermine. A great diamond glittered on his thumb, and I could see by the bumps on the gloves' fingers that he had rings beneath them as well. He looked like the sort of man who would know every coin by name.

Dela Mota fixed me with a cold beady eye and I looked back at him perhaps a little more coolly than was entirely courteous.

He said in a thin voice, 'I am new to this Committee and I wish to form my own judgement on the men who serve it.'

That in itself made me bristle. I serve the Republic of Venice, not the men of the Committee, and I have followed my own conscience rather than my orders before now. But dela Mota did not seem to notice that I stiffened. He steepled his fingers together and continued, 'You are a bastard son of Signor Domenico Bono, yes?'

I wonder if all illegitimate sons are as sensitive as me. Whenever I am asked that question in that typical superior, drawling tone I want to grab the questioner by the lapels and shake him and yell into his face, 'Listen, you ignorant idiot, my father loved my mother. He would have married her if he could!'

'That is correct, my lord,' I said, setting my jaw.

Dela Mota consulted the secretary in an undertone, then pressed on. 'Your mother was Elisaveta, called L'Estari, licensed prostitute.'

She was a courtesan. She was his mistress. She lived in the house he gave her. She bore him his first son. From the time he set up her household until the day she died she never lay with another man.

I kept myself very still. 'Yes, my lord.'

His eyebrows were dark and hairy, like two caterpillars crawling across his face above his thin nose. He lifted them now. 'Most noble bastards use their father's name. To advance them in life, shall we say? Your father is one of the Forty, it would do you good to make your relationship to him public. Why do you call yourself D'Estari?'

That was none of his business. 'My father and mother decided it, my lord, and I have seen no reason to change it.'

'Humph.' He sat for a moment, considering his next question. I looked into his face with hatred, wondering how many bastards he had littered about Venice. Had his maids and his girl-slaves laid newborn infants before the church door? The next time I was at liberty I would amuse myself by digging out some real filth about Signor dela Mota and splattering it all around the Rialto market. The streets would buzz with it as far as Spinalunga.

'Is your father aware of the work you undertake for the Committee?'

'Only in part, my lord. My lord the Doge approached me personally after his election to ask me if I would act as an agent of the Republic.'

Dela Mota looked startled and turned to the Chairman for confirmation. After a moment he said, 'Why did the Doge know of you?'

'I operated as a freelance in the Aegean for some time, working against the pirates,' I said. 'In one operation I saved a Dandolo ship with a very valuable cargo. This was before my lord was elected Doge. He thanked me personally and employed me sometimes after that to protect his convoys.'

He nodded, pursing his lips. 'That is all,' he said, sitting back and nodding to the Chairman. There was a rustle and the Committee members looked at each other. Then the secretary prompted, 'My lords: Monemvasia.'

The next series of questions was as bad as I had expected. It really hadn't been my fault, but it is hard to explain field work to a quintet of noble merchants sitting in a comfortable chamber. I did not come off smelling of roses, but in the end they seemed more or less satisfied that there was nothing I could have done differently.

At last the Chairman said, 'Well, Marcello.' My Christian name now. Thank God for that. I bowed. 'We did not recall you simply to put you on the griddle over Monemvasia.' He looked at a paper before him. 'I understand that you speak both Arabic and Sicilian dialect.'

For a moment I didn't reply. My stomach turned over. I could feel the blood draining out of my face, and I put my hand to my forehead to conceal it. The Chairman was watching me with his eyebrows raised, and I swallowed hard and managed an answer. 'Yes, my lord, that is correct.'

'How do you come to speak Sicilian?' demanded dela Mota.

You fat-arsed lapdog, read my papers if you want to know. Why make me tell you? I would have liked to grind his face in the dirt. I said evenly, 'I was a slave in Sicily for nearly two years, my lord.'

'A slave?' he sounded astonished. 'A Venetian citizen a slave?'

'My ship was wrecked,' I said. 'The survivors were picked up by Barbary pirates and they sold us. I was a slave worker in a sugar factory for six seasons.'

'How did you escape?' he asked, his caterpillar brows arching skywards.

Vicarious excitement was what he was after. He was not going to get it from me. I appealed to the Chairman. 'Is this relevant, my lord?'

Dela Mota looked offended, but the Chairman nodded. 'Signor dela Mota,' he said, 'the secretary will explain to you later, if you wish. Ser D'Estari's full history is known to us. Marcello,' he said, 'you are aware that the Emperor Michael of Byzantium is intriguing against Charles of Anjou, King of Sicily.'

'Yes, my lord. It is his only hope to prevent the invasion.'

'We have reason to believe that the Emperor is fomenting conspiracy in Sicily itself. The King of Aragon is involved. We know that Byzantine gold is entering Sicily. We are seriously concerned. If there should be a rebellion in Sicily, it might prejudice the joint Venetian and Angevin attack on the Empire. We have tried to warn King Charles, directly and through our connections at the Angevin court, but he will not listen to us. Immediate action is required.'

'In Sicily,' I said, with a sinking heart. I had hoped that I would never have to set foot on that accursed island again. Could I refuse the assignment? I wanted to.

'In Sicily. King Charles's invasion fleet is assembling off Messina and his land forces are in Messina and across the straits in Naples. The fleet will sail in the spring to rendezvous with ours off Corfu. Signor Vallerio Dolfin,' Dolfin inclined his head to me and I acknowledged him with a small bow, 'has been appointed the Republic's naval advisor to the Angevin invasion force. He will be going to Sicily within the week. We wish you to go with him and work as our agent to uncover the network by which Byzantine gold is distributed. If you can discover the agents of conspiracy and remove them, so much the better.' He leant forward, holding my eyes. 'Without the Angevins we cannot make a direct attack on Byzantium. With them, we stand a chance of recovering all our possessions in the Aegean. Do you understand, Marcello?'

Of course I understood. The ambition of Venice is to control Mediterranean trade. To do that we need to control the ports, and as much of the hinterland as counts. 'Yes, my lord,' I said. 'But just because Byzantine gold is making its way into Sicily, it doesn't mean that Charles's expedition is doomed.'

'No. And that is why we are sending you to make sure that wherever that gold is going, it does us no harm. The Angevin fleet must sail in the spring, Marcello. It must sail.' He nodded to the secretary, who came to me with a thick bundle of papers. Agents' reports, copy bills of lading, notes of ship movements, lists of names.

'Signor Dolfin will be resident in Messina,' said the Chairman. 'It will be difficult for him to find reason to leave that city. We will rely on you for intelligence from the rest of the island. You will report to Signor Dolfin unofficially, by whatever method you think fit. Officially the Republic will not know of your presence in Sicily.'

Typical. Diplomatic immunity for the noble lord in charge, and nothing for the poor hapless agent. I said, 'I understand, my lord.'

'It will be better, my lord, if you deal with Ser D'Estari in private,' said the Chairman, turning to Vallerio Dolfin. He jumped and bowed. I would have said that he was nervous. 'The fewer people know of any detail, the better. He is experienced in these matters. He will explain to you what you need to do.'

'Yes, my lord,' said Dolfin, bowing again. I swear he was pale.

'My lord,' I said, and the Committee swung as one man to look at me. 'My lord, the Byzantine Emperor's treasury is deep, and it takes a decoy to catch a duck. Will funds be available to me?'

There was a rustle from the Committee members. Dela Mota looked as though he had smelt a fart. The Chairman frowned, then said, 'If it is necessary.'

'It will be necessary,' I assured him. 'I will need access to gold: Byzantine gold, for preference.'

'You might abscond with it and vanish!' exclaimed dela Mota.

'My lord Chairman knows me better,' I said, looking into the Chairman's eyes. He held my gaze for a moment, then nodded. Dela Mota subsided, muttering, and to conceal my pleasure at having put him down I turned to Signor Dolfin and said, 'I will wait on you at Ca' Dolfin later in the day, my lord, if it please you.'

He nodded slowly, still looking apprehensive. The Chairman consulted the secretary, then said, 'Thank you, Marcello. That will be all.'

Outside the chamber in the corridor over the Piazzetta the air still smelt of smoke and burning flesh. I stood leaning against a wall, my arms wrapped tight around myself, trying not to shiver.

Sicily. And with Fiammetta's father.

THREE

W hen I mention Lucia, people start making assumptions. Perhaps I am married and the various girls I visit around the Mediterranean are simply victims of a philandering and faithless nature. Wrong. I'm not married, at least. Or perhaps I like my creature comforts and so I keep a woman at home, a slave perhaps, to cook and clean and warm my bed. Wrong again. I could afford a girl-slave, even a pretty one: but this is not the explanation either. Venice is the only port that I don't have a girl in.

Lucia must be well into her sixties. I have begun to notice that she looks older each time I return from another long absence. She stoops almost double now, and the lines multiply on her face like spiders' webs in an unswept room. I suppose she will die in the foreseeable future and one day when I come back the house will be cold and dark. I don't like to think about it. When my mother was a courtesan Lucia was her tiring-maid, and a good one. When my father set my mother up as his mistress Lucia became her housemaid. She brought me into the world. I still sleep in the bed where I was born in the house that was my mother's, and Lucia is still my housemaid. She knows everything about me, and she is unshockable.

When I came into the house she was mending a tear in a shirt sleeve, a memento of the crossbow bolt at Monemvasia. It's amazing how many of my clothes she has had to stitch, one way and another. She frowned when she saw my face.

'Marco.' My mother used to call me Marco, and Lucia still does. Nobody else does. 'Bad news?'

I shook my head and said, 'Yes,' giving out mixed messages, as usual. She raised her eyebrows, but said nothing else. She never says much. A tiring-woman either chatters non-stop, or she learns silence. 'I have to go to Sicily.'

'Why?'

Good question. I couldn't answer it at once. I sat down on the stone bench in the wall and looked up at the painted beams of the ceiling. Then I said, 'Fiammetta's father is being sent there.' I would have told someone else that I was a patriot and that it sounded like an important mission, or that I didn't want to be afraid of a place just because it had bad memories, or that I thought some of the Byzantine gold might stick to my pocket. Any of these would have been partly true. But I always told Lucia the real truth.

She looked at me in silence. Her face was pale and pouchy under her thick black veil. After a moment she said, 'I'll get you something to eat,' set down her mending on the little carved table by her stool and went slowly towards the kitchen.

Seeing Vallerio Dolfin had thrown me into a quicksand of memory. Every time I struggled to escape from it it sucked me in deeper. I looked at the stairs with out-of-focus eyes and saw my mother.

'Mama, I'm sleepy.' A nine-year-old whine. 'I want to go to bed.'

She leans over me, dark-haired, dark-eyed, with skin whiter than the clouds. She is thirty-five years old and the most beautiful woman in the world. 'You'll have to sleep down here, caro mio. *Your father is coming.'*

I know already. I know because of her intricately braided hair, the dangling earrings of Byzantine filigree, the subtle paint on her eyelids, the embroidered shift of cotton so gossamer fine that her body gleams through it like the foam on surf. She always looks more beautiful when my father comes. I hate it that she loves him more than me.

The sound of a boat tying up outside. My mother kisses me briefly and rumples my hair then runs to the door and opens it herself, as if she cannot afford a maid. My father stands there, flinging back the hood of his furred velvet cloak. He glances over his shoulder as he comes in, then he embraces my mother and she clings to him. He kisses her and his big ringed hand touches her breast and she makes a little smothered sound as if he has hurt her. I huddle further back into the window seat. He doesn't see me. He stoops and catches her into his arms and lifts her, moving towards the stairs to the upper chamber as if steered by wires. He murmurs to her, 'Elisaveta, Elisaveta, mia bella, carissima,' *and she sighs and stretches up her parting lips.*

They vanish upwards into the shadows, trailing the sounds of their pleasure like gauzy scarves. I wrap my arms around my knees and stare at the staircase, suppressing the tears that scald my eyes.

I hate him.

★   ★   ★

I presented myself at Ca' Dolfin about halfway through the afternoon and was admitted at once. The steward must have been expecting me, for he showed me straight upstairs, above the counting-house and storerooms to the *piano nobile*, the great first-floor reception chamber. I looked around curiously as we ascended. It is odd to have been on the top floor of a house and never have seen the main staircase.

I knew the Dolfin family was wealthy, one of Venice's premier clans, and the house proved it. It was spacious and well appointed, floored with marble and terracotta and polished wood, hung with rich tapestries. The balusters of the stairs were gilded and the wooden roof-beams were painted in brilliant colours. I have more subdued taste, and I preferred my father's house.

The steward showed me into the *piano nobile*, which was empty even of servants. Good: my business was private. He bowed and abandoned me, saying that he would inform the master that I had arrived. I didn't mind waiting, because there was plenty to look at. I sat experimentally in one of two carved wooden chairs with cushions of scarlet Damascus silk embroidered with gold, and ran my hand over the smooth surface of a long table of pale oak from Dalmatia. The walls were covered in tapestries of hunting scenes, and on the wall opposite the window there was even a painting, of the discovery of the body of St Mark. I went and admired it, for paintings in private houses are rare. It was new and the figures were brightly coloured against a burnished gold ground, rather like the new mosaic in the Basilica. Heavy fragrant candles were burning on either side of its gilded wood frame, though it was still light.

The shutters that kept out the draughts from the balcony were half closed, and I pulled them back. The view was splendid, out across the Grand Canal towards the Rialto Bridge. What city in the world is like Venice? Before the bridge and beyond it lay palazzo after splendid palazzo, rows of marble arches and colour-washed stucco and rosy brick, and between them was the most unusual and splendid main street in the world, the Grand Canal. It was thronged with gondolas, barges, sandalos and skiffs, and the air was blue with the shouts of the gondoliers and the bargemen.

It was cold, but I went out onto the balcony. A young lady appeared at the upper window of a palazzo opposite, warmly wrapped in a gown of silk lined with squirrel, lifting her hands to her hair to fix a slipping amber comb. She saw me and smiled, lifting her arched elegant eyebrows suggestively. Normally I would have responded with alacrity, but I couldn't, not here, in Ca' Dolfin. I walked to the end, where the palazzo overhung a little side canal, then leant on the rail and looked down. The ring where I had tied up my sandalo was still there. If I looked up I would see the bottom of Fiammetta's balcony, her tiny roof garden, overhung with the dead brown stems of honeysuckle.

Movement behind me. I took a quick deep breath and composed my face as I turned. Then I stood entirely still. The world blackened. Through a long tunnel of darkness I saw Fiammetta standing before me, brighter than a seraphim, glowing, inestimable. Giant fists grasped my chest, squeezing so tightly that I could not breathe. My heart fluttered and lurched like a wounded bird.

She was whiter than her linen. I suppose she was as startled as me. But she recovered more quickly. After only half a dozen gasps she said, 'Marcello.'

The same voice, quick and light, complex and sweet as a nightingale's. I still couldn't speak. She hesitated, then went on, 'My father sent me to say he'll be with you soon. He – he is with my husband.'

I shook myself back to life. She was turning as if she would leave me. I took a quick step towards her and said, 'Fiammetta.'

She stopped moving, but she did not turn back. Her silver-gilt hair tumbled down her shoulders onto her robe of heavy dark blue silk, ringleted and wreathed with pearls, moonbeams coiled onto midnight. I didn't dare to touch her. I hunted for words. Normally words are easy for me. It made me angry to be tongue-tied.

At last I said, 'Fiammetta. Are you happy?'

She turned then and looked at me. Her dark blue robe was embroidered with crystal and jet, and beneath it she wore a snowy camise edged with a tiny, delicate frill. Her white throat rose from the white linen like a column of ivory. There was a fine chain around her neck made of jet and diamond and pearl strung onto gold, and it glittered as it lifted and fell with the movement of her breathing breasts. Heavy pearls hung from her ears and her eyes were brighter than sapphires. She was like a painting of the Virgin, a miniature of such beauty that its frame is made of massy gold and set with gems. I would have scoured the world for jewels fit to adorn her image.

Her face was very still, as it had been the day she married. She said, 'Why should you care, Marcello, after so many years?'

Fiammetta, I have lurked outside your husband's house to

catch sight of you as you get into your gondola. I know everything about you that a skilled agent can discover. I know you are childless. I know your husband keeps a gaggle of mistresses, I know you beat the slave who dresses your hair. But I don't know your heart, I don't know if you have changed, I only know that I am the same.

I made my lips move in a wry smile and said, 'I'm stubborn.'

No answering smile touched her face. She went to the parapet and took hold of it with her soft white hands and looked down onto the Grand Canal. Her wedding ring was a band of red gold, set with a square-cut diamond. Her expression was quite opaque. Did she hate me, or yearn for me, or had she just forgotten me?

She had not answered, but I had to seize my chance. I took another step towards her, so close that I could have reached out and touched her perfect face. In a low voice I said, 'Fiammetta, my offer still stands. Say the word, and I'll take you anywhere in the world. I've got plenty of money, we could live well.' I expected her to slap my face, but she neither moved nor spoke. Her eyes were as clear as glass. I did not know if she had even heard me. Another step, and I was so close that I could smell her perfume, lilies and ambergris. Was she shivering? 'Fiammetta.'

'Ser D'Estari,' said a loud male voice within the room. I moved violently away from Fiammetta and stood for a second with my eyes shut tightly, gasping. Then I controlled myself and called, 'Here, Signor. We were admiring the view.'

Vallerio Dolfin appeared in the doorway and joined us on the balcony. He was dressed for comfort and leisure in a thick loose robe of scarlet wool lined with marten skins, a matching scarlet hood worn as a hat, and red slippers. 'Splendid, isn't it?' he agreed cheerfully. To Fiammetta he said, 'Thank you, my dear, for amusing my guest. Off with you now. Ask your noble husband to join us.' She gave him a pale smile and lifted her heavy skirts and left us without a backward glance. My heart followed her.

'My daughter Fiammetta,' he said. 'Wife of Aliusio Contarini. He is here with her, I shall introduce you presently. Lovely woman, isn't she? The picture of her mother, God rest her soul. I was lucky in my first marriage.' He rattled on as men will when they are nervous, talking about his dead wife, about Fiammetta, about his second wife and their brood. He said it was cold and we should move inside. I followed him obediently, saying nothing.

Her balcony, warm and heavy-scented with summer. A glowing, golden moon lifting above the ragged fringe of buildings on the horizon. The sounds of the city night below us, cats and dogs wailing and barking, oars splashing on the Grand Canal. My arms around her, thin and wiry: I am eighteen and still growing. Her face turned up to mine, whiter than the moon. The moonlight and her hair pouring together over my caressing hands.

'I love you.' Between kisses. We are both gasping. 'I love you, I love you.'

'Marcello, my darling, my sweetheart.'

Kiss after kiss, succulent and trembling. She is wearing just her shift and a shawl over her narrow shoulders. Her girl's breasts are as round as peaches, firm and tipped with hardness like lemons warm with the sun. My hand moves from her hair, cups one tender swell, strokes it. Her head rolls back and her tongue quivers in my mouth. I want to take her, I ache for her, but she is just fourteen and a virgin and I love her too much.

'Fiammetta, my little flame. Come away with me.'

Her eyes are wide open, I can see the stars in them. For a moment she says nothing. Then her lips move, hesitantly. 'Where?'

'Anywhere. Wherever you want. Rome, Avignon, Constantinople, Acre.' I can't believe that she's listening. My heart is shaking me. 'Anywhere. Come with me.'

'Now?' she asks, looking over her shoulder at the door to her little room where her duenna is sleeping. 'Now?'

This was impulse, I'm not prepared. I have no money with me, nothing. How can it be now? The whole city would be hunting us in the morning. 'Tomorrow,' I say earnestly. 'Tomorrow night I'll come for you. I'll bring all my money, my mother's jewels, there'll be plenty. I'll get a better boat. We'll be out of the city before the dawn.' I gaze in wonder into her eyes, which are shining with tears and the constellations. 'We'll get married. We'll be happy. Fiammetta, I love you.'

'Marcello, mio amore. Marcello.' Her white eyelids shut out the stars. Her arms around me, her lips on my lips, her breast against mine.

Her father was speaking seriously now. I made myself listen. '– not familiar with this sort of work.'

'Don't worry, my lord,' I said, with brazen confidence. 'I'll take care of most things. You can do your job as our advisor to the French fleet and wait to hear from me. When you need to take action, I'll tell you.'

'How?' he asked, looking genuinely puzzled. 'How will you contact me? Surely you won't just walk in to the residency in Messina?'

I found myself smiling at his innocence. 'I'll get messages to you,' I explained. 'We'll arrange a place to leave them and a system of signals. I can't tell you exactly how at this point: it'll depend on the geography. When you get to Sicily you'll hear from me.'

'We won't travel together?'

'No, my lord, of course not. And we must arrange a password, so that you know the message is from me.'

'A password?'

'Something easy to remember. Your daughter's name.' I should have blushed for shame, but I am hardened to deception. Signor Dolfin was looking stunned, as if all this was too much. I didn't feel like making it any easier for him, so I said, 'Are you taking a guard with you, my lord?'

'A guard?' he repeated blankly.

'I need to know how many men I can call on in case of need,' I explained.

Dolfin looked as though he was about to say that Venice had no intention of getting embroiled in violence. But then the door opened and a young nobleman breezed into the room, dressed to kill in a tunic of yellow Greek silk lined with sable, a woven-gold girdle and short soft leather boots that blazed a fashionable red. Even his purse was made of chamois leather and embroidered with gold. His glossy black hair fell to his shoulders in suspiciously regular, tong-shaped curls, and I could smell his pomade.

I knew exactly who he was. He was the tall, dark, handsome young scion of the great Contarinis to whom Signor Dolfin had married his daughter. At their wedding women around me had cooed in astonishment and delight, admiring the beauty of the bride and groom: an allegory of light and dark, Fiammetta all in cloth of silver and her husband in jet-encrusted black. And I had stood, silently fighting tears, clenching my fists as I willed her to turn my way, to look at me just once, just once more. And she had looked at me, and it hadn't helped.

'Aliusio, this is Ser Marcello D'Estari,' Dolfin was saying. 'Ser D'Estari, my son-in-law Aliusio Contarini.' I bowed, wishing that he was dead. Why had Dolfin asked him to join us, anyway?

'This all sounds very exciting,' Contarini gushed. 'Secret work on behalf of the State! I am looking forward to it.'

My researches into Fiammetta's household had convinced me of her husband's deep stupidity. I frowned in disbelief and disapproval. Signor Dolfin saw my expression and looked first uncomfortable, then defensive. 'I am too old,' he said, 'for cloak and dagger work. I shall take Aliusio with me to Sicily and if you need active assistance you shall use him.'

'I do hope you will,' said Contarini with enthusiasm, tapping the gilded hilt of his sword. 'I am ready for anything.'

No such polished peacock could be ready for the sort of dirty dust-up that I tend to get into, though his fistful of rings might come in handy for punching. His idea of fighting was probably a street brawl between the Contarinis and some other noble house, the sort of thing that young bloods get taken up for in the Piazza from time to time, all flashing swords and posturing and swirling cloaks. While I thought of some easy complaisant answer I felt myself beginning to smirk beneath my urbane mask. How often had I wished that Fiammetta was a widow? And here was her husband eager to assist me in what promised to be a difficult and dangerous mission.

Perhaps, for once, Dame Fortune had dealt me a promising hand.

FOUR

xperience tells me that I can grow a beard thick enough to conceal my lean, rather recognisable jaw in about three weeks. I retired for the purpose to the little port of Naupaktos on the southern flank of the Greek mainland. Italians call it Lepanto. It was a pleasant, quiet place to change identity, and when I felt ready to move on I could get a ferry to Patras and head from there to Bari and on round to Sicily.

On arrival I took a room in the lower town among the Greek merchant captains and fishermen. I presented myself as a landlubber who didn't like the look of the weather. The weather obliged, remaining resolutely foul the whole time I was there.

I can pass for a Greek without problems. My mother was from Negroponte and I have the accent of Euboea. Normally I just tell people the truth, which is that my mother was three-quarters Greek and my father Italian, without specifying what sort of Italian or where I was born. If they want to go into details, there are plenty of places I know in Greece in enough depth to pass as my home town, including a few choice bits of elderly gossip just in case I encounter another native.

My room was at the top of a smallish house, owned in time-honoured fashion by a respectable widow. Not many people except respectable widows and widowers have rooms to spare, especially in little places like Naupaktos. The room had a view over the harbour and in the summer it would have been charming, but at Epiphany it was draughty and damp. I bought a rug of bright Arahova wool to keep the chill off the bed. At least the situation meant the room got plenty of light, so I didn't ruin my precious eyes poring over heaps of papers in the gloom.

I had with me the essence of what Venice knew about the conspiracy in Sicily. There wasn't much. Byzantine ships were probably carrying gold and silver direct from Constantinople to Palermo. Some Genoese and Pisan vessels had also been involved. This could appear sinister, but in my view it was inevitable. If you want to move goods or funds about the Mediterranean you are more than likely to use the ships of one of the Italian naval powers, and if Venice is out of the picture that leaves you with Genoa and Pisa to choose from. I didn't want to read more into it than that.

The Aragonese angle was intriguing. King Pere of Aragon's wife, the Infanta Constance, had a claim to the throne of Sicily and it was common knowledge that Pere meant to try to seize it in her name as soon as King Charles's back was turned. King Pere was lurking in North Africa at the moment, pretending to be on Crusade but in reality keeping himself in an ideal place to launch an invasion of the island. Our agents suggested that he was also involved in the Sicilian conspiracy. Again, this seemed unlikely to me. The Byzantine Emperor would be sending his gold in the hope that a rebellion might keep King Charles at home. But if I was the King of Aragon I would want King Charles as far away as possible before I attacked. If he was embroiled in war with Constantinople it would be ideal. I didn't understand how Aragon and Byzantium could both be aiming for the same outcome.

One thing did seem clear. The Sicilians themselves favoured the Queen of Aragon as their next ruler. They wanted to kick out Charles's Angevin Frenchmen, and the sooner the better. The reports said that the French governed Sicily badly: 'rapacious' and 'corrupt' were terms that appeared regularly. I had spent two years there, but I had nothing to add to what I read. You don't gain a clear understanding of domestic political issues when you are struggling for your life in a sugar factory. All I knew was that as far as I was concerned, the Sicilians deserved everything they got.

In general all the information I had was no more than background, interesting enough but useless when it came to arranging an operation. Our agents' suspicions centred on Palermo: surprise, surprise. But there was one very useful titbit. I read it with greed and lovingly burned the paper afterwards.

'One phrase appears to have particular importance, the name of "John of Procida". I once heard a suspect saying, "John of Procida sent me." Note that John of Procida is the Chancellor of Aragon, which may or may not be significant.'

There were other advantages to my lodgings apart from privacy and good natural light. The respectable widow had a brood of children littered around the town, half a dozen assorted sons and daughters, and one still living at home with her, a girl of fifteen or so called Angela. Fifteen is old for a girl not to be married. I guessed that the widow had her eye on this last child as the stay of her old age, someone to look after her when she was past looking after herself.

This would have been a waste. Angela was an advantage in my eyes because she was delectable, honey-gold and nubile as a water-nymph. She was a modest girl, who always wrapped up her red-brown hair in swathes of veil whenever she went out and didn't stray further than the fish market or the church, where she went regularly to hear Mass. Most of the local lads whistled after her in the street but did little more. They knew perfectly well what her mother had in mind for her, and they also knew that the nice little house already belonged to the widow's eldest son and that Angela was likely to come with no dowry other than her person. It was sad to imagine her as a maiden aunt in one of her siblings' houses, growing dry and threadbare and gummy, gossiping as she twirled her distaff on the doorstep.

I would have liked to console her, but I didn't get the chance. A widowed mother who lets out rooms on a short-term basis knows how to cope with single male lodgers, and I never, ever saw Angela on my own. It was mildly frustrating, but after a week I met a fisherman's wife in the market who provided me with a welcoming distraction whenever her husband was out in the boat. She smelt less of fish than might be expected, and her body was very white. I don't think a beard suits me, but she seemed to have no objections. She received my attentions with the enthusiasm I have come to expect and took the edge off my desire for Angela.

After a couple of weeks I was ready to head for Sicily and start work. I destroyed my papers and packed my bags and told the widow I would be leaving the next day. She was polite enough to express regret. I must have paid the rent too readily by half.

I went down to the harbour to negotiate a passage to Patras. I had felt quite relaxed during my thinking time, but now my stomach began to curl like shavings from a plane. It was hard to focus on the job in hand. I went to find the fisherman's wife to distract myself, but her husband was at home and I stayed away. My mind kept filling up with images of Fiammetta and the galley I had rowed to escape from Venice and my enforced stay in Sicily. There was no chance that anyone on the island would recognise me, and I had been free for so many years that they would have no claim on me anyway, but the memories pounded on my shuttered brain like battering rams.

Normally I would have stayed out all evening, drinking the thin local wine in a pleasant tavern and enjoying a meal while I talked to the company. But the thought that I would sail for Sicily tomorrow made me lose my appetite. About an hour before sunset, my ferry arranged, I wandered back through the narrow dim streets of the port to the widow's house.

I move quietly as a matter of course, and the door didn't creak as I entered. The place smelt of steam and soap, like washing-day. It was dark inside the shuttered ground floor. My eyes adjusted fast and I put my hand to the curtain that kept the draughts from the door out of the main living room. Then I heard a splash and something made me put my eye to the gap between the curtain and the wall.

My breath hissed between my teeth. Angela was standing over a big bucket of hot water. She was wearing her shift, but it was half off her, damp and clinging to her round hips like the drapery on a pagan statue. Her hair was piled on the top of her head and she was soaping her breasts. Their pink tips were swollen and stiff with the gentle caress of the water. She didn't know I was standing there. I swallowed hard. My fingers tingled with lust.

She hummed a little tune to herself and rubbed the soap between her hands, then put her palms to her breasts again. They were clean already, she was doing it because it gave her pleasure. She half closed her ivory eyelids and eased down her shift. It fell to the damp floor at her feet. The soap gleamed in the dark curls at the join of her thighs. She pushed her right hand between her legs and sighed as she rubbed it to and fro.

She had to be alone. My luck was in. I could hardly creep up on her, this would have to be a direct assault. I took firm hold of the curtain and flung it back rattling on its rings.

She threw up her head and covered herself with her hands. Her mouth opened to scream, but before the sound came out I was on her, silencing her with my lips. For a moment she struggled. Then I touched the stiff peak of her soapy breast and suddenly she was limp against me, slippery as a mermaid and whimpering with readiness.

'Where's your mother?' I hissed. I am nothing if not cautious.

Her sloe eyes opened wide. 'My sister's baby is coming, she's gone to bring it. She thought you would be gone till after dark.'

'She won't disturb us, then.' Perfect. Perfect! I picked her up: she was light. I kissed her as I carried her across the room and up the stairs. It's a knack. In my little cold room I laid her on the bed. I knew I was right to buy the rug.

For some time everything went according to the rule. When I stripped she gasped, which is always pleasantly flattering, and reached out for me as if she was going to touch a holy relic. Between her slender thighs the moisture wasn't just soap. Her body was the colour of unleavened bread and she tasted sweet. I am fastidious, I always prefer a clean girl. I locked her heels behind my knees and waited a moment, savouring her openness. Then I began to move.

She cried out, not a sound of pleasure. I hesitated and drew back a little. My blood thumped in my temples and my throat. I tried again and again she whimpered, clinging to me and biting her lip.

My heaving chest brushed against her taut nipples. I said softly, 'You're a virgin.'

She nodded. There were tears in her eyes. If she had asked me to stop, perhaps I would have done, I don't know. But she didn't ask me, and I wanted her. She would probably never marry, anyway. I took hold of her wrists and held them, gently but firmly, and then I took what I wanted.

I could have had Fiammetta, that moonlit night on her balcony, and I didn't. She could have been mine, mine by the oldest rite of all, and out of a boy's idiot dreams of chivalry I let her walk away and take her maidenhead to Aliusio Contarini. I was a fool. I have never stopped regretting it.

Angela cried a little at first, but then what I was doing to her took the pain away. After a few moments I let go of her wrists and she reached up for me, her dark eyes wide with amazement. I like pleasing women. As I watched her face I promised myself that whatever happened to her after this, nobody would ever make her feel what I was making her feel now.

Afterwards she cried again, especially when I reminded her that I was leaving in the morning. She seemed to think that what we had done meant I would marry her. I got out of that in the end by saying that I was already married. I gave her gold instead, which didn't insult her as much as you might have expected, and the rug, which had a little scarlet stain on it. Something for her to remember me by.

She hid the gold so that her mother wouldn't find it. Then she dressed and dried her cheeks and went off to her sister's house, where her family was expecting her. I retired to bed. It was cold without the rug, but my smugness kept off the chill.

Unfortunately, I dreamt of Fiammetta.

FIVE

A ll around the Mediterranean people say of Venetians that they are born with webbed feet. We know more about ships than any other nation, and we have plenty of them, too. Even so, I gasped when the wide-bottomed ferry boat that had carried me from Reggio came within sight of Messina harbour.

The choppy blue water was seething with activity. The ferry could barely squeeze between the vast numbers of Angevin vessels that filled up the harbour behind the mole and spilled out into the Straits. It was as busy as the Arsenal when war breaks out, though not as organised. All around the shelter of the bay the water was dotted with galleys, rocking at anchor or moving unhurriedly from place to place. I counted almost forty of them in that one anchorage. They were long, lean vessels, built for speed, with narrow prows that extended into deadly iron-clad ramming spurs. Banks of oars were stacked on the decks and the crews were busy carrying stores aboard and trimming the ships up for sea, tarring the planks, scraping the hull, painting fresh eyes on either side of the prow to avert bad luck. The masts were struck and the sails furled on the decks, but at each high curving stern a long pennant flew, brilliant blue and gold, the arms of Charles of Anjou.

Forty galleys! It would cost the whole of the revenue of Sicily to equip them and keep them at sea for six months. Venice could hardly compete with those numbers, and King Charles's fleet was not yet fully assembled. No wonder the Byzantine Emperor was apprehensive.

As we came into harbour I saw several Venetian war-vessels berthed along the mole and an elegant galley with the gold Lion of St Mark fluttering at its prow tied up at the harbour wall. It must have been the Government ship that had brought Vallerio Dolfin and his entourage to their posting. There were more than a dozen great French carracks tied up too, big cargo ships with high wooden castles at prow and stern, and provisions were being loaded into their massive bellies by rope and crane and muscle. The little local fishing fleet was squeezed into a corner of the harbour, so close together they were practically stacked one atop the other like hats on a hawker's back or melon shells after a feast.

At last I tore my eyes from the wonderful spectacle of the fleet and turned my attention to Messina. The last time I was in Sicily I was not interested in seeing the sights, and so I couldn't say whether it had changed much in ten years.

Messina is a big, busy town. It controls the Straits between Sicily and Naples, which means that its garrison can keep an eye on and potentially stop every ship that wants to sail up the west coast of Italy. When the Normans were kings of Sicily they lived on the island, in their Palermo palace, and under their rule Messina was quiet and respectable. Now it was loud and raw. Charles of Anjou didn't like Sicily. He'd hardly ever visited it, and he wouldn't have dreamed of living there. As far as he was concerned the island was nothing more than a source of revenue. He administered it through justiciars, whose agents travelled to and fro to his court at Naples to get their orders and make their reports. That meant a lot of governmental coming and going through Messina, and the town was garrisoned and growing accordingly.

The town was dominated by the bulk of the old castle, called Mategriffon, built a hundred years ago by King Richard of England. Now the Angevin flag fluttered from the battlements, and the sun shone from the helmets of soldiers patrolling to and fro on the wallwalks. The town beneath the castle looked quite new, but then Messina was plagued with violent earthquakes. It had probably been rebuilt since I fled Sicily. Far off to the left, beyond the mountains that hemmed in the town, the peak of Etna loomed through the clouds, smoking threateningly. Sicilians are mad. Who would live on the slopes of a fiery mountain that could bring Hell to earth on a whim, without allowing you any time to prepare to meet your God?

I sauntered down the gangplank looking insouciant and feeling sick. I had no girl to go to in Messina. On my last visit no girl would have looked at me, a stinking, infested, half-naked refugee, thin as a starving wolf, with sunken flanks and the furious, demented glare of a hunted man in my hollow eyes. I shuddered, but no one in Messina knew me. The only thing that troubled me was my memories.

Once on dry land I stood to one side and stroked my new beard thoughtfully, weighing up the sights before me and considering which way to go. I was rather proud of the beard. I had dyed it black to conceal the red-gold lights which betray my blond Venetian father, and it was glossy with a blue sheen to it and looked authentically Levantine. My clothes were good, too. I looked distinctly unSicilian. Sicily is a very polyglot, mongrel place, you see all sorts of people there – dark native Sicilians, turbaned Arabs, narrow-eyed Greeks, tall broad-shouldered descendants of the Norman kings, fair-haired Germans and any number of hybrids – but they all look uniquely like Sicilians, with little oddities to their dress and deportment which set them apart from other examples of their various races. I, on the other hand, was pretending for the moment to be a Greek from Constantinople, and I looked the part. I wore a splendid Phrygian cap made of scarlet felt on my dark hair. My blue-black beard was carefully trimmed and my clothes were heavy and complicated and made in the most part of silk of Byzantine manufacture, Thebes silk, not the Eastern silk that comes through Outremer or the Italian and indeed Sicilian stuff which many Westerners wear now. I liked my outer tunic particularly. It was dark red, ochre dipped in purple, and the silk was patterned heavily with birds and beasts. It drew glances.

People pressed up to me, offering accommodation at inns, taverns, eating shops and private houses. They made it clear that with the French army assembling any sort of bed was at a premium, and they were only doing me this favour because I looked a desirable tenant. After not long a small fight broke out between the representatives of two of the local *hosterie*, each of which claimed to be the cheapest, cleanest and most welcoming place on the sea front. I don't know what they were fighting about, I had not shown interest in either. I prefer to stay in a private house when I can: there are fewer people about you.

I entered into negotiations with a couple of the house owners and settled on one in the end that promised every comfort and convenience: my own room, and a privy in the yard outside that only served half a dozen other houses. The price made me whistle, but I could see for myself that the town was very full. The representative was apparently the householder's brother, operating on commission. I gave him a tip and let him carry my bags. We walked along side by side, watching the shipping.

You couldn't take two steps along the harbour front without

34

running into a train of mules or an oxcart laden with dried peas and flour and barrels of wine and salted fish, and the air was full of shouts in French and Italian and Sicilian dialect, mostly curses with a few instructions inserted for good measure. There were a great many French soldiers about, dressed in mail and helmets and looking tough, even those who were not involved in the lading of the ships. The place stank of spoiled food and overworked people and the dung of the pack beasts.

'That's a big fleet,' I observed to my companion.

Like most obvious remarks, this one was well received. 'We've never seen anything like it,' he said, and spat on the ground. 'Frenchmen. They're worse than locusts. They're stripping the land bare to feed their army. We'll have nothing but dust to eat when they're done.'

It was interesting that he felt free to criticise the French to a stranger. I said, 'Do you always speak ill of your overlords?'

He hardly missed a beat. 'You are Greek,' he said. It was obvious to him that a Greek would abhor the French. I raised my eyebrows, but I didn't correct him.

As we were about to leave the harbourside a French sergeant stepped in front of me and looked me up and down in that particular arrogant, hostile way that stupid men in authority seem to assume as a matter of course. He wore patched chain mail with rust spots, four days' worth of stubble, broken veins in his cheeks and a drunkard's splotchy nose. If I was his captain I would have told him to keep his equipment cleaner. The only parts of him that shone were the blade of his dagger and the hilt of his sword.

He addressed me in French. Another example of arrogance, but from what I had heard it was typical of the occupying Angevin troops. Fortunately I understand French well, though I don't pretend to be fluent. 'Name and business?' he demanded.

I glanced at my companion, who was looking extremely uncomfortable, and hesitated before I replied. The sergeant put his hand threateningly to the hilt of his sword and whistled shrilly through his teeth. From a tavern nearby another three or four mail-clad soldiers heaved themselves to their feet and began to move towards me. One of them was clapping his fist into his open palm and grinning at me like a snarling dog. The sergeant repeated, 'Name and business, stupid.'

A merchant would look nervous, and I did. 'Basil Eleftheriades,' I replied quickly in French that was Greek-accented but understandable. 'Of Eleftheriades, Manuelos and Company.

35

Dealer in silks and precious stuffs.' I swallowed and fumbled in my purse, feeling for silver. 'No need to bother your men, sergeant,' I said confidingly as coins changed hands. 'Let them go back to their drinking.'

He curled his lip, somewhat mollified. 'On your way,' he said, stepping back and jerking his thumb over his shoulder. 'But watch out. We don't like to see men wearing swords around here. It's asking for trouble.'

I looked down at my sword belt and the sword hanging from it. It was a rather fragile, pretty object with a gilded handle, entirely suitable for a wealthy merchant on his travels. My real sword was wrapped up in my baggage. I said meekly, 'Thank you for the warning, sergeant,' and slithered past him. I walked like a small man, with my shoulders and head stooped. It takes a handsbreadth from your height and looks entirely natural. As I went away from the soldiers I looked no taller than my Sicilian companion. In fact I am a little above middle height. Lucia says I should have been as tall as my father, but circumstances stunted me.

'Bastards,' said my Sicilian friend, when the Frenchmen were out of earshot.

I admit I had not been favourably impressed. But I said nothing. Merchants are not people who make a habit of interrupting the status quo.

The room was ghastly. It was at the top of a precarious house that seemed to be built out of mud like a swallow's nest, and it managed to be both cold and stuffy and damp at the same time. Even with my artificial stoop I brushed my head against the ceiling, and greasy stains on the bare rafters showed that other inhabitants had also done so. The bed was a lumpy straw-stuffed mattress, the window a hole. It had an unrivalled view over the local midden. Forget descending six flights of rickety stairs to go to the overpopulated privy, I would just piss out of the window.

However, it was quietly located, and the man who owned the house was more than half blind. This and the fact that I did not intend to remain long in Messina recommended it to me sufficiently to remain, though I beat them down hard on price. Price is important to me. Whenever I make a report I have to account to the Republic's auditors for every copper coin that has passed through my fingers, and if they think I have overspent I get short shrift. Venice is fussy about Government property and profligacy is theft. Anyone convicted of theft from the Serene Republic is likely to spend the rest of a rather short life regretting it.

I did not unpack my bags, but fastened them up more securely, not because I was afraid that my landlord was a thief but to try to stop the cockroaches from getting in. Then I changed into duller clothes and put a battered grey cloak and a linen coif under my arm. I fastened on my everyday sword as well. When a soldier tells me that he doesn't like to see people going armed I know that arms are even more necessary than usual.

Out in the streets of the town I found a quiet corner, slung on the cloak and tied the coif over my hair. I now looked different again, not like a wealthy silk merchant, more like a bearded nobody. Then I began to poke around the town.

It was full of Frenchmen, and I mean full. Everywhere I went I heard their voices, loud and raucous as blackbirds proving that they own their patch of garden. I went as far as the city walls, looked at the number of men guarding them, and shook my head. If I were going to start a conspiracy against King Charles, I most certainly would not choose to start it here. Palermo was a better bet.

The Venetian delegation had been installed in a fine house not far from the castle. It had the look of a property that has been recently confiscated: a family badge over the heavy bronze-studded doors was roughly effaced with whitewash. I asked an old woman going past with a basket full of spinach on her back what place it was.

She looked up at the house with difficulty, because she was bowed under the weight of salad, and said, 'It was Messer Corlei's house. He fell behind with his taxes, poor man. No fault of his, he was an honest merchant. And he got on the wrong side of the Governor.' She spat, copiously. 'And the French dogs flung him and his family into the street and took his house. Now they lend it to their accursed Venetian friends.' Her snarl showed a mouth full of stumps the colour of the spinach leaves.

Well, people never admit to falling behind with taxes on purpose, do they? The first thing anyone does when the tax collector appears is to claim injured innocence. But confiscation of the family property is a fairly drastic step, especially for a well-born family as this one must have been. The French seemed quite as high-handed as they had been represented. And I didn't like the tone of the old woman's voice when she spoke of Venice. I wanted to ask her something else, but she had gone on her way.

There was a church a little way down the street. I found out its name and then returned to the residency and left a message with the porter: Signor Dolfin should meet Fiammetta at Vespers tomorrow. The porter raised his brows intelligently and gave me the sort of sly man-to-man look reserved for pimps. I began to regret the choice of code name.

As I left the building Aliusio Contarini came towards it. He was dressed in a green silk robe, a fur-lined cloak and a hat made out of green silk to match the robe and edged with sable. He was wearing enough perfume for a small harem, and he had two rich young French officers with him. Like many well-born military men the Frenchmen sported civilian clothes, long silk tunics split to the thigh to show off the fur lining and the tall leather boots beneath, but each of them wore some piece of luxury armour as an ostentatious token of their army connections. One had a chased and gilded scale-armour corselet which looked as if it had come straight from Constantinople, and the other wore brilliantly polished steel arm-guards and gauntlets backed with chain-mail. They were talking to Aliusio in a mixture of bad French and bad Italian on the subject of the local whores. I leant against the wall with my arms folded and stared at them insolently.

Aliusio felt me examining him, turned and demanded angrily, 'What are you looking at, fellow?'

Just as stupid as I thought. Change my hair and my beard and he didn't know me from Adam. I raised my brows at him and made him a little ironic bow and went away. It was tempting to get into a fight with him right now and rid the world of a pestilential parasite, but the young Frenchmen with him swaggered with the assurance of soldiers who can look after themselves and I don't like long odds.

Plenty of sleep appealed, but getting it was tricky. The neighbourhood proved to be busier at night than in the daytime. One of the lower local tarts seemed to have her pitch right against the wall of the house below my window. A salubrious spot, just beside the midden, but she did brisk business anyway. What with the grunts of her customers as they rooted under her skirts and her shrill arguments with her bully, and the wails of cats either mating or fighting, and the snores of my landlord on the next floor down and the domestic dispute in the hovel over the road, it took me some time to get to sleep. But I was up before dawn all the same. I had work to do.

I was back at the little church at the end of the day, just before Vespers began to ring. I took up position in a shadowed corner and watched for Signor Dolfin.

The congregation ambled in, chattering together as congregations do. There are always a few pious ones, women with their heads swathed in black, men kneeling or prostrating themselves, but most people come together to meet and gossip before they enjoy their evening's *passeggiata*. The place was full of coloured hoods and the brightly-patterned scarves that the women used to cover their hair, all bobbing up and down in eager conversation. Nearly everyone was Sicilian. I suppose the French had their own favoured places of worship.

Perhaps it wasn't a good meeting place after all. If Vallerio Dolfin entered in his persona as Venetian Special Delegate, complete with entourage, nobody in the church would look at anything else. A private word with him would be impossible. I might have to disappoint him and try again.

The service began and the noise level diminished slightly. I watched out for Signor Dolfin and went through the motions, crossing myself occasionally. Then I saw him, and I smiled in reluctant admiration. He had come alone, dressed in a quiet cloak with a deep hood, and he was standing at the back of the nave beside a big pillar. He had more sense than I had expected. I oozed backwards and brought myself up next to his shoulder.

'Signor Dolfin.' He jumped nearly out of his cloak. Beneath the hood his eyes were wide open and his lips were dry. He looked terrified. He looked at me and frowned, not recognising me at once. I raised my eyebrows and grinned at him and his face changed again as he realised that I was me.

'Where have you been?' he demanded in an undertone. 'We have been here two weeks.'

'Listen.' I wasn't going to justify myself to him. He had addressed me in Venetian dialect, but I replied in the Italian of Tuscany to confuse anyone who might be listening. 'Here are instructions for our contact.' I pressed a paper into his hand. 'If there is a message for you, there will be a light on the hill they call the Hog's Back at midnight. It's visible from the window of your residence, I checked. The signal is written in there. I will check for messages regularly in case you want me, and there's a message waiting for you now so that you know you have found the place.' He looked down at the piece of paper and shook his head. 'Listen,' I insisted, 'signor, listen. Memorise what is on that paper and burn it. Do you understand me? Burn it.'

He hesitated. Then he said, 'I will tell Aliusio –'

'No.' He lifted his eyes to mine. They were blue, like his

daughter's. He looked insulted. 'Signor, the noble Ser Contarini is young. He is thoughtless. Keep the information to yourself until he is needed.'

Someone came too close for comfort. My voice changed to a wheedle, my Italian to Sicilian. 'A fair creature, I promise you, noble sir. Only thirteen years old, and a virgin, my word and faith upon it.' Dolfin's face was a picture. He couldn't have looked more offended if I had really been offering him my little sister. The person behind us moved away and I leant forward and touched his arm and spoke in Venetian this time: I wanted him to remember it. 'Signor Dolfin. Tell Aliusio nothing. Memorise my instructions and burn them. I am leaving Messina tomorrow, but you will hear from me.' I glanced from side to side, then said, 'Now tell me to get out.' I felt almost sorry for him, he looked so apprehensive.

For a moment he gaped, then he pulled himself together. 'You disgusting object,' he said, striking at my arm with his hand, 'how dare you? Leave me alone!'

I winked at him, then melted into the crowd.

Six

I passed the sugar factory on the road from Messina to Palermo. It looked just as I remembered, even to the spikes set on the top of its high walls to keep the slaves from climbing their way out. I stopped my horse in the road outside and listened, my spine prickling. I could hear the groan of the huge presses turning, turning, and sometimes the groans of the slaves who turned them.

My hand itched to strike a spark from my flint and send the whole place up in smoke, but I resisted. The overseers would escape with their skins and leave the slaves to fry, which would be an odd sort of vengeance for an ex-slave to take.

I travelled alone, on a skinny hired horse whose iron spine was already rubbing right through saddle cloth and saddle and expressing an interest in my testicles. Normally I would have gone from Messina to Palermo by sea, since the road journey was both arduous and potentially hazardous, but I wanted to judge the mood of the island's people for myself. I wore my battered grey cloak and a heavy woollen hood and looked as mean as possible. I was concerned about the entrepreneurial interest of any French soldiers I might encounter, and I wanted to give the impression of a nobody who didn't have much but was prepared to be awkward to hold on to it.

Where was Basil Eleftheriades? His outer shell was in my saddle bags, neatly folded and wrapped in coarse linen to fool a quick look. There were only two reasons why I had adopted his persona at all. The first was that there are many people in harbour towns who make it their business to watch those who disembark. If they can pigeonhole you easily, they won't worry about you. If you look like a misfit, then you will attract further attention. I was confident that on my arrival at Messina I would have been easily pigeonholed – wealthy Greek merchant – and, I hoped, forgotten.

The second reason was just as straightforward. I had lines of credit arranged at Venetian banks in Messina and Palermo in the name of Basil Eleftheriades and my alternative alias, whom I had not yet found occasion to unroll. I needed access to funds. Only a fool travels with everything he possesses: what are banks for?

The Byzantine gold was not with the banks, of course. Vallerio Dolfin was holding it. The Security Committee wanted to keep me from temptation.

Sicily is a fertile country, and its hills are beautiful. Spring comes early there, and although it was only the end of January the bare red earth smelled of warmth and green things waiting to sprout. Between the fields there were hedges of thorns, or walls of tumbled earth and great lumps of pumice cleared from the ground, and the hedges were shiny with buds and the walls were bright with spring flowers, anemones and narcissi, turning their sweet-scented faces to the sun. A gentle, mild wind blew in off the sea, bringing a fresh briny smell as an appealing counterpoint to the unmistakable whiffs of spring given off by the land. It was such a beautiful day that I felt my spirits begin to lift, and I pursed my lips and whistled merrily.

The Palermo road was busy with traffic carrying more supplies into Messina. Carts laden with hay and grain were pulled by heavy-headed white oxen with knowing liquid eyes. Knock-kneed, evil-tempered mules carried ten great jars of wine or oil apiece. Herds of little mountain sheep bleated mournfully, and there was even a flock of geese. The geese were almost too much for my wretched horse. As the noisy birds flooded round its hocks it crouched down in the road, shivering and clearly almost on the point of flight. I held on to the reins like grim death and stuck my feet out in the stirrups. Venetians are brought up to swim, not to ride. Give me a leaky boat any day.

After a while I stopped whistling, because the Sicilians didn't seem to share my good humour. A lot of them were driving their beasts and carts under armed escort, and even those that weren't looked sullen and browbeaten. They were also very thin. Spring is always a lean time, when the stores are going or gone and nothing has begun to grow yet to replace them, but I didn't expect to see hunger in as fertile a place as Sicily. And yet these peasants had the sharp cheekbones and narrow faces of want.

My own face looking at me out of my mother's antique silver mirror. A fifteen-year-old face, spotted with unhealthy pimples, and all points and corners, like a fox. My dark eyes glitter with specks the colour of amber in blue-shadowed sockets, and my nose is as sharp as the prow of a galley. The famine in Venice is terrible.

I am apprenticed to a goldsmith. He is wealthy, so we don't starve, but he puts his family first and there is less for the servants and the apprentices. Also I save some of my food and take it home for Lucia when I can. You might have expected that my father would look after her, but my mother is several years dead, may her spirit rest in the arms of the Virgin, and he has a pretty new young wife and a new legitimate son and other things on his noble mind.

I sympathised with the peasants' hunger, and it was easy to see the cause of it. For years they had laboured under foreign kings, first the Emperor Frederick and now the Angevins. They should have been prosperous and content, but their masters took most of what they grew. Enough to feed fifty families must have been flowing into Messina daily, all so that King Charles could conquer Constantinople. Hapless people, oppressed and beaten down by their overlords. Venice orders these things better. I would have pitied them, but I hated Sicily, and King Charles was my country's ally.

As I got further from the city the traffic grew less until I was alone on the road. The day drew on and I found myself feeling peckish. There was a pasty in one saddlebag, purchased before I left Messina, but I had bought it around the corner from my appalling room and I only wanted to eat it as a last resort. It was probably made out of dog, or cat if I was really unlucky. A little township with a friendly tavern was what I had in mind as an ideal location for my lunch.

Over the brow of the next hill I saw a farm beside the road. It was a huddle of low buildings, some made of timber and plaster, some cobbled together from the local stone. It was surrounded by olive groves and orchards of almond and orange trees. The almond trees were just beginning to come into blossom, starred with white on their bare black branches, and the olive trees were bright with buds. A donkey was tethered near the house beside a dark-eyed cow whose belly was great with this season's calf.

At first I could see nobody, and I imagined the family within their house, seated around their long table eating their lunch of vegetables and bread. For a few hundred yards I thought that perhaps they would give me something to eat. Peasant families are often warmly hospitable. However, as I descended this seemed less likely. The road wound towards the farm and revealed the farmyard between the house and the ramshackle timber barn. There were a number of horses there, and men jumping about in what appeared from a distance to be some sort of game. The sun gleamed on mail and a couple of coloured surcoats. It appeared that the French had got as far as this place in their provisioning exercise.

I wouldn't have gone near the place if I could have avoided it, but the road went right past and I didn't trust myself to ride across ploughed fields. I passed through a little vineyard and the olive grove, then entered the orchard. The sweet smell of the blossom surrounded me. Then I left the shelter of the trees, and the farmyard was right in front of me.

There were half a dozen Frenchmen there, a sergeant and a handful of his men. They were standing in a rough circle, laughing as they pushed a man between them so hard that he staggered with every shove. He was dressed in just his shirt, and his naked legs and feet looked pathetic. Small nervous chickens scuttled complaining away from him as he reeled from side to side. As I got closer I saw that he was an idiot, with an idiot's good-natured slack-lipped face and dim anxious eyes. He was blubbering like a child as they mauled him. They were goading him with the points of their daggers, too, and his coarse shirt was stained with little patches of red.

Strong people torment weak ones because it amuses them, but even so I found this hard to understand. I caught up the hood of my cloak to hide my face. There wasn't anything I could do to help, one man against six, and I didn't want to attract attention. If I could have gone around by another way I would have done.

Before the door of the farmhouse was a middle-aged couple, wringing their hands. I suppose they were the idiot's parents. The woman was on her knees, crying and pleading: not with one of the soldiers, but with another young man who was standing before the door with his hands spread across it, gripping the jamb on either side with white knuckles. His eyes were shut and he was shaking his averted head.

The French sergeant caught the idiot in his turn and looked towards the door. He snarled impatiently and flung the poor creature into the centre of their circle so hard that he fell to the ground and crouched there shivering and bleeding. His weeping was a thin keening like a dog whimpering. The sergeant drew his sword and took a menacing step forward. He said in bad Sicilian, 'You want me to kill him?'

My horse plodded on. A lean pig heaved itself up from its dust bath in the road to get out of my way. I would be riding almost through the farmyard in a moment. One or two of the soldiers had already spared me a glance, but it seemed that they wouldn't bother me if I didn't bother them. I still didn't understand what was going on. Half of me wanted to know, the other half wished I was somewhere else.

The old woman was still importuning the young man in the doorway. His face contorted and he shook his head again and again. The sergeant jabbed the idiot with his sword, producing a shrill, wordless yelp. At this the young man jerked his hands violently from the door, slammed his fists onto the wall and hid his head.

I understood when another figure came out of the farmhouse, a young woman in a coarse gown. There was a toddler hiding in her skirts. Perhaps she was the young man's wife, perhaps his sister. She was pale to her lips, as well she might be, with six hungry Frenchmen waiting for her. They cried out welcomingly in French and the sergeant went and grabbed her by the wrist and pulled open the front of her gown. The young man swung around and stood with his back to the wall, his fingers clutching at the plaster like claws, his lips drawn back from his clenched teeth.

There was nothing I could do. Soldiers are the same everywhere, and life is cheap. I had seen the same and worse all across Europe, wherever overlords were careless of their subjects. Venice would not benefit if I got myself killed trying uselessly to save one young peasant woman. I gritted my teeth and put my heels into my horse.

The French soldiers didn't worry about me. I had made no move to interfere, and they had other things on their minds. Two of them threatened the young man with their naked swords. One kept an eye on the parents. Another plucked the screaming child from its mother's skirts. The sergeant put his sword back in the scabbard and began to open his clothing.

Strangely, now, what I remember most clearly is not the woman's plight but the man's. He stood there with a sword at his throat, quite still, watching while the soldiers prepared to rape her. I suppose he stood there, after I had ridden past, until they were all finished, and then picked up the pieces. I remember his face. It was white as a sheet of paper lit from within by the smouldering of his rage. His eyes were like holes torn in the page. His anger blazed through them.

When you put a paper in the hearth it lies for a few seconds untouched and pristine with the fire glowing below it. Then, suddenly, incandescence: light and heat and a crackle of flame. The page lifts itself and snaps upwards in the ecstasy of its own destruction.

Now I believed the Security Committee. I believed that our alliance with the Angevins was at risk. It was not the Byzantine Emperor's gold, or Pere of Aragon's ambitions for a new kingdom, that would fuel rebellion. The young man's face had revealed it. It was hatred of the French that would set fire to Sicily.

SEVEN

I n the summer heat the reek of the Vucciria bazaar must be stifling. In mid-February, though, its smell is not exactly bad, just strong and confusing. Everything with an odour leaves its mark on the air. The most rare and costly perfumes, attar of roses, spikenard and myrrh, vie for nose space with the acrid tang of cheap spirits, the friendly reek of animal dung, the warm aroma of food of all kinds, the sweet mind-numbing smell of the kif the Arab boy-prostitutes smoke to make their job bearable, and above everything a tang of fish and salt blowing up from the nearby harbour.

The bazaar stall-holders said that times had changed since the good old days of King William, when the Court was based in Palermo and wealthy Norman nobles spent their livings on Oriental luxuries almost inconceivable in the castles of the colder North. Now the pleasure-palace of La Cuba was empty and the silk works, which King Roger used as an unofficial supplementary harem, was just a silk works. But still the city hosted a garrison of more than two thousand French soldiers and officers, and even if cloth-of-gold sales had fallen off, business in the bazaar was buoyant.

Everything in the world was for sale there. From where I sat, nursing a cup of bitter orange juice sweetened with sugar and sheltering my purse from the attentions of the bazaar thieves, I could see stalls selling silk cloth from Palermo and Greece and velvet from Italy, strong red broadcloth made of English wool, silver plate from Germany and jet and amber from the Baltic, medallions with the portraits of saints to keep you safe on a journey or ward off the fever, the myriad little bottles and jars of an apothecary's stock, spices from the East and relics from Outremer, oranges, almonds, sweetmeats, millet, copperware and the little snails the Sicilians love. The narrow choked streets rang with the noise of hawkers and bargainers and laughter.

I could also see a young woman selling flowers. She was there every day, from about halfway through the morning until dark. It puzzled me how she made her living, for flowers are cheap. Today she had hyacinths and anemones the colours of jewels, posies of spring flowers from the edges of the fields, celandines and primroses, sheaves of reeds from the salt marshes to strew on floors, bundles of new herbs and green branches to freshen your bedchamber.

As I watched a couple of customers came up to her. She sold a respectable housewife several bunches of herbs, savory, rosemary and lovage, then fell into discussion of the relative merits of anemones and her other flowers with a good-looking French officer. Her face was lively and animated, with a bright, eager smile. The Frenchman said something that made her laugh and blush. Her shawl fell back from her head, revealing light brown hair, shading towards gold: a surprise, when her eyes were as dark as an Arab's. No doubt some warrior from the blond North had made a contribution to her ancestry. There were cheap silver hoops in her pretty ears. She sold the Frenchman a posy of dark purple violets and he pinned them to his cloak and bowed to her. She smiled back at him and bobbed a little curtsey. That was surprising too. Most women in Palermo wouldn't give a Frenchman the time of day.

Why was I watching a flower-girl? Because I was depressed, lonely and unsuccessful, and she was an attractive cheerful thing to watch. She wasn't beautiful, or even exactly pretty, but she had a neat round figure like a robin and her ready smile made me think she would be welcoming. If I had had the luxury of my own persona I would have set about her with the intention of boarding and carrying her.

But I was still disguised, bluebeard wrapped in a thick cloak, the Venetian agent trying to claw his way into the Palermitan conspiracy against the French. I had trimmed my beard three times and redyed the roots twice, and I was heartily sick of it. What would be the point of making approaches to a girl if I had to change my name and drop her the moment I had success?

I finished my juice and called for another. When the server came I jerked my head at the girl and said, 'She's here every day.'

He raised his brows at me. Men always think the worst of each other. 'That's Caterina,' he said. 'Everyone knows her. Try your luck if you want, signor, but you'll be the first in the bazaar.'

'A virtuous maiden, then,' I remarked glumly.

'Not a maiden. She's a widow.'

He went away and left me stirring my juice with my finger and looking moodily at the young widow. She looked barely into her twenties, and I had thought she was unmarried because of her energy. Married women of any age are usually tired, worn out with childbearing and the cares of their house and husband, and their beauty rapidly deserts them. Except for my Fiammetta, whose loveliness was like unchanging gold.

My Fiammetta! Sometimes I was as foolish as a mooncalf. Why should she not be lovely, with nothing to do all day except tend to her pristine person? I jabbed at a piece of floating orange flesh and drank the sharp juice all in one gulp. My bowels were aching and my abdomen taut with the need for a woman. Four weeks of uninterrupted failure urged me to seek physical comfort.

Well, there were plenty of whores in Palermo. I've never liked having to pay for it, but my balls were full and I wanted to stay anonymous. I slammed the cup down and left the tavern.

I looked once more at the flower-girl. To my surprise, she was looking at me. For a moment our eyes met. She didn't look encouraging, just curious. She raised her brows and held out a bunch of hyacinths and I shook my head and turned away.

As in most cities, in Palermo you can find whores of all kinds close to the harbour, and that's the way I headed now. The twisting, sloping streets of the Vucciria bazaar find their way eventually to the sea, to the crowded, dirty anchorage called La Calza. I shouldered my way through throngs of cheerful, noisy people. In Sicily they dine well at midday and then sleep, even in the cooler seasons, and everyone was out and about, heading homewards for their meal or towards a hospitable tavern.

A man pushed past me with a freshly-killed lamb slung over his shoulder and turned suddenly to greet a friend. I ducked before the lamb's flying feet knocked off my expensive Greek hat, and as I straightened I felt the familiar touch of a pickpocket. Now, a real merchant from Constantinople would have failed to notice it, but I didn't know how long I might have to make my way in this town and I couldn't afford to lose any money. I reached behind me with my left hand and caught the pickpocket by the wrist, then turned with my right hand on my sword and a smile on my face.

The pickpocket was a boy no taller than my chest. His face was thick with grime, snot ran from his nose and his clothes were no more than a collection of rags. He stared at me in horror, as well he might. I was holding his life in my hands.

'Looking for something?' I enquired.

He shook his head, appalled and mute. A man leant out from a herbalist's shop just in front of me and yelled, 'Have you caught that little fox Menego? Hold on to him! I'll call the watch –'

'Is that Menego?' called another voice. 'It's about time –'

'The lord Santucci's just down the street,' suggested someone else. 'Get one of his bodyguard to –'

The boy twisted around and pulled frantically at his wrist. He was thin, so thin that his belly was bloated. I jerked his arm and he moaned with fear and turned to look at me. I winked at him, then stumbled artificially and let him go. He gasped and fled through the growing crowd like a cat with its tail afire.

'Signor!' called the herbalist. 'What happened?'

I sat up. A couple of big men in some lord's livery dropped their heavy staves and grabbed my elbows to give me a boost, then officiously helped me to dust myself off. In a heavier Greek accent than usual I said, 'I think he tripped me.'

'That little devil!'

'Never gets his come-uppance –'

'You must be shocked, signor,' suggested the herbalist, with a covetous look at my silk hat. 'Will you step into my house and breathe some aromatics to help you recover?'

'Forget aromatics,' said the tavern keeper next door. 'You need a drink, signor. And a bit of my wife's stew. It would revive a corpse.'

'Thank you,' I said politely. 'But I'm not hungry.'

I thanked the lord's men, avoided the commiserations of their master and continued on my way down to the harbour, ignoring the other offers of hospitality that came my way. I really wasn't hungry. On reflection I didn't want a whore, either. I reached the seafront and mooched along the broad cobbled street between the two waterfront churches, stepping over nets and floats and the detritus of the morning's fish market. My eyes ranged over the still water of the harbour, as if I was expecting that some sort of lead might jump out of the water like a fish and land in my arms.

I wasn't completely clueless. Oh, no. I knew that something was going on. I have a nose for intrigue, and the smell was strong in Palermo. It led me to the taverns where I would find the ringleaders. But firm evidence, that was hard. Sicilians are natural conspirators. They love whispering for its own sake, they can make a conspiracy out of nothing, and when it comes to a real secret they are as silent as the grave. Since my arrival in Palermo I had manoeuvred myself gently from place to place, keeping my eyes peeled and occasionally dropping the name of 'John of Procida' where I thought I might be on to a winner, but nothing. No response.

It was not enough to report back to Vallerio Dolfin in generalities. It was my job to infiltrate, not to confirm what we already suspected. And that meant I had to make personal contact with the conspirators, whoever they were.

I could have told Dolfin that the agents of King Pere of Aragon were active in Palermo, but that was hardly a secret. Pere's messengers were received openly in the houses of some of the noblest native Sicilians. Their cover story was that they were discussing plans for a North African Crusade. I don't think even the French were convinced, but they weren't doing anything illegal and the governor had taken no action. Anyway, my job was to find out where the Byzantine gold was going, and I still didn't believe that Aragon and Byzantium were hand in glove.

It was small things that made me suspicious. The taverns I was interested in were the ones that had not welcomed me and which never seemed to harbour any Frenchmen, but it wasn't that which stuck in my mind. It was that I had seen groups of men engaged in deep quiet conversation, and among them were several whose daggers looked as though they had been made in Lombardy or even north of the Alps. None of them wore swords. The French patrols in Palermo confiscated swords worn by Sicilians, which to a Sicilian male is little short of castration.

Why should a Sicilian wear a dagger from Mainz? Most of what they don't make themselves they import from Spain. The Germans and the Lombards make excellent weapons and sell them widely, but more often to France and England than to the South. That one man might wear one was possible, but that two or three in one group should have such weapons was too coincidental. I didn't think, though, that this would be sufficient evidence to convince Dolfin, never mind the French.

The harbour was full of ships, mostly French ships of war, just sailed over from Provence on their way to the great muster at Messina. They were big weatherly sailing ships, horse-transports and troop-carriers, not the light galleys, which wouldn't sail in the uncertain weather of February. They would leave with the galleys in the middle of April for their rendezvous with the

Venetian fleet. When they went, most of the French soldiers from the Sicilian garrisons would go with them.

And nobody would be sad to see the backs of them. In my single month in Sicily I too had developed a cordial dislike of the French. They were cruel and greedy. They oppressed rich and poor alike. What I had seen at the peasant farm outside Messina was repeated daily across the country, while the rich suffered injustice and extortion on a truly magnificent scale.

In Venice, where the merchants are noblemen, we are very careful of money. Taxes are on the whole small and fairly levied, and fines are suited to the culprit's pocket. If you strip a man naked as a punishment he must steal again to clothe himself, and then what have you achieved? But Venice is a republic, and republics care for their people. The Angevins served a monarch, and they had no such restraint. If a noble misbehaved or refused to pay their swingeing taxes and duties they would fling him into prison and keep him there until he paid a massive ransom or died of misery. People said that they used torture, too, and it was not hard to believe it.

Of course there were individual Frenchmen to whom this did not apply, but I had seen relatively few of them. Certainly the brutish, the callous and the plain bad outnumbered the good by a large factor. When I was in a weak mood I regretted that Venice was driven to ally herself with Charles and his rapacious ministers to reclaim her Eastern possessions. We deserved better.

No point in standing staring at the sea and brooding. I pulled myself together and looked around me.

Coming towards me was a group of Aragonese, looking like foreigners. They were talking together in low voices. This is unusual for Spaniards, who are often as loud as jays, and in itself caught my attention. They stood for a few minutes looking furtive. Then a couple of them disengaged themselves and set off up the sloping narrow streets towards the Vucciria bazaar. I only hesitated for a moment before following them.

They seemed uncertain of their way, and several times asked shopkeepers and passers-by for directions. This didn't surprise me, since King Pere's men normally kept to the better parts of the city. This pair looked uncomfortable and self-conscious. If I had been a cutpurse I would have picked them off at once. One of them wore a florid hat with a feather, which made it child's play to follow them. I slipped from one side of the street to the other, keeping the feather in the corner of my eye.

You can imagine how I felt when I saw them hesitate outside one of the taverns I had been watching. I wanted to cheer and wave my hood in the air. They were looking up at its sign, a brightly-daubed piglet on a spit. Nothing fools people as much as what I did next, which was to push past them in the doorway and walk boldly in, trying to keep the grin off my face.

The interior of the tavern was gloomy. Light came from an open jug-and-bottle counter at the front and from a doorway at the back which led through to a courtyard. Sounds pretty? Forget it: it was full of garbage, general detritus, broken jars and the privy. Not a place to enjoy a glass of wine beneath the dangling vine.

I sat down near the fire, which was central. I could watch all around me without looking too obvious. I ordered a jug of red and sipped it cautiously. My heart was hammering so hard it made the wine ripple in the cup.

The Aragonese came in, as I knew they would. One of them called the landlord and whispered in his ear. The man's face changed. His eyes flickered towards a table in the corner of the room, where two men were sitting eating a plate of the tavern's speciality, suckling-pig with herbs. One of them was wearing a Mainz dagger. My self-satisfaction knew no bounds.

The Aragonese went over to the table and spoke to the men there. I was too far away to follow the conversation, but my eyes are good and I could make out the faces in the gloom.

One of the Sicilians was a big man with broad shoulders and a slight stoop. He wore a coif over his shaggy hair, but the white ribbons tied under his chin could not conceal the fierceness of his face. He had narrow eyes in deep pouches of flesh and all the skin of his face looked about to sag, as if it had given up the hopeless struggle of clinging to his bones. Every movement he made seemed to be barely suppressing violence, and his big red hands shifted on the table constantly, powerful fingers mauling hapless pieces of bread into crumbs.

The other man was small and thin, forty perhaps, with a clever, prissy face and unnervingly good teeth. He looked like a clerk or a schoolmaster, a faded grey man. As the Aragonese sat down he broke himself off a piece of suckling-pig and put it to his lips, moving with quick precision.

The novice-master, tall and thin as a skeleton. His lips are pursed into a tight knot and his elegant grey eyebrows are arched skywards. I tremble before him.

'Marcello, why did you run away?'
I look at the ground. Monks like him think that unhappiness is sent
by God to curb our pride.
'Marcello, your father has sent you here for your own protection. This
is a place of safety for you, and one where you may learn much that will
be of help to you in your future life. Why did you disobey your father
and run away?'
I am as dumb as an ox. I want my mother. My grief for her fills me
like molten lead. If I were only a little less stubborn I would cry for her.
'Disobedience is a grievous sin,' the novice-master says. 'Take off your
robe.' He opens his desk and lifts the birch from it, moving with quick
precision.

I dragged myself back to the present and stifled a shudder. The
Aragonese were talking eagerly to the Sicilians: the big man was
answering them. I expected them to look as if they were in
agreement, but they did not.

After a moment one of the Aragonese took a leather bag from
his pocket and placed it on the table. I could sense the heavy
chink of gold. The Sicilians stared at the bag, then exchanged a
silent look. Their faces were eloquent. They wanted the gold, but
they would not take it.

The little schoolmasterly Sicilian spoke for the first time. His
voice was very quiet and he pushed the bag back towards the
Aragonese and turned from them in dismissal. One of them began
to protest, and the big man shifted in his seat and loosened his
dagger in its sheath. The Aragonese looked first startled, then
insulted. They put their noses haughtily in the air and left.

Why in the name of St Matthew the tax-gatherer should the
Sicilians refuse Aragonese gold? I strained to hear over the sleepy
pre-siesta hum of conversation in the tavern.

I was rewarded. The big Sicilian said in a growl that carried
over to the fire, 'Whoreson Spanish dogs. What do they think
they are about, offering us crumbs from the Emperor's table? We
need the whole loaf!' And he swept the shards of his disembowel-
led bread from the table to the floor.

Nobody paid any attention. But I drained my cup and got
happily to my feet. It is always pleasant to discover that your
suspicions were solidly founded. I had heard enough. Soon I
would present myself as alias number two, an Emissary of the
Emperor Michael to the Palermitan resistance.

First, it was time to leave Palermo. I would go back to Messina,

contact Dolfin and collect the Byzantine gold which I would
need for the next stage. Then I could lose the beard! When I was
a safe distance down the street, I cheered.

EIGHT

M eet Nicetas Demetriou, extremely clean-shaven and, dare I say it, handsome gem factor and supposed agent of the Byzantine Emperor Michael. Nicetas has all the distinguishing features of a Byzantine agent, that is, a very comprehensive alibi and a large quantity of gold concealed about his person. With any luck nobody will look far enough beyond the moneybag to detect the Venetian connection.

I returned to Palermo in my new persona within the week. What would a gem factor do on arriving in a large port where he intended to undertake some private business? First, he would acquire comfortable lodgings. He would not dive off in the direction of a low tavern in the bazaar. I left my baggage with the ship factor and spent an entire morning ambling about the narrow streets of the jewellers' quarter, discussing amethysts and chalcedony with Jewish merchants and holding pearls up to the light. I didn't work for a goldsmith for four years for nothing.

In the course of my ambling I found myself chatting to a Greek merchant, a long-standing resident of Palermo, whose last daughter had just married and gone to live with her husband's family. With insufficient children to fill the space, he wanted to let out the top floor of his house. I went back to have lunch with him and his grey-haired, enormous-bosomed wife, inspected the room and pronounced it ideal. It was big enough to have a separate area for eating and sleeping, and there was a little fireplace set into the wall with a crook to hold up a saucepan. The house was splendid, with a staircase both front and rear, and you might have imagined that he and his wife and two married sons would enjoy the chance to occupy it. But when I suggested that, he laughed. 'You don't get rich enough to own this sort of house without letting out everything you can,' he told me, emitting a sort of wheezy chuckle. 'You youngsters are all the same. Getting and spending is all one to you.'

I have plenty of savings in a number of banks in Venice and I am extremely conscious of the need to anticipate flood tides. But I tried to look careless.

'If you like,' his wife offered, 'I can have one of our women clean for you. Or bring up your water from the well, when she's fetching ours.'

'For a consideration,' her husband said quickly.

'I'd like to have water fetched.' It is a real chore hauling jars up the stairs. 'But I'll look after myself for cleaning.'

'Do you want meals?' asked the wife.

The husband's eyes lit up. I could see him adding a whacking mark-up to the cost of the food he and his household ate. The slaves' food for nothing, all paid for by the lodger! I shook my head. 'The room has a fire,' I said, 'I'll do my own cooking.'

In fact I had no intention of doing any such thing. I negotiated with the merchant for one of his slaves to run to the harbour and collect my baggage from the ship factor. Then I set off for the bazaar. My mother used to say that men follow their pricks the way dogs follow their noses. And she knew what she was talking about.

I arrived just as things began to liven up again after siesta. Caterina was still on her corner, selling flowers. She had narcissi today. Their heavy scent cut through the bazaar's olfactory morass with a blade of sweetness as sharp as their pointed leaves. I went and leant against a wall close to her and appraised her with my eyes.

She looked just as she had before. Small, lively, quick-moving. Her dress was made of homespun, coarse pale-brown fabric a little lighter than her fine pale hair, which was decently hidden under a dark shawl. The dress was not a flattering colour, but she had done her best with the cut. It clung to her slender waist and outlined the rich curves of her breasts and hips. She must have been wearing heavy petticoats beneath it, to make it swing so seductively. Why did a virtuous widow bother?

One of the other stallholders, a massive Arab with a turban the size of a pumpkin, was laughing with her about something. She seemed to spend most of the time laughing. There was something touching about her cheerfulness. I put back my hood and watched her, my head on one side, waiting.

She noticed me quite soon. She frowned briefly, as if trying to place me, but then her face cleared. She raised her brows at me in a cool, dismissive gesture and turned to serve a customer.

I was next in the queue. When she saw me she pressed her lips

57

together in anticipation of disapproval, then smiled a very professional stallholder's smile. 'Good day, signor,' she said. 'What can I give you? The narcissi are sweet today.'

'Lilies,' I said.

'I haven't got any lilies,' she told me, and added as if I were an idiot, 'it's not the season.'

'I can see two,' I said, and let my eyes lower to where the swell of her bosom just showed above the wide neck of her gown.

She bridled and narrowed her eyes at me. 'They're not for sale,' she said.

'Roses then,' I suggested, moving my gaze to her lips.

'They're not for sale either,' she said, frowning delightfully. 'What do you take me for?'

I looked back into her dark eyes. They were sparkling with mischief, or with annoyance, it was hard to tell. In a couple of breaths I might get my face thoroughly slapped. Well, it was worth the risk. 'I thought,' I said with a smile, 'that you looked like a businesswoman. Someone who would listen carefully to a suggestion that might be to her advantage.'

Suddenly she was very still and her eyes were shielded. There was a tension between us. You can't mistake that feeling, like a drawn bowstring, like a sail stretched twanging-taut by a strong wind. Her lips parted. They were good lips, a clear pale red, well defined and charmingly full. It would be a pleasure to kiss them. They were probably her best feature, though you could have made a case for her eyes.

The parted lips moved. 'Go on.'

'I've just arrived from Greece,' I said. 'My name's Nicetas. I deal in gems. I've taken a room here for a few weeks. My servant died at the last port and I need someone to look after the room for me. And to look after me, of course.' Somehow I didn't want to lie to her more than I had to.

She was looking at me intently. Her eyes were as dark as chestnuts. She said after a long moment, 'Why ask me?'

'I liked the look of you. And they say you're a widow.'

'You want a – a housekeeper? And you'd pay me?' She was tempted. I could see she was tempted. I assumed it was the thought of my purse, rather than my person, that tempted her.

'That's the deal.'

'What did your servant die of?' she asked me, sharp as a knife. 'Is it catching?'

'I don't think it was catching,' I said, 'just fatal.' And I grinned.

She made a face, sticking out her tongue in silent disgust. Then she said quickly, 'I can't cook.'

'We'll send to the cookshop.'

She grinned now. 'I'm a slut. Hopeless. Filthy.'

'I'm not fussy.'

She flung back her head and laughed. Her shawl fell back and her bright hair glowed in the sun. 'Don't try to fool me,' she crowed. 'You're just after my body, aren't you?'

'Curses. You guessed. Well, that was the idea.'

She laughed again, but then her face changed. The colour left her cheeks. She caught up her shawl and held it close to her face and said in a voice that sounded suddenly vulnerable and distressed, 'I'm not a whore.'

'I know,' I said gently. The distress faded from her face, but she looked puzzled now and confused. 'Listen,' I said, 'if you're not interested, I'll apologise and be on my way.' She said nothing. I tried to catch her eye, but she was looking down at the flowers around her feet. Her face was still pale. There was no way for me to tell what she was thinking. I said, 'I apologise,' and turned to leave.

'Wait,' said her voice behind me.

She was whiter than the narcissi. It seemed to be hard for her to make her lips move. 'I'm interested,' she said. I started to speak, but she went on, riding straight over me. 'Come back here at sunset. I need to think. I'll want to ask you questions. Will you come back here at sunset?'

Oh, the old D'Estari charm never fails. I gave her my most glinting smile and said, 'Yes.' Then I stooped and picked up an armful of narcissi. I felt in my purse for a gold coin, one of the Security Committee's finest, and tossed it to her. It was a Byzantine coin, bigger than my thumbnail, and heavy, not like one of the tiny local gold coins disparagingly called 'sequins'. She caught it and stared. Greek coins are good all over the Mediterranean, and this one would have bought the whole of her stock. I said, 'I'll come back at sunset for the change,' and went on my way.

A misuse of the Republic's funds? I think not. A happy agent is an efficient agent. We need to be fed well and exercised regularly, like racehorses. Otherwise we atrophy.

On the way back to my lodgings I bought a large crock to put the narcissi in. They made the big, airy room smell wonderful. I bent my face to the bowl and drew in a deep lungful of their sweet fragrance to try to still my nerves. My next interview was unlikely to be so enjoyable.

The tavern was fuller than when I had last seen it. My two targets were not at the table in the corner and I seemed to be out of luck. Dispirited, I ordered a drink and a snack and sat down near the jug-and-bottle counter, wondering whether I dared to give their descriptions to the landlord and ask where I could find them.

He brought over my jug of Greek wine (I was sticking to my character) and a plate of olives. As he set them down I said, 'I'm looking for someone.'

'Aren't we all,' the landlord said.

'Listen.' I caught his arm. He looked down at me in surprise. 'One of two men. One of them is smallish, thin, scholarly-looking, grey hair. The other is big, broad-shouldered, dark hair that curls. Both of them maybe forty. Do you know them?'

'I get all sorts in here,' the landlord said dismissively.

He tried to pull his sleeve free. I shook my head and slipped a coin into his palm and dropped my voice. 'John of Procida told me I might find them at the sign of the spitted pig,' I murmured.

There was a brief silence. I don't know which did it, the name or the money, but the landlord said, 'Stay around, and you may be in luck.'

He wasn't wrong. Before I had finished the olives my two marks came in, this time in the company of three or four others. They made a motley crowd, young and old, some clearly wealthy, others squalidly poor. They sat down at the corner table and started to talk in low voices.

At once the landlord was there, leaning over the little scholarly man. They both looked at me. No point in waiting. I got to my feet and walked over to the table.

The big man was holding his dagger. As I came up he started to play the old game of nerves that involves jabbing the point between the spread fingers of your left hand, faster and faster. To do it well requires a cool head and excellent coordination. I know, I'm good at it. The threat was obvious.

Six pairs of eyes fixed on me, cold and unwelcoming. The scholarly man said, 'Prunio says you were looking for me.'

Christ, he even sounded like the novice-master. That prim, clipped voice brought up the hairs on the back of my neck. I said, 'If you're expecting a message from John of Procida, I'm looking for you.'

His face didn't change. 'I might be. Where are you from?'

My accent might have told him that. He was talking in Sicilian and I was replying in a mixture of Tuscan Italian and dialect, with heavy overtones of Greece. They all had to concentrate to understand me. I said, 'Constantinopolis.'

He had good control, but his men didn't. At this news they rustled and cawed like a treeful of crows. His grey brows came down tight and they fell silent, suddenly chastened. 'Who sent you?' he asked.

'Listen,' I said arrogantly, 'you want the message or you don't.'

Without warning the big man plucked his dagger from the table and flung it. I just managed to stand still as it whipped past my face and stuck quivering in the pillar behind me. The men around the table laughed nervously and the big man said, 'Watch your tongue, Greek. If we want to know who sent you, we'll find out.'

My heart was hammering. The knife had shaved the pile from my hood as it passed. I remembered who I was supposed to be and said angrily, 'If you don't want the message, the Devil take you,' and made a Greek but unmistakably filthy gesture.

At this they all snarled and began to surge to their feet, but the little man stopped them with a wave of his hand. 'What sort of a Greek are you?' he asked, sounding almost amused. 'I heard they were all silver-mouthed diplomats.'

'Do you want this bog-poxed message?' I demanded, leaning on the table. 'Or shall I take it back to Constantinople?'

'Let's hear it,' he said, sitting back.

'Give me the counterword,' I snapped.

This was a gamble. For all I knew he might already have used it, and I had missed it. But I sensed that until now he had been playing with me.

The patron saint of spies was watching me that day. The little man frowned at me, then nodded slowly. 'John of Procida is witnessing a treaty,' he said evenly.

I drew out a bag from my bosom. They all froze, staring at it intently. The big man said, 'At last.'

'The message is, "Keep up the good work".' I put the bag down on the table. 'My principal is eager to see the French kept where they are. He looks to you.'

The little man reached out for the bag and opened it. His face cleared as he saw the gold within. He said with inexpressible satisfaction in his voice, 'Tell your master he can rely on us. We'll keep the French out of his hair.'

There was a silence. They expected me to go. I hesitated, then said, 'There's more where that came from.'

Another silence. Then the big man said, 'What do you mean?'

It was time to start throwing my weight around. 'That's only half of what I brought with me,' I said. 'Aren't you going to ask me to sit down?'

That was pushing it. Instantly the big man was up and grabbing at my tunic, thrusting me back against the pillar and breathing garlic sauce into my face. I didn't try to fight him, though if he had only known it he was in a perfect position to get my knee right in his family jewels. 'Are you holding out on us, you son of a Greek whore?' he snarled. 'What are you talking about?'

'Blasio,' said the little grey man, getting up, 'gently.' The big man's lips writhed back from his teeth like a dog's, but he let go of me and sullenly sat down.

I dusted my tunic in a pointed manner and raised my brows at the absence of a seat. At last one of them shifted reluctantly up. I sat down, folded my hands in front of me and smiled. 'At least I know one of your names,' I said brightly.

'I'm Andrea,' said the little grey man thinly. 'Blasio is my deputy. And you?'

'My name's Nicetas,' I said. 'Your most humble servant.'

'Enough of the jokes,' said Andrea. His narrow pinched voice made my stomach heave. 'If you're keeping back gold your principal gave you, we want it.'

'What's to stop us taking you now and finding out where it is?' demanded Blasio. He was very, very angry. 'You think we couldn't make you talk?'

'If you ever want more from the same source, you'll leave me undamaged,' I said. 'My principal expects me to report back in one piece. You won't risk it.'

Andrea exchanged a cold, unreadable glance with Blasio. They had the air of men who had worked together for a long time and knew each other's minds like brothers. He said, 'Speak.'

I licked my lips and leant forward, opening my hands to them. 'Listen.' My voice had changed too. I sounded earnest and eager. 'I know what you're fighting for. I want to help.'

'You want to *what?*' Blasio sounded astonished.

'I want to be involved. Look, I'm from Greece. The French have been there, you know, and they were as bad as they are here. I hate them. It's taken me months to get this courier mission. I only wanted Sicily. I want to help you. Use me.'

My words bubbled up like water from a spring and my eyes blazed sincerity. I saw Andrea, cold devil that he was, suppressing a smile. 'We don't need you.'

'You need the gold,' I reminded him.

'If you want to help us, you'll give us the gold,' he said, and his men grinned at each other at this impeccable display of logic. 'And if you don't, I'll get word back to your principal some other way. He'll hear that you've been lining your purse at his expense. From what I hear, the Greeks know how to punish that sort of treason.' All round the table his men were nodding like idiots, amazed by his powers of argument.

I looked dashed, as if I hadn't thought of any of this. Then I said again, 'Look, I'm offering you my sword. I'm young, I've got plenty of courage, I'll do whatever you ask me to, just as long as it's against the French.'

'We don't need you,' Blasio repeated wearily.

'I came through Messina on my way here,' I said. 'I saw the size of that army and that navy. You need every man you can get.'

There was a pause, during which Andrea and Blasio talked with their eyes. Then Andrea said, 'How do I know you're not a double agent?'

'A what?' I asked, dumbly.

He rolled his eyes, annoyed despite himself by my simplicity. 'How do I know that you're who you say you are?' he explained with strained patience. 'That you're telling me the truth?'

That floored Nicetas, who was a young man of energy rather than thought. I opened my mouth as if I was going to reply, thought better of it and said with a totally blank look, 'I don't know. How can I prove it?' I shrugged and tried a charming smile. 'I could ask you to trust me.'

Blasio laughed outright at that, and most of the others let out grim chuckles. Andrea shook his head slowly, his cold eyes fixed on my face.

I looked helpless. 'I don't know,' I said. 'I can't prove anything. Set me a test or something. I'll do anything you say.'

There was another of those chilling intervals of quiet. Then Andrea said, 'I'll think about it. I tell you what, Nicetas.' His voice had changed. A patronising edge had crept into it, and I knew I had won. Once your enemy despises you he will underestimate you, and then you have the upper hand. 'Tell me where I can find you. In a day or two I'll let you know my decision. If I'm interested I'll ask you to meet me. Bring the rest of the gold with you then.'

'But –'

'Take it or leave it,' he said. 'If you run with the gold, your principal will hear of it. Bring it with you when I send for you.' I scowled and sighed like a frustrated child, then nodded angrily. 'Where are you lodging?'

I told him how to find the merchant's house. He nodded. 'What's your cover?'

'Gem factor,' I said airily.

He raised his brows. 'How come you know enough for that?'

'That's my secret,' I said, putting my nose in the air. I got to my feet and turned as a young hothead would, to have the last word. 'Listen, you'd be mad not to use me. Think about it.'

As I swaggered off I could see out of the corner of my eye Andrea and Blasio shaking their heads in disbelief. I hoped I hadn't overdone it. I was pretty sure it would be all right, though. Andrea looked hooked. No cold manipulative organiser can ever resist the offer of an expendable resource at no additional cost.

Outside the tavern I looked about for the sun and couldn't see it, because it had dipped behind buildings. Nearly sunset! I headed back towards the bazaar with a spring in my step.

I hurried along feeling proud of myself. After a while, though, a healthy element of self-doubt began to build up. What had I really achieved, apart from making a handful of tavern thugs angry? I now knew the names of two men who were self-professed anti-French agitators. Wonderful. I didn't know how to find them if they wanted to avoid me. I didn't know who organised them or what their intentions were. Above all, I didn't understand their motives. They had before my very eyes refused gold offered them by the Aragonese. But they had seized grate-fully on gold supposedly from my purported principal the Byzantine Emperor. If they needed money, why turn down Aragon's? I still had a great deal of work to do.

By the time I reached Caterina's pitch I had worked myself up into a fine state of gloom and I was more than ready to seek oblivion in the arms of a cheerful blonde widow.

But Caterina was not there. Her pitch was empty.

NINE

I nstantly, irrepressibly, panic.

The new, seaworthy boat is tied up below the balcony, rocking gently. It is heavy with the weight of my inheritance, all the gold I possess and my mother's jewels. There's a rug lined with squirrel skin, too. I am afraid for Fiammetta's tender body, chilled by the dawn winds of the lagoon.

I toss up the grapnel and start to climb up, hand over hand, my brain teeming with the future. We'll go to Greece first, over to Epirus. Nobody will find us there. Then somewhere that Fiammetta would like. Constantinople perhaps, she's a city girl. It should be safe as long as we steer clear of the Venetian quarter. I will be the most wanted man in Venice within the hour. Her noble father and her noble fiancé will be shouting out to see my blood on the pillars of punishment. Nobody steals a virgin heiress and gets away with it.

Nobody until Marcello D'Estari.

I sling myself up onto the balcony and drop to a crouch behind a plant pot. The balcony is empty. I whistle our signal.

Nobody comes. I wait, I try again, I wait. Nobody. Fear sits in my stomach like a writhing knot of mating snakes. Foolhardy, I creep to the shutter of Fiammetta's little chamber and put my hands to it and listen.

Can I hear breathing within, movement? Desperate, I whisper, 'Fiammetta.'

No reply: but now I am sure I can hear something. Her duenna is deaf as a post. I speak again, louder now. 'Fiammetta. It's me, Marcello.'

The next sound is unmistakable. A wracked, smothered sob. I catch at the handle of the shutter and pull at it, ready to die if only I can help her. It is bolted on the inside. Heedless, I shake at it. 'Fiammetta!'

She does not come. I stand by the shutter, my hands spread flat upon it, unbelieving, cold and sick. Time passes. The sobbing within continues. I sink gradually to my knees, my palms and my forehead pressed to the pitiless wood, my eyelids squeezed shut against the tears, whispering her name.

When the dawn comes I get to my feet, stiff and trembling. I could hurl myself from the balcony, but the fall to the Grand Canal wouldn't kill me. I could hang myself from my rope, but my corpse would accuse her, and I love her too much to give her shame. I slither down into the boat and untie it. Its contents mock me.

The boat drifts out into the Grand Canal and down it to the Bacino. Transparent dawn rises over the Piazza San Marco, drawing back the starry blue mantle of the night with a silver thread. The sky in the east turns white, then pink, then gold. The domes of the Basilica begin to glow as if they are gilded like the heavenly spheres. So much beauty. But my darkened eyes cannot see it.

I lie in the bottom of the boat with my good cloak dragging in the bilges, staring up at the sky as the sun rises. My life is over.

I pushed back my hood and raked my hand hard through my lion's mane of hair. It wasn't the same, not the same. I said to a man filleting his last tuna fish, a blue and silver monster a good bit bigger than he was, 'Have you seen Caterina?'

'She just went to pack up her pitch,' said the stallholder, and then, 'Are you all right, signor?'

Yes, fine, and feeling like a fool. I bit the inside of my cheek and leant up against one of the walls of the bazaar, ostentatiously relaxed. A number of the stall-holders were giving me frankly curious glances. Who was this good-looking young Greek waiting for the bazaar's virtuous widow? I slung my cloak around myself in a devil-may-care sweep and posed.

Within moments I saw her, hurrying back through the crowd. She was flushed, but when she saw me her cheeks paled. She came to me at once, saying, 'Have you been waiting? I'm sorry, I had to –' She began to fumble in the pocket of her heavy apron. 'Do you want your change? I went to the money-table for it.'

'Not now.' I offered her my arm. 'Shall we go?'

'Wait.' She drew back. 'I have some questions for you first, you remember.'

'Here?' I asked, surprised. If people wanted to overhear they could.

'Here,' she confirmed. 'If I don't like the answers, I won't go a step with you.'

Another interrogation! I shrugged and tried to look confident. 'Off you go.'

She folded her hands before her, like a child reciting the catechism. 'Well,' she began, 'first, are you married?'

'What's that got to do with anything?'

'I don't believe in adultery,' she explained candidly.

I smiled. 'Don't worry. I'm not married.'

She frowned at me. 'Swear!'

I crossed myself Greek-fashion, right to left. This was easy, at least. 'I swear by all the saints.'

For a moment she still looked unconvinced. 'I suppose you're an Eastern Christian,' she said. 'Our priest says they're not true Christians. He says they're heretics. Can I believe a heretic?'

I said nothing. In general I eschew religious debate. In any case she seemed resolved to continue, because she drew down her brows and looked vague for a moment then said, 'Do you have bad breath?'

Bless her. I grinned and said, 'Only you can tell,' and I leant forward and breathed on her.

She flinched at first, then stiffened and sniffed. I seemed to pass muster: she raised her light-brown brows approvingly. 'All right,' she said carefully. 'Now, when you fart in bed, does it stain the sheets?'

'What?' I couldn't control myself, I was laughing. What would anyone do? I fell against the wall, gasping for breath. 'As far as I am aware, not guilty,' I croaked.

She watched me soberly while I recovered my composure. Then she said, 'All right. I'll come with you and look at the place. Just look, mind.'

'Is that it?' I was surprised. 'What about all the standard stuff?'

'What, like what do you do, and how much is it worth? Oh, I'll ask them later. Those were the really important questions.'

I offered her my arm again and this time she took it. She had rather big hands with square palms, and her fingers and nails were stained with the juice of plants. She saw me look and said self-consciously, 'I've only just cleared up. I haven't had a chance to wash.'

We walked through the bazaar in silence. Everyone we passed stared and one or two of them actually called out in surprise. Caterina pulled her shawl up around her head and her back stiffened, but she did not seem ashamed. I wanted to ask her about herself, how long she had been a widow, how she lived, but she seemed to have hidden herself in a shell of coolness which I was reluctant to break.

At last we moved into quieter, residential streets. I stopped and said, 'Would you like to eat before we go to the house?'

She turned to face me. 'Look,' she said, 'we're going to look at the place, yes? Just look at it. I might not want to do this at all. Don't take anything for granted.'

'All your friends in the bazaar will think you've done it,' I said.

'They would believe me if I said I turned straight round and walked out,' she insisted. Perhaps she was right, too. Who knows?

I didn't know what to make of her. Not a trollop, not a virgin. I didn't know if I was seducing her, buying her or doing her a favour. I shrugged and we went on to the merchant's house, still in silence.

The merchant's face said that he thought I was a sly dog. His fat wife obviously disapproved, but Caterina dropped her a most humble curtsey and she looked a little mollified. I showed my housekeeper the way up the back stairs that led to my room. The fragrance of the narcissi wafted down to meet us.

As we went up the stairs she shook herself free of my arm. I thought she was trembling, though I wasn't sure. Certainly she seemed in a state of extreme nervous tension. It made me uncomfortable. I don't like to feel like a villain.

She looked around the room with a sort of quivering eagerness, then buried her face in the crock of narcissi and inhaled their scent. Apparently to the flowers she said, 'How long do you think you will be here?'

'Hard to say. Depends on business.' In fact it depended on the sailing time of the Angevin fleet. 'Perhaps till the middle of April or thereabouts.'

'And what will you pay me?' She swung round now and fixed her dark eyes on me. Her full lips were folded into a pale line.

'Six silver pieces a day,' I suggested. She wouldn't earn half that from the flowers. It was about what a skilled whore might take in an evening, but I didn't want to tell her how I had calculated it.

She was tempted, so tempted, but her face was full of doubt and conflict. I didn't understand. She swallowed hard and said, 'I think we ought to try it just for tonight. To see – to see how it goes. And in the morning I'll decide.'

Did she think that she wouldn't be able to bear my company? I was hardly flattered, but I couldn't really insist on anything more. I said, 'All right.'

'I won't do anything – disgusting,' she added suddenly. There was a line of red on her cheekbones.

'Like what?' I asked innocently.

'Oh –' She had no idea. Her blush deepened. 'And I want payment in advance,' she said, squaring her jaw.

'Blood of Christ!' All this prevarication was making me angry. 'Keep the change as a down payment, if you want.'

'No!' she shouted, suddenly almost in tears. She dragged a little leather bag from her apron and flung it to the floorboards. 'Here's the change. Take it, take it, I don't want it. I just want one day's payment in advance. I'm not a cheat!'

'All right, all right! Calm down.' I picked up the purse and opened it. What was left of the Byzantine coin was now in Sicilian money. I found six silver pieces and counted them out. I held them out to her and she snatched them like a thief and turned away to hide them in some secret compartment of her gown.

She stood then with her back to me. I could see her shoulders shaking. Her breathing rocked her. Her fear made me feel hollow and weary. I waited, hoping she would turn and face me, but she stayed where she was.

At last I said gently, 'Look, Caterina, I don't think this is going to work.'

She turned at that. Her eyes were incredibly bright. 'Not work?' Her voice was trembling too. 'What do you mean?'

'I don't want to make you do something that you're unhappy about.'

'Unhappy?' she repeated, shaking her head slowly and gazing at me. 'Unhappy? Oh, you stupid, stupid man.'

Before I had time to do more than gape she flew across the room and caught hold of my head in her hands, pulling down my lips to hers. She almost knocked the breath out of me. I was astonished, but her enthusiasm was infectious.

We did it on the floor, rolling in the dust like urchins, our clothes around our waists. When I entered her she gave a great cry of joy and triumph. Her soft white body was sweetly responsive to every impulse. I tried to please her, and I know I did.

It was over quickly. We lay together in a bundle of twisted clothes, glistening. My seed sank into the floorboards. She arched her back against me and purred.

I stroked her hair. 'You sound like a kitten, a little girl-kitten. *Gattina.*' She said nothing, but her face was transfigured with fulfilment.

'*Gattina*,' I said, 'I don't understand you.'

At that she turned her head and smiled. 'I know,' she said. 'If I hadn't been so nervous I would have laughed.'

'Explain,' I snarled, thrusting my hips against her so that she winced.

She smiled again and looked up at the ceiling. 'You don't know anything about me,' she said, and I nodded. 'I live with my husband's kin. They hate me. He wedded me against their wills, because I had no dowry. But he loved me. And when he died, for shame his mother let me live with them, but she makes my life wretched. She still hates me, the old sow. We didn't have any children, you see. Even the maid has a pallet, but I sleep on the bare floorboards. That's why I keep the stall, it gets me away from them. If I had enough to leave I would, but I have nothing but what I can earn. I thought of being a whore.' Her eyes were clear and frank. 'But I – couldn't bear the thought of doing it with just anyone. But when you came, I, I liked you, and it seemed like an offer from Heaven.'

She moved against me and put her hand on my naked hip. It slid slowly towards the hollow of my loins, making me shiver. 'And,' she whispered, 'my husband has been dead two years, and I wanted it so much.'

I shook my head in disbelief. 'Why all that fuss about the money?'

'Oh, blessed Virgin.' She started to laugh. 'Like I said, I liked you. I was afraid if I didn't take it I'd end up just letting you have me for nothing. That wouldn't be businesslike, would it?'

'No, indeed.' Her hand was still between my legs, moving in an encouraging fashion. I was beginning to respond. I pulled away and rolled to my feet, holding out my hand to help her up. 'Beds are more comfortable,' I said. 'Floors are hard on the knees.'

'Your knees, my backside,' she said, brushing the dust from her silky haunches.

As she got up I said, 'You'll stay?'

She grinned at me as she began to unfasten her crumpled gown. 'I'll tell you in the morning,' she said. 'This is your chance to prove yourself, Nicetas.'

I never could resist a challenge.

TEN

I woke with a start. The shutters were open and the sun was pouring in. What sort of an agent lets a woman put him so soundly to sleep that she can get up without waking him? I sat up, shaking my head and shoving my hair out of my eyes.

Caterina was already dressed. She smiled at me. 'There's nothing to eat,' she said. 'A man who's worked as hard as you needs food. Will you give me some housekeeping money?'

'Take the purse,' I slurred. I was still fogged with sleep and sensual pleasure.

It was hard to find it in the mess of my clothes, but after a while she chirruped with success and stowed the little bag in her apron. She brought in firewood from the landing and made up the fire, then put a jar of water into the cauldron. 'When it starts to boil,' she said as she went to the door, 'stir it so it doesn't stick.'

I got up unsteadily and went over to the window to piss. The bed looked like a battlefield, sheets and blankets awry and twisted, pillows everywhere. The linen was damp and salty and stained. It was without doubt the most comfortable bed in the world. I collapsed back to the crumpled sheets and closed my eyes.

She returned singing and woke me. She set down a big basket and washed her face and hands in the steaming water. Then she took a straw-jacketed crock out of the basket and poured from it into a couple of cheap clay cups.

The wine was as sweet as milk and as strong as blood. I gasped and drained the cup. She refilled it and brought me a honey-cake, still warm and fragrant from the baker's oven. The crumbs fell into the bed.

While I ate the cake Caterina was slowly shedding her clothes. She stripped to her shift, then stopped and looked at me, anxious and shy of the sunlight. Last night it had been dark. I sucked leftover honey from my fingers and smiled at her. 'Take it off, *gattina*.'

'You'll be tired out,' she said timidly.

71

'I'll show you how to fix it,' I offered. She swallowed, then took off the crumpled shift. She had a blonde's skin, like transparent alabaster filled with wine. Her breasts were glorious. I pulled back the sheet and she got in beside me. She was quivering with eagerness. What must it have been like to go without for two years? I couldn't imagine it. When I was a slave it was different. A day was infinity, and absence of women was the least of my worries. Since then I had made up for it.

I kissed her mouth and throat and breasts. Her head moved on the pillow as if she was in pain. Everything I did inflamed her, but I had made all the running last night. This morning I wanted her to do something for me. I lay back and guided her head towards my loins.

She was startled at first. Her husband might have been energetic, but I don't think he tried anything but the Holy Church approved, classic man on top position. Well, I like to use my imagination. After a little while she got the hang of it and began even to enjoy herself. Certainly she had the desired effect on me. At last I pulled her away and said through my teeth, 'Come on, gattina. On top of me.'

'On top?' she squeaked, wide-eyed. 'Like a man?'

'Not exactly,' I said, getting her into position. Her wide eyes opened wider as she sensed her own power. I took her gorgeous breasts in my hands and she flung back her head and cried out. The curtain of her hair swept against my thighs. She moved with urgent desire, calling on the saints.

'What was your husband like?' I asked injudiciously afterwards, when she lay panting on top of me.

She rolled away from me. 'I loved him,' she said.

It would have done my pride good if she had confirmed that he wasn't a patch on me in bed. But I would never hear it, she was too loyal. It touched me. I stroked her hair apologetically. She lay still and did not look at me. There was silence. Then she said, 'Do you think it's right to marry for love?'

I wiped sweat from my forehead with the back of my hand. Fiammetta glowed before me. What would I have felt if it had been her slender body arching as it impaled itself upon me? Bliss? Wonder? Fear?

'Do you?' Caterina insisted, turning now to look at me.

I shook my head and said, 'I can't tell you.' My voice betrayed the hollow ache of my heart. Caterina asked nothing more, she was absorbed in her own loss. We lay in the warmth of our mingling breath, wet with each other's juices, and separated by our sorrows as completely as if a naked sword lay between us.

Several days passed. I heard nothing from Andrea, but this did not surprise me. He would be trying all his sources to see what he could discover about this Nicetas, messenger of the Emperor and wild-eyed anti-French fanatic.

After that uncomfortable morning Caterina and I came to an understanding. We were cautious. I did not mention her dead husband, and she did not enquire into the state of my heart. We continued to enjoy each other's bodies with hectic abandon. I paid her and gave her money for housekeeping, and she looked after the room – rather desultorily, for she was somewhat of a slut as she had admitted – washed my linen, and cooked me some of the most delicious meals I have ever eaten.

It was Lent, but that was no handicap in Sicily, where there are more sorts of fish than anywhere else in the Mediterranean. Caterina thoroughly enjoyed spending my money on food, and we ate glorious stews of fish fragranced generously with saffron, giant eels roasted with ginger and galingale, tuna fish as dark and rich as venison, sea bass made into patties green with fresh herbs, swordfish with pine nuts and raisins, prawns and clams and nameless things I didn't enquire about, just guzzled.

We developed a rather restful domestic routine. Every morning Caterina went to market to buy the ingredients for our lunch, and I went out and pretended to be a gem factor. In fact of course I was continuing to investigate Palermo for further signs of conspiracy. I did, however, buy some gems here and there, which I told Caterina were samples. They were stones that were currently fashionable in Venice. Why not turn a profit when you can?

I returned a little after noon and we would eat our wonderful meal and then retire to bed for a siesta, along with a little gentle exercise to aid the digestion. In the evening I went out again until curfew and Caterina would either go and gossip with friends or sit on our little balcony and sew. She spent her first week's wages on a massive bale of fabric from which she intended to make herself a truly splendid dress for the Easter Monday procession. It had been a torment to her since her husband died not to have a new dress on the most festive occasion of the year. She chose a mixture of silk and wool, heavy and smooth and glossy, dark golden like saffron strands and patterned with two colours of green. When she held it up against her face the reflection of the light from the gleaming fabric touched her skin with gold and showed up the glittering blonde highlights in her hair. It made a pool of colour on the bare wooden floor of our room, like trapped sunlight, while she crawled around on it and cut it out with her new pair of shears. Stitching the dress was complicated, and it kept her quiet for hours at a time and made her eyes go pink.

The presence of food in the apartment soon brought up mice and cockroaches, and Caterina brought home a little brindled kitten to keep them down. I thought it ate more of our fish than our vermin, but it was company for her and I didn't complain.

I had to stop wearing my sword. The French soldiers weren't supposed to give foreigners trouble, but it seemed that if they saw you more than once you stopped being a foreigner. On the third day my sword was actually confiscated by a brutal idiot of a sergeant and it took all the Greek hauteur I could command to frighten a callow young officer into giving it back to me. I didn't want to risk losing it for good. I couldn't have bought a replacement, it was illegal to sell arms in Palermo. So, like the native Sicilians, I left it at home. I was so accustomed to wearing it that for a day I walked with a list, like an ill-stowed carrack.

I complained about my treatment to Caterina, but she was surprisingly unsympathetic. 'They have to do their jobs,' she said.

'They're all power-crazed louts,' I said, keeping to character. 'I hate them.'

'Hate the ones who've done something to you,' she advised me, 'and not the others. Some of the French are all right. There was a young officer who used to buy flowers from me –'

'Tall? Good looking? Chestnut coloured hair?'

'How do you know?' she demanded, taken aback.

'Oh,' I grinned at her, 'I kept a weather eye on you for a while before I decided you were the one for me, my beauty.'

She tossed her head, not certain whether I was flattering her or mocking her. 'Well, yes, him,' she admitted. 'His name was Jacques of Vaison. I liked him. He asked me to – well, you know – a couple of times, but when I said no he was always nice about it.' She looked at me out of the corners of her sleepy dark eyes. 'If you hadn't come along,' she teased, 'I think I might have tried him instead. And when I was in the market today I saw him, and he said –'

'If he comes near you, I'll kill him,' I said, only half joking now.

'Green eyes! I'm not your wife, why should you care what I do when you're out?'

She was right, of course, but I did care. No man wants to be a cuckold, even unofficially. 'Don't I pay you enough to ensure myself the exclusive right to your services?' I demanded.

She kept me waiting for a while, then laughed at me. 'I could be just trying to put the price up,' she said merrily. 'Don't worry, Nico. I'm a simple girl. I couldn't cope with more than one man at once. I'd get all muddled.' And she came and kissed me and reassured me.

After more than a week I was beginning to believe that Andrea had resolved to do without the rest of the Greek gold. This was not good, and I wandered the streets of Palermo in the warm spring evening racking my brains for a way to recover the ground I seemed to have lost. Should I go to the Pig and look for Andrea? No; if he didn't want me to find him, there was no point in looking.

I walked through one of the little squares opening out of the confused narrow backstreets in the area around the governor's residence, the old palace and fortress of the Norman kings. The piazza was neat and well-kept, shaded by a tall spreading plane tree, with a well in one corner. A lot of the French lived in that part of the city, and a group of them were playing bowls on the dust of the square, noisily enjoying themselves. The space they were occupying should have housed a local craftsman, and while they were there none of the local women would dare to come to the well to draw water or do their washing. But what could anyone do?

One of them was the sergeant who had confiscated my sword. He had a little Sicilian boy fetching his balls for him, and every time the child came back he clipped him around the ear. The boy's face was smeared with blood. I just walked past. In Palermo, you got used to that sort of thing quickly.

One of the Frenchmen called out, 'Hey, Petrot, isn't that the Greek who gave you trouble the other day? How about teaching him a lesson?'

I should have speeded up at this point, but I wanted to be able to look at myself in a mirror afterwards. I stopped and turned around, wishing I had my sword. The sergeant looked at me and moved his face in an odd hybrid of snarl and smile. 'Certainly is,' he said. 'But we're in the middle of a game. He'll keep to another

time.' His smile broadened, revealing vile teeth. I bowed ironically to him and went straight home.

On my return Caterina met me at the top of the stairs. Her
face was tense and anxious, and she was clutching the kitten so
tightly that it was squeaking with protest.

She did not usually fuss. I ran the rest of the way up. 'What's
the matter, *gattina*?'

She chewed her lip before she replied. 'Nico, a man came with
a message for you. He said you were to meet Andrea this evening
at the same place. He said not to forget the rest of the message.
Not me, I mean you. That was his message, that you shouldn't
forget the rest of the message.'

She looked confused, but I understood her. It was the gold
they were interested in. 'When did he come?'

'Ages ago, not long after you left.' I didn't wait, just turned on
the stairs and started back down. If I ran I would just have time
to get to my banker before he shut up shop. Caterina hurried to
the top of the stairs and called down after me, 'Nico!'

'What?'

She hesitated. 'Nico, the man who came, I know him. He's a
villain, he and a friend of his used to run a racket in the
marketplace. Why are you going to talk to someone like that?'

I didn't answer her, just started to descend the stairs again. She
dropped the protesting kitten and followed me. 'Nico —'

I must have looked angry and impatient, because she took a
step back and wrapped her arms around herself protectively. She
knew that she had no right to ask me anything. She was my
housekeeper and my bedwarmer, not my wife. For a while she
struggled with herself, fighting against questions that bubbled to
make themselves heard. Then she said simply, 'Be careful.'

'I'm always careful,' I said carelessly.

She looked as though she didn't believe me.

ELEVEN

All the way to my banker's office I knew that someone was following me. When I turned a corner I could see him out of the corner of my eye, hanging back in the belief that I wouldn't notice him, and in the crowds hurrying to be home before curfew he kept having to stretch upwards to keep me in sight. I thought of stopping to confront him, or alternatively of carrying out some simple manoeuvre to give him the slip, but in the end I let him alone. No doubt he was one of Andrea's men, just checking that I was fulfilling my promise.

The bank was near the harbour, beside the larger of the two shoreline churches. It was a big building, built unusually out of brick, striking enough to catch the attention of wealthy travellers disembarking, and the presence of two large and heavily-armed guards on either side of the door revealed that the banker took his responsibilities seriously. However, it wasn't at present the most popular establishment in town. The banker had well-established Byzantine connections, and since Venice signed the alliance with the Angevins he had been seeing much of his clientele turn elsewhere. I was with him some time, enjoying wine and sweetmeats and exchanging pleasantries. Anyone who cared to deposit substantial quantities of Greek gold was very welcome to him.

When I finally came out with my passport to success stowed safely inside my tunic the twilight had evaporated. Curfew was ringing from the tower of the governor's palace, echoed by the warning shouts from every French garrison post, and the streets were rapidly emptying of people as the law-abiding hurried to their homes.

Mournfully, I considered the darkness. In Venice, it is the job of every parish priest to trot around in the evenings and ensure that candles are lit in the little shrines that stand on every street corner. The narrow lanes and calles are illuminated by a faint gentle flicker. You can see where you are going, spot where footpads might be lurking, and avoid tripping into the canals. The only other city I know so, literally, enlightened is Constantinople, where the streets are lit by splendid bronze lanterns. The rest of the Mediterranean from Gibraltar to Gaza lapses into barbarous gloom after dark.

In barbarous gloom I groped my way to the Spitted Pig. Palermo is a big, busy city, exciting during the day, at night plain dangerous. The doorways and alley mouths are inhabited, some by beggars sleeping rough and cats taking a rest between mousing and caterwauling, some by men intent on parting your purse from your belt and quite possibly your soul from your body. The French soldiers didn't patrol after curfew, just stood in their little guard houses trying to look tough. A man alone was fair game, and my tunic was stuffed with gold. No wonder Caterina had looked anxious.

Fortunately I have a good nose for trouble, which usually allows me to avoid it. Mind you, in a town where the standard Lenten fare is fish with garlic sauce you don't need to have much of a nose to smell trouble coming. It generally knocks you over with the sheer force of its personality before anyone lays a hand on you.

I arrived at the tavern whole, if a little breathless. It was quiet, as it should have been. Nobody was in it but the landlord Prunio and Andrea and his mob, sitting around a big table close to the fire in the guttering light of a single tallow lantern. Their presence there after curfew had rung would have been enough to prove them conspirators, if there had been any Frenchmen there to see it.

They were eating, but they all stopped and stared at me in unwelcoming silence when I came in. I sauntered over to them, looking supercilious and wondering which of them was the marketplace bully who had frightened Caterina.

Andrea set down his clay cup. 'Nicetas,' he said coolly. 'Glad to see you got here safely. The streets can be dangerous at night.' His thin grey voice still brought up the hairs on the back of my neck. 'Let's see the gold.'

'Not until you tell me what's going on,' I said. 'You've kept me waiting a week.'

Andrea smiled thinly. 'I've been considering your offer of assistance,' he said. 'I decided we ought to let you have the chance to prove yourself worthy.'

Prove myself worthy! What did he think his sneaking little

conspiracy was, a holy order? But I didn't show my scorn. I grabbed the bench and hauled it out, then flung myself down upon it, the picture of eagerness. 'How? You know I will. Tell me what you want me to do!'

'I thought we would use your own idea,' said Andrea. I frowned. I remembered perfectly well that I hadn't suggested anything, but madcap young Nicetas wouldn't. Andrea looked at me in silence for a moment. Then his narrow, pursed lips formed themselves into a smile. It looked unnatural on his grey, thin face. 'I want you to kill someone.'

My face became very still. Here was the young enthusiast brought to bay. Behind my mask of apprehension my mind was working fast. Murder! I had no immunity: to all intents and purposes I wasn't a Venetian at the moment. If I was taken up for a killing I would die for it, hung from a French noose on the gallows outside the governor's palace. And besides, I have never liked killing in cold blood.

But I didn't have any choice. My orders were to infiltrate the conspiracy, and if murder was the entry fee I would have to pay. Right now I needed to concentrate on making them believe in Nicetas. I folded my hands on the table in front of me and chewed my lip, then said, 'When?'

I was proud of my voice: just enough nervousness beneath the bluster. Andrea kept me waiting for an answer and I licked my lips. When he thought I was well stewed he said, 'Tonight. No time like the present.'

The Devil take him! He was a professional, all right. No time for me to plan anything smart to get out of it. I said, 'I haven't got my sword with me.'

'You've got a dagger,' Andrea said. 'That's all most of us have these days. It'll do the job. An inch of steel in the right place will do the job. You don't want a big noisy sword for a midnight killing.'

He was talking man to boy. Nicetas would be bound to object, and I bristled accordingly. 'What's wrong? You think I've never killed a man? I'll show you. Tell me who!'

'Anyone you like,' Andrea said, and beside me Blasio gave a low, satisfied laugh.

'I'd rather not kill anyone I like,' I joked feebly, trying to buy myself time. I was truly surprised. Shocked. I was beginning to realise quite how devious Andrea was. They weren't even going to select a target for me. There would be no excuse, no 'I was only following orders'. My choice, my responsibility. I swallowed and said, 'A Frenchman?'

'If you like,' said Andrea, offhand and uninterested. 'It's up to you.'

'I've not been here long,' I said, fumbling for excuses. 'I don't know where they lodge. I don't know how to find them at night.'

'Don't worry,' said Blasio, taking a draught of his wine. 'We'll know.'

There was a silence. Then one of the others, a good-looking youngster with an aristocratic air, grinned at me and stretched. He was enjoying my discomfiture, curse him. 'Who'll it be?' he asked.

Trapped like a fox in the snare. No way out. I shook my head and screwed up my nerve. By the thief that mocked Christ, I couldn't fail this far down the line. 'There's a French sergeant,' I said. 'Name of Petrot. What about him?'

They all laughed. 'Good choice,' said Blasio. 'He's a bastard, right enough.'

'Lodges outside the castle, too,' said another of them.

'Him, then,' I said. I was almost certainly going to have to go through with this. I might as well pick someone who could give me trouble if he remained on the scene. I offered up a silent prayer to Saint Mark. Besides being my name saint he took special care of Venice, and he could explain to our Judge that I was only doing what I had to. Thank God I didn't have to tell Dolfin or the Security Committee why I needed to kill a Frenchman to assist Venice's alliance with the French.

'Right,' Andrea said, relaxing. 'That's agreed, then. You kill Petrot, and I'll think about involving you in our work from now on.' His expression was smooth with satisfaction, like a cat before a fire. He must have suspected me of being a French agent. The French are patriots and like their countrymen. One Frenchman might kill another over a woman or a dice game or because he is in a drunken fury, but not just to keep his cover intact. Andrea probably felt he could be sure that whoever Nicetas was, he wasn't in French pay. 'Now,' he said, 'hand over the gold. Then you can have something to eat until it's time to go. Prunio, what have you got?'

'I don't know where Petrot lodges,' I said hesitantly.

'We all know,' grinned Blasio. 'We'll walk along with you and keep an eye on things.'

'Got to make sure it goes according to plan,' said another of them.

I nodded dumbly and reached inside my tunic for the gold. It was heavy in my hands. I wondered if thirty pieces of silver were so heavy. Andrea opened the purse and poured the glittering coins into his palm, smiling quietly to himself. The others pushed a little closer, gazing. 'We'll put this to good use,' he said.

'For what?' I asked bluntly.

He smiled at me. The Devil must smile so when he sees a mortal sin. 'I'll tell you after you've killed Petrot.'

'You can talk to us while we wait,' said Blasio. The landlord came with food, bread and olives and the inevitable Lenten pickled herring and dried salt cod. It didn't look very appetising to a man who was used to Caterina's cooking and was going to have to carry out an assassination within a few hours. Blasio grabbed a handful of olives and crammed them into his mouth. Through them he said, 'We were wanting to know about Caterina.' He spat out one stone after another onto the table.

'Caterina? What's it to you?' I snapped.

'If you wanted a girl for your bed,' Andrea said thinly, 'aren't there enough whores in Palermo? Why pick an honest widow?'

'Listen.' I let my anger show. It was a relief. 'I'm a gem factor, right? I've got plenty of money, right? Why have a common slut when I can have a nice girl who knows how to cook?' Once the anger was released it was hard to rein in. 'What's your problem?' I demanded. 'Leave my private life alone. My tastes are up to me.'

Andrea arched his half-moon brows. 'Very touchy,' he said. 'I'm not ready to leave it quite yet, Nicetas. Tell me why you hate the French.'

'What?'

'What did they do to you?'

'It's none of your business,' I told him, turning my back.

His cold voice pursued me. 'We've got the gold now,' he said. 'I call the tune, Nicetas. Explain what the French did to you, if you want to help us fight them.'

I swallowed hard. I had prepared the story with care, but it had to look convincing. In a thick, clotted voice I said, 'I'm from the Morea. From Monemvasia. Until recently the town was held by the French. You know what they're like.'

The conspirators nodded. Their eyes glittered as they watched me. I thought I had their sympathy, but I hadn't earned it yet. Andrea said, 'I've heard of Monemvasia. It's back in Greek hands now, I understand.'

I nodded. 'That's right.'

'So why this enthusiasm, Nicetas?'

'Before the French left, a – a French officer raped my sister. He was the second in command, there was nothing we could do. He saw her in the streets and sent his men to take her. He –' I shut my eyes tightly. 'He got her pregnant. She tried to get rid of it and the abortionist – killed her.'

A long silence. Nobody laughed. I must have sounded suitably harrowed. Andrea said after a while, 'How old was she?'

'Fourteen,' I choked. 'Fourteen years old, and a virgin.'

Another silence. Andrea stared at me with odd, greedy eyes. One of the other men asked, 'Did you kill the Frenchman?'

'If I had, perhaps I wouldn't feel this way.' I shook my head. 'The French left and I lost my chance. He got away from me. I –' I left the words hanging and buried my face in my hands. Then I caught in a deep breath and snarled to the empty air, 'We are a noble house. He dishonoured us! I am the eldest, it was my place.'

They nodded slowly. Sicilians understand honour. Even Andrea looked as if he believed me at last. He said, 'Well, now we know. No more questions, Nicetas. Have some food.' He tore a hunk off the loaf and turned to speak to his neighbour.

I sat with my head hanging and toyed with a cup of rough wine. Time crawled, and the Sicilians let me alone. Perhaps they thought that I was dwelling on the past dishonour of my fictitious sister and anticipating my imminent revenge. In fact I was dreading what was about to happen. It wasn't that I really cared about the sergeant. The sum total of human evil would be somewhat reduced once I had killed him, and the average intelligence of the French army marginally increased. But only a madman really enjoys killing people.

I needed something to do. After a while I got out my dagger and tested its edge against the heavy wooden table, then said, 'Does anyone have a strop?'

Blasio passed me a sliver of whetstone in silence. I sat and ground the dagger blade against it, quiet and absorbed. Nobody talked to me. Nobody talked about anything interesting, either, though my ears were wide open. They were still being cautious. They would not trust me until the Frenchman was dead.

At last Blasio went over to the window and looked up at the sky. 'Past midnight,' he said. 'Time to go.'

Andrea did not accompany us. The genius behind the operation was far too valuable to risk himself on a murder foray. That was a pity. If he had come with us I might have been able to arrange for some sort of accident to happen to him.

The streets were quieter now. Even the thieves had gone home to bed. I followed the broad shadow of Blasio's shoulders away from the harbour through narrow alleys and side streets, lost within a hundred paces. Occasionally we crossed a piazza or a main street which I recognised: then all was confusion again. The moon had risen, and its blue light streamed across the silent city, casting sharp shadows. We were heading west, towards the quarter near the governor's palace.

There were more guard posts in this part of town. We passed quite close to one, a little island of golden lamplight in the dark of the streets. Presently Blasio and another of the men conferred briefly. Then he whispered to me, 'There.'

A tall building, big, high windows, typical soldier's lodging. I nodded. 'That's where he lodges,' hissed Blasio. 'Front room on the upper floor, there, where you see the balcony. There're a lot of soldiers on the lower floor.'

'Does he have his own room?'

Another brief conference. 'Probably. He's senior sergeant in the building. Maybe one other in the billet.'

I studied the building. My conscience twinges had stopped, though my blood was racing with nervous energy. This was a job to be done, and a tricky one. 'Any suggestions for getting in?'

Blasio looked at me. He seemed a bit surprised, by the coolness of my tone or the fact that I was asking his advice, I don't know. He said, 'There's a broken shutter there, third window along. Once you're in the staircase is right ahead of you.'

We went over to the building and I tugged at the shutter. It swung back without a creak. The window was as high as my head. I signalled to Blasio and he made a stirrup and hoisted me up.

Inside, the silence of a lot of men sleeping. Murmurs, snoring, sighs. I swung my leg over the windowsill and landed silently on the floorboards, dropping to a crouch so my silhouette would not show. Nobody stirred. A single ray of moonlight fell through the shutter and illuminated a carpet of bodies. One or two of the soldiers had their women with them, soft faces next to stubble. I crept through them to the stairs and began to climb.

Half way up a step gave a violent squeal. I froze while the sleepers below me grumbled and turned over. Nobody woke.

At the top of the stairs I hesitated. I knew which door to open, only one could give onto the room at the front of the house. I began to think about the possible other person sharing the room. This could be difficult. Killing in silence is harder than you might imagine. Perhaps Andrea's men were going to get two French lives for the price of one.

Well, no point in waiting on the landing until I lost my nerve. I eased my dagger from its sheath, put my hand to the latch and lifted it. It raised without a sound. The door opened enough to admit me. I moved like a wraith.

The shutters were open and blue moonlight poured into the room. The brightness fell over a bed, centrally placed. There was one figure in it. I breathed a silent sigh of relief. The person in the bed was turned away from me. Unpleasant, but shamefully easy. In two paces I was at the bed, stooping over it. My dagger flashed silver in the moonlight, then drove between the figure's shoulder blades. At the same moment my hand clamped over its mouth to stifle any involuntary cry.

As soon as I touched the face I knew I had made a terrible mistake. It was too late. The hilt of my dagger was against the blanket and a dark stain was already spreading around it. The figure arched and shuddered and thrashed for a moment, then lay still.

I swallowed, hardly able to breathe. I took my hand away from the gaping mouth and hesitantly rolled the body over. Glowing moonlight fell on the face.

It was a young girl, no more than sixteen years old. Her dark eyes were wide open, ringed with white, glazing as I watched. I turned my head away violently, afraid of her innocent, accusing stare. My heart rattled in my ears.

Movement outside the shutters! Stifling a gasp, I flung myself back into the shadows. My eyes ached and stung with tears of desperate, furious remorse. A burly naked figure blocked out the moonlight as it moved slowly into the room. No mistake this time, this was the Frenchman. I could see his shadowed face. I should have jumped him at once, but I was shaken and incompetent.

He looked at the bed and hesitated. I don't know what warned him, but he turned and stared straight at me. His mouth opened.

I leapt. He flung up one arm but I caught it with my left hand and knocked it violently aside. I loathed him as if he had made me kill the girl himself. He was about to cry out. I snarled and slashed my dagger across his throat.

He stood upright, clawing at the open lips of the wound. His mouth was moving, making the shapes of words, but no air gave them sound. Blood spurted in pulsing jets, catching my face, my hands, my tunic. The breath bubbled from his cloven windpipe. After an infinite moment he fell to the floor, struggling.

I ran straight to the window and out onto the balcony. His blood would drip through the floorboards and waken whoever was lying underneath, if the thump of his fall had not woken them already. I swung over the balcony, hung by my hands and dropped.

Blasio appeared from the shadows and caught at me. He pulled me away into the maze of little streets. Behind us I heard sleepy cries growing into a full-throated crescendo of amazement and horror.

We ran in silence. For a while my clothes dripped a spoor of the sergeant's blood. At the central crossroads we stopped, gasping in the moonlight.

'Run,' Blasio said in a quick undertone. 'Can you find your way home?'

'Home?' I repeated. I was still fuddled with horror. 'But —'

'You'll hear from us,' said Blasio. 'My word on it.'

They left me. I heard the hue and cry raised and I ran from it, hurrying back to the merchant's quarter. I slipped the catch on the door and slithered inside. Nobody in the house stirred as I staggered up the stairs.

When I reached the top I thought about how I must look, plastered with blood like a demon. I hesitated. Then the door that separated us from the staircase opened and Caterina stood there, wrapped in a blanket, her eyes wide. Moonlight flooded through the open doorway, fringing her dishevelled hair with silver.

I didn't say anything. I couldn't. She stared at my face, then at my tunic. The blood on it looked black and glistening in the blue moonlight. In a dull flat voice she said, 'You're hurt.'

I shook my head dumbly. She caught me by the arm and drew me through the door, her face twisting as she felt the blood on her hands. 'Take your clothes off,' she said softly.

I obeyed her. I was trembling. When I was naked she took me to the window and examined me, going over every inch of me, testing my bloodstained skin with her strong hard fingers. When she was assured that I was unhurt she gave a long, shuddering sigh.

'Wash,' she said, 'and then come to bed. It's late.'

I understood her. I was not excused explanations, but they were deferred for now. I washed myself, ruining three rags. The hue and cry was beneath us in the streets, Frenchmen shouting and calling out, dogs barking and whining, torchlight bobbing, yellow against the blue of the moon.

At last I was clean. I walked unsteadily to the bed and Caterina drew back the blanket for me. I crept in and lay huddled and shivering, like a child expecting to be beaten. When she stroked my hair I pressed my face to her soft neck and clung to her. Her body was warm and resilient with life. I shuddered and held her more tightly and she stroked and stroked my hair and said nothing. After a while the hue and cry below us died down and she fell asleep.

I did not sleep. I was afraid of my dreams.

TWELVE

By the time she woke up I had my story straight.

It was a grey morning, threatening rain. It felt almost like Venice. Caterina had slept in my arms all night. Or was I in hers? In any case, when she stirred in the dawn and opened her eyes I just held her tighter.

She sighed and gave a huge yawn. The kitten, which had been asleep at the end of the bed, sensed that she was awake and stomped over the covers to demand attention. For once she ignored it. Her dark eyes looked into mine, but she said nothing.

'Do you still want an explanation?' I asked her softly.

'It's up to you.'

Her face was very still. I didn't know what she was thinking. 'If I say nothing, what then?'

She looked away and made a little helpless movement. 'I don't know. I'll probably leave. I don't think I can bear not knowing what is going on.'

It felt as if she was about to pull away from me. I didn't want her to. 'All right.' Her eyes returned quickly to mine. 'Look, Caterina, I'm not really a gem merchant.'

'Go on,' she said, pursing her lips. Her tone was faintly jocular and there were the beginnings of a sparkle in her eyes. I was glad she still had a sense of humour.

It was time for my carefully prepared story. 'I do deal in gems,' I said, 'but not the way you think. I – smuggle them. I'm here looking for new supply sources and men prepared to be couriers.'

She was looking puzzled. Her feathery brows drew down over her eyes and she pushed her hair back from her forehead with her hand. It hurt me more than I expected to lie to her. I really wanted to tell her everything and put the burden of my conscience onto her white shoulders. But that luxury was denied me. After a moment she put her head on one side and said, 'Why do you want to smuggle gems?'

'Taxes are high in Byzantium,' I said, truthfully. She looked even more puzzled at this. For her, taxes were something that happened to other people. 'It's as if someone came to you at the end of every day in the market and took away one coin in ten,' I explained.

'One in ten? That's awful!' she exclaimed. 'What for?'

'Oh,' I shrugged, 'the defence of the State. The Civil Service. The Emperor's slippers. I don't know.'

She frowned and freed herself from my arms. 'So why did you come home covered in blood?'

'Caterina, the work I do is risky. You remember the man who came for me?' I could see by the shadow on her face that she remembered. 'He's typical. I was meeting him and some others,' I said cautiously, 'in a tavern. On business. On the way back someone tried to – to rob me. And I killed him. It was a bit – messy. Hence the blood.'

Her expression did not lighten. 'Was the hue and cry for you?'

I shook my head. To my own astonishment, I found myself unable to look into her eyes. 'I don't know what that was about,' I lied. 'But what would you do if you heard the hue and cry and you were covered in blood? I ran.' I glanced over at the pile of bloodstained clothes on the floor. 'You'd better get rid of that tunic,' I suggested. 'If the French saw it they'd take me up for – for whatever it was they were chasing last night.'

She was chewing her lower lip. Her fair brows were knitted, furrowing her forehead. She looked about six years old. After a moment she said in a very small voice, 'Nico, I don't know if you're telling me the truth.'

'Why should I lie to you?' I asked, unanswerably.

'I don't know.' Suddenly she moved close to me and buried her head in my shoulder, squeezing me tight with her round white arms. 'I told you to be careful,' she said. 'I told you so.'

'Don't ever, ever say I told you so.' I caught her by the shoulders and pulled her away from me, trying to smile as if I hadn't a care in the world. 'It doesn't do any good. Don't say it, *gattina*.'

She covered her mouth with her hand, eyes twinkling. I seemed to have struck a chord. 'I'm sorry,' she said through her fingers. 'I know it's bad. My husband used to say that anyone who said I told you so ought to be hung up by their tongue until they repented it.'

'I'm not sure I'd go quite so far,' I said, catching her back into my arms.

I tried to be cheerful, but it was hopeless. I kept seeing the dead girl's eyes, dark like Caterina's, staring sightlessly upwards at the moonlight. Stupid, stupid, stupid. She had been slight, small, her shape nothing like a burly French sergeant. The most obvious mistake, and irreparable. I wanted to weep.

Caterina tried to interest me in a little early-morning excitement, but I was as unresponsive as flat dough. After a while she was worried and asked me, 'What's wrong?'

I shook my head. 'I got a fright last night,' I admitted, quite truthfully. 'I think I need some air.'

She shrugged and got up. 'Whatever you want,' she said, 'but you're not going out in this.' She stirred my wrecked tunic with her toe. 'I think I'll burn it,' she said thoughtfully. 'I'll make you a new one. It won't take long.'

I dressed in my spare tunic and went out. The streets were becoming busy with the day's traffic. People were grumbling about the appalling weather, as townsfolk do who don't have crops that need rain to grow. Personally I felt as if I deserved thunder, lightning and hailstones, never mind some heavy cloud. I knew what I needed: I needed to confess. I was burning to tell someone what I had done, and more than that, I was in dire need of God's forgiveness. But I didn't dare go to a priest in Sicily. He wouldn't understand the necessities of State that had driven me to kill not just my target but an innocent girl. He might impose some appalling penance, something I couldn't hide. Confession would have to wait. There was a priest at my local church of Santi Apostoli who knew me. He had a good grasp of my priorities.

So for the time being I walked the streets of Palermo like one damned, which I certainly would have been if I had been smitten with lightning or a rock had fallen on my head. The Angevins were out in force, stopping people at random, searching them for weapons, demanding whether anyone knew anything about last night. Nobody did. The soldiers were rough and brutal, and the faces of the Palermitans were closed. Even if anyone had known it was me the French sought, they would have said nothing.

The bells were tolling in all the churches I passed. Presently I stopped before the glorious dome-topped campanile of the church named for the Norman admiral who had it built, Santa Maria del Ammiraglio. The bells caught at me. I slipped inside with the other worshippers.

The interlaced, receding arches and pillars of the wonderful building burned with gold mosaic. Upon its glittering ground stood the figures of saints and angels, filling every niche. Even the narrow curving squinches were filled with the figures of seraphim, their six great wings lapping against the stone on either side, every feather shown clear and bright.

I walked slowly forward past the broad square pillars that held up the high dome. From it Christ Pantocrator looked down at me, stern and unforgiving. I flinched from him. The brilliance of the mosaic reminded me not of the fires of Heaven but the flames of Hell. I craved an image of a friendly saint, someone who would help me and carry my prayers before the Lord. But it was Lent, and the statues of Saint and Saviour in the aisles were swathed in black and the doors of their shrines were closed. There was nobody I could pray to apart from the flat bright pictures of the mosaic, and the Pantocrator made me afraid. I crossed myself, forgetting in my perturbation of spirit to do it right to left. Then I went sadly to the door.

In the narthex there were more mosaics, this time of the donor and his patron King Roger. Like the rest, they were splendid. They rivalled even the new work in St Mark's. I read the inscription on the patron's memorial, written in good Greek. Sicilians have always been cultured. *Grant him the forgiveness of his sins as Thou only, oh God, hast power to do.* I bit my knuckle and slipped out of the building as the choir began to chant Matins, saluting the day that the Lord had made.

Outside the threatened rain had started, a thin miserable drizzle. In all the houses along the street people were pushing herbs and plants in pots outside to benefit from the rare bounty of water from the sky. It suited my mood. I stood in the little square outside the church and moped.

A pair of feet appeared before me. I looked up quickly, sharp and angry at being interrupted. The feet belonged to a boy, a thin clever-looking thing of twelve or thirteen. He said, 'Andrea wants you.'

'Does he,' I replied coldly. 'Where? The Pig?'

'No. Follow me,' said the boy. He didn't wait for me to agree, just turned and set off through the narrow crowded streets. I followed, watching my footing. The cobbles were slippery with rain and the red earth was quickly turning to mud. I felt my remorse altering within me, metamorphosing by some strange magic of the spirit into anger, which a man need not be ashamed to feel. By the time the boy stopped at the door of a small, clean house in a respectable street I was shivering not with the fear of damnation, but with barely contained rage.

The boy, clearly a native, opened the door and led me inside. It was small and clean. My anger left me no space to congratulate myself on having penetrated the Holy of Holies. As soon as I was shown into the room where Andrea sat with Blasio and a few others I demanded, 'Did you know he would have a girl with him?'

Andrea gave me one of his icy smiles. 'You killed her too, I hear. Well done.'

'Well done? She couldn't have been more than sixteen! Was she Sicilian?'

'Came from the market quarter,' said one of the men easily. 'Perina, her name was. A little whore, but cheerful, she was.'

'Sicilian, French, no matter,' said Andrea. 'Any woman who lets a Frenchman have her deserves to get a sword where he puts his prick.'

The others growled in agreement. I couldn't believe my ears. This was fanaticism gone mad. Fortunately the character of Nicetas allowed me to display my disapproval. I hurled myself at Andrea, foaming with rage. Blasio caught me by the arms and wrestled me back. Andrea never moved, just looked at me with his cold eyes. 'You dog,' I spluttered, 'are you talking about my sister?'

'They raped your sister,' Andrea said. 'Not her fault. Perina was sleeping with the enemy. She should have known better.' He watched me heaving under Blasio's huge hands and shook his head. 'Nicetas,' he said after a moment, 'you did well. But if you want to work with us you're going to have to control your temper.'

I took a deep breath and pulled free of Blasio's hands. 'Sorry,' I said sullenly.

'Sit down,' Andrea said. I obeyed him and he nodded. 'All right. Time you met the rest of us.' He introduced me to the other men in the room. 'This is Zanino.' A thin, ferrety, poverty-stricken man with a permanent sense of humour failure. 'Pietro.' A well set up youngster whose gold-embroidered tunic and carefully-cut hair gave him the look of wealth. A wag. He was the one who had asked me with relish whom I had chosen to kill. 'Bartolo.' The one who had known Perina. He looked like a hard case. My money was on him as the racket-runner. 'Giovanni.' A respectable-looking fellow of middle years. You could have taken him for a merchant. 'There's one of them from each quarter of the city,' Andrea explained. 'They pass on our plans to their own networks. It keeps Blasio and myself, ah, anonymous.'

It made good sense. I nodded, concealing my glee. At last I was making progress. Infiltrate the network, those were my orders: find out where the gold is going and stop it.

Andrea's boy servant came in with a trayful of wooden cups and a big jar of wine. He set it down on the floor: there was no table and half of us were standing. He poured the wine and brought it round to us. I noticed that when he handed Andrea his cup their fingers touched and their eyes met in a way that made my guts tingle with loathing. I looked quickly around at the others, but either they hadn't noticed or they took their leader's proclivities for granted. Palermo in some ways is still more than half an Arab city, and Arabs think that if a man wants something he should take it. I suppose I shouldn't have been surprised that their vicious beliefs rubbed off onto the other inhabitants.

'Can you get us more gold?' demanded Zanino. He looked as though he wanted it for himself.

I shrugged. 'I'll have to go to the mainland and report. If I can tell my principal that you are going to achieve what he wants, maybe. What did the last lot go on? There was enough to hire a small army.'

Andrea smiled in his supercilious way. 'We don't need men,' he said softly. 'We have every man on the island. We outnumber them ten to one.'

'They're soldiers,' I said. 'Numbers aren't everything.'

'That's why we need weapons.'

'Weapons,' I breathed, leaning forward. This was new, but somehow I wasn't surprised. 'You can't get weapons in Palermo.'

'Not legally,' agreed Pietro.

'Andrea has arranged for us to ship weapons from the mainland,' Blasio said. 'We've had a couple of shipments already on credit,' he gestured at the German dagger he wore on his hip, 'and the next one arrives next week. They want paying this time. We were wondering how we would manage.'

'We thought we were going to have to rob a French supply train,' put in Bartolo. 'But you saved us the trouble.'

That explained the German weapons I had seen. I felt very satisfied, as anyone would when their hunch is proved to be correct. 'And when you've got them?' I asked breathlessly, maintaining Nicetas's excitable character. 'What then?'

'What would you do?' asked Andrea, his head on one side.

I pursed my lips in thought. This might be my chance to sort out the last thing that had been bothering me. 'Well, if it was me, I'd get together with the Aragonese once the French have left the island for Byzantium. But my principal wouldn't like to hear me say that.'

Behind me Blasio spat hard. 'The Aragonese? Pah.'

Suddenly they were animated, leaning forward, speaking all at once. 'The Aragonese just want to put another foreign king over us.' 'One overlord's just like another.' 'It would be out of the saucepan and into the fire.' 'We don't work with the poxy Spanish, they're as bad as the French.'

'I don't understand,' I said at last, flinging up my hands in confusion. 'I thought you wanted Pere of Aragon as King. What alternative is there?'

'We can rule ourselves,' said Andrea quietly.

'Rule *yourselves*? But –'

'We can be a Commune.'

'What's a Commune?'

'Oh, you Greeks.' He curled his lip. 'You've knelt to your Emperor for so long you've forgotten there's any other way to live. You don't have to crawl to an overlord. We can be independent cities, governing ourselves. Like Venice does.'

I tried to look blank and ignorant. They didn't know that I was an expert on matters Venetian. 'Venice has a Duke,' I said. 'Doesn't it?'

'The Doge doesn't run Venice,' said Andrea pityingly. 'He's a salaried governor. He can't take gifts or receive ambassadors alone. He doesn't make decisions on his own. He's got councils of advisors. We can be like that. No overlords. No corruption. We can control ourselves!'

They all sighed with the glory of the vision, and indeed the whole thing had a sort of mad appeal. After all, what Andrea said about Venice was true. I serve Venice with a light heart, even when my work is dirty, because I know that it is the best governed state in the Mediterranean. I don't mean just for patricians like my father, but for all its people: nobles, merchants, tradesmen. Even the prostitutes are better off there than anywhere else, as my mother knew.

It's not just a question of street lighting, nor hospitals and orphanages, nor the organisation that means that even in the worst floods and famines relatively few of our people starve.

Venice is a place where tens of thousands of merchants and artisans can make a decent living without being afraid that some sword-bearing lout with a gold circlet on his hair will ride down on them and steal everything they have. But we are an ancient Republic with an empire and the wealth to look after our own defence. We have a merchant fleet as great as any in the world and a vast population, nearly two hundred thousand people, and all of them busy making money and paying their taxes and tithes. How could Andrea imagine a government like Venice's for Palermo? Palermo was just a single city, full of people scarcely more than peasants, who wouldn't have known what an election was, never mind how to put in place the sort of checks and balances that Venice has used for years to keep the Doges honest.

They didn't stand a chance. But they weren't to know it. I shook my head, pretending to be a puzzled Greek. 'You've got to have an overlord,' I said. 'Who'd protect you?'

'We'll be vassals of the Pope,' said Andrea with determination.

I flung back my head and laughed heartily. Andrea had gone beyond the bounds of credulity. 'The Pope? He'd never accept you. He's French. He'll support Charles of Anjou until he dies.'

This cast a damper on their elevation. Andrea scowled at me. 'What do you know about the Pope, Greek heretic?' he demanded.

Better not tread on any toes. I looked hunted and admitted, 'Well, not much.'

'We'll be a republic by Whitsuntide,' said Blasio. His wrestler's face was glowing with hope. 'No more King, Charles or Pere. Government for the people.'

The others were all nodding and murmuring with eagerness, but I was puzzled by the timing. Did they mean to rise against the French, or didn't they? 'Whitsuntide?' I said. 'That could be too late. All the French in the island will have gone to attack Constantinople. I'd have to go back when the fleet sails.'

Andrea looked at me with narrow eyes. 'If you want to help us kill Frenchmen,' he said slowly, 'I promise you you'll have your chance. Before the Angevin fleet sails for Corfu we will attack. I have contacts in other cities all over the island. It'll be a general rebellion. They won't know what's hit them.'

'Kill them all,' muttered wizened, furious Zanino. He looked as if he was anticipating the slaughter with more glee than the freedom that would come after it.

'We'll dip them in tar and use them as torches,' suggested Pietro.

'We have to land the weapons before we do anything,' said Andrea, bringing his people back to their senses. 'We've got enough now to pay for the first shipment. The second will still pose a problem. Nicetas, you've heard our plans. What more can you get out of your principal?'

They really only had me there to extract more money from me. Well, fine. If they needed me, all the better. I hemmed and hawed and sucked my teeth. 'I won't have time to hear from Constantinople,' I said. 'I'll have to go back to my master on the mainland and try to convince him. It could take me a couple of weeks.'

Andrea nodded. 'Not to worry. The second shipment is planned for some time around Palm Sunday. I'll be making the arrangements fairly soon. Nicetas, tomorrow I am meeting our shippers to finalise the first deal. Come with me and observe. You'll be able to give your master plenty of food for thought. We're doing this properly.'

I looked eager, and I was. 'I'll be there. When shall I meet you?'

'Come to the Pig at noon.'

There wasn't much more to say and after a little while I made my salutations and left. It was almost time for lunch, and I wandered home through the damp streets planning my next move.

Nobody in Venice was expecting a general armed rising of the Sicilians. An attack by Aragon was what the Security Committee was looking for. If that was how we felt, how must the French feel? They despised the Sicilians, as their treatment of them showed. They did not consider the islanders a threat. How would I convince them at third hand that they needed to do something, and fast?

At least I had the chance of a personal visit to Messina to talk to Dolfin. If I was going to achieve anything he would have to be part of it. When I knew more about the arms shipments I could lay my plans.

Outside my house I saw a French officer standing looking up at the balcony. I knew him. It was the good-looking chestnut-haired bastard who had bought a posy from Caterina weeks ago. He turned and saw me watching him and raised his perfectly arched brows in a way that would have had me drawing my sword if I'd been wearing one. I wasn't, and he was, so instead I just went into the house.

As I climbed the stairs I could smell cooking. It smelt good, as always. I walked in with my nose twitching and demanded, 'What's for lunch?'

'It should be blood pudding,' Caterina replied from her stool where she sat sewing, 'seeing how much of the stuff I had to clean up this morning.'

She meant to make me laugh, but I thought at once of Perina. My face must have changed, because Caterina got up quickly, looking remorseful. 'I meant it as a joke,' she said. She held out her sewing. It was fine wool, amber gold. 'Look, it's a new tunic for you. Don't you like the colour? It's like the flecks in your eyes.'

I admired it, trying to sound cheerful. She showed me the shape of it and held it against me to check the size. As she did so she talked rapidly to me. 'You had a lucky escape last night,' she said. 'Someone killed a French sergeant in his lodging over towards the harbour. Can you believe it? Crept into his room in the night and killed him, just like that. That's who the French were looking for. If they'd caught you they'd have thought it was you, I'm certain.'

'Who do they think did it?' I asked.

'Nobody knows. They think it couldn't be a Sicilian, because he had a girl with him, one of the little whores from the market, and she was killed too. Mustapha who keeps the spice stall told me they think it was an Aragonese spy.'

I raised my eyebrows. Caterina's offhand reference to the dead girl as a whore didn't make me feel any better. I didn't say anything and she ran on breathlessly, 'Anyway, I burned your tunic, like you said.'

She sounded as if she was trying to talk herself out of an entirely natural suspicion. It was time to change the subject. I said, 'What was that red-headed Frenchman doing looking up at our balcony?'

She flushed, then grinned. 'You saw him? I told him to leave before midday.'

'He was here? Caterina –'

'He followed me back from the market like a stray dog. What can I do? I couldn't make him stop, could I? And I told him to go away.'

'What did he want? As if I couldn't guess.'

'He wanted to know why I went with you when I turned him down. That was all. And I told him, and he went away. Nothing happened. He didn't lay a finger on me.' She smiled at me coaxingly. 'Don't you believe me, Nico?'

'I suppose so,' I said, scowling at her. I was thinking of what Andrea had said about girls who sleep with Frenchmen. Caterina's admirer could be dangerous for her. It was unlike me to miss an opportunity to receive a compliment, but in my anxiety I forgot to ask Caterina what she had told the red-headed Frenchman when he asked her why she had chosen me.

Now it was her turn to change the subject. 'So what do you think of your new tunic? It'll be nicer than the old one. I'll embroider the neck for you and the sleeves.' She looked up at me and suddenly her eyes stopped sparkling and became soft and warm. 'I thought,' she said timidly, 'I thought I'd embroider a kitten on it somewhere, so, so you'd remember, later, who made it for you.'

I knew that look, I knew the sound of that voice. I wanted to avoid her falling in love with me. It would not be convenient or sensible, and it could hurt her. So instead of responding I shrugged, 'If you want,' and went over to the cooking pot to investigate lunch.

She hesitated, then flung down the sewing and came and snatched the spoon from my hand. She looked offended, not upset. 'Thief,' she said. 'I don't know why I put up with you.'

'Because I pay you six silver pieces a day,' I reminded her. 'And because I'm good on the mattress.'

'You weren't this morning,' she accused me.

'I'll make it up to you now.' And I was ready to. Seeing the Frenchman outside had administered a salutory jolt of jealousy. I grappled with her and we reeled together over to the bed.

As I took her she clutched me and her dark eyes opened wide and glazed over with pleasure. It made her look like Perina. I buried my head in her shoulder and rutted like a stag, hiding myself from horror. I was so engrossed I forgot to withdraw. It was bliss, like Heaven's gates opening for me. She seemed to be happy, too. Afterwards we fell asleep, and the lunch burned to the pot.

THIRTEEN

The arms runners were Pisans. No surprises there. They were a canny bunch, who appeared to spend our entire meeting drinking but remained suspiciously sober throughout. We paid them half of the agreed fee, the balance to be handed over when we picked up the goods.

I was interested to note that the amount which changed hands was not big enough to account for half of what I had brought with me. Where had the rest gone, I wondered? It would be nice to think that some of it had stuck to Andrea's fingers. My cynicism tells me that nobody, however idealistic, is immune to the lure of gold.

The drop was to take place at a small cove not far outside Palermo. We arranged a simple system of light signals to indicate when we were in position and it was safe to come in. I asked a few really stupid questions to give Andrea the impression that I'd never done this sort of thing before.

We left the Pisans still drinking and went out from the crowded, stuffy tavern into the streets, which were quiet with siesta. The weather was bright and hot, a premonition of the steel-strong sunshine that beats down onto Sicily from May to November. The refuse in the gutters and between the tight-packed wooden buildings was beginning to smell ripe. Andrea retreated under the shade of an awning. He looked like a lizard in its lair.

'Well?' he said. 'Will you be able to convince your master?'

I shrugged. 'I'll do my best. I can't make promises.'

'We need that gold,' he insisted.

We do, or I do? How much was he making out of this? I shrugged again and looked equivocal. He gave me a narrow look from under his heavy lids and then asked, 'You sail tomorrow, you said. When will you be back?'

'A week or so.'

'You'll miss the drop.'

'Can't be helped.' I had no intention of missing the second one. In fact I had every intention of making it a good deal more exciting for Andrea and his men than the first seemed likely to be.

He continued to watch me like a cat waiting for a mouse to emerge from its hole. Finally he said, 'You can come to my house when you get back and let me know how things went.' He made this sound like a favour. I nodded and he turned without another word and went away.

He was not walking in the direction either of his house or of the Spitted Pig. Something inside me was curious about where he was going and wanted to follow him, but he looked over his shoulder as if assuring himself that I was off about my business. It is hard to follow someone who knows where you were to begin with, and I decided to leave indulging my curiosity for another occasion.

Besides, I had other things on my mind. I was concerned that my absence would enable the good-looking young French officer to descend upon Caterina and press his point in a way that she couldn't refuse. I wanted to ensure, if I could, that she had the strength of character to resist him until I returned. I have always believed that women remember their men better if they have something tangible to jog their memories. So on the way home I walked along the street where the goldsmiths kept their shops.

It was a little wider than many streets in Palermo, as befitted its exalted merchandise. Two men would have been hard put to span it, even with outstretched arms. The cobbles were in good repair, and a gutter ran down the centre of the street, scoured clean by yesterday's rain. The shops were low, squat buildings, with windows opening onto the street to display their wares. Butchers and tailors have windows as big as they can, or sometimes just have the whole front of the shop open, but these windows were small. Goldsmiths don't want casual passers-by leaning in and relieving them of some little object the value of twenty oxen.

Many of the little windows were closed and shuttered or barred for siesta, but one or two of the shops were open. The first that I passed was selling rubbish, strings of tawdry beads and gold chains that were patently pinchbeck. I curled my lip at the owner as he held out a string of 'real lapis from Egypt' (clay painted blue) and he spat and cursed me. Fakers don't like customers who know their business.

The second place was different altogether. It was a smallish building, its stucco frontage neatly painted white, and the cobbles were swept clean around the door and the open counter so that the potential customer might not be put off by treading unexpectedly in dog dung. Inside the walls were hung with canvas cleverly painted in rich dark colours to mimic damask and tapestry. The place looked inviting, and through an open door at the rear I could just see the owner's workshop. Sunshine poured into it through the window and his bench was neatly laid with tiny tools. He was a tidy worker, always a good sign. I remembered how I used to enjoy grading the raw gems on my desk exactly by size and colour to choose the best matches for a brooch or a pendant. My master said I had a good eye.

I walked into the shop. Instantly the owner materialised from nowhere. You could see he was the owner. He was an Arab, bearded and turbaned, with the squint of a man used to close work, and he wore silk and heavy rings. Showing off the stock, my master used to call it. The rings were fine, all of gold, and one of them was set with a pearl that would have bought the whole contents of the shop down the road. He looked me up and down and smiled unctuously. He seemed to be alone, but no doubt his guard was lurking somewhere in the background. All goldsmiths keep guards, the bigger the better, but some are more discreet than others.

'My lord,' he said, bowing lower than I would have expected given my dress. 'How can I serve you?'

I explained what I wanted and was frank with him about what I was prepared to pay. He bowed his head and steepled his fingers together, then drew a key from the loop on his enamelled belt, unlocked the cabinet where the finished pieces were kept and began to draw out rolls of fine linen, looking inside them and muttering, keeping some, replacing others.

Presently he had a selection and he unrolled them on the counter by the window, where the hot afternoon sunlight would show off the stones to their best advantage. He lent me a little silver-bound crystal for my eye so that I could admire the workmanship.

I understand jewels and gold. Like most courtesans my mother loved such things, and as a special treat she would show me her favourite pieces and tell me the story of the giver. I was always fascinated, particularly when the giver wasn't my father. And what I learnt in my four years' apprenticeship to a very wealthy goldsmith has never left me. This man's work was good. The settings were strong and looked delicate and though the stones were not large, given my budget, they were of good quality. We discussed each item and within a few minutes he was treating me as an equal, which I also liked. I detest being talked down to.

What really took my eye was a little necklace. It was a fine gold chain, carrying clusters of gold filigree beads and seed pearls and a pendant of garnet and pearl. A pretty bauble, with distinguished workmanship and the appropriate message, too. Pearl for purity, garnet for faithfulness. It wasn't the dearest thing I saw, but it was just right. At last I expressed an interest and the other pieces were put away and the bargaining began.

Both of us were expert and determined. The goldsmith clapped his hands for a servant and called for sherbet, as an Arab will the moment the sun is hot enough to warm you through your clothes. I don't particularly like sherbet, which tends to make me sneeze. But I did not want to insult him by asking for intoxicating spirits, so I drank the stuff and ate some of the little sticky sweetmeats that came with it. We were served from a chased silver tray, proving his wealth.

At last we reached an accommodation. I offered to pay what he had originally asked, and as well as the necklace he gave me, out of sheer generosity, a pair of charming earrings, slender hoops of gold with a pendant pearl. They would complement the necklace perfectly. I dusted the powdered sugar from my hands and he sent for water and napkins and gave the jewels to an apprentice to wrap.

'Have you been in the trade yourself, my lord?' he asked.

I admitted that I had, for a while. He asked me if I would be interested in seeing the commissions he had on hand, in case I ever wanted something more splendid. He intimated that the necklace must be for my mistress, and a gift for my wife might also be appropriate. I gladly agreed, for I had admired his work, and we went through together into the workshop.

An apprentice had spread out his work in hand on the bench. If I had been a thief I would have noted with satisfaction that the surface of the apprentice's pallet in the corner of the room was rumpled, showing that the work-in-progress box was normally hidden beneath it. There was a beautiful dagger-hilt, silver gilt and set with onyxes, and a stand for a drinking-horn. And a large object, which he unwrapped with pride.

'A headdress,' he said, holding it out, 'for a noble bride.'

My master is nervous. He brushes at some invisible speck on the front of my tunic and licks his hand to flatten my unruly hair. 'Now,' he says, 'when Signor Dolfin comes, no jesting, not a word out of place, or I will beat you until you can't sit down.'

The noble lord comes in at last, smooth with the assurance of his wealth. Half his household is with him, his treasurer, his bodyguard, a few grooms and valets, all standing out in the street because there is insufficient room in the shop. And two women, veiled and swathed in heavy cloaks.

My master brings forward the commission and Signor Dolfin admires it. It is beautiful indeed, a crown of fine arched gold wreathed with pearls. I chose the pearls. Signor Dolfin says, 'My daughter must try it on. Fiammetta.'

The smaller of the ladies puts back her heavy hood and removes her veil. Hair paler and brighter than the gold of her wedding crown spills out onto her slender shoulders. Her skin is whiter than tinted marble. I stare, astonished at her beauty.

My master sets the wreath on her hair. If it were made of diamond it would be quenched by her. She smiles to feel its weight and I run for a mirror to show her herself. I hold the mirror up at the level of my chin, hoping that she will look at me. She does, she does. She raises her eyes to mine, radiant with simple delight. They are bluer than lapis. I am lost, possessed.

'Marcello,' says my master, 'show the signorina how to set the crown.'

I lift off the heavy gold, shivering as the gossamer of her tumbling hair caresses my fingers. Thinking fast, I give the crown a little twist so that when she comes to set it on her hair it will not lie evenly. I must put my hands to her head to adjust it. I am so close to her that I can feel the warmth of her skin.

She looks up and smiles at me. My incandescent longing reflects from her brilliant eyes and scalds me.

It is her bridal crown. In three weeks she will marry. It is unthinkable, impossible. It is heresy even to imagine that she will ever belong to anyone but me.

Messina was more crowded, more ill-tempered than a month ago. I arrived on a short hop from the mainland, swathed in a cloak and a large hat to maintain my incognito. My first move was to make sure that no one was following me. My second was to set up a light signal and a message on the Hog's Back.

A different meeting place this time, a small church just outside the town. I was there early, waiting for Vespers to sound and wondering whether the necklace and earrings would work on Caterina. She had been absolutely delighted with them. I got the feeling that her husband had not given her gold since he gave her a ring. But she had smiled at me as if she fully understood my intention, and she looked inclined to tease me. The last thing she had said to me was, 'I wonder what I shall do for company? Just me and the cat –'

She was a bonny girl. I was fond of her. I easily become fond of cheerful, accommodating girls. I only wished that she would stay light-hearted. When girls begin to get hopeful and serious, I begin to tire of them.

A couple of horses were approaching, fine beasts with scarlet saddles and bells on their gold-studded bridles. A young groom dressed in the Dolfin house livery was running behind afoot. Dolfin didn't seem concerned to escape attention; anyone who had seen him riding out of the Venetian residency would recognise that rig. And two horses? He had brought his son-in-law. My mouth filled with the taste of bile.

They dismounted and gave the reins to the panting groom. They hadn't seen me, waiting in the shadow of a tall buttress. After a few moments they set off around the church to look for me. I walked round in the opposite direction and met them on the far side. Both of them jumped when I appeared before them and pulled off my hat, allowing the strong rays of the setting sun to slant across my face. Dolfin was wearing his heavy subfusc cloak, but Aliusio glowed like a bright insect in a tunic dyed with saffron and his usual scarlet boots. Perfect taste, as always.

I did not attempt to conceal my displeasure. 'Signor Dolfin,' I said, 'the message was for you alone.'

Dolfin was no pickled innocent, he was a successful politician. He knew that the best form of defence is attack. 'I have told you before,' he snapped, 'that Aliusio has my full confidence. And where by the face of God have you been? We have –'

'I have uncovered a network of Sicilians who intend to prevent the French fleet from sailing,' I interrupted him, speaking steadily. 'I know where the gold went. I need more.'

Dolfin looked interested, but Aliusio had only heard one word. 'More?' he squeaked. 'You've already had enough to –'

'Ser D'Estari,' said Dolfin. It was interesting that although he had confidence in his son-in-law he did not hesitate to interrupt him. 'The gold is a potential problem. But a bigger one is the French. My best efforts cannot convince them that there is a risk of rebellion among the Sicilians. Some accept that Aragon poses a threat, but by no means all. What do you expect? We have offered no proof. Their king will not listen to us, and they follow his lead.'

'I can deal with that,' I said. 'And as for the gold, not all of it will be spent. We can recover at least half of it if we are clever. Listen to me.' I explained my plan. We would intercept the second weapons shipment, capture the weapons and retrieve the half of our gold that had not yet been passed to the shippers. The weapons would be ours to sell, we might even make a profit. 'But above all,' I said, 'we must capture the leaders of the resistance. If you hand them over to the French everything will be revealed. The French will have to believe you and be on their guard.'

Aliusio laughed. 'I wouldn't be the Sicilians,' he said. 'The French will —'

I ignored him. 'Signor Dolfin,' I said, 'do you agree to my proposal?'

He looked heavy and tired. 'I will not take part in any operation of this kind,' he said. 'I will let you have my men at your disposal. Aliusio will command them.'

'And capture gold, weapons, conspirators and all,' chirruped Aliusio. Arrogant idiot! What did he know about this sort of work? He sounded as if it were all some young nobles' prank. I would have liked to bring him face to face with Blasio's dagger and see if he felt like laughing.

I ignored him and kept my eyes fixed on Dolfin. 'And the gold, signor? I must take it back with me. As much as I had before. Without it, nothing will happen.'

There was a pause. Then Dolfin said, 'It will be provided. I will leave it in the agreed place and set up a signal for you.' He rubbed his hand across his big square chin. 'For your own sake, Ser D'Estari, I hope that you can give good account of where it has gone. This expedition has cost the Republic much already, and I am afraid that we are throwing good money after bad.'

He suspected me of keeping the gold for myself, I knew it. 'I can't exactly get a receipt from a rebel,' I said acidly. 'If we do not act, signor, the Angevin fleet will never leave Messina. All of the Republic's investment will be lost. We both have our orders.'

His heavy face did not change. Even Aliusio's idiot good spirits seemed dashed by his sobriety. After a moment he said, 'You are right. We have our orders. And for all our sakes, I hope we succeed.'

FOURTEEN

Caterina welcomed me back with such enthusiasm that I at once felt confident that my gift had worked. She dashed down the stairs to meet me, the earrings jumping in her ears and the little necklace winking at her throat, and flung herself into my arms.

She put all her energy into proving that she had missed me desperately. I had missed her, too, and was happy to show her how much.

It was a hot day, with a damp humid spring wind blowing. It would have made us filthy-tempered if we had not had other things on our minds. Our naked skin was damp with perspiration and we stuck together like mating octopi. She said, 'I can't bear you lying on me, you great sweaty oaf,' and made me lie back on the sheet while she climbed aboard my single-masted, heavy-ballasted ship. A violent squall resulted which flung her from side to side, gasping. Beads of moisture gathered beneath her heavy breasts and in the small of her back under the tawny shawl of her swinging hair. She was naked but for the necklace and earrings, and she looked so eminently desirable that I lost all self-control and rebelled against her.

'I'll show you what great sweaty oafs can do,' I said, rolling her over and pinning her to the mattress and doing what I wanted, for a change. She arched her back, thrusting up her nipples to within reach of my mouth. Her moans proved that I pleased her.

'A message came for you,' she said when I had finished.

I was still holding her down. My head was hanging and sweat was dripping slowly from the end of my galley-beak nose and landing on the flushed glistening skin between her breasts. I frowned at her. 'What?'

'A boy brought a message. He came yesterday. He said if you were back some time today there was a meeting at the Pig this afternoon.' She smiled ruefully. 'He said it was important, Nico, or I wouldn't have told you.'

'Oh.' Business closed in on me. I rolled off her and sprawled beside her, offering my damp limbs to the slight breeze that did not cool them at all.

My eyes were shut. There was a pause. Then she touched my collarbone with her hard fingertips, tracing along its length. Her fingers dipped into the hollow of my throat, feeling my thumping pulse, then trailed up the cords of my neck to my ear. I thought of the dead Frenchman and shivered.

She stroked the straight dark bars of my eyebrows and the lashes of my closed eyes. I flinched and turned my head away. Her face suddenly pressed to my shoulder. 'Nico, if that's the place where you went before, you will be careful, won't you?'

I rolled upright and sat looking down at her. She looked back at me as if she expected a beating. 'Caterina,' I said, 'I don't answer to you.'

'I know.' Her full lips were taut, as if she were trying to prevent them from trembling. 'It's just that –' Her eyes glittered. She looked at me for a moment in silence, then suddenly got up and began to reach for her clothes. Her voice changed, becoming bright and brittle. 'It's just that I don't want to have to clear up all that mess again.' She pulled on her shift, reached under the bed and tossed a bundle of brightly dyed linen onto it. 'Here,' she said carelessly, 'I finished it. If you wear it tonight and get it all over blood I shan't make you another.'

I unwrapped the parcel, feeling guilty. It was my new tunic of amber-coloured wool, embroidered on the neck and sleeves with yellow and brown and green thread. On one shoulder there was a pretty little working of a tabby and white kitten, looking out with a quizzical expression. I said in a subdued voice, 'Thank you, *gattina*.'

She watched me examine it. Then she said, 'Nico, the French found the man who killed the sergeant last week.'

I kept the shock from my eyes and sounded bored. 'Oh? Who was it?'

'A boy,' she said, 'just fifteen. They say he did it because the sergeant misused his little brother.' I tried not to look interested. I already knew the penalty. There was a cold sticky lump in my throat.

She was watching me without the shadow of a smile. I knew she suspected me; she might be naïve, but she wasn't stupid. She waited for me to speak, but I said nothing. Then she said very evenly, 'They hanged him on Sunday, Nico.'

I looked away and made a business of dressing. Caterina's face did not change. I pulled my tunic over my head and said from underneath it, 'Why the significant look?'

She inspected her hands and pushed back the rims of her nails. Then she looked up again at me. Her eyes glittered like obsidian. 'Nico,' she said, 'when you came back all bloody I believed you. I still want to believe you. But I –'

'Listen,' I said, going to her and taking her hands. I made myself look into her eyes, though it was hard. 'I told you what happened. Why would I kill a Frenchman? *Gattina*, don't fret. I know how to look after myself.' She did not seem reassured. 'I'm sorry I have to go,' I whispered, and I leant forward and kissed her.

Her eyes closed and she made a little sound halfway between a sigh and a sob as she reached up for me. Her hands buried themselves in my hair, holding my lips on hers. I don't understand women, I never will. I knew I hadn't convinced her. If I found a woman had lied to me I would drop her instantly. Caterina thought I was certainly a liar and probably a murderer and she still clutched me as if my body were her soul's salvation. It took some strength to detach her hands so that I could leave.

The usual gang were at the Pig when I arrived. The low grimy rafters of the room where we met were dripping with the humidity of the hot wind, and every face within doors was shiny and sallow with the unhealthy heat. I saluted my colleagues brightly and asked, 'Did the drop go well?'

'Fine,' said Blasio curtly. He despised me, and his voice showed it.

'We had a bit of trouble with a French patrol,' Andrea put in, concerned for accuracy. 'We'll have to change the drop site next time.' He pushed a cup of wine across to me. 'Have you got the gold?'

The tension around the table was tangible. I let them stew for a moment. Nicetas's behaviour was based as closely as I was able on Aliusio Contarini, and I am sure he never missed an opportunity to make an impression. When I could feel that I was within two breaths of exhausting their patience, I said, 'Of course I have it.'

They relaxed, congratulating each other. Even Andrea's smile looked natural. 'How much did you get?' he asked.

'The same as last time. Half I brought back with me: half I pick up when I go back to report before the operation.' He looked even more pleased, and I wondered what sort of bargain he was striking with this time's suppliers. 'But,' I went on, 'if we were having trouble with the French, I'm worried.'

'They're all as thick as cowpats,' said Pietro dismissively. 'Couldn't see their hands in front of their faces. No problems.'

'But you had trouble,' I insisted. 'If you're going to change the location, why not let me choose the new one?'

'You?' Blasio was scathing. 'You don't know the island.'

'Sometimes a fresh eye sees more clearly,' I said sententiously.

Andrea arched one grey eyebrow. 'There could be something in that,' he said thoughtfully. 'And I do need something to keep you busy.' Condescending slimy lizard. 'You have a look', he went on, 'if you want. It should be somewhere up the coast, no more than two hours from Palermo, probably in the direction of Cefalù. When you've found the place, let me know and Blasio and I will come and inspect it.'

Blasio nodded. I got the feeling that he still didn't like me.

There was a little more conversation. They were all loud and cheerful, pleased with the news about the money. Then I said diffidently into one of those little gaps of silence, 'Caterina tells me that the French think they've solved Petrot's murder.'

That sobered them up. Zanino drew his dagger and stuck it into the table. He almost gibbered with fury. 'The boy came from my quarter,' he said. 'He couldn't have done it, he was at home in bed, his whole family were witnesses. The bastards never listen. Find a likely man and hang him, and let the law smother.'

The others joined in, muttering imprecations and curses against the French. Andrea was silent for a while. Then he said, 'When we have dealt with them as they deserve and taken control of the city these wrongs will be righted. We can't bring the dead to life, but we can punish the killers and institute justice.'

They all nodded like a pew full of dozing monks. I kept my face blank, hiding my scowl of disbelief. They had made me kill the sergeant, it was their fault the boy had been executed. I was bound to be sympathetic to their republicanism, and the French were, without doubt, highly objectionable, but right now they had their priorities all wrong.

'Such a shame,' Andrea murmured. 'Such a young man, too.'

Something in his voice made me shudder. I didn't want to stay there any longer, and now I was accepted by them as much as I was ever likely to be I didn't have to. I got to my feet and made my excuses and left.

Once I was outside the clammy atmosphere seemed to lighten somewhat. I was going to return to Caterina's welcoming bed, but a thought struck me. Instead I retreated under the deep shade of a nearby doorway and waited.

I can be as patient as Fate when I need to be. Time passed. The siesta hour was over. Bartolo and Zanino left, still deep in conversation, and then Pietro and Giovanni, who looked as though they were going off to get drunk. No sign of Andrea. I waited still. The sun crawled towards the horizon and was hidden by a cloud of sticky grey, as if all the sweat of the city had vapourised and spread itself across the sky.

Presently, with a few hours still to sunset, Andrea and Blasio emerged. They spoke on the doorstep for a little while. Then they separated. I followed Andrea as he walked purposefully away from the Pig and up into the twisting Vucciria streets. I was careful, which was just as well. He glanced behind him from time to time, almost unconsciously, just making sure. I am certain he never saw me.

He went through the bazaar and across the main crossroads, then on into the western quarter of the city, the palace quarter. I shadowed him, drawing a little closer now. In the same square where I had encountered Petrot playing bowls with his cronies he stopped to sluice his face and hands at the well, then combed his fingers carefully through his thin greying hair. He looked at himself in the well and straightened the neck of his simple tunic. Was he planning a smart visit?

Apparently he was; but it wasn't the sort of visit I had expected. In the next square he stopped before a large building that looked as if it might almost be a nobleman's house. It was tall and roofed with red tiles and the shutters that closed its big windows were decorated with wrought ironwork. Very elegant. But there was ironwork decoration on the heavy door, too, and the central motif revealed the house's provenance. No nobleman that I have ever known would choose to ornament his front door with a large, grotesquely erect phallus. The house was a brothel, and it looked like an expensive one. The Security Committee's precious gold was certainly finding its way into some salubrious haunts.

Andrea paused, brushed at his clothes and knocked. A little flap in the door flew open, followed by the door itself, and he went in. He hadn't spoken: they must know him.

I gave him a moment, then went to the door and knocked.

Brothels are nothing new to me. Not that I use them myself, but the girls inside them are often valuable sources of information for an agent. Prostitutes are usually either vulnerable or venal, and whatever Andrea was there for, I was fairly sure I could find a girl who could be charmed or bribed into telling me about it.

The little spy hole opened and I felt myself scrutinised. Somebody grunted.

'Good day. I'm looking for entertainment,' I said blandly.

There was a short silence. I must have passed muster, because the phallic door swung silently open. I walked in and it closed behind me. The porter folded his arms and stared at me. He was a big man, more muscle than fat, who looked as if he might be half Negro or Moor. His bald, shining scalp glistened and his arms were like tree trunks. I said, 'Can you –' but he scowled and shook his head, grunting again. He didn't need to open his mouth to show me that he had no tongue.

Well, that was one way of ensuring client confidentiality. I raised my eyebrows and concentrated on my surroundings. The hallway was grand, with tapestries decorating the walls and a carved polished wooden staircase, for all the world like the nobleman's house which the brothel superficially resembled. There the resemblance ended. Everywhere I have been the design of a brothel is fundamentally the same; one big public room where the customers can go to have a drink and make their selection, and myriad little booths in which they can satisfy their desires in as much privacy as the place affords. In the cheaper places the booths are made of wattle or even of cheap cloth, but this hallway had real walls with lots of carved wooden doors. An expensive place, then. I looked forward to meeting its employees. If they were as handsome as the surroundings, they might even tempt me to break my usual rule.

Expensive, no doubt. As it proved, the brothel was specialist, too. I had just finished looking around when a voice fluted in front of me, 'Welcome, signor. What can we offer you?'

I looked down and stepped back as if struck. I was expecting a madam, or at least one of the girls. Wrong, Marcello, try again. It was a boy, a pretty dark-haired boy of twelve or thirteen, with eyes as dark as Caterina's outlined with kohl to make them look bigger and rouge on his cheeks. There was a garland of fresh flowers on his curled scented hair and he was stark naked, not a stitch. He simpered smilingly up at me and struck a coy but revealing pose.

It took all the control I had not to recoil. I just managed to keep myself still. If I wanted to appear as a prospective customer, I had to look as if this sort of thing was to my taste.

Movement before me made me catch the boy by the shoulder and turn towards the wall, lifting my hood. Not a moment too soon. Andrea came out of a door that presumably led to the reception room and went straight to the stairs. Walking beside him was another boy, younger than the one I was holding, no more than ten years old, blonder than a cherub and dressed in the sort of carefully arranged rags that I would have called alluring if they were on a teenage girl. As they began to ascend the stairs the child slid his hand up under Andrea's tunic.

I couldn't stay in there. But I had to know something about it. I made myself say to the painted boy, 'I – I'm just looking. Tell me some prices.'

'What do you want, signor?'

I shrugged, trying to look as if I just didn't dare give words to my salacious desires. The boy slid a coquettish glance at me from beneath his lowered lids and then, to help me out, made some suggestions.

I listened, feeling as if I wanted to vomit. At last I gasped, 'Sorry, I don't think I can afford it,' and got to the door.

It took me a little while to recover. I stood across the road, shaking. I was afraid my clothes would be contaminated with the boy's scent. If the Forty's police had got wind of such a place in Venice, they would have closed it down at once and kept the whole city amused for weeks by the punishments of the pro-curers. No doubt there are men in Venice with such tastes – I have heard rumours from time to time – but they have to bury them deep. We take the protection of children of both sexes very seriously.

All the same, I was right to have asked the prices. The place was extortionate, as well it might be. The children were presum-ably slaves, and pretty boy-slaves don't come cheaply. The bribes to the French authorities would also have to be massive. Andrea certainly nurtured expensive tastes.

Nothing would have made me move from the spot until I knew more about him. I waited while the afternoon crawled on. Other customers came and went from the boy-brothel. My weary, disgusted eyes registered a couple of high-ranking French officers, a wealthy Arab merchant who looked suspiciously like the man who had sold me Caterina's necklace, more than one nobleman and a man in cleric's robes who was presumably concerned with the cure of the boys' immortal souls. I am hard to shock, but I was amazed to see people walking into that place in broad daylight.

I waited still. Presently Andrea emerged. All agents are practised at spotting their quarry even through disguises, and without that practice I would hardly have recognised him. He had changed his clothes and was now wearing a long blue silk robe and a smart felt hat, like a nobleman. The blond cherub was with him, carrying an unlit torch, and so was another child, a little older and brown-haired.

I followed Andrea and his link boys southwards through the narrow streets to the Santa Agata gate. Beyond it were the beginnings of the hills, the smart suburb where the noblemen had their palazzi. As we climbed I felt a faint breeze, a blissful relief after the stifling heat of the day.

There were no shops here and fewer people. Most of them were the liveried servants of noble houses, out running errands or finding the excuse to meet their friends in the street and gossip. Once or twice a noble entourage passed us. There was a lady in a litter curtained with silk and carried by a matched team of Moorish slaves. I could hear her whispering and laughing to her maids, but I couldn't see her face. There were half a dozen young noblemen riding back from the hunt, calling out jokes to each other. Their hawks were sleeping on their saddle-bows and their kill of hares and partridges bumped behind them. They looked flushed and fresh from their exercise, but their horses trailed their hooves in the dust of the street, their huntsmen staggered with weariness from running the whole day afoot, and their exhausted hounds were panting and freckled with mud.

Andrea did not look out of place, although he was on foot. He climbed to the very fringes of the quarter, where water from the mountain springs ran down each side of the street and the houses were more like country villas, set in broad walled gardens. At one of the biggest of these great houses he presented himself at the porter's lodge. The wall was so high and the lodge so distant from the house that you could only just see the tall red roof through the sheltering blossom-trees.

The house's owner must be an important man. Despite the lateness of the hour petitioners were still waiting at the gate, and they clamoured for attention as Andrea spoke to the porter. They were ignored, but he was admitted without delay. His pretty torchbearers accompanied him. Behind him the gate slammed shut.

I came up to the house and touched one of the petitioners on the arm. 'Who lives here?' I asked, in a thick Spanish accent.

The man stared at me with the scorn reserved for foreigners. 'My lord Resetto,' he said. 'Guglielmo Resetto. You ought to know that, Spaniard!'

'Guglielmo Resetto?' I repeated. I sounded dumbfounded, and I wasn't pretending.

'Yes,' he said impatiently, and added in an undertone, 'son of a Spanish whore.'

'*Gracias*,' I said, and withdrew. My head was spinning. The Resetti were one of the chief families in Palermo, and I knew from my earlier researches that the lord Guglielmo Resetto was hand in glove with the agents of Aragon. What double game was Andrea playing?

If I had been in Venice I would have been into the servants' quarters in less time than it takes to pickle a herring. My experience and a certain unscrupulous charm serves me well in gaining access to the back rooms of noble houses, just as my father's birth and my educated upbringing helps me to infiltrate the front rooms. I have contacts among the high-placed servants in pretty well every palazzo along the Grand Canal. A few well-chosen words in the ear of the master's valet and a few well-chosen coins in his palm and I would have all the information that I needed.

But in a foreign country these things work differently. It would take weeks to suborn even one servant of a noble Sicilian house without giving rise to suspicion, and I did not have that sort of time.

I walked slowly around the estate, considering its high, serious wall. There was a tradesmen's entrance, but it was locked and the lodge was empty. Behind it a dog's chain rattled and I heard a faint, subterranean growl. Another dog barked furiously a little way across the park-like garden. I didn't fancy climbing in. But I did find a tree close to the wall which offered enough easy footholds for me to shin up it and get an uninterrupted view of the house.

It was a tall, elegant palace, three storeys high. It was shaped like a letter E without the central stroke, with its wings pointing towards the lovely park behind it. In the courtyard between the wings there was a pavement of herringbone terracotta tiles and a tall, elegant fountain lifted on twisted marble columns and inlaid with brilliantly coloured mosaic. The walls were washed with red and white stucco and over the doorway was a big escutcheon with the arms of the Resetti painted upon it. The windows were beautiful, row upon row of elegant pointed Moorish arches in white marble, decorated with chevrons and chequer patterns after the Norman taste. This charming mansion must have been built in the days of the Norman kings, when every nobleman on the island was as rich as a prince. Today, with the kings gone and the nobles labouring under Angevin taxes, it looked a little sad and dilapidated. In a couple of places the plaster had dropped from the walls, and two of the spouts in the fountain weren't working. But the garden was still glorious, just beginning to brighten with the spring green. The last breath of the evening wind brought me the fragrance of the blossom on the early-flowering fruit trees.

Twilight was coming, and the breeze dropped as if the sunset had killed it. I wiped the sweat from my forehead and flapped my tunic to move the air underneath it. Vespers rang in the church a little way down the hill, and answering bells jangled all over the city. The sound reached up into the stifling sky. Candles began to be lit in the upper chamber of the house, above the great room on the first floor. Faint strains of music floated to my ears. Andrea's arrival seemed to have precipitated a private party. I thought of the children who had accompanied him and shuddered.

What was I waiting for? He would probably be there all night. It was getting late and I was tired, and the threatening stillness of the air told me that a storm was coming. I wasn't going to sit in a tree until morning getting soaked, and I didn't want to have to fight my way back across Palermo after curfew. I abandoned my fruitless watch and began the long walk home, my eyes gazing into nothingness as I tried to think of my next move.

FIFTEEN

I had never seen Caterina angry before, but she was angry now. The shape of her face changed. Her lips made a thin white line and the peak of her hair rose above her tight brows. I didn't know exactly why she was angry, but I thought I was going to find out. No wonder there had been no smell of supper cooking.

Right. I was hardly through the door when it started. 'Have you had a profitable afternoon?'

I raised my brows and didn't answer. I don't answer questions asked in that tone of voice. There was a jug of wine in the niche by the fireplace, and I went over to it and poured some. I got the feeling I would need it.

'Nico,' she said. Her voice was trembling. 'Nico, I know I gave you that message when we maybe hadn't quite finished, but did that really mean you had to go off to a brothel?'

News travels fast. I drank some of the wine. 'Who says I was at a brothel?'

'It's not that far from the bazaar, is it?' She was getting shrill now. 'I went out to get us something nice for this evening and what happens? What happens? People sidling up to me and saying, "Hey, Caterina, do you know where your fancy man went this afternoon?" and *laughing* at me!'

I was sorry if she had been embarrassed, but I wasn't going to be blamed. 'Did any of your so-called friends bother to tell you how long I was in there?'

'Oh, so you did go in! You're not even trying to deny it!' She shook her head ferociously. Her cheeks were flushed and her eyes were fierce as a falcon's. 'By Satan's horns, Nicetas, by the Virgin's tits, couldn't you have waited until it was dark?'

'Caterina, shut up,' I said sharply. Enough is enough, and if she went on I was going to lose my temper too.

'How long were you in there?' she shouted. 'How long does it take? Long enough for you to empty your bollocks, I'll bet!'

'What are you, a fishwife?' I yelled back.

She screamed with rage and grabbed up a heavy crock, one she used for steeping the washing. She was a strong girl. When she flung it at my head I didn't hesitate, I dropped straight to the floorboards and laced my fingers over the back of my neck. My cup broke and wine went everywhere. The crock struck the wall just behind where my head had been and shattered into a million fragments.

Clay settled into my hair and the folds of my new tunic. I waited to see if any other missiles would follow, but there was silence. I lifted my head. Across the room Caterina was staring at me, her chest heaving and her face streaked with tears of rage. 'Boys,' she hissed. 'Boys, Nico! Bollocks of Christ, as if women wouldn't be bad enough. *Boys!*' A trickle of snot began to run from her nose.

I got slowly to my feet. Where I had lain on the floor there was a Marcello-shaped gap in the carpet of clay fragments and dust. At another time it might have made me laugh, and as it was my lips twisted in a wry smile. Caterina was glaring at me and sniffing hard. I thought she was past the angry stage and onto the crying. I said, trying to sound soothing, 'You don't really believe that, Caterina.'

It was the wrong tone altogether. Her tears evaporated beneath a white-hot flare of indignation. 'I don't know what to believe!' she exclaimed furiously. 'But when people tell me where they saw you going I believe that I'm living with a Christ-cursed boy-bugger!'

I hit her. I took two quick steps across the room and hit her in the face, hard enough to make her stagger. She came upright, clutching her cheek and staring at me. Her mouth was open to speak. I pointed my finger between her white-ringed eyes and said, 'Don't you ever, ever say that again.'

If she had argued I would have kept on hitting her until she shut up. It must have showed in my face, because she folded her lips tightly together and drew away from me, shivering. A dribble of bright blood joined the snot beneath her nose.

Once someone has been violent there's no point in trying to talk reasonably. I was still shaking with rage and loathing. I gave Caterina one last glare and lunged for the door.

Out in the street I flung back my head and took a deep, deep breath. The air was hot and sticky and clung to my lungs like burrs. If only it would thunder. I went a little way down the street to our local tavern and called for a cup of wine and stood outside.

The owner was a middle-aged woman, a thin parched creature, but good-natured. She brought me better wine than I had asked for. 'Trouble upstairs?' she asked, sympathetically enough.

I suppose the whole street had heard us. I drank the wine in one gulp, paid for it and left. Sympathy was not what I wanted. I made my way to the bazaar, where I could find some solitude, at least until curfew.

It was well nigh dark. I found an open tavern and bought a jug of wine and then sat outside on a well head and began to drink it. The shops were shutting around me. It was the time of day when I had come back for Caterina, that first evening when she went home with me.

I wished now that I hadn't hit her. I'd never made a habit of violence. In fact, thinking back, I couldn't remember a single other occasion on which I had hit a woman. But at the time it was inevitable, and it could have been a lot worse. There are some subjects on which I am barely rational. I tried to concentrate on the wine and forget the pain I had seen in Caterina's dark eyes.

A pair of feet in front of me. Respectable feet, clad in soft leather shoes and well-fitted hose. A voice said softly, 'Marcello D'Estari.'

Never, never recognise your name. I took another pull at my jug of wine, ignoring whoever had spoken. My blood pounded in my ears.

'Marcello,' said the voice again. I let my eyes come into focus and said in a hostile tone, 'Are you talking to me?'

Then I saw who was standing in front of me. He was ten years older. His hair was grey and he was wearing a nobleman's livery, but after one glance I knew him. I couldn't believe it.

My face showed no recognition. I was not yet drunk enough to be careless. I said, 'You've made a mistake, friend.' Then I looked into his eyes. He looked hurt and puzzled, like a dog. I looked significantly down at the brick of the well head, picked up the jug and went straight into the tavern.

I had drawn an arrow in spilled wine on the brick pointing to the tavern door. After a moment he followed me in. I was in a dark, secret corner, but he found me.

'Marcello,' he said again. 'It is you.'

'Antonio,' I said. He sat down suddenly on the bench, as if his legs had been cut away. His face looked as grey as his hair.

'You escaped,' he murmured as I offered him the jug. 'You escaped.'

'You're still a slave.' He wore expensive livery like an important servant, but he was branded on the back of his hand with a noble's house mark.

He shook his head. 'Yes and no. I could buy myself out, but –' His voice faded away. He looked into my eyes. 'Did Marco escape with you?' he asked. He looked both hopeful and hopeless.

'No. I'm sorry, Antonio. He's dead.'

His face twitched, a sort of spasm of regret. You might have expected more reaction from a man being told that his younger brother was dead, but Antonio had had a long time to prepare himself. 'I guessed it. Or I half knew it. I was sent to Messina on business a couple of years ago, I went past the factory and enquired about Venetian slaves called Marco. They said there weren't any. And I guessed you had escaped and I hoped he had, but he was always unlucky.'

He was quite right. Until I tried it on my own after he died, Marco's bad luck had stuck to me too.

The holding pen is half below ground, dim and cold and stinking of sweat and shit and fear. They fling me down the steps and I land on my face in the filthy straw. The familiar smell fills me with hopelessness. For a moment I don't move.

Another body lands beside me. It's Marco, groaning and whimpering. I try to sit up. The pain enfolds me, driving me back to the floor. I try again and this time I manage it.

Marco's back looks like the offal that no one will buy, bad tripe, leftovers, lungs. It is still running with blood. He moans and shuffles a little way on his elbows, then begins to weep. My back is in the same state as his, and we are both equally exhausted. But I know that it's not the pain that makes him weep, it's the guilt. I put my hand in his hair, trying to comfort him. Around us eyes glitter in the shadows, but nobody says anything.

Out of the depths of the darkness a figure materialises. Antonio, carrying a bucket of water. I reach for it with a husky whimper of need, but he shoulders me away and leans over his brother. 'Oh, Christ in Heaven,' he whispers. 'Oh, Marco, Marco.' He cups water in his palm and holds it to Marco's dry lips. Marco drinks, drinks again, then crawls into his big brother's lap and cries like a child.

Antonio turns on me like an angry beast. 'Marcello,' he grates, 'this is your fault, curse you, your fault. I told you not to try it.'

He might be our accountant, but he is twice my size. On the ship I

118

was afraid of him, but what point is there in fear here, with my back in ribbons and only horror in front of me? I snatch the bucket from him and push my face into the filthy water, drinking like a camel. Men can die of thirst after floggings. Antonio grabs me by the hair and pulls me harshly away.

'Your fault,' he repeats, and begins to bathe Marco's face with the water.

Marco chokes back his tears and opens his eyes. 'Not his fault,' he stammers at last. 'My fault. I got cramp. He came back for me.' Antonio lifts his eyes to mine. He looks as if he is in pain. I turn my head away, ashamed. Heroism is stupid when it fails. Marco presses on, 'He could have let me sink. He came back, and they got him too.'

I reach out to put my hand on Marco's flayed shoulder, then think better of it. I would go back for him again, if I had to. You don't leave your oar mate to drown. 'Never mind, Marco Uno.' Since I joined the ship he has been Marco Uno and I have been Marco Due, two Venetian name saints on one oar. We should have had the safest ship in the Mediterranean. Holy Saint Mark, where were you looking? 'Never mind,' I say again. 'We're still alive.' But this hardly seems like comfort.

There was a long silence. I imagined Antonio's memories were much the same as mine, though who's to know? At last he shifted uncomfortably and drank deeply from the jug. Then, looking down at the scarred surface of the filthy table, he asked softly, 'Was it quick?'

I knew at once what he meant, and it took me a hair's-breadth too long to answer, so that when I said, 'Yes,' he must have realised that I was lying. He looked at me with those great dog's eyes. Marco had had the same eyes, big and brown, though his had always sparkled with devilment. He hadn't been a sober, cautious old stick like his brother the accountant.

Marco's brother the accountant deserved better than a lie. I took the jug from him, drained it and called for more. Then I said steadily, 'It was an accident, Antonio. In the sugar presses. He was badly hurt. He died quite soon.' Nothing I could have said would have done justice to Marco's suffering, in any case.

Antonio took a deep breath and let it out. The wine came and he drank some. Then he said, 'How did you escape?'

The overseer – I forced the memory down, stifling it. 'I don't want to talk about it.' Change the subject, fast. 'What about you, Antonio? What happened to you?'

He shrugged, unconsciously spreading the fingers of his left hand and examining the brand on the back of it. 'A noble family bought me.' He named them. 'There was a good market in literate men at the time. I'm still in the family: steward, now.' His eyes caught mine and flitted away. 'I could have bought myself out a couple of years ago,' he said hesitantly, 'but it's a good place to save, as good as a free man, and I wanted to have enough to –'

His face crumpled. I finished for him, 'To buy Marco out if he was still alive.'

He nodded, his eyes shut. I didn't enlighten him on what Marco might have been like if he'd still been alive after ten years in the sugar factory. I was going to say that the Republic would probably free him, but then a thought crossed my mind. I struggled with it briefly, but it made itself heard in the end. 'Antonio, I imagine you have good connections among the other noble houses.'

My voice betrayed business. He looked up at me, squinting through the dark of the tavern. All he said was, 'Of course.'

I don't know how I had the face to ask him to help me. But needs must. At least I knew I could trust him. I leant a little towards him and said, 'Antonio, I'm engaged in secret work on behalf of the State. That's why I didn't seem to recognise you. I'm operating under an alias. I need to find out about Guglielmo Resetto.'

Antonio's eyes were very steady. He seemed to give my request some thought. Then he said, 'What exactly do you need to know?'

'There's a man called Andrea,' I said. 'He went there this evening with two brothel boys. Is Resetto a paederast?'

One of Antonio's brows appeared to be trying to crawl off his forehead, which I took to be assent. I plunged on. 'I need to know why Andrea goes there. If it's just – vice, God curse them, or something more.'

'What do you suspect?' asked Antonio, cool as a judge.

'That it's to do with Aragon,' I said. 'Antonio, can you find it out?'

I expected him to bargain, but he didn't. He just nodded. 'You won't regret it,' I said. 'I'm in contact with our ambassador here in Sicily. I'll have you freed, Antonio, whenever you want.'

'That would be good,' Antonio said steadily, 'but I'm doing it for Marco, Marco *Due*, and for you, not for my freedom. It's important, you say.'

To the Republic, or to me? It was both. My hatred for Andrea had become personal. 'It's important.'

'Then I'll do it.'

We made arrangements to pass messages. Antonio knew Palermo like the back of his hand, his suggestions were excellent.

A bell sounded in the distance and nearby a French soldier shouted a warning from his guard post. Curfew! Antonio, ever orthodox, leapt to his feet.

'Don't go,' I said. 'I'll come home with you, it'll be safe. We've hardly talked.'

He shook his head. 'I mustn't be abroad after curfew.'

It would have been easy to despise him. He would never take a risk. He wouldn't come with Marco and me when we escaped. But then he was alive and Marco was dead. I took his hand and said, 'I'll check for messages every day.'

'It may take a few days,' Antonio said. 'I'll have to find some excuse to go there.' He hesitated, then reached out for me. We embraced, briefly, awkwardly. Then he turned without another word and left the tavern.

I stood in the close humid air of the narrow street, irresolute. My clothes were sticking to me. I glanced up at the sky and saw it covered with a thick layer of gloomy cloud, blotting out the stars.

'Oi, you!' yelled the Frenchman from his post. 'Didn't you hear curfew? Get off the streets!'

There was nothing left for me to do but go home. I was dreading it.

Sixteen

All the way up the stairs I was arguing with myself.
Self-interest told me that I should exert myself to make Caterina stay. After all, it pointed out, she was good-natured and cheerful, pleasant to look at and an excellent cook. She was also one of the most rewarding girls that I had ever bedded. She made my life in Palermo comfortable.

The better side of me was adamant that if she wanted to leave I should let her. She was probably falling in love with me, as girls have a habit of doing, and since it would get her nowhere the sooner we broke it off the better. For her, that is.

But I knew that she enjoyed living with me. I didn't believe that she could bring herself to go back to her husband's hateful family, even if they would have her. So if she left me she would look for another man whom she could serve in a similar capacity, and it would be surprising if she didn't consider the French officer, Jacques of Vaison. That would be hard for my pride, and it could be dangerous for her.

All in all the arguments seemed to come down on the side of keeping her with me. Somehow I never doubted that she would be there for me to persuade. And she was.

She was standing beside a bundle of her belongings, unfastening one of the gold and pearl earrings I had given her. A single bright candle stood on the little table she used for her sewing, illuminating the other earring and the necklace. Beside the jewels was the leather purse she used for the housekeeping money. I didn't need to be told that it contained everything I'd paid her that she hadn't already earned. She was so honest she almost compensated for me.

I didn't speak, and she took her hands from her ear and looked at me in silence. The light of the candle glowed on her still face. She had cleaned up the blood, and only a redness on her cheekbone showed where my blow had landed. That was honest too. A lot of women would have let the blood stay as a reproach, and stained their cheeks with tears as well as bruises. Her restraint made me feel much, much worse. It's never easy for me to apologise, but I had to. I swallowed, then said, 'Caterina, I'm sorry I hit you.'

She nodded, still in silence, and put her hands back to her ear. She removed the earring and laid it on the table, then stooped to pick up her bundle. Thunder rumbled, making us jump, and the roof tiles began to rattle under the onslaught of the rain.

I said, 'Don't go.' She must have wanted to be convinced. If she had really meant to leave me, she would have been gone before I came back.

She shut her eyes for a moment, then slung the bundle on to her shoulder and came towards me, her eyes firmly fixed on the door. I said, 'Caterina, listen. Let me explain. I was following someone. He went in there and I followed him. I didn't know what sort of a place it was, I thought it was just a brothel.' That hadn't come out quite right, but I ploughed on regardless. She walked past me as if she hadn't heard a word. 'I was out in the time it takes to ask the prices,' I finished.

Her hand was on the latch. 'Don't go,' I said again, and now I really meant it. My voice was hollow with earnestness. 'Please.'

She hesitated and closed her eyes. The bundle quivered in her hand and slid towards the floor. She stood with her back to me and said very clearly, 'My husband Francescino was a mule driver.' This was news to me, and I wasn't sure why it was relevant, but as long as she was talking she wasn't leaving. 'He had to go long journeys. Lots of things come to Palermo and he took them all over the island, far off places: Enna, Syracusa even. He told me that in all his travels he was never unfaithful to me.' She lifted the bundle again. 'The thing is, I believed him.'

'Caterina!' I jumped after her and caught the bundle from her hand. 'Is that what's bothering you? Look, I swear, I swear by the head of the Virgin, since we met you've been the only girl I –'

'Oh, Nico!' She shook her head at my foolishness. 'It's not what you do. It's not even that you hit me,' she stiffened slightly, 'though you don't have any right to hit me, you know. I know a husband has the right to beat his wife if she displeases him, but we aren't even married. It's that you tell me lies.'

I put the bundle on the floor and pushed it away with my foot. I couldn't deny it, so why bother? I was close enough to her now to follow another line of argument. It wasn't exactly fair play, but I was sure that it would be convincing. With my right hand I reached out and stroked the soft curve of her chin, slipping my fingers up towards her ear. She closed her eyes and turned her head away. My hand moved below the weight of her heavy hair and caressed the nub of her neckbone. Lightning briefly outlined us in fire, and immediately afterwards the thunder crashed overhead and the rain hit the roof above us with redoubled force.

Tears squeezed from between Caterina's closed eyelids. Her lips parted and her breathing was uneven. Through the fabric of her gown and shift the peaks of her nipples stood up, hard with excitement. I put my palm onto one stiff point and caressed it gently.

Her ragged breathing turned to sobs. I said nothing, just drew her into my arms and turned her face up to mine. All down the length of my body her softness pressed against me. Her open lips begged for me to kiss them. I did.

After a few minutes I said softly, '*Gattina*, don't go.'

She opened her eyes and looked up at me. One of her hands was in my hair, the other around my shoulders. She did not pull away, but she took a deep, shuddering breath and whispered, 'Why did you hit me?'

I couldn't look into her eyes. I shook my head.

'Tell me,' she insisted. 'Tell me.'

'Tomorrow,' I suggested helplessly. 'We'll go out of the city, we'll take a trip into the country. I want to look at the coast, it's for business.' Her expression was sceptical. 'Truly, Caterina, it is. We'll take some food and ride along the coast and have a good time. Will you? Will you come with me?'

'And you'll tell me,' she said. 'You'll explain.'

'If you want.' I'd think of some way out of it.

'Promise.'

I hate promises, especially when I don't intend to keep them, but I didn't seem to be able to get out of this one. I crossed myself Greek-fashion. 'I promise.'

'Swear!' Her hands knotted in my hair and tugged so sharply that I gasped. 'Swear, Nico, swear by the Wounds of Christ.'

'And would you believe a Greek heretic?' I teased her gently.

Her eyes closed and she rested her forehead against my chest. Here it comes, I thought, waiting for the tears, the confession of love, the wretchedness and complexity and misery that would follow. Love was the one thing I would never lie to a woman about.

I was wrong again, as so often with Caterina. In some ways she really was an exceptional girl. For a moment she stood very still, her face hidden from me. Then she pulled back a little way and straightened. Her face was set and determined. She caught hold of my wrist and put my hand on her breast. Her other hand slid up under my tunic and I gasped as she grasped me. Again the lightning blinded us and the thunder deafened us. When it died away she said over the hammering of the rain on the roof, 'Nico, come to bed with me. Now, Nico.'

Not even, 'Nico, make love to me.' Was she trying to protect me, or herself, by not uttering that fateful word? In either case, she was wasting her effort. I was not at risk, and as I caught her up in my arms and carried her to the bed her rapt, helpless face told me that it was already too late for her.

The following morning she went to market early and bought food for our day in the country while I went to a stable to negotiate for a quiet, gentle horse that was strong enough to carry two. I was generous with tips. The last thing I wanted was to have to carry Caterina before me on the back of some wicked old screw.

For once a horse dealer was honest. I ended up with a big soft old grey with a backside wide enough to roll dice on and a mouth like a pat of butter. We put our basket of food on the crupper and I hoisted Caterina up before me and we laughed like a pair of country fools on holiday as we rode out of the city towards Cefalù.

After an hour or so the roads had quietened. The market garden business was past us, and we were out in the country proper. On the fertile ground around Palermo orchards flourished, and we rode through thick groves of orange and lemon, almond and apple and cherry. The heavy blossom filled the air with scent and the early bees thrummed past us, honey-bags bulging.

It was a glorious spring morning, with a mild fresh breeze in place of the appalling humidity of the day before. The world glittered with droplets, washed clean and sparkling like another Eden. Yellow and white flowers bloomed everywhere on the stony banks on either side of the muddy track, and the birds were singing. Caterina cried out with excitement at each bend in the road and wriggled in my lap, eager as a child. When she was turned away from me it was easy to forget that her left eye was blackening.

'Nico,' she said to me at last as the grey ambled steadily onwards.

'Mmm?'

'Does the motion remind you of anything?'

I laughed. 'Insatiable woman.'

She twisted round to face me. 'No, I mean it. I mean, if I sat astride you, couldn't we –'

'Forget it, *gattina*. I'm no horseman. I seriously doubt that you'd get my attention.'

'How much do you bet?' Her hand was on my thigh and ascending.

I bet nothing, which was just as well. However, I resisted her until we came to a cherry orchard where the new grass beneath the trees was as bright and as soft as silk in the skein. Then I leapt from the horse and flung her to the ground onto a cushion of sweet violets. Her hat rolled aside and her gilded hair spread out on the damp grass. She laughed and held out her hands to me as I dropped onto her like a hawk onto a pigeon. I pulled open the front of her gown, and the petals of the cherry blossom tumbled slowly down upon her, catching like snowflakes in her tangled tresses and settling on her skin, as pale and silky as her naked breasts.

The sun was strong and bright when we set off again. We spread our clothes out to dry off, though the grass stains would take some cleaning. The road wound down to the rocky coast and then kept close to it. It was a brilliantly clear day, and I could almost have sworn that from the tops of the hills we could see the massive cape of Cefalù, like the head and shoulders of a giant.

We passed one little rock-and-shingle bay after another. I examined them with a sailor's eye. It had to be a place that a ship would find easy to recognise. Too many of them looked the same. Besides, I was concerned that on this orientation our lights might be visible from Palermo. Palermo lies in a broad, sheltered bay, opening out to the east, and the tower of the castle commands the coastline for miles.

The going became harder for the horse. It put its head down as we climbed mountain foothills. We passed through a couple of tiny villages, just a huddle of buildings made of rock and roofed with branches, where children ran out into the street to stare at us as if we were a nine days' wonder. Then we left the cultivated lands and climbed through rough grass and fragrant scrub to the shoulder of a headland.

A spike of mountain, thrusting out northwards into the sea, cut off the view of Palermo. It was crested with a tall cairn, an unmistakable sea mark. I drew rein on the top of the headland and looked down into the sea on either side. There was a slight breeze, just enough to lift the sea into little waves. It was transparent blue, green and white where it crested into foam around the rocks. A little way below us, on the side away from Palermo, lay a small bay. The water was deep until quite close in to land, then suddenly flattened out to a sheltered pebbly cove ideal for boats.

For a while Caterina sat patiently. Then she said, 'What are you looking at?'

'The currents,' I explained. 'I'm looking to see whether a boat could easily come in this side of the headland, away from the city.'

She sat very quietly under her straw hat, which was tied to her head with her shawl, and looked at me with big serious eyes. She believed me, apparently.

In fact the location was excellent. A boat approaching from the mainland of Italy could take its bearings from the mountain behind Cefalù and then sail straight across the broad, shallow bay between Cefalù and the headland. We should be far enough from the Cefalù garrison not to fear that they would see our lights, but in any case we were sheltered from them by a little prong of land. I didn't really see how it could be improved from the Palermitans' viewpoint. However, I needed to check whether the bay would also make a good trap.

I put my heels into the horse and guided it down the steep wall of the bay towards the sea. That was ideal, too. One ship could startle the arms dealers into flight, while the two dozen men I had at my disposal could keep twice that number pinned down between the precipitous rocks if they had bows and spears enough. We could capture every member of the Palermo resistance that was involved in the operation. I reflected with pleasure that Andrea had supervised in person last time.

'Why are we coming down here?' asked Caterina.

'It looks like a nice place for lunch,' I said disingenuously. She caught my eye and frowned, and I grinned at her. 'I want a closer look at it,' I said.

At close quarters it was still ideal. Sheltered, secret and deadly. I had all the information I needed, and I felt as if the morning had been well spent. I tied the horse in the shade and Caterina pulled some scrubby grass and new shoots for it. Then we took our basket and went down on to the sand-and-shingle beach.

It was just warm enough to be really pleasant clothed and unclothed. I announced my intention of going for a swim before we ate and at once began to take off my tunic. Caterina watched, wide-eyed, as I stripped and waded into the gentle curls of the surf. The dark blue water was icy cold, but it was a keen pleasure to me to feel it abrading the dirt from my skin. Anyone who has suffered the inevitable, impotent filth of slavery can never be too clean.

I stood up in the shallows. 'Come in!' I called to Caterina.

'I can't swim,' she called back.

I cajoled and wheedled and told her that salt water was good for bruises. At last, with many an anxious glance over her shoulder, she tentatively removed her gown and then pulled off her shift. She waded tiptoe into the waves, squeaking with the cold. Even her nipples came out in goosepimples. I ran to put my arm round her and support her against the buffeting of the surf. She clung to me and kissed me lasciviously, but the cold water had reduced my enthusiasm to the size of a wizened acorn and I did nothing but return the kisses.

After a while we scrambled back to our lunch, salty and thirsty. The sun dried our skins as we ate and drank. Then I rested my head on my folded tunic and took Caterina into my arm and we drifted off on the sounds of the waves into a light refreshing sleep.

When I woke she was propped on her elbows, watching me. Her bruised face rebuked me. 'Tell me,' she said.

I had hoped she would forget. I hid my face in my folded arms. She said, quiet and determined, 'Nico, you promised.'

The overseer is grunting like a rutting boar. He is almost there. My mouth is full of blood, my blood. I am biting my forearm, hard, gagging myself with my own flesh.

At last it is over. He lifts his hideous weight from me and slumps to the filthy mattress with a satisfied sound. I shut my eyes and lie absolutely still. This may be my last chance, I think he is beginning to be bored with me. I have done everything I can to exhaust him. I have forced myself to offer him pleasure, as if I actually wanted to be in his loathsome bed. If he sends me back to the barracks now I will hang myself in self-hatred and despair. Fall asleep, you bastard. Fall asleep.

His breathing becomes steady and regular. After a moment he rolls onto his back and starts to snore. He is a huge strong man and his snores rumble like distant thunder. I begin to get up, very very slowly, keeping my right hand still so that the chain fastening me to the bed head will not jingle.

I can't get off the bed without waking him, I know, I've tried it. The keys and his dagger are hanging on the door of the room, safely away from the bed. I have to make sure that he won't wake up. I am shaking from head to foot with hatred and terror and the desire for revenge.

The straw rustles. I am on my knees beside him, crouching like a frog. My belly quakes as I prepare myself. Then I leap. I fling my heels in the air and bring my feet down together, as hard as I can, onto his great bulging belly.

He rocks upright, wheezing, his eyes blind and bulbous. I hit him in the throat with my left fist. His Adam's apple fractures sickeningly and I snarl with grim approval. He reels back, mouth gaping as he strains for air. I force him down to the mattress and thrust my manacled fist right into his open mouth. His teeth chip and shatter as they gnash against the metal cuff. My hand pushes his tongue down his throat, choking him.

I can't believe how long it takes him to die. As long as it used to take him to take his vile pleasure from me. I enjoy every minute of it.

At last the breath rattles out of his spasming lungs and he is still. I withdraw my hand, feeling sick now. I half-push, half-lower his body to the floor so that I can move the bed and get to the keys. Every scrape of wood, every chink of metal makes my heart stop. If they find me I will beg in vain for a death as quick as his.

At last the manacle is off and the overseer's dagger is in my hand. His tiny window opens onto the outside world, beyond the walls, beyond the dogs. I can see the lights of Messina through it, and the moon.

The dagger itches against my palm. Before I crawl through the window and flee, I do to his corpse what I always wanted to do to his living body. It disappoints me that there isn't more blood.

I couldn't tell it the way I remembered it. The story emerged in jerks, lame and halting. As I spoke Caterina watched me in utter silence. At one point she folded her hands over her mouth. Then she began to shake.

At last I said, 'If you ever breathe a word of this, Caterina, I'll kill you.' I suppose I didn't mean it, though I thought I did when I said it.

'Oh, I wouldn't. I wouldn't. Oh, Nico, I'm so sorry. I'm sorry for everything.' You would have thought that it had all been her fault. She reached out for me, groping through tears. At first I turned from her, but she stroked my hair and my cheek and at last I buried my head in her lap and let her hold me. It wasn't enough, but it helped.

She was naked and so was I. After some time the smell of her lap, honey and musk and brine, penetrated my foul memories. I crawled up her soft body and pushed her down onto my tunic and cloak.

At the end I was smeared with dark blood. Caterina lifted her head to smile at me, saw the state of my loins and blenched. 'Oh,' she cried, 'oh, holy Virgin, how terrible! It's bad luck! Oh, wash it off, Nico, please, please, straight away.'

I kissed her and tried to reassure her. 'Don't worry,' I said. 'I'm in the right place for it.' I waded into the sea and washed myself clean. I was glad for the blood. I don't like to beget bastards, and I was afraid that with Caterina I might have forgotten myself once too often.

When I emerged she had pulled on her clothes and was sitting with her face hidden in her hands, weeping. I squatted down beside her and said, 'Don't worry, *gattina*. It's not your fault.'

'But it's bad luck,' she insisted. 'I'm so sorry, Nico, I should have known –'

'Hush.' I pulled her head onto my shoulder. 'It's because I told you that dreadful story. That's why it happened. Ask anyone, they'll tell you. Bad luck works both ways.'

I didn't believe a word of it. But it seemed to make Caterina feel better, and somehow in comforting her I found that I had comforted myself as well.

Seventeen

'They're Genoese,' Blasio said as we made our way through the crowded streets towards our rendezvous. 'Just as greedy as the Pisans, but they're offering us more at one drop. Swords and spears mostly, some crossbows. It's a good deal.'

Genoese. A little warning prickle began between my shoulder blades. I said nothing, just nodded.

'Quite odd that you should pick on St Margaret's Bay,' said Andrea. He was in a good mood, which made him even more creepy. Every time I looked at him I thought of the naked painted boy in the brothel. 'It was the very place Blasio and I had in mind. If I'm honest, Nicetas, I didn't think you'd have the sense to choose it.'

'I'm glad I surprised you, then,' I said acidly.

We were meeting the Genoese by the bridge over the river Oreto. It had been built by the same Norman lord as the church of Santa Maria, so they called it the Admiral's Bridge. It was somewhat out of the way, being well beyond the town walls, but because of that it was relatively unfrequented and there was a little tavern beside the river with a walled garden which Andrea liked to use for private meetings. Besides which, the landlord was Giovanni's brother and therefore entirely trustworthy.

It was a long walk. Everywhere was now as dry as if the storm had never happened, and the road was carpeted with a thick layer of silky white dust. There was quite a lot of traffic, people and animals on their way to market in Palermo, and every passer-by flung up a plume of smoky white that hung in the air and caught in our mouths and noses. Because of the dust we went most of the way in silence. When a flock of sheep passed us, bleating and jockeying each other as if they wanted to see who could get slaughtered first, I cast a fold of my cloak over my nose and mouth. After the sheep had passed I left it there. Once or twice Andrea murmured something to Blasio, who replied equally

131

softly. We were almost there when Andrea said to me, 'I hear that you and Caterina have been having disagreements.'

I stared at him, then lowered my cloak. 'What business is it of yours?' I demanded. I remembered Caterina shouting in her strong determined voice, 'Boys, Nico! Boys!' What had Andrea discovered?

'I make all sorts of things my business,' he said quietly. 'And I'm sure that you do the same.' His black lizard's eyes were fixed on mine. I was as certain as I could be that he knew I had been to the boy-brothel after him.

'We did have a spat a few days ago,' I said, trying to sound offhand. 'But we made it up. She came out into the country with me to look for the landing-place –'

'You never told her why?' Blasio sounded furious.

'Of course I didn't. What d'you take me for? She thinks we went for a country ride and so I could give her one on the beach. Which I did.' I gave Blasio what I hoped was a man-to-man look, but he didn't seem impressed.

'What did you argue about?' asked Andrea.

'Andrea,' I said, 'in the Devil's name, shut up. Curiosity killed the cat.'

'So it did,' he agreed. 'Which of us miaows, do you think, Nicetas?'

I looked at him narrowly for a few minutes, then dropped my eyes. Blasio gnawed at his thumbnail, glaring at me from under his heavy brows. He appeared confused, which in itself was interesting. Close as those two were, it seemed that Andrea's Aragonese connections were personal to him. He couldn't have had that high an opinion of Blasio's intellect, if he felt safe to raise the subject before his very eyes. Mind you, Blasio hero-worshipped him, as strong violent men sometimes do idolise little clever weaklings.

The bridge was before us, busy with traffic. It was a fine bridge, ten feet wide if it was an inch and resting on three sturdy stone arches. The parapets were low enough not to interfere with the burdens the pack-horses carried. There was a French guard post at the city end of it, collecting tolls. So much for a cartload of fodder, so much for firewood, so much for beasts. A herd of the little scrubby Sicilian cattle was crossing the bridge as we approached, heading like the sheep for the abattoir, and the three of us stopped and leant on the parapet to wait for our road to be clear.

We watched the Frenchmen on duty. They were half a dozen young soldiers, lazy and slapdash, who clearly thought that this sort of job was beneath them. Like most of the French soldiery they were dressed in coarse woollen hose, padded linen gambesons to stop their armour from chafing, and hauberks of chain-mail that covered them from shoulder to knee. Because they were young and fancied themselves, they had sprigs of fresh flowers tucked into their helmets and decorative drapes of once-bright, now-grubby cloth swept across their shoulders. They collected the tolls in an offhand, haphazard way, but they showed eager interest when the cattle-drover's wife, a handsome young woman, tried to pass them.

'Stop,' said the senior soldier, catching her by the arm. 'We have to search you.'

'Search me?' She glanced at her husband, horrified.

'You might have concealed weapons,' said the young soldier smugly. He grinned at his friends, put his hands on the woman's body and ran them all over her. There wasn't anything her husband could do; he just stood there, pale with anger.

The soldier didn't try to lift her skirt or open her gown, but Blasio stared through narrow furious eyes, hissing and muttering beneath his breath as if the cattle-drover's wife were his sister.

'They really are the spawn of the Devil, aren't they,' I said softly, keeping in character. 'I swear, if I had my sword, for two pence I'd –'

'Shut up,' hissed Blasio, rounding on me. 'You young fool, you talk out of your arse. What do you know? We've lived like this for fifteen years. Save your energy. You'll need it when we take them. Proper revenge, little Greek, all of them, not just these few.'

I scowled at him and subsided. I looked over the river, which was high with the rain, to the tavern on the far side. Andrea looked too and said, 'They're ahead of us,' pointing to a group of three men about to go inside. They had come by boat, a little lean rowing-launch that looked as if it belonged to a ship of war. It was tied up just below the tavern.

One of them, a tall man, pulled off his hat to wipe the back of his hand across his brow. His faded ash-blond hair caught the sun. I couldn't see his face, but even at that distance I recognised the easy, confident swing of his stride. Daniele Filippo.

The first thing that crossed my mind was a surge of anger that Daniele had cheated when we made our bet. He had had inside information, sure enough. Then anger gave way to fear. There was no chance of preserving my incognito with Daniele there. Suddenly I was sick and light-headed with the panicky whirling of my blood. I had to think fast.

The beasts had crossed, leaving the bridge studded with cow pats. Andrea and Blasio straightened and Andrea said to me, 'Come on.'

I lurched, doubling up over my stomach as if someone had hit me. Andrea said, 'What's the matter?' in a voice that was suddenly sharp and suspicious.

'Christ,' I gasped, 'my guts.' I let myself fold to the ground, retching. My hair hid my face. Beneath its cover I stuck two fingers down my throat hard, with the usual result.

Blasio's big hand grabbed my shoulder and pulled me upright. He got my puke on his hands and thrust me away from him, cursing. I reeled back against the parapet of the bridge, gasping. 'Bad shellfish,' I hazarded wildly.

Andrea said, 'I don't want to keep them waiting. Pull yourself together.'

I did exactly the opposite and let myself go, racking my diaphragm with violent cramps. Amazingly enough it worked. Andrea had to sidestep smartly to avoid the next ejection. He gave an exclamation of disgust. I stood bent in two, clutching my guts and moaning.

'Andrea,' Blasio said, 'we can't wait for this.'

'Christ's twitching prick,' said Andrea, who had a fruity line in blasphemy. 'Nicetas, when you've got rid of whatever it is, you know where we are.'

'Oh God,' I whimpered, 'the other end as well.' I lifted my head pathetically. 'Where can I go?'

'There's a whole river right there,' said Blasio. He wiped his hand on the stones of the bridge and then took Andrea by the arm. They gave me a last disgusted look and moved away.

I moaned and retched my guts up all the time it took for them to cross the bridge and head towards the tavern. The young French soldiers on the guard post didn't blink an eye as the leader of the Palermo resistance movement walked past their noses. They were much more interested in my contortions, and a couple of them started to lay bets on the quality and content of the next heave.

When Andrea and Blasio were on the far side I let them see me scrambling down to the rocky river bed and disappearing beneath one of the arches of the bridge with a pained, purposeful look on my face. Then I went to find a source of clean water to wash away the taste of puke.

★ ★ ★

I waited on the city side of the bridge for the meeting to be over. I was anxious. Andrea had certainly been suspicious at first, and I didn't know whether my energetic convulsions would have convinced him. Something else was needed.

An opportunity presented itself. Just as I saw the big and small figures of Andrea and Blasio emerging from the tavern, a couple of Sicilians came to cross the bridge. They were peasants of the poorer sort, walking to the city with their surplus produce on their backs to sell – a few eggs, a scrawny chicken, some clay jars of honey. One was a stooped, greying man and the other a girl, his daughter I guessed, a ripe round dark little thing of maybe fourteen years. The soldiers saw her coming and nudged each other. 'Here comes Rubea,' said one of them. It seemed that the girl was familiar to them and they had a bet on concerning the number of kisses they might be able to extract from her.

I thought the girl knew what they had in mind. When she appeared over the sharp crown of the bridge she was clinging as close to her father as the foal does to the mare, and she kept her downcast eyes on the road. As she drew closer the soldiers rallied her, calling out to her, offering her free passage and no tolls in recompense for kisses. She looked once at her father and shook her head.

Then the young Angevins got tough, threatening unless she obliged them to empty their baskets into the river, to charge them double, to chuck her aged father over the parapet. It was all I needed. I strutted up to the ringleader of the soldiers and said in French, 'Leave her alone, you donkey's arse.'

He stared at me, utterly astonished to encounter resistance of any sort. He looked me up and down, trying to place me from my clothes and failing. 'Who the hell are you?' he demanded. 'You smell of puke.'

The peasants scuttled away behind me, taking the chance to avoid their tolls as well as the girl's harassment. I silently hoped that the guard had changed before they made their return journey. To the young soldier I said, 'If I smell of puke, you smell of donkey shit. That's because you're a donkey's arse. Or perhaps a donkey got you on your mother, which must make you a mule's arse if your mother was a mare.'

He yelled with rage and swung for me. I ducked and hit him in the stomach as I came up. My fist came into sharp contact with his mail hauberk, hurting me a good deal more than it hurt him. Well, it all added verisimilitude to the character of Nicetas as an impetuous idiot. I cursed, then with the hand that wasn't skinned and stinging I hit him on the chin instead. His men were slow to react, but as he tottered and swore they snarled and drew their swords.

Suddenly Andrea was there, catching me and thrusting me back into Blasio's bearlike grip. He helped the young Frenchman to stand up and dusted him down, chattering in bad French. 'So sorry, my lord sergeant, I am so sorry. A stupid young man, stupid, shouldn't be out on his own. Allow me −' Silver changed hands. The soldier looked happier at once. Andrea grovelled a little more, then jerked his head at Blasio.

They towed me away from the bridge. At a little distance, when we were out of sight of the Frenchmen, Andrea made another gesture to Blasio. The big man jerked my arms behind my back and held them and Andrea stood in front of me, looking up at me with his black glittering eyes. 'What in the name of God do you think you were doing?' he demanded, and went on without waiting for an answer. 'Did you make yourself sick just so you could be left alone to have a go at those young French fools? Are you mad? They could have killed you, and then where would our gold be?'

'I didn't make myself sick,' I muttered sullenly. I tugged against Blasio's hands, but he was as strong as a castle keep.

'By the swollen tits of the Magdalene,' Andrea said softly, 'Nicetas, you must learn to do as you are told.' He struck me in the face. I snarled and heaved and tried to kick him. He hit me twice more. When blood began to run from my lip he stopped and took a step back, a little out of breath. I fought Blasio for a moment, cursing them both. Then Andrea drew his dagger and I stopped struggling, though I was still simmering like a boiling pot. 'Do you understand?' he asked icily. 'I want discipline from you. You could prejudice everything with your foolishness.'

'Let me go, curse you,' I said to Blasio. Andrea nodded at him and he released me. He looked mildly disappointed. I imagined that he had been hoping for a chance to rough me up personally.

I bent my head, trying to staunch the blood from my lip. It wasn't serious, but I didn't want to drip on my new tunic and give Caterina the excuse to shy another heavy kitchen utensil at my head. 'Now,' Andrea said, 'will you behave?' I nodded sullenly and said nothing. I hoped that all this rigmarole might have allayed his suspicions.

'Come with us then. I need to tell you the operational details. Then you go and get us the gold.' He sheathed his dagger and shot me a hard, determined look. 'And keep yourself under control from now on.'

EIGHTEEN

A few days later I was sure that Andrea still suspected me. Under the circumstances I didn't want to go to Messina again. I had said that my master was on the mainland, and that's where I went to pick up the last of the Greek gold.

If Andrea had me followed, the man was good at his job. I noticed nothing. But I remained extremely cautious. I waited two days before setting in train the system of light signals which would summon Dolfin to join me from across the Straits of Messina. He responded instantly; someone must have been watching. He would be able to join me next day.

On that day I spent several hours skulking around Reggio, ensuring that nobody was on my tail, before making my way to our rendezvous. Dolfin came with Aliusio, which I supposed was inevitable. After all, the young bantam was charged with carrying out the operation, Saint Mark preserve us all.

In a reasonably decent portside tavern we sat and looked at each other. Dolfin was dressed in a respectable but threadbare grey tunic that looked as if it must have been borrowed from the caretaker at the Venetian residency. To me he still had the arrogant air of a nobleman attempting incognito, but perhaps that was because I knew him. He appeared to have been biting something bitter. He looked pinched and strained.

Aliusio was overdressed as usual, this time at the opposite extreme. He had taken the secrecy of our meeting to heart. He wore an enormous sweep of dusty black cloak to cover up his bright clothes, and had the hood raised although we were indoors. His air screamed 'secret business'.

'For the Virgin's sake put your hood back,' I said fractiously. 'You look like an agent of the Devil.'

'I didn't want to look conspicuous,' he said, unfortunately without a trace of irony. He flung back his hood theatrically and scowled at me. His black hair was crowned with a thin gold fillet and carefully curled. The smell of his perfume made me feel sick.

'What progress have you made?' Dolfin demanded. 'Ser D'Estari, it is less than two weeks to Easter. The fleet is almost ready to sail. They are talking about leaving halfway through April.' He pursed his already tight lips. 'I begin to think that you have invented this whole conspiracy. We have laid out a vast amount of gold in order to prevent some alleged insurrection, of which I have no certainty at all. I must insist that you give an account of yourself.'

He wasn't going to shake me. 'Signor Dolfin,' I said, 'there is no need for me to give an account to anyone. We will soon have all the evidence we need, enough to satisfy the Doge himself, never mind the Security Committee. On Palm Sunday the resistance in Palermo are receiving a shipment of weapons, just as I told you. We are here to decide on how the delivery is to be interrupted and the leaders of the conspirators captured.' I leant a little closer to him and added, 'The man in charge already knows when the French fleet intends to sail. He has intelligence in Messina. They plan to attack just before, when the French are at their most preoccupied.'

'It is not enough to make assertions,' Dolfin said angrily. 'Tell me who these agents are, who in Messina is passing information back to Palermo, then perhaps I could give some credence to what I say to the French. As it is they think I am simply a scaremonger. What am I to do? Without proof I am not believed, I am turning into a laughing stock.'

'After all,' interposed Aliusio, 'even if they did believe that the Sicilians might revolt, what on earth would happen? A bunch of peasants, rising against the entire Angevin army? They'd be put down in the time it takes to skin a cat. I can understand why the French aren't worried.'

'We are talking about determined, well-organised, armed resistance,' I reminded him. 'Not a crowd of excited peasants with mattocks and hoes. If we can successfully interrupt this arms delivery and capture the leader we'll stand a chance of convincing the French that they need to do something.'

'Do what?' asked Dolfin, making a helpless gesture. 'What can the French do, if the revolt is secret?'

I raised my brows at his naïveté. 'Find out from the leaders who their counterparts are in the other main towns,' I said. 'Take them, make them confess. Execute them, if they want. The fact of discovery of the resistance will shock the people into keeping quiet.' As I spoke I realised how brutal I sounded, like the worst sort of Frenchman. I wasn't usually so callous. Dolfin, however, just nodded quietly, as if he understood.

There wasn't any point in further argument. I began to make a rough map of the bay on the table top with pieces of bread and crumbs. 'Look,' I said. 'This is St Margaret's Bay. It's on the headland, the first headland to the east of Palermo, the first bay that is concealed from the Palermo garrison.'

'Our pilot will know it,' said Aliusio confidently. 'He has sailed these waters for years.'

'Good.' I was relieved. I didn't trust Aliusio to find his foot in a fog. 'Now, listen. The arms runners are Genoese –'

'Genoa!' exclaimed Aliusio, so loudly that I winced and held up my hand to try to quieten him. 'Those bastards! They'd do anything to hit at Venice. We should –'

'It's nothing to do with Venice,' I said through my teeth. 'They're in it for the money. They're just turning a profit, the way you or I might. They have no idea that Venice is involved. Forget them, they're not important. It's the men on the shore that are important.'

He fell silent and pouted. He obviously thought that the Genoese involvement was adding insult to injury. I watched him for a moment, trying to see whether he was really paying attention. Then I began to explain. 'They'll bring in the arms in small boats,' I said. 'The resistance will be on the land. I'll be with them. The Genoese will signal the shore when they arrive, three long flashes. We'll signal back with three short. Then they'll come in and start the drop.'

'Three long flashes and three short,' Aliusio repeated.

'What I want you to do,' I said, 'is have all your men except for one boat on the shore, just over the crest of the headland from the bay. When you see the signals, get your people around the bay. There's only one track down to it and it's steep, a dry river bed. If you block that they're trapped, there are cliffs and rocks all around the bay. The boat is to scare the Genoese into moving straight off, otherwise they might be able to take the Palermitans off by boat.' He was frowning. At least he seemed to be listening. 'When you've got them trapped, keep them there. Don't shoot into them if you can avoid it. We want them alive, and one of them will be me.'

'And we wouldn't want any accidents, would we?' asked Aliusio nastily. He obviously disliked me as much as I did him.

'There'll probably be about a dozen of them,' I said. 'Your

men will outnumber them, but be careful. They'll be desperate, they could fight like rats in a trap. Kill some of them if you have to to persuade the others to submit. I'll try to get hold of Andrea, the leader, and keep him safe on one side. Tell your men that one of them will be a Venetian and they should help me when they find me.'

'How will they know you?'

'The password is "Fiammetta",' I said, trying to suppress a grin.

Aliusio's face stiffened. He had given his wife no children and had betrayed her with the Saints knew how many women, but it's a husband's duty to be jealous. 'Fiammetta?' he repeated in a cold angry voice. 'Why that password?'

'I agreed it with Signor Dolfin,' I said honestly. He looked sharply across at his father-in-law, then back at me. His expression relaxed somewhat. 'Now,' I suggested, 'you repeat back to me what we've agreed.'

Aliusio looked startled, then began to do as he was told. He hesitated and stumbled and needed correction. I tried to be patient. He was hopeless, but he was all I had got.

There was so much that could go wrong. Clouds over the moon, mistaken places, incorrect signals, panic, clumsiness and simple stupidity. And this operation was important to me. Not because of Venice, but because of Andrea. I hated him. I wanted to deliver him to the French torturers and let them screw the truth out of him, and if that meant that the rest of the Sicilian resistance was doomed, so be it. My hatred drove me forward, though the whole thing was fraught with risk for me. Daniele would be on the Genoese ship, and he knew me. The thought of being unmasked wrenched me with fear.

My father's palazzo rears up before me, huge and overwhelming. I run up to the porter's lodge, shivering, and ask for Signor Domenico Bono.

'He's away,' the porter says. 'Not expected back till the day after tomorrow.'

I stare at him, horrified. I can't believe it. I open my mouth to say, But my mother's sick and she wants him, she needs him. But I can't say that to a stranger. It would have been hard enough to say it to my father.

'Who wants him?' asks the porter, a kindly soul. He cranes out of the lodge window to look down at me better. 'Do you want to leave a message?'

What message? How can I leave a message that he will understand and no one else? I stand racking my brains and fighting tears. Then I think, Well, nobody in his house knows about me. So if I leave a message from Marcello, that will work. I frame the words and am about to speak. Then behind me a shrill woman's voice cries, 'Catch that child!'

A strong hand on my arm. I squirm and struggle, but the young page holds me tightly. He drags me before a handsome, angry-looking woman dressed like a queen in pearls and velvet. I know her. It is my father's wife, the ogress, the witch, the she-devil that my mother threatens me with when I am bad. She is my mother's age, but as unlike her as the dark is unlike the light. She is staring at me as if I am a portent or a demon from Hell, and I stare back, dumbstruck with terror.

'Look at his face,' she whispers at last. 'Domenico's very features. God in Heaven, it is my husband's bastard! I knew it!'

She raises her hand to hit me. I writhe like a worm and bite the page's wrist. He curses and lets me go and I flee, darting away from the groping arms that try to trap me. Her voice behind me cuts through the air, shrill with hatred and fury. 'Catch him! Follow him! Track him down!'

I have not left my message. My sick mother will not have her wish, and I have been seen and recognised and brought ill fortune on us all. I could die for shame.

At last Aliusio got everything straight. I would have written it down for him, but he had forgotten all the letters his tutor had ever beaten into him. I made him repeat it twice, so that I knew it was set in his thick head. Then I turned to Signor Dolfin. 'My lord, there is another matter I need to discuss with you.'

'My head is aching,' Aliusio complained.

'Go and take some air, then,' snapped Dolfin. He had been impatient with his son-in-law's endless repetitions and confusion. 'What?' he asked me sharply.

'My lord,' I said, with careful courtesy. 'There is an additional complexity. I have found a Venetian citizen in Palermo, enslaved. He is helping me with information about Andrea and his connection with Aragon. I have – taken the liberty of promising him that when he has helped me, the Republic will purchase his freedom.'

Dolfin's grey brows came down hard. 'A slave? What sort of a man is he?'

'He is steward of a noble house. He was the captain's clerk and accountant on a war-galley many years ago.'

'A steward?' Dolfin sounded horrified. 'But a steward is a very valuable slave. It would cost a great deal to redeem him.'

I couldn't believe my ears. 'Signor, he is a citizen of the

Republic. He has been a slave for ten years, and now he is helping me. Surely the Republic would not grudge the cost of his freedom?'

Dolfin shook his head. 'I don't know,' he muttered. 'Ser D'Estari, you put me in an invidious position. I did not come here with authority to decide on the expenditure of the Republic's funds for any cause other than that of obstructing the Emperor's conspiracy. I dare not exceed that authority.'

I sympathised, knowing how unreasonable the city's treasurers could be, but I despised his lack of resolution. 'He's a Venetian citizen,' I repeated.

'The State can't afford to redeem every Venetian citizen that has the bad luck to become a slave,' snapped Dolfin, turning to the attack as he always did when pressed. 'It has been years since we have redeemed prisoners of war, you know, taken in direct battle fighting for the Republic. I cannot promise to redeem your man, Ser D'Estari. I will not promise. If you gave him your word, that is between you and him. Do not seek to involve me.'

Miserable gutless worm. I could have had your daughter on the balcony over your head, you timid old man, I thought. I wished again that I had. I said aloud, 'I did give him my word, signor, expecting that there would be no difficulty with the State. If you are reluctant, I will draw on my own funds.' That startled him. Had he thought I was a pauper? 'And when we are back in Venice I will present the facts to the Committee and let them decide whether they wish to reimburse me. I will tell them that you refused.'

'Are you threatening me?' demanded Dolfin, surging up from his stool.

'No,' I said evenly. Lying again, Marcello.

NINETEEN

I stood on the beach where Caterina and I had lain and wrapped my cloak more tightly around me. My face was swathed in black, just in case Daniele should be on one of the boats bringing the arms to land.

Everything was going smoothly so far. We had encountered no French patrols as we left Palermo or on the road to the bay. The weather was perfect, with a steady soft breeze out at sea to bring the Genoese straight to us and a glowing gibbous moon. Small waves ran in to the shore, curled into foam that was blue-white with moonlight, and sighed onto the pebbles. The bright moon quenched the brilliance of the stars, but around the edges of the sky they sparkled as thickly as wet shells on a sandy beach. It was a balmy, beautiful night, a night to walk with a pretty girl beneath the glittering sky, to put back the veil from her hair and touch her white throat, to kiss her until her limbs melted and then lie her down and show her gleaming body to the chaste moon.

I looked out to sea for the Genoese signal. My nerves tempted me to scan the rocky crags around the bay for the concealed Venetian land forces, but I resisted.

My lips still burned with the memory of Caterina's goodbye. I had made light of things as usual, but her intuition had told her that tonight was important. She had clung to me and pressed her lips to mine with a desperate urgency that betrayed her feelings more than any words could. But she had learnt from our disagreements. All she had said was, 'See you later.' No questions, no exhortations to be careful. Just, 'See you later,' and that heart-searching, breath-stopping kiss.

She was turning herself into a secret agent's perfect companion. I really would regret it when the time came to part company with her. It would be nice to be able to roll her up, like a summer cloak, carry her about with me and unroll her whenever the occasion allowed. Impossible, alas. Ah well.

To keep my mind from my nerves I allowed myself to

succumb to the lure of the moonlight. I let myself think of Caterina in bed. I compared her with all the other women I could remember, all the way back to Boneta, the blowsy lusty laundry maid who had first taken me in hand before I was fifteen. Caterina was up with the leaders. She didn't have the prettiest face or the loveliest body, but she put such life and energy into everything she did that it raised her above the commonplace. She made me laugh, too.

Enough dreaming. There, out at sea, I could just make out the shape of a little lean galley, low in the water. I knew her lines. It was the same ship that I had seen refitting in Naxos harbour three months ago, Daniele's galley the *Basilisk*. She was running under sail, but as I watched the sheets came down, with such elegant swiftness that I suppressed an admiring whistle, and the moonlight flashed on quick turbulence as her oars came out. They were muffled and hit the water with hardly a sound. Her rowing–master knew his job and so did her captain. She turned on her heel like a water gnat and came in towards the bay in eerie silence.

Just before the little galley came into the calm between the high rock walls of the bay she backed water and lay still, rising and falling gently on the slight swell. Around me there was movement as the Palermitans came to stand at the water's edge, looking eagerly outward. One of the mules picketed at the back of the bay snorted and let out its shrill braying whinny and someone cursed and ran back to silence it.

'They'll be making sure it's safe to come in,' said Andrea's voice in my ear, soft as a breath.

I nodded. Then from the masthead of the Genoese galley a light shone and was extinguished, three times.

'Reply,' said Andrea, and Blasio lifted the dark lantern in his hand and opened the little grille three times in the counter signal.

For a moment nothing happened. Then there was movement on the galley's decks and a launch splashed into the water. Phosphorescence gleamed briefly about her as she settled. Men ran down into her and boxes began to be passed from hand to hand. We heard the drop of another boat on the other side of the galley.

The first boat came towards us through the still water of the bay. Pietro and a couple of his young friends hitched up their tunics into their belts and ran out into the icy waves to catch it and drag it to land. Andrea pushed back his hood to show his face and walked forward with Blasio beside him. 'Welcome,' he said.

Daniele jumped from the prow of the boat and splashed through the shallows to shore. He was swathed in a heavy cloak, but his head was bare, and the moon gleamed unmistakably in his blond hair. I retreated a little, though there was no reason why he should look at me. He took Andrea's hand and inclined his head civilly. 'Here we are, then,' he said. 'Everything as agreed. Have you got the gold?' His Sicilian was good. Agents have to be polyglot.

Andrea produced a leather bag, the property of the Security Committee of the Serene Republic, had he but known it. He held it up, swinging in the moonlight. Daniele reached out for it. Andrea let him take it, then said in a cool voice, 'Count it, by all means. You'll be waiting on the beach until the delivery is over, in any case.'

A steel blade gleamed. Blasio had a dagger in his hand, just touching Daniele's ribs. Daniele looked down at the dagger and laughed, looking unconcerned. 'Don't you trust us?' he asked, as if nothing could have surprised him more. 'What a sad and sorry world this is. Well, I don't mind waiting here and letting my friends do the work.'

He made a signal to the men in the boat and they began to unload the cargo and hand it to the Palermitans, who carried it back to the beach. I ran forward to help as well, not wanting to look out of place. I felt excited with the promise of additional success. I had expected Daniele to head back to the *Basilisk* with the gold at once, out of our reach. If he was still on the beach we could recover gold and weapons and conspirators all together. I stooped down with Giovanni to heft one of the heavy wooden boxes. Come on, Aliusio, I thought. What are you waiting for?

As each box landed Pietro prised off the lid with a crowbar and Andrea checked the contents. Swords bundled together like firewood, daggers like kindling, all carefully wrapped in oiled linen to keep the sea water out. Lighter boxes contained crossbows and their strings in leather bags. Crate after crate of quarrels for the crossbows, some with heavy narrow armour-piercing heads. Venice's gold had gone a long way. There were about a dozen of us on the beach and we worked like dogs, heaving the heavy boxes from the waterline to the waiting mules.

Still no sign of Aliusio. I stopped work, as if the operation would slow down noticeably just because I wasn't fetching and carrying. I was sweating under the dark fabric that concealed my face, not with fatigue but with fear of failure. Where in the name of Saint Mark was he? He was supposed to move in as soon as the signals had been given.

Both the Genoese boats came to land with another load. As the conspirators began to unload them one of the boatswains said, 'That's it.'

That's it? Everything over? I couldn't believe it had gone so quickly, and no sign of the Venetians. The Genoese hurried to help us unload the crates from the boats, one after another. They carried some of them up on to the beach for us. I suppose they were eager to be gone. I helped to lug off a box of swords, shuddering with impotent rage.

'Well,' said Daniele to Andrea. Neither of them had carried a thing, and I thought that Daniele was laughing. 'Well, there you are. Everything as agreed. You get a fair deal when you deal with Genoa.'

Andrea frowned. He had been reckoning the crates on his fingers. 'It seems to be all there,' he said at last. Blasio nodded and stepped back from Daniele. The reflection of the moon gleamed blue on his dagger blade, then darkened as he sheathed it. 'Fair enough,' Andrea went on. 'It's been good doing business –'

Suddenly through the night a horn squealed, cracking the air with urgency. Daniele hid the gold in a fold of his tunic and swung around, drawing his sword. His frowning face was a tense patchwork of shadows. 'You Sicilian dog,' he said to Andrea, 'what's going on?'

Andrea looked momentarily nonplussed. All around the beach men dropped their burdens and pulled out their swords, staring wildly about them in the moonlight. I frowned up at the cliffs, trying to see Aliusio's men.

'Daniele,' shouted one of the Genoese sailors on the beach. 'She's signalling. Quick, to the boats!'

Daniele glanced quickly out at the Genoese ship, cursed and turned to run. Blasio grabbed at his arm, snarling, 'You aren't going yet, you dog. What are you trying to –'

Without a word Daniele turned, his sword a blue arc in the moonlit air. Blasio shouted and met steel with steel. Suddenly the whole beach was confusion as two boatsful of Genoese leapt forward to protect Daniele and the Palermitans jumped in to back up Blasio.

I stood back and watched with an admiring smile. It was perfect. Set one against the other! I was ready to congratulate Aliusio personally for showing more initiative than I could ever have given him credit for. But then –

Movement out at sea and on the walls of the bay. My head swivelled as I tried to take everything in. It didn't look right. I stared out to sea and my jaw dropped. The Genoese boats were still beached and the three sharp cutters racing around the point could only be Aliusio's.

Three boats? Why three? He only had two dozen men in all. If they were manning the boats that meant there were only a handful on the walls of the bay, not half enough to keep down twelve angry rebels. Then I saw what the boats were doing. They were heading for the beached Genoese launches.

From the walls of the bay came the sound of rocks showering down the cliffs as men scrambled down towards the beach, then a shrill shout. I thought I recognised Aliusio's voice. 'St Mark!' it yelled. 'Venice!' The idiot, announcing his presence as if he were making a grand entrance at one of the Doge's parties!

'*Venice?*' repeated Daniele in a voice that echoed from the cliffs. 'Venice?' He stared into Blasio's face across their drawn swords. 'What treachery is this?'

Blasio looked dumbstruck. He wasn't quick. Andrea reacted faster. 'The Venetians are on the side of the French. We're betrayed. You, too,' he said to Daniele. He waved his arm. 'Defend yourselves!' he shouted. 'Watch the mules! Keep the weapons safe!'

'Back to the boats,' Daniele yelled. He rallied his countrymen, shouting to the boatswain of one of the launches. I stood with my sword in my hand, wondering what in the Devil's name was going on and trying to think of some way of getting things back on track.

The Venetian boats were heading towards the shore. It looked as though they would arrive before the Genoese had shoved off. If they did, everything might still work. I began to move surreptitiously towards Andrea, determined to get my hands on him personally. Daniele ran right past me without a glance of recognition and my heart soared.

But I had reckoned without the *Basilisk*. Its crew had also heard Aliusio's yell. It turned and skidded across the surface of the shallow bay like a waterborne scorpion. Men were shouting orders and running to and fro on its decks. With my hand extended to grab Andrea's tunic I stopped as I heard an order from the galley: 'Fire!'

A streak of blue lightning seemed to skim the surface of the bay. A bolt from a ballista, a giant crossbow loaded with a thick six-foot spear. It struck home on one of the Venetian boats. The appalling shriek of the man in its way was rapidly joined by cries of dismay from the others. Those bolts are heavy and the Genoese marksmanship was excellent. The bolt had gone right through its human target and fractured the shell of the boat. It went straight down, as small boats will, sprinkling the still surface of the bay with the heads of swimming men like poppy seeds on a loaf.

The Genoese on the beach and on the galley cheered. One of their launches was afloat now and the men in it were tugging at the oars, swinging her round to drive back for the galley and safety. The two remaining Venetian boats were backing water while the men in them shouted in confusion. Idiots! At last one went back to pick up the men from the first boat and the other came towards the shore, slower now.

At that moment Aliusio yelled again from the walls of the bay and he and his handful of men leapt down onto the beach and ran towards us. He must have been mad, seeing his boats in disarray, to launch a direct attack on land. If he had stayed put, at least he could have held the path. I didn't have time to worry about it. The Genoese continued to retreat to their remaining launch, and the Palermitans saw Aliusio's men running towards them and snarled with fury and leapt to the attack.

I hung back. I didn't dare join in and fight with the Venetians in case they lost, as seemed inevitable, and I was unmasked. They fought bravely, but there weren't enough of them. After I saw the first couple killed I looked desperately out to sea, but things were no better there. The Venetian boat was still some distance offshore, and now it seemed to be hesitating.

Near me the Genoese boat was ready to leave, all except for Daniele. The boatswain was calling to him. He ran towards them across the beach. Then from nowhere one of the Venetians dashed over to cut him off. Their swords flashed in the moonlight. Daniele was expert. In three swift strokes he wrong-footed his opponent and with a twist of his wrist struck away his sword.

I couldn't stand and watch while Daniele skewered one of my countrymen. With a shout I leapt forward, barged the defenceless Venetian aside and took Daniele's blow on the blade of my own sword. The Venetian staggered and caught at my clothes, trying to right himself. As he fell he pulled me off my balance and ripped the black cloths from my face.

Daniele's sword sizzled against mine and dragged it down to the pebbles. I gasped as I tried to resist him, but I was shaken and he was too strong. He stamped his foot on the flat of my blade, wrenching it from my hand. On one knee, panting, disarmed and helpless, I looked up to see death descending.

Into Daniele's blue eyes. He stood over me for a second, his sword raised, his mouth open, staring in recognition and disbelief. Then without a word he hurdled over me and dashed to the boat. He and the boatswain ran it into the sea and leapt over the gunwale.

I staggered up, shaking, and grabbed my sword. Near me the Venetian I had saved was also pushing himself to his feet, sword in hand. I registered with unsurprised resignation that he was wearing red boots. The life I had saved was Aliusio's.

Aliusio turned and looked at me. His mouth opened to speak. Brainless fool! He had caused this mess, and in a moment he would condemn me along with him. I raised my sword and yelled in wordless fury and lunged at him.

Our swords met with a hissing crash. Aliusio's face was a picture of astonishment. By God, I hated him! I let my anger flow through me and fought him in bitter earnest. He retreated towards the sea, parrying my furious blows. He wasn't a bad swordsman, but I was better; faster, stronger, more deadly. In a few moments, I promised myself, I would free Fiammetta for ever. I slashed at his face and he jerked back, but not fast enough. The point of my sword drew a line of red from jaw to temple and he whimpered with surprise and pain. Our swords locked together and I snarled as I twisted the hilt from his hand. I flung his weapon away behind me and it clattered on the pebbles. He stepped back and back, defenceless, gasping. The point of my sword was poised at his throat.

'Go on, Nicetas,' yelled someone, 'kill him!'

I glanced over my shoulder. Aliusio was the only Venetian on the beach still alive, and the victorious resistance were watching to see what I would do to him. I turned back and met his terrified eyes.

I couldn't do it. I didn't have enough anger left to kill him in hot blood, and in cold blood I just couldn't. I tried to make my hand move, but it stayed still. I bared my teeth in a snarl of impotent frustration and Aliusio flinched, perhaps thinking the expression meant his death. Blood coursed from the wound on his face and dripped to the pebbles.

'Go on,' someone called again, laughing out loud now. That had to be Pietro. 'What's the problem?'

I lifted my sword, feeling trapped. At that moment Aliusio gave a little moan of panic, turned and fled. He ran straight into the waves, flung himself forward in a shallow dive and began to swim frantically towards the Venetian boat.

Pietro ran up to stand beside me. 'You let him go,' he gasped. 'Why?'

I shrugged. 'They didn't get what they came for,' I said, concealing my rage beneath a cloak of indifference.

'Will the galley fire again?' asked Andrea eagerly, baring his teeth.

'They're busy taking in the boats,' rumbled Blasio. 'If the Venetians are quick they'll be able to get away.'

He was right. The Venetian boats, heavily loaded with Aliusio and the survivors of the ballista's target, turned tail and scooted out of the bay and around the headland. The galley made no attempt to stop them. The second boat, the boat with Daniele in it, was alongside now, and the crew were scrambling up the boarding-ropes. The moonlight gleamed on silver hair as Daniele jumped onto the deck and turned to look back at the beach where we stood.

Andrea lifted his hand and waved. A stir of movement showed that Daniele was waving back.

I ought to have been worrying about what I would do to retrieve Aliusio's appalling failure. But I could only think about Daniele.

Why had he let me go?

TWENTY

O f course we had to get the weapons into the city as well, which could have posed an even bigger problem than getting them ashore. But I had to accept that Andrea was a good organiser. We drove the mules back almost all the way to the city and then turned off into some farm and found waiting for us in the yard half a dozen great ox-carts laden with bundles of firewood. They had special slings between the axles for some boxes and others could be concealed within the load. The whole of our night's labour vanished into those carts before the dawn broke, and we were ready to make our way through the city gates with the normal morning rush.

It would look odd to have too many men with each cart. The distribution of the weapons was already arranged, one each to Zanino and Bartolo's quarters, two to Pietro and Giovanni's, and so a man from the quarter jumped up with each driver and the rest of us set off afoot. We would filter in through the gates a few at a time, without drawing attention to ourselves.

Andrea and Blasio elected to walk along with me. I hardly noticed, I was still half stunned with failure. I couldn't make myself think of what I should do next, my mind was far too busy reviewing what had happened and trying to determine whether anything that I could have done would have changed things.

Most of all I regretted not having killed Aliusio while I had the chance. It would have been utterly excusable, with the resistance baying for his blood just behind me. And he had deserved to die. He had ignored my clear instructions and caused the failure of the whole operation, not to speak of the deaths of several Venetians who were now lying on a remote Sicilian beach, unshrived, unburied, unmourned. Besides, who would have known who had killed him? But I had let him go, just as I had let Fiammetta go to his bed a virgin. Soft-hearted and stupid.

Andrea interrupted my self recriminations. 'Nicetas.'

'Mm?' I yawned hugely. Dawn was breaking in streaks of pink and gold, and we were all tired.

'What do you think was happening there? What in the name of Saint Anthony were those Venetians doing?'

I shrugged, a carefree Greek. 'I suppose,' I said, 'that the Venetians are in league with the French. But I reckon they were there to try to catch the Genoese. They're enemies, aren't they?'

'What, Venice and Genoa?' He looked thoughtful. 'I suppose they are. But as far as I know they aren't at war, not right now.'

'They're both cities full of pirates,' I said. 'They don't need open war to attack each other. You saw the way the Venetians went for the Genoese boats.'

'Until that ballista stopped them,' Andrea chuckled unpleasantly. 'Shame they know how to swim, or we could really have had a laugh.' I wanted to break his neck.

It was coming up to dawn. The sky was a thin translucent blue, threaded with pink and gold, and the pale stone walls of the city glowed in the growing daylight. The setting moon hung over the gate, huge and sightless. Ahead of us the bell sounded for the opening of the gates. For a moment nothing happened. Then from behind the wall came the sound of the heavy bars being slid back, and the gates creaked open in the arched gateway.

The first of our carts paid its toll and rumbled through. The soldiers on duty were sleepy and lazy, and they didn't even bother to jab their spears through its load. I watched and stifled a shiver. Within a couple of days every able-bodied Sicilian in Palermo would have a sword under his mattress.

Andrea smiled with quiet satisfaction as the carts passed through one by one. Blasio stood beside him, for all the world like the little man's huge misshapen dawn shadow. When the last cart was through Andrea sighed and said, 'Well, it's a well-earned rest for me. Good morning to you, Nicetas.' He lifted one prissy eyebrow. 'Tell me,' he said, 'are you intending to return and brief your master following the success of the operation?'

'I hadn't thought of it,' I said. 'I wouldn't like to miss anything.' In fact I had arranged to meet Antonio later in the day and I hoped he would be able to tell me some more secrets about Andrea. Besides, the last thing I wanted to do at present was to meet Dolfin and be confronted with the evidence of my own foolishness in the person of his incompetent and still breathing son-in-law.

'You'd have time if you wanted,' Andrea insisted. 'We're planning the rising for the Saturday after Easter. They'll all be here then, every one of them, ready for us. You could be back by then.'

'Anyone would think you were trying to get rid of me, now I've brought you the money,' I said testily. Andrea bared his teeth in what passed for a smile. 'Well,' I said stubbornly, 'I've done my bit. Now I want my revenge on the French, like you said. I'm staying.'

'Please yourself,' Andrea said, with a casual shrug. 'Council of war a week today: on Easter Monday, before the procession. Will you be there?'

'You can bet on it,' I said. 'I'm just looking forward to the day when I can wear my sword.'

Blasio sneered at me. 'If you're so hot for blood,' he asked, 'why did you let that Venetian go? He was the only one that got off the beach.'

'Yes, why?' echoed Andrea.

I frowned. On this occasion perhaps honesty was the best policy. 'I can't tell you,' I said. 'I don't know. I meant to kill him, I just – didn't. And then he ran, like a snivelling coward. These cursed Venetians are all the same, they have flippers instead of feet. I wasn't going to follow him into the sea.'

'Well,' Blasio said, 'you'd better not be so hesitant when we come to take the French.'

'Rely on me,' I said.

Andrea regarded me steadily. 'I might,' he said after a moment. 'I just might. You've been more help than I expected, Nicetas, when you remember to do what you're told. How would you like to form part of our travelling company?'

'Your what?'

'A lot of our men won't want to leave the city,' Andrea explained. There he was right. The political horizon of most people doesn't extend beyond their local campanile. 'They see us as liberating Palermo, not Sicily. If we can become a Commune and rule ourselves, that's all they want. But you have to see the bigger picture. Most of the cities will rise with us, but some of them may need some help. I want to get together a company of men who are prepared to go where they're needed and stiffen the resistance.'

'Like where?' I asked suspiciously.

Andrea frowned and pursed his lips. 'Messina,' he said at last.

'*Messina?*' I almost shouted, and Blasio raised his big hand as if he would cuff me to make me keep quiet. I lowered my voice. 'By Saint Demetrius,' I hissed, 'I thought you had Messina all sewn up. It's got more Frenchmen than anywhere and the whole of the fleet! If it stays loyal –'

'That's why I want a striking force,' Andrea said with bare patience. 'The Messinese are timid. They have a lot to lose. But if we can start things, it'll be like setting sparks to kindling. What do you say, Nicetas? It'll give you the chance to kill even more Frenchmen.'

'I'll think about it,' I said. That wasn't a lie, either.

I walked back to my lodging through the narrow streets, which were becoming crowded with people going about their business. The whole way I was thinking hard. The time was coming for me to shed my alias and get back to my countrymen in Messina. I didn't want to be involved in any general massacre of the French, and I needed to warn Dolfin that it was time to leave before the worst happened. I wondered if I could suggest to him that he leave his hopeless son-in-law behind.

On the doorstep I met my landlord the merchant. He gave me a puzzled look and said, 'Out all night?'

'Up early,' I corrected him.

He scowled, obviously well aware that I hadn't gone out that morning. I think I was turning out not to be the tenant of his dreams. I went past him to the stairs.

If I was planning to leave, I ought to tell Caterina. Things could become unpleasant for her if the resistance thought she had been hand in glove with a man who was, in essence, an Angevin spy. I should give her the chance to get away from me. It didn't suit me to lose her, but for once I ought to be unselfish.

The door at the top of the stairs opened and Caterina stuck her head out. She looked pale and anxious. When she saw me her face blossomed into a smile of relief. 'Oh, Nico,' she said, 'I'm so pleased to see you. I've got you breakfast.'

'I'm pleased to see you too,' I said.

'You don't look well,' she said, taking me by the arm to guide me through the door as if I were a child or an old man. 'Are you all right? Are you hurt?'

'I'm just tired,' I said. 'Would you mind if I got some sleep?'

'No, no, of course.' She steered me over to the bed and helped me off with my clothes. I slipped beneath the covers into the little warm nest she had occupied all night. The sheets smelt of her.

She pulled the blanket up around my ears and kissed me, then went over to her seat by the balcony and picked up her sewing. Her dress for Easter was nearly finished. The light of early morning struck the bright fabric and bounced up onto her face, outlining her cheeks and lips with gold. I watched her take one stitch, then fell asleep.

I dreamed so vividly that I seemed to be awake. The Venetian attack on the beach happened again and this time I was ready. When I had Aliusio at my mercy I didn't hesitate, just thrust my sword into his belly and grinned at his expression of incredulity as his guts spilled over his hands.

Then I was back in Venice, climbing hand over hand up my rope to Fiammetta's balcony. Behind me the city glowed in the dawn like a pink pearl. She was there, holding out her hands to me. 'Marcello, *mio amore*. You have freed me. I am yours.'

She moved into my arms. Our clothes vanished like smoke and we were naked in my bed and she was lying beneath me, white thighs parted, rosy nipples taut with her pleasure, crying out as I poured all my love into her and gasped her name.

Cat naps are surprisingly refreshing. The sun was still climbing when I woke and Caterina was still stitching her dress, embroidering the hem with gold thread.

'You're going to look like a statue of the Virgin dressed for Assumption in that,' I said, sitting up. 'Try it on for me, go on.'

'No. It's for Easter. It would be bad luck, in Holy Week.' She folded up the sewing and came over to the bed to hand me a cup of wine. I drank it gratefully. She put her hand on my naked shoulder and ran it down my body, below the sheets.

Her face changed as she felt the stickiness on my loins. 'Eurgh,' she said, pulling her hand away. I laughed, but she didn't look amused. 'Nico,' she said after a moment, 'I would have thought you would dream in Greek.'

Saint Mark protect me, what had I said in my sleep? I said easily, 'I've been in Sicily for months, *gattina*. No wonder if I dream in Sicilian.'

'Not Sicilian. Italian, some other Italian. I couldn't understand it.' She looked suspicious and sad.

'I've been all over Italy,' I said.

'Who's Fiammetta?' she asked me, looking straight into my eyes.

'Just a girl I knew,' I replied, trying to look innocent.

'You obviously like dreaming about her,' Caterina said, with a mournful look at the stained sheets.

'What is this, an Inquisition?' I reached up and caught hold of her, pulling her down to the bed. 'Come here, jealous. If I was with a woman last night, why would I have had that sort of dream?'

She didn't resist me. Fortunately I had enough energy left to prove my continuing regard for her. It didn't quite compare to the seraphic ecstasy of my dream of Fiammetta, but it had the distinct advantage of being real.

She lay in my arm afterwards, her head pillowed on my shoulder. I looked up at the ceiling, wondering how to tell her that within two weeks I would be gone. I could feel her dark eyes watching me. Possible words flitted into my mind like bats, tumbled over themselves a couple of times and vanished.

I needn't have worried. She had a sixth sense for this sort of thing. She took a deep, deep breath and said, 'Nico, something's wrong. Are you going to tell me what it is?'

It's always easier to answer a question than to volunteer bad news. I said, not looking at her, 'My work here is nearly finished, *gattina*. I'll be leaving Palermo within a week of Easter.'

There was a long silence. She seemed to shrink, as if her flesh drew away from me wherever I touched her. When at last I looked at her she wasn't looking at me. She said into mid-air, 'Nico, take me with you.'

For a moment I was tempted. But how could I take her? I was going back to Venice, not to Greece. Every lie I had told her would be exposed. I didn't need a housekeeper in Venice, Lucia did everything for me, and I didn't want a bedwarmer. It was impossible. I shook my head and said, 'No, Caterina, I can't.'

At that she pulled away from me altogether and sat up. She hitched her dress back up onto her shoulders and pulled it down around her feet. She still didn't look at me. 'You're married,' she said, in a flat exhausted voice.

'I'm not married,' I told her testily. 'I just can't.'

Suddenly she was desperate. She caught hold of my hands and looked into my face and her eyes were so beseeching that I turned my head away. 'I'll be good,' she promised. Her words tumbled over themselves and her hands gripped mine feverishly tight. 'Oh, Nico, I'll stay where you want me to, and I'll never ask any questions, and I'll never bother you, I swear it. Please take me. Please. Don't leave me here.'

I steeled myself, freed my fingers from hers and gently cupped her face between my hands. 'Caterina,' I said, as gently as I could, 'it's not possible. I can't do it.' I wanted to say that I would be generous to her, but it was too distasteful to mention money now. I just said again, 'I can't. I'm sorry.'

'Are you?' Her eyes were full of tears, but she was fighting them. I admired her courage. 'Are you sorry? Or will you forget me the moment you're gone?'

'I will be sorry,' I said, quite honestly. 'And I won't forget you.'

She pulled my hands away from her face and set her jaw. Her lips folded into a white line, as they had done when she was angry with me. She said resolutely, 'Well, Nico, in that case, I think I'd better leave you straight away.'

I was taken aback. To be honest, my pride was somewhat shaken. 'What? What will you do? Go back to your husband's family?'

'No.' She lifted her chin and looked me in the eye. 'I'll go to Jacques of Vaison. He still wants me, you know. You're not the only man in the world.' She spoke brazenly, but there was a little shiver in her bright voice.

'Caterina.' My voice was very steady. 'Look, listen to me. Don't go to the Frenchman.'

Her hair tumbled over her shoulders as she shook her head. 'Now who's jealous? By the Virgin, Nico, you are awful about Frenchmen. There's nothing wrong with Jacques. He's as good-looking as you, and he's generous. And at least I think he's not a born liar. I'd know where he'd be every night.'

'It's not jealousy.' I turned my head aside, trying to hide my agitation. I couldn't tell her of the danger, I couldn't tell her what Andrea had said to me. She liked the French, she might betray the resistance before I was ready, and in betraying them betray me to them. 'It's just that – people don't like Sicilian girls going with Frenchmen. It could get you into trouble.'

'If I cared what people thought, I wouldn't have come to you,' she said bluntly.

'Don't go to him,' I begged. 'Caterina, don't. Find another man. Or I'll pay you, if you want your own place. How much do I have to give you to –'

'Nico!' Suddenly the tears were running down her cheeks. 'I

told you, I told you when I came, I'm not doing it for money. I'm not a whore! How dare you?'

'I'm sorry,' I said helplessly. 'I didn't mean it like that. But still –'

'What right have you got to tell me what to do?' she raged weakly. 'How can you? How dare you be jealous when you've just said you don't want me? All you ever do is lie to me! If you don't want me to go to him –' She hesitated, then her resistance collapsed. She clutched my hands and pulled them to her lips and kissed them fervently. 'Nico, please,' she sobbed. 'Take me with you, please, please.'

I caught her and pulled her against my shoulder. She clung to me, weeping. Her face was hot and wet against my neck. I held her with a desperate, delicate tenderness until she was still. Then I gently pushed her back and kissed the tracks of tears on her cheeks. I didn't know what to say. I could offer her nothing, I couldn't persuade her, and apologies were worse than meaningless. All that came out in the end was, 'I didn't mean to hurt you.'

She must have understood that the situation was hopeless, and what I said touched her pride. She tossed her head and wiped her hand hard across her streaked face. 'Nothing to do with you,' she said briskly. 'My own fault. It's not as if you promised me anything, is it?' She looked at her possessions, tumbled about our room in casual disarray. 'I suppose I ought to sort things out,' she said in a dead, flat voice.

'Don't go now,' I suggested. I reached out and touched her breast, just touched it with the tips of my fingers. 'Tomorrow, Caterina. Stay one more night.'

'It ought to be now,' she murmured, but I knew I had tempted her. For a moment she said nothing. Then she looked me in the eye and said, 'All right. I'll go out now and find Jacques and tell him I'll come to him tomorrow.' She took a deep breath and closed her eyes for a moment. The effort of setting aside her pain was visible. 'I'll cook you something special for dinner,' she said at last. 'What would you like?'

'You,' I said. 'On a stick.'

She managed a grin and said, 'That comes after the fruit.' Then her eyes filled with tears and she jumped to her feet and bustled about the room, picking up her shopping basket and her house-keeping money. She didn't look at me until she was ready to go out. Then she asked with an attempt at defiance, 'What will you do while I'm gone?'

'I've got an appointment,' I said. 'I should be back by Vespers.'
She nodded. Her lower lip was quivering. 'All right,' she said.
'I'll see you then.' She walked swiftly to the door and out without
a backward glance.

Twenty-one

I waited for Antonio at our agreed rendezvous, under a big plane tree in a quiet square by the city walls, close to the Santa Agata gate. It would be an easy walk for him, down from the exalted heights where his masters lived.

It was the hour of siesta, and now, more than halfway through March, it began to be clear why Sicilians took their midday rest so seriously. The strong sun lanced downwards, striking rods of heat through my amber tunic. There were no leaves open yet to provide shade. I stood the heat for a little while, then walked over to the centre of the square. In this part of Palermo there was plenty of running water, and the square was decorated with a fine marble fountain, inlaid here and there with brightly-coloured mosaic in geometric patterns. It was a pretty thing, and the water it spouted was blissfully cool and sweet. But it couldn't cheer me up.

I was morose and subdued. I don't know why it should have bothered me that Caterina was leaving. I had more or less planned it. But I could have wished that she was going to anyone, anyone, even Aliusio, rather than Jacques of Vaison. I had a bad feeling about him.

Also, I wasn't sanguine about what Antonio might have found out. He had always hated to look ignorant, and it was quite possible that his good connections in noble houses in Palermo were so much hot air. Besides which, I had bad news for him, and that never makes me eager to see anyone.

He came towards me at last, yawning. At siesta he could be absent from his house without anyone remarking on it, but it was hard on him. He had been in Sicily for ten years, and he was used to sleeping in the afternoon. I was tired, guilt-ridden, depressed and fractious, but at least I wasn't expecting another nap.

'You look as if you've lost a florin and found a pin,' he said to me as he sat down, tugging at the neck of his shirt.

'Cheer me up, then,' I said. I wasn't in the mood for sharing my troubles.

He yawned again, exhaustively. Yawns are contagious, and I screwed up my face and gaped in sympathy. When he said, 'I think I will,' I almost choked.

'What have you got?' I demanded, when my mouth was my own again.

He smiled at me. It was good to see him smile. I sat forward, eager and attentive. 'Believe it or not,' he said, 'I was at Resetto's house only yesterday. I spoke to his valet. Very informative, I can tell you.'

'Tell me, tell me.'

He frowned and from the folds of his tunic drew out a little notebook. I was surprised. Like most agents, I tend to rely on my memory, which is excellent. I only have to scan a document once to remember most of it, and I can recall maps and plans at sight. The idea of writing something down so I don't forget it has always been foreign to me. But then Antonio was a clerk, and clerks get accustomed to the written word. I folded my arms and tried to conceal my impatience while he licked his finger and flicked slowly through the pages.

'Well,' he said at last, 'first, did you know that Resetto is deeply involved in the movement to put Pere of Aragon on the throne?'

'Yes,' I said, and then added, 'How deeply?'

'He has been promised the governorship of Palermo,' said Antonio, consulting his notes. I nodded slowly, impressed despite myself. Andrea was certainly moving in exalted circles.

Antonio turned another page. 'You were right about his being a paederast,' he said. A crooked smile touched one corner of his mouth. 'Oh, I got full details of that.' He looked up at me from under his brows. 'Federico, that's his valet, is young,' he explained. 'Used to be his lover. Still jealous of the boys. What a situation, eh?' My face must have shown my feelings, because Antonio's expression became even more wry. 'Wouldn't happen in Venice. Is that what you're thinking, Marcello?'

'I know what would happen to them in Venice if it came out,' I said coldly.

'Hmm. I'm not sure that it would. Resetto keeps his tastes fairly private; and besides, he's rich enough for it not to be a problem. When did you ever see one of the Forty burnt between the pillars?'

He had a point, though I didn't like it. I grumped and he gave a little half smile. 'Well, anyway, this Andrea.' I sat up and took even more notice. 'He's been coming to the house for about six months. Originally Federico thought he was just a procurer, he always came with a pretty boy or two in tow. But recently he's thought there was more to it. The trouble is that your man is extremely careful. He never talks about anything other than boys and buggery when there are servants and slaves around to hear.'

My lips twisted in a curse. Trust Andrea to cover his tracks. Antonio let me mutter for a moment, then said, 'But not everyone is so careful.'

'Look, Antonio, out with it,' I said. 'I'm bursting.'

He looked very pleased with himself. 'There was a Spanish duke there yesterday, or a count, some nobleman, anyway. He's another one of the boy-lovers, no wonder he and Resetto are so close. He talks quite freely in front of Federico because they've been to bed together.'

'Christ's wounds.' I was sickened, but I had to listen. 'Your friend Federico is quite open about all this, then.'

'Everyone knows it,' said Antonio. I could hardly believe how offhand he was. 'Things are different in Sicily, Marcello. They don't make so much of this. Anyway, yesterday Resetto and the Spanish duke were talking about your man Andrea. Apparently he's organising something, Federico doesn't know what, but something that could destabilise French government in Palermo.'

I raised my brows, trying not to give anything away. Antonio looked at me hard for a moment, then went on. 'Anyway, he seems to have given some promise that he'll help Aragon take over Palermo, which is half-way to holding Sicily.'

My breathing was shallow. Andrea was going to help Pere of Aragon gain control of Palermo? He was using every man in the city as his puppet. They would rise against the French, put themselves in danger and be killed, and in place of the Commune they hoped for he would bring in another king. I said softly, 'What's in it for him?'

'Two things,' Federico said. Antonio turned another page. 'One is the post of customs master for Palermo.'

I whistled soundlessly. Officials like that always do very well for themselves. 'What's the other?'

'You'll love this.' Antonio looked up into my face. 'There used to be a school in Palermo under the Norman kings, a school for indigent boys. It's, ah, lapsed under Charles of Anjou. Any governor appointed by Pere of Aragon would refound the school and put your friend Andrea in charge.' He smiled coldly at me. 'Very public-spirited, eh?'

I laughed. It was profoundly unfunny, but what else could I do? The opportunity to coin money and as many boys to abuse as his black heart desired. It was perfect. He was even more of a villain than I had thought him.

In the long silence that followed I tried to decide what I should do with this information. Tell the resistance? Tell which of them? Blasio? He'd never believe me. Which of them would hear something from me against Andrea?

'Marcello,' Antonio said.

I jumped. 'Sorry. Antonio, you've done so well I can hardly believe it. Thank you.'

He inclined his head to me civilly. 'I hope it helps,' he said.

There was another silence, full of unspoken words. At last I said with some difficulty, 'Antonio, I saw the Venetian ambassador. I'm afraid he – declined to put forward the Republic's money to redeem you.'

Antonio smiled at me. There was more than a touch of sourness in his expression. 'I'm not surprised,' he said. 'To be honest, Marcello, I thought you were promising more than you could make good. As I said, I did it for Marco.'

I was nettled. 'Listen. I said you'd get your freedom, and you will. It might take a little longer than I expected, but it'll happen, Antonio, if I have to pay for it myself.'

He shrugged. 'Don't worry,' he said. 'I can afford to buy myself out. I couldn't go at the moment, in any case. There's a lot happening in my house. They need me.'

'They need you?' I was incredulous. 'Antonio, don't you have anyone back in Venice who might need you more?'

Suddenly his eyes were very cold and level. 'Did you make it your business to find out about my family when you got back?' he demanded.

I felt shame staining my cheeks. I had had other things on my mind when I returned to Venice. At last I confessed, 'No.'

'Then shut your mouth,' he said.

'I'm sorry.' I was, too. He looked away. After a moment I said, 'I mean it. I'm nearly out of credit now, I couldn't buy you out right away. But I will, Antonio, if you want your freedom. I promised.'

He bit thoughtfully at his thumbnail. I couldn't understand his hesitation. How could anyone who was a slave not want to be free? At last he said, 'All right. When you can do it, Marcello, approach the head of my house.' He actually smiled at me. 'I will be grateful,' he said, as if I might be doubting it.

There didn't seem to be much left to say. I got to my feet and held out my hand. Antonio got up too and clasped it. He seemed to be struggling for words. Then he swallowed hard and said, 'Marcello, I wasn't just to you after the wreck. I know you tried to help Marco.' His voice became thick and blurred. 'I apologise.'

I shook my head and put my arms around him. He was weeping. I suppose that for years he had hoped that Marco was alive, and only now was he able to grieve for him properly. I held him for a moment. It was like comforting a bear. After a little while he pulled away and wiped the tears from his cheeks and left me without another word.

She was cooking my favourite dish, swordfish with pine nuts. God help me, I would miss her cooking. I came in and said, as usual, 'That smells good.'

'Only the best for the condemned man,' said Caterina. She glanced at me over her shoulder. She was wearing a bright, brittle smile. 'Well, I saw Jacques,' she announced. 'He said he was glad I've come to my senses.'

'Don't talk about him,' I said fiercely. I went quickly over to her and pulled her away from the pan and kissed her. Her arms went around my neck.

Somehow during that evening we found time to eat the swordfish before it was quite spoiled. Afterwards we coupled and then I fell asleep. Soon she woke me and we did it again. Caterina was inexhaustible, and she had learnt enough about me to be able to arouse me over and over, through the twilight and into the night. The Easter moon rose outside the window and glowed in upon us, turning our conjoined bodies to silver. Midnight came and still Caterina's eagerness kept me awake and active, long after I should have been spent.

At last, though, we were both worn out. She pressed close to me and laid her head on my chest and I held her as sleep overcame us.

I don't remember my dreams. But when I woke in the early morning Caterina was already awake, looking at me with lines of tension around her dark eyes. She said very softly, 'I don't believe that you're even really called Nico.'

Fatigue and misery pressed down on me. 'Oh, *gattina* –'

'Don't!' she said imperiously. 'Don't, Nico, don't. I can't bear it.' She clutched me and pressed her mouth to mine. With hands and lips she roused me and thrust herself onto me. It was desperate, driven, physical pleasure, so intense that it hurt, and utterly joyless.

Then she got up, abandoning me without a kiss or a touch. She gathered her belongings together into a bundle. I sat in bed with my arms around my knees, watching her. The silence drew out. Presently I said, 'That dress. You've been sewing it for ages. I think it's a real shame I haven't seen you wearing it.'

'If you want to,' she said, 'come to the Santo Spirito procession on Easter Monday. Everyone has a new dress for that. I'm going to be the envy of every girl from the market. You can come and watch me show myself off.'

'I'll come,' I promised. 'I wouldn't miss it for the world.'

Something glittered on the little sewing-table. I frowned at it. It was the necklace and earrings I had given her. I got up naked from the bed and went to pick them up, and she looked at me with a hunted expression.

'Don't you want them?' I asked. I sounded hurt and disconsolate, like a little boy. Absurd.

'You might need them for the next bedwarmer,' she said, looking at the floor.

'Caterina, don't be a fool. I gave them to you. They're yours.' She didn't move. I went over to her and held the sparkling gold out on the palm of my hand. Somehow I was reluctant to fasten the chain around her neck. She looked at them and after a long moment of silence picked up the earrings and slipped them into her ears. Then she turned her back to me and stood expectantly, waiting for me to put the necklace on her.

I obliged. The skin of her neck was warm beneath my fingers and beneath her hair she smelt delicious. She had enjoyed me half a dozen times in the last few hours, and the perfume of her body was concentrated, warm and sensual and satisfied. I would have liked to kiss her nape, but I resisted.

'Don't let that Frenchman get his sticky fingers on them,' I said, drawing back a little. 'They're all the same. He'd sell them to pay his gambling debts.'

She shook her head, declining to argue with me. Everything she owned was wrapped up in one big heap. She looked around the room and laughed ruefully. 'Well,' she said, 'I don't know what sort of a housekeeper I was. It looks a lot tidier without me.'

'Caterina,' I said softly, 'I will really miss you.'

For a moment she didn't reply. Then she looked at me and said, shaking her head, 'Nico, have you ever told me the truth?'

She turned her back and picked up her bundle and headed for the door. I stood still, burning with her reproach. I had deserved it, but it hurt all the same. Then I darted naked after her. 'Caterina,' I said, standing behind her.

She hesitated and stopped. Then she turned and looked at me, cautious, suspicious, afraid that I would hurt her again. I couldn't let her go without giving her something. I said, 'Caterina. It's Marcello. My real name. It's Marcello.' I sounded weary, tense and desperate.

Her face changed, wariness vanishing into desolate softness. She said, 'Oh,' almost as if she was in pain. Then she wiped her eyes and smiled and said, 'Why is it that I believe you when you speak like that?'

'Because it's the truth,' I said.

She gave a little half laugh. 'Marcello,' she said softly, looking into my eyes. 'Marcello.' She rolled the name on her tongue as if she were tasting it. Her Sicilian accent was charming. 'I like that so much better than Nico,' she went on. 'Nico sounds like the tumbler's monkey.'

'Caterina –' I stretched out my hand to her. I still don't know why.

She flinched, almost as if I were going to hit her again, and pulled away. 'No,' she said, sounding suddenly afraid and defensive. 'No.' She took a couple of steps towards the door. I stood very still and watched her. Her knuckles whitened on the knot of her bundle and she said, 'Goodbye, Marcello.'

'A goodbye kiss,' I suggested, stepping towards her.

'No.' She caught hold of my hand and pulled it to her lips and kissed it. For a moment she held it, bowed over it. Then she pressed it quickly to her cheek, dropped it as if it were scalding hot and ran out of the door and down the stairs.

I listened to her footsteps descending, then went to the balcony and stood there to watch her going down the street. A woman passing underneath looked up and saw me there bare as a worm and laughed and made some coarse suggestion. I ignored her, but when Caterina appeared in the street she didn't look up at me. She had one hand pressed over her face, and she turned and ran away as fast as she could carry her enormous bundle.

I watched until she was out of sight. My guts felt cold and empty, as if I had been purged. Then I went back to the warm bed, which still smelled of her, and pulled the covers over my head to shut out the sun. I still had a lot of sleep to catch up on, and I was exhausted with goodbyes, and anything was better than being awake.

TWENTY-TWO

I had plenty of time now to think, and that's what I did. Eventually I realised that the obvious step was to kill Andrea. Forget trying to explain his duplicity to the resistance, this was simpler. Dead, he could not lead the Palermitans into revolt, export rebellion to Messina, betray his unsuspecting followers to the Aragonese or debauch a potentially unlimited number of indigent schoolboys. I should have recognised it sooner, but as I have said, I don't like killing in cold blood.

If I murdered Andrea I would far exceed my instructions from the Security Committee. They had envisaged a bit of undercover work resulting in a report to the French that would allow them, the island's masters, to take any necessary action. But I didn't really care. I was on my own anyway, and the operation was already a disaster, and I found Andrea repugnant.

It took me a couple of days to think this decision through. They were not pleasant days. The room seemed empty and reproachful and I spent a lot of time out of it, strolling aimlessly around Palermo and brooding. I forgot to feed the kitten, and it left home. Not so much of a problem. I was eating in cookshops the whole time and the mice and cockroaches would soon evacuate all by themselves for want of food. I took my linen to a laundress to wash. Caterina had done a better job. When she washed my shirts, they had ended up smelling of lavender.

Once I had decided on Andrea's death at least I had something to do. However, I had set myself a difficult task. I knew where he lived, but his little house in a quiet street was like a pocket fortress behind its simple facade. The doors were barred and the shutters bolted and the watchdog was the size of a small volcano. I spent a long time lurking in the streets outside to see if I could catch him alone, but whenever he set foot out of doors he had Blasio with him. Not once did he set off for the boy-brothel, well dressed, unaccompanied and vulnerable. He seemed to be growing more cautious as the day assigned for the rebellion drew nearer.

I saw Caterina several times. The first time we came face to face quite by chance in a busy street in the bazaar. In fact she almost ran into me. She recoiled, gripping the handle of her shopping basket as if it were a rope to draw her from the jaws of Hell. Then she squared her shoulders and smiled at me and said, 'Hello, M–' She stopped herself before she said my real name aloud.

'How are you?' I asked her. She looked all right, but I wouldn't say blooming. Her cheeks were lacking their roses and there were streaks under her eyes. If that Frenchman was mistreating her, I would strangle the bastard.

She smiled again. 'Fine,' she said brightly, 'just fine.'

I thought of her in bed with Jacques of Vaison and struggled to stop my lip curling with entirely misplaced jealousy. My toes curled instead. The words, 'Is he any good?' fought to make themselves heard. No doubt Jacques felt exactly the same.

'I wonder,' she said, 'if I could come by one day and collect the kitten. We've got mice.'

'I'm sorry,' I confessed. 'It seems to have left home.'

She raised her brows and sighed, suggesting that nothing had changed and I was still hopeless. We stood and shuffled a little, uncomfortably. Then she said, 'Well, I ought to be getting along.'

'Goodbye,' I said. She smiled at me, just a twitch of her sweet lips, and sidled past me. I looked around and saw a number of the bazaar stallholders watching our encounter with interest. I snarled at them and went on my way.

The next time I saw her she didn't see me. She was heading through the narrow streets in the quarter where the soldiers lodged, on her way to the old royal palace that was the Angevin military headquarters. She was carrying her basket and something in it covered with a cloth. I hesitated for a moment, then followed her.

She was heading for the palace itself, which was no surprise. As an officer that's where Jacques would be posted. From the outside it was an odd-looking building, a square, heavy, formidable Norman keep with a few decorations that were supposed to make it look like a palace. It reminded me of a soldier guarding his lord at a wedding, dressed in full armour with a garland of flowers around his helmet and streamers on his spear. I had heard that the palace was fabulous inside, with painted reception chambers and a chapel that glittered with so much gold and precious stones that you might imagine yourself already in Heaven. But you wouldn't have guessed at this hidden luxury from its outward appearance.

Caterina went up to the great gatehouse and spoke cheerfully to the soldiers on duty there. She was always bold-faced with Frenchmen. One of them went off, presumably to call for Jacques, and the others enjoyed her company. I stood in the deep shade of one of the buttresses and eavesdropped. Call it habit.

'Make the most of us,' one of them was saying in flawed but fast Sicilian. 'Only a couple of weeks and we'll all be off to the East.'

'Not Jacques,' said Caterina. 'He says he's staying here.'

'Lucky bastard,' said another of the soldiers, in French this time. 'Whose arse did he lick to get to stay home?'

'No fighting, no booty, no promotion,' said the first succinctly, encapsulating the professional soldier's attitude to battle. He said again to Caterina, 'Well, pretty, are you going to be parading out to Saint Esprit on Easter Monday?'

'Saint Esprit? Oh, you mean Santo Spirito. Yes, of course. Nobody misses it.'

'We'll all be there,' grinned one of them. 'What are you going to be wearing? We'll look out for you.'

'You'd better not,' said a cheerful French voice. I drew back further into the shade and watched Jacques of Vaison emerge from the gatehouse to claim his prize. He pulled Caterina straight into his arms and kissed her thoroughly. He was the sort of man who opens his well-cut lips wide and slobbers over his girl. I have more subtlety and style.

The soldiers laughed and made admiring comments as long as the clinch lasted. Jacques ran his gauntleted hands down Caterina's back to her bottom and squeezed it tightly. She didn't seem to mind. At last they separated and Caterina gave a theatrical gasp. Jacques laughed and kissed her hand. I found it intensely annoying that he seemed to be a pleasant, nice-looking young man who was really fond of her.

He opened the basket and exclaimed over its contents. 'Look at this!' he said to his men. 'She's spoiling me. You'll have me fatter than Captain le Gras by Easter, *ma petite*.' He picked the basket up and took her hand. 'Come inside and help me eat it,' he suggested.

'You don't want her to help you eat your lunch, you want her to help you siesta,' said one of the soldiers. Jacques laughed and Caterina blushed, but neither of them denied it. She followed him through the gatehouse, swishing her skirt and smiling flirtatiously over her shoulder at the soldiers.

She looked happy, but it left a bad taste in my mouth. She wouldn't have gone to him if it hadn't been for me, and I was afraid that by going to him she had begun to turn herself into a whore. At the moment it was one man at a time. But when Jacques had tired of her, or been posted somewhere else, or fallen to a Sicilian sword, what then? I didn't like to think that the respectable young widow I had bedded would end up on the streets.

So, I had made my decision. Now I had to implement it, and turn myself from agent to self-appointed assassin.

Throughout what was left of Holy Week I tried to find an opportunity to catch Andrea alone. I failed. Whenever I saw him he was in company. If I hadn't cared about my own life I could have killed him anyway, but I didn't feel that the safety of the French in Sicily demanded that level of commitment from me.

On Good Friday one of Andrea's boy servants found me at the merchant's house and told me where our Easter Monday meeting would be. The boy also told me to dress up. 'Look as if you're going on to the procession,' he said. 'Best clothes for everyone, master's orders.'

If I had my way his master wouldn't give any more orders. But an assassin's job is not always easy.

It felt strange on Easter Sunday to hear the bells announcing that Christ was risen and to know that I couldn't receive Mass. Like most people I know I only taste the Body of Christ once a year, at Easter, and I make my confession just before that so that I can hear the Easter Mass with a clear conscience.

Not this year. This year I was unshriven, stained, corrupted. I should have stayed away from church altogether, but somehow I couldn't.

I could have gone to the Admiral's Church, but something drew me to the Cathedral instead. I was probably subconsciously hoping to see Caterina, since the Cathedral was close to the palace and the soldiers' quarter.

Palermo Cathedral is an astonishing building. It is huge, and its great bulk overshadows everything else in the city apart from the palace on its little knoll. In the hot sunlight its golden stone forms sharp lights and shades, and every inch of its three splendid apses and its magnificent twin towers is chased with the finest carvings to be seen anywhere in Sicily. Once you enter its great portal the light is quenched; the interior is dim and gloomy, and the brilliant shafts of sunlight falling through the high windows seem to fall like water on the stone.

The portentous size of the building was suitably chastening. I padded through the crowds of kneeling worshippers and found myself a place on the cold stone in one of the aisles, close to the tombs of the Norman kings, sleeping securely in their colossal porphyry sarcophagi.

The priest and cantor were singing the Easter responsory. I listened to the ebb and flow of the chant, my nostrils full of the pungent smell of incense. My spirit felt as heavy as one of those massive marble tombs, weighed down with the death of Perina and Caterina's tears.

I wanted to compose myself to pray, but it was hard. I needed help. I got to my feet and wandered through the crowded church. At last I found what I sought, a mosaic portrait of the repentant Magdalen. She wore a red robe and her long unbound hair glowed almost as brightly as the gilded background of the mosaic. Repentant she might be, and a saint she certainly was, but the artist had taken pleasure in showing her dressed as befitted her previous occupation. Her dress clung to her elegant limbs and outlined the curves of her small, high breasts. No doubt she had made herself a good living, before she had met Our Lord and changed her ways. She would understand me.

I knelt before her, lifted my joined hands in supplication, and prayed for my mother's soul.

'Well, there we are.' She flings back her deep hood and lets her hair spill onto her shoulders. It is the colour of a raven's wing, glossy and curling. 'All over for another year.'

'Was he horrible?' I ask timidly. I hate confession, and it always amazes me that my mother is so cheerful about it.

'Oh, just as usual. A little discussion about the true meaning of penitence. We both know the facts: things won't ever change.' She takes off her heavy cloak and hands it to Lucia. They smile at each other, a smile of shared secrets.

'Unless Father marries you,' I say boldly.

Mother takes a deep breath and comes over to me. She holds both my hands and looks into my face. Her eyes are like the night. I feel as though my middle is melting.

'*Marco,*' *she says very gently,* '*you know it won't be. Your father has a wife.*'

'*I'll kill her,*' *I blurt out.* '*She's horrible. She'd hurt us if she found out about us. I'll kill her, and then Father will marry you.*'

'*Hush, hush!*' *For a moment she is about to embrace me, but I am stiff and twitching with anger and eleven-year-old resentment.* '*Don't say things like that. Two wrongs don't make a right, Marco.*' *She gets to her feet and draws her hand over her forehead.* '*I wish your father could be here more,*' *she says, half to me, half to herself.* '*You should have a man to look to.*'

'*I'm a man!*' *I shout, and I run over and catch hold of her.* '*I'll look after you, Mamma, you and Lucia too. I don't need him. Him and his ogress of a wife! We don't need him.*'

She shakes her head slowly. '*Marcello,* caro mio,' *she says,* '*you're wrong. I need your father.*'

The man who was away on business when she was ill, who left her to suffer and die with just her maid and her child to comfort her when what she wanted was him. When I was a boy I hated him, and it used to be hard for me not to curse him as I prayed for her. But an older, wiser Marcello understood that life is not so simple.

I prayed with all my heart that my mother's soul might be redeemed from the sin of her life and attain Paradise. Then I offered up a short, uncomfortable prayer for my father, too, and hoped that back at home in Venice he was doing the same thing for me. I needed his prayers.

I was finding it hard to sleep without Caterina's warm soft body next to me. I tossed and dozed for most of the night and didn't wake on the morning of Easter Monday until the sun was high. Outside the bells were ringing, not the disciplined, steady chime of yesterday, but a full-throated jangle of enjoyment. A party of Sicilians went by under the window, noisy and cheerful, blowing squeaky musical instruments and banging little drums. One of them was playing a hurdy-gurdy and singing. After yesterday's great religious celebration they were all getting themselves in the right frame of mind for a day of fun and feasting, crowned with a pleasant walk in the warm evening sunshine out to the church of Santo Spirito for Vespers.

I got up, frowsty, and poured some water into the pot over the fire to heat up. I hate shaving with cold water. The mice had been at my leftover loaf during the night, but I ate it anyway.

By the time I was shaved and clean the noise outside was beginning to die down as people went to find their lunch. I considered my available wardrobe. Dress up, Andrea had said. I had three options. There was the robe of ochre-and-purple patterned Greek silk I had worn for my earlier alias, but that would be a bit excessive. There was the amber-coloured wool tunic Caterina had embroidered for me, but I wore it every day. My spare everyday tunic didn't stand a chance. It was worn at the elbow and patched on the shoulder, another of Lucia's attempts to make good a hole put there by someone with deadly intent.

The best choice was my other silk tunic, a handsome but subdued affair of dark green heavy plain silk lined with blue. It was quite long, to the mid-calf, but slashed almost to the crotch to make it possible to stride out in it, or ride. There was a fine band of gold embroidery on the hem, including right around the slash on both sides, and finishing off the sleeves and neck. I had brought it in case of attendance at smart diplomatic events. Chance would have been a fine thing.

I began with a pair of very respectable and well-fitting dark blue hose, followed them with a clean shirt and fastened it carefully at throat and cuffs, then pulled the tunic over my head. I was shocked to notice a moth hole, but fortunately it was in one armpit so it wasn't likely that anyone else would see it. I added my best pair of leather boots, made of glove-dyed doeskin and laced tightly on the ankle to display my elegant leg, and finished off the whole ensemble with a belt of red patterned and embroidered leather studded with blue and white enamel plaques.

Rustling like a nobleman I strolled towards our rendezvous, a tavern beyond the city walls not far from Santo Spirito. I thought I looked fine, which was just as well. I intended to go on to the procession afterwards, see Caterina and remind her what she was missing. My sword would have been the finishing touch, but I didn't dare wear it where the French would see. My dagger would have to do.

Only five days to the planned date for the rebellion. I didn't have long to remove Andrea from the scene. I wondered if today might offer me my chance. So many people, surely I would be able to get up close enough to him to slip a blade between his ribs? In enough of a crowd I could even pretend it hadn't been me that did it.

When I arrived at the tavern the landlord showed me into a private room. It was small and bare, just a plain board table and a couple of stools. There was a narrow window covered in parchment leading onto the street and no fire in the grate. Pietro was there already, playing knucklebones with himself. He welcomed me cheerfully and challenged me to a game. He looked even more like a young nobleman today, dressed in bright silk with a wreath of flowers on his hair. His tunic was similar to mine, but you could see that he was the real thing. His shirt was the finest cambric, embroidered all around the neck with sprays of foliage so cunningly worked that it looked alive, and beneath his heavy damask outer tunic he wore a second under-tunic of the softest carded silk in a wonderful shade halfway between green and gold. The glistening blue lining of my tunic looked like second best in comparison.

'Not so many of us today,' he said. 'No Bartolo, no Giovanni. Just you and me and Zanino.'

'Why's that, then?'

'We're going to be talking about Messina. Bartolo's not interested, he just wants to run his rackets in the market without the French to interfere, and Giovanni's far too respected in Palermo to go far outside.' He grinned at me. 'That's what he says. I say he's scared. What do you think?'

'Why are you interested in Messina?' I asked him.

'Same as you. I hate the French. And it'll be a laugh.' He tossed the knucklebone in the air and made a clean sweep. 'My father would have piglets if he knew I was doing this,' he said with a grin. 'He makes his money selling to the French garrison.'

The door opened and Zanino came in. He looked even more silent, shifty and dangerous than usual. His idea of festive dress was a tunic that wasn't frayed at the hem. He and Pietro were an ill-assorted pair.

'Where's Andrea?' he demanded. Pietro shrugged. I frowned, suddenly struck with an idea.

'Listen,' I said hesitantly, 'both of you, I wanted to ask you something.' My voice showed that it was serious. They both looked at me suspiciously, but with interest. 'Well,' I said, 'I was wondering if there was any reason why Andrea should be talking to men of King Pere's faction.'

Pietro looked puzzled, Zanino shocked and angry. 'What?' he demanded. 'Those bastard Spanish, they shouldn't have anything to do with us.'

This was a promising reaction. I watched Zanino's face carefully. He was violent enough in his nature to be effective if he was really incensed. 'Well,' I said, 'I understand that Andrea has been spending time at the house of Guglielmo Resetto.'

'Resetto?' Pietro laughed. 'That's nothing to do with Spain, Nicetas. Resetto's a boy-lover. They all stick together, you know. He probably invites our leader to his private parties.'

'With a Spanish nobleman?' I asked, lifting my brows.

Zanino looked shocked and almost convinced. In a few minutes I would have had him. But then the door opened and Blasio came in with Andrea behind him. We all turned and I suppose we looked startled or defensive, because Andrea's face changed at once, becoming hard and suspicious.

'What's going on?' he asked sharply.

'Just discussing politics,' Zanino said. That was promising too. He was covering up for me.

'Well,' said Andrea, 'I've got another person for our meeting. We'll have to get to Messina fast when the time comes. We'll need a ship. I've been discussing transport with one of our contacts. He's come too.' He opened the door and gestured in a tall figure. I knew who it was before he put back his hood.

Daniele. I had been feeling almost successful. Now I could barely keep back a flinch of fear. I couldn't get to the door, Blasio was right in front of it. I sidled towards the window and put my hand to my dagger.

Daniele was looking right at me. His face was a picture, intense suppressed amusement and a good deal of real sympathy at seeing a fellow agent in a very tight corner indeed. He raised his blond eyebrows at me and then said conversationally to Andrea, 'Tell me, did you know that this man is Marcello D'Estari, a Venetian agent?'

There was a moment of petrified stillness. Everybody stared at me as if I had grown horns. Daniele smiled ruefully and shook his head at me. Pietro said in a stunned voice, 'A Venetian? But he's a Greek.'

Andrea said nothing, but his black lizard's eyes swivelled to me and narrowed. I opened my mouth to deny it, to try to cover myself, but one look at his face told me it was hopeless. Why should he concern himself with me? He had got the gold from me, and that's all he wanted. He said, 'Blasio, kill him.'

Blasio's eyes lit up and he reached for his dagger. Zanino was between me and the window. I grabbed him by the shoulders and flung him at the table. He hit it and it skidded across the room and struck Blasio amidships. He threw the knife anyway, but he was shaken and it missed me. Once it had stuck in the wall it was safe for me to move. I plunged my dagger through the parchment of the window and hurled myself into the ragged gap. Hands caught at my disappearing ankles. Someone got a good grip on the top of my boot, but I kicked out and whoever it was yelped, Pietro I think. Then I was free. I picked myself up from the dust of the street and began to run.

They were after me in moments. I headed for the nearest group of buildings and darted around a corner. Outside the walls of the city there were not that many houses, not much cover for a hunted man. I glanced around, jumped up onto a hen house and swung myself up onto the nearest roof.

Pursuers rarely look up. Agents learn this early in life, or they tend to have short and uncomfortable lives. From my position on the rickety tiles on top of a little scrubby building I looked down in comparative safety as the four of them dashed around the corner and stood panting and looking around for me.

'The Devil take him,' said Andrea. 'A Venetian! He could betray us to the French tomorrow.' He fell silent, his face working in thought.

'Kill them all today, then,' gasped Zanino, frothing with rage. 'Do it now.'

'Shut up,' said Andrea. 'The other cities aren't ready. It has to be everywhere.' He caught Pietro by the arm. 'Get back to the city,' he said. 'Find our best men. One of them to watch his lodgings. Others on the gates. Don't let him back in.'

'I don't want to miss the procession,' protested Pietro.

'Would you miss your neck if the French stretched it?' snapped Andrea. 'Do as I tell you!'

I had my dagger in my hand. Now I rose silently to my knees, lifted it by the blade and held it poised, ready to fling it straight into Andrea's heart. But as I was about to throw Blasio came between me and my target. I cursed and slid back down to lie on the roof on my belly. I wanted Andrea, not his ape.

Pietro ran off towards the city gates, grumbling. The others went away from me. I sat up on the roof and breathed hard.

I was on my own. I couldn't get back to my lodgings. I doubted that I would be able to get back into the city in safety. It was time to leave: get to Messina and warn Dolfin and the French governor there.

But I felt bad about abandoning every Frenchman in Palermo to the tender mercies of the resistance. If only there was some way that I could pass on a warning. Dolfin had failed to persuade the French of the danger. Perhaps I should make a direct attempt myself.

Andrea and Blasio were far away. I stood up and stretched, then pulled off my tunic and turned it inside out. The simplest measures are often the most effective. They would be looking for me in a green tunic and now it was blue.

Not far from me was the road that ran out to the church of Santo Spirito. It was full of people, singing as they walked out from the city for their Easter Monday jaunt. Among them were clusters of Frenchmen, soldiers on duty keeping an eye out for trouble and parties of officers going to enjoy the spectacle of all the prettiest girls in Palermo and the countryside wearing their best dresses and showing themselves to the crowds. Caterina would be among them, and Jacques of Vaison with her. He was an officer, and what I had seen of him suggested that he was sensible and competent. I would swallow my pride, get her to introduce us and explain the situation to him. All I had to do was remain incognito in the crowd until I could find him. With a bodyguard of Frenchmen I could even get back into Palermo in safety. We could turn the tables on the resistance.

I swung down off the roof and began to make my way to the road. My spine prickled. I wished I had eyes in the back of my neck.

TWENTY-THREE

I hid myself among the people and let their cheerful flow carry me along. I glanced from side to side until my head started to ache.

The crowd was moving at no more than a gentle saunter, like a flock of multi-coloured, ambling birds. We bunched closely together to pass under the stripy shade of a long line of cypress trees, the avenue which led to the Piazza Santo Spirito and the church itself. Then the people spilled outwards, laughing, as we reached the piazza.

I looked around among the brightly-dressed crowd for Caterina and her fancy man. I didn't see either of them, but I did see Zanino, curse him. He saw me too and lunged towards me, his hand going to his dagger. I melted into the crowd at once, but he would warn the others that I was around. I needed somewhere safe, a vantage point where I could spy out Jacques of Vaison without the others seeing me. The crowd protected me, but if I was discovered among this press it would be as easy for them to kill me as I had hoped it would be for me to kill Andrea. I huddled close to one of the cypresses to protect my back and looked around, craning over the heads of the people round me.

Across the piazza was the church of Santo Spirito. It was a plain, severe building of pale local stone, rectangular like an old-fashioned basilica, not particularly tall and without florid ornamentation. I rather liked it. It had been built without towers or anywhere to hang the bell, and next to it someone had erected a separate bell tower, a squat, rather crazy wooden campanile that looked fit to fall over in the next earthquake. That would do, if I could get to it. I slipped circumspectly through the crowd to the little door at the base of the campanile, glanced from side to side one last time, and squeezed in.

It was a good hiding place as well as a good vantage point. Beside the tower there was a big cypress tree, so close that its branches brushed against the beams. It would give me a second escape route if anyone saw me. I ran quickly up the shaky stairs, squeezed up through the trapdoor onto the rickety little wooden roof by the bell and craned over the parapet to look down.

What I saw was enough to make me laugh aloud. There below me were Andrea and Blasio, keeping close together as usual, and at a little distance Zanino and one or two other men that I recognised as members of the resistance, moving to and fro through the crowd looking for me. Not one of them thought of looking up. At one stage Andrea was standing right underneath me. If I had had a big enough rock I could have dropped it on his head. The temptation to aim a little coin at his bald patch was almost irresistible. I folded my hands on the parapet and smirked. He thought his mob was professional! He was going to find out just what professional meant.

They continued to quarter the crowd, their heads swivelling in a search pattern. I turned my attention away from them and began to look for Caterina and Jacques. If I could find them I would keep my eye on them and descend a little later, when it looked safe to approach them and speak.

Beneath me in the open dusty piazza were thousands of people. It looked like half of Palermo, together with all the peasants from the hinterland who could grant themselves a day's holiday. The noise was incredible, like a flock of roosting rooks, and the colours were enough to make you giddy.

Everyone was there, from the lowest to the highest. The noble ladies were dressed in their best, dragging rustling trains of silk after them through the dust, showing off their corseted waists and their white bosoms in low-cut, tight-fitting gowns, with strings of gold and pearls draped around their bare necks and veils of translucent chiffon hiding their plaited and coiffed hair. Young noble girls wore simpler gowns, but their long hair hung loose behind them, confined only by a simple gold fillet around their brows. I saw one delicious little thing, no more than fourteen years old, with a curtain of dark-red hair hanging to her knees. Even the peasant women were brightly dressed in red and yellow and green, with clean white aprons tied tightly to show off a narrow waist and their hair decorated with their gayest scarves or fresh meadow flowers.

The women moved through the crowd like giant butterflies, escorted by their menfolk, all groomed and preened as sleek as starlings. The noblemen outdid their ladies in the richness of their patterned damask tunics and the splendid sweep of their silken cloaks lined with fur. But there was no hierarchy today. The rich strolled next to peasants whose Sunday best consisted of a scarlet girdle tied over an everyday tunic.

People were singing, cheerful irreligious songs about spring and the pleasures of the flesh. Here and there there was a real musician, and in one corner of the piazza a little band struck up with shawms and recorders and a tabor and everyone drew back to make space for an impromptu dance floor. Amid cheering and whistles several couples stepped into the space and raised their hands above their heads, clapping the time. Some of the women had little Moorish sistra, and the bright tinkling sound cut through the noise of the crowd. They began to pace out a simple folk dance.

The dancers were as odd an assortment as the crowd itself: a nobleman and his lady, a peasant farmer dancing with his little daughter, a great fat merchant in ermine-trimmed velvet with his even fatter wife, and –

– and Caterina. Her new dress glittered in the bright sunlight. I remembered its vivid colour, golden saffron patterned with green. The bodice was skin-tight, laced with scarlet silk. It pushed up her lovely breasts until a man could have lost himself in the silken crease between them, but in fact what nestled in that delicious crease was the little pendant I had given her. She tossed her head and I saw the pearl earrings flashing in her ears. I felt a surge of satisfaction that Jacques of Vaison hadn't bought her anything she preferred. Yet.

It was good to see her enjoying herself, filled again with energy and enthusiasm, though it made delicate threads of regret tug at me. I turned my attention to her partner. Jacques of Vaison, dressed for holiday in a bright tunic, debonairly striped in blue and white. There was a garland of flowers on his shining chestnut hair – anemones, mostly, dark red and blue. Of course, Caterina knew all about flowers; she would have made the garland for him. His long sword was his only concession to military attire, and though it marked him out as a Frenchman the other dancers did not scorn him. He looked cool, handsome and cheerful, the dog. He was absolutely riveted by Caterina's bosom. Every time she turned in front of him his eyes moved and his head swivelled to follow the gleam of her white cleavage. At one point he reached out to catch her and kiss her, but she pulled coquettishly away from him, swished her skirt and leant back, snapping her fingers and laughing.

At last he grabbed her and leaned over her to whisper in her ear. She blushed. I knew as if I had overheard him that he was telling her he had to have her and he wanted to go home.

She looked disappointed, I'm sure of it. Her dark eyes searched the crowd. I hoped that she was looking for me. But Jacques whispered again and she turned her face up to him for a kiss and moved into his arm and left the dance.

They couldn't go back to the city already! How would I manage to speak to Jacques? I craned over the edge of the tower. Andrea was still below me, standing on the church steps with Blasio, sweeping the crowd with his black eyes. Zanino was with them, muttering some craziness in his rusty voice. I cursed and struck the parapet with my clenched fist. Alternative plans flashed through my mind. Wait today until it was safe, then get over the city walls during the night and go to Jacques's lodging. I knew where it was well enough. Caterina's presence should be enough to ensure me a hearing. Warn Jacques of the danger, then get a fast ship to Messina.

The figures of Jacques and Caterina reached the avenue of cypresses on the road to the city. Her bright yellow dress stood out from the other dresses as much as she could have wanted. I watched them until they vanished among the crowd.

Beneath me the tower shuddered slightly as someone climbed the steps inside. I tensed and dropped to one knee, putting my eye to a cranny in the floorboards. No need to worry, it was only a fat friar wheezing his way up to the bell chamber to ring for Vespers. I got silently to my feet and returned to my watching of the crowd.

People had seen the friar going into the tower. They began to move towards the church, ready to go in for the service. Perhaps all would be well. When they had gone I would hurry down from the tower and run after Jacques and Caterina. They were strolling, hand in hand. I might catch them before they reached the city gates.

A party of Frenchmen were on the church steps, four or five together, standing beside Andrea and Zanino. They had the slightly wild-eyed look of soldiers who know that their posting is coming up and are determined to have a really good time before the worst happens. A couple of them were flushed, as if they had been drinking. Andrea slid his eyes sideways at them and moved a little away, and Zanino's leathery face convulsed with hatred.

A pretty young peasant girl came up the steps on her husband's arm. He was just a boy, fair-faced and fresh-looking. He was unarmed, the peasants weren't allowed to bring weapons when they came near the city, not even the dagger that every civilised man carries to cut his meat. One of the soldiers eyed up the youth's wife and shouted in a coarse voice, 'Here's one to search for weapons, Drouet!'

I could have warned them that this was not a good idea. Unfortunately it was impossible. The Frenchman called Drouet, a thick-featured sergeant of the worst kind, leered at the girl, grabbed her from her husband's arm and thrust his hand into her bosom. The laces of her gown broke and she shrieked as her white breasts were suddenly bared to the gaze of a riveted, horrified crowd.

For a moment there was silence. Beneath me the friar, unaware of what was happening outside, began to toll the bell. It rocked behind me, clanging the call to prayer, dinning in my ears so that I could hardly hear it when the boy shrieked, 'You bastard!' and jumped for the sergeant. I looked to see him spitted at once on the Angevin's sword, but I was wrong. The boy had a knife in his hand. Zanino's knife. It flashed in the evening sunlight, then vanished into the sergeant's chest. He screamed and fell. The boy stood over him, white-faced and stained with blood, apparently stunned by what he had done. The girl rocked back, screaming.

The other Frenchmen roared with rage and went for their swords. They didn't stand a chance. The Sicilians near by, peasants mostly, swarmed over them and overwhelmed them and jumped to their feet, dabbled with blood and yelling with pride, waving the French weapons like trophies. Others ran up and began to kick the bodies of the fallen Frenchmen, though they were already dead.

Andrea and Blasio seemed to have faded away. Andrea didn't believe in risking himself unnecessarily. Not so Zanino. He had a bloody Angevin sword in his hand and he jumped onto the bodies of the Frenchmen and shrieked, 'Death to the French!'

Death! The men in the crowd took up the cry. The noblemen shouted, just like the peasants. Some of them were city men with daggers, some, miraculously enough, seemed to have swords. Had Zanino arranged for the men of his quarter to come armed? No time to worry about it. Zanino meant the massacre of the French to happen now.

Below me more Frenchmen were running through the crowd, trying to reach their dead compatriots. The Sicilians flowed over them like a river. One or two of them drew together, back to back in little pockets of resistance, fighting until sheer numbers and anger overwhelmed them. If there were women with the Frenchmen, the mob slaughtered them as well. It didn't seem to make any difference whether they were Frenchwomen or natives. Some Sicilians were killed too and their wives shrieked and wailed over their corpses. Other women snatched up the weapons of the fallen and fought beside their men. No doubt they also had reason to hate the French.

I tore myself from the hideous but riveting view from the parapet and scrambled down the ladder into the bell chamber. The friar, astonished, stopped ringing Vespers and stared at me. Then he heard the sounds of bloodshed outside and went white. I carried on down the stairs, bouncing off the walls until I hurled myself out of the little door onto the church steps.

Right in front of me lay the bodies of the first Frenchmen to die, the sergeant Drouet and his friends. The mob had taken out its hatred on them. They were extremely dead. By the door of the church the young peasant was standing with his arms around his pretty wife, staring at the corpses and shaking. I don't think he had intended to make history.

I glanced around, looking for Andrea. A riot would be a good opportunity to kill him. He would certainly kill me if he could. But I couldn't see anyone I knew. The great mass of the Sicilians was moving away towards the town, waving its weapons in the air. Every now and again someone would yell in a voice of brass, 'Death to the French!' and the whole mob would reply, '*Death!*'

Suddenly, like thunder from a clear sky, I thought of Caterina, strolling back arm in arm with her French lover towards the city gates. If the mob took them they would both die. I broke into a run and soon came up with the people at the rear of the crowd. I began to fling them aside, shouldering through them. They shouted angrily at me and I shouted back in Sicilian fluent and furious enough for them to let me past. 'I've lost my girl,' I yelled. 'Where is she? Let me through!'

There must have been more than a thousand people surging towards the city walls. More than ten thousand, perhaps. How can you tell, when you're in the middle of them? Dead Frenchmen littered our path, some stripped of their armour, naked and bloody with wounds like gaping mouths. Moving with that mob was like being part of a battering ram. I kept pushing my way past one Sicilian after another, looking from side to side, trying to spot

Jacques's blue and white tunic or Caterina's yellow skirt. I couldn't see them.

The walls loomed up before us. I wondered briefly how the mob would pass the gates if the French closed the portcullis against them. But by the time I reached them the gates stood open for the Sicilians to pour through. Bodies had been rolled aside, their wounds showing that they had been trapped by the falling portcullis before somebody managed to kill the guards and raise it again. Perhaps people on the inside had seen what was happening and come to help.

When I got through the gates I stopped for a moment, struck with horror. There must have been twenty Frenchmen on gate duty and they were scattered on the cobbles below the gateway, dead or nearly dead. A couple of them were crying out with the pain of their wounds. As I watched a Sicilian woman stepped out of her way to cut their throats, then waved her bloody dagger in the air and ran to catch up with her companions, shouting with pride.

One of the French guards was pinned to a nearby door by a spear, bristling with crossbow bolts. They must have dragged him up there as an impromptu target. I stared, forgetting everything. One of the bolts was stuck through his open mouth.

The crowd flooded past me and spread out into the narrow streets of the city. I could hear distant shouting and shrieking. I knew what would be happening. The men were racing home for their arms, arms I had helped to provide, and then back into the streets to hunt down the Frenchmen. I sobbed with sudden hopelessness and took to my heels again, running and ducking through the alleyways towards the quarter where Jacques of Vaison lived. Perhaps he had got there in time, perhaps he had got his men and Caterina away to the safety of the royal palace. But as I ran I knew the chances were small. The French had been out in the city having a good time, their last holiday before most of them were sent off to fight against Constantinople. They were scattered and vulnerable, and every man in Palermo was ready to kill them.

I ran into a small piazza. It was packed with people, a mob in full cry. They were all armed and foaming with excitement. In their midst they had a French officer, a middle-aged man of good bearing. They had stripped him half naked and were trying to make him dance by stabbing at his feet with swords. He was snarling at them and refusing to move, though his bare feet bled like Christ's. His men were sprawled behind him. The people had seen to them first.

'Tell you what, Frenchman,' shouted one man in the crowd, 'save yourself. Say something in Sicilian.'

'What do you want me to say?' demanded the Frenchman scornfully. His Sicilian was accented, but good.

The crowd laughed at him. A woman yelled, 'Say *ciciri!*'

Clever and cruel. The Frenchman hasn't been born that can manage the Italian *ch* sound. The French officer must have known, but he set his jaw and tried it all the same. Silence fell on the mob as he opened his mouth. They swayed forward like leashed hounds, eyes stretched wide, waiting eagerly for him to fail. '*Shishiri.*'

They screamed with laughter and rage and descended on him. I ran on. Every street was strewn with corpses, some just dead, others horribly dead. Now the Sicilians had their own arms they were less fussy about stripping their victims. I found one Frenchman who had fallen on top of his sword. I pulled it out from under him and wiped its bloody hilt on his tunic. I felt safer with the long blade in my hand.

Nearly there, and still I hadn't seen anything of Jacques. I was quivering with absurd hope. I dashed around the last corner and stopped dead.

It was a small court, pretty, with climbing plants up the walls and a well in the centre with an ornamental wellhead. There was only one way out, which meant there was only one way in, too. The French must have hoped it would be defensible. They were lying across the entryway, their corpses heaped one on another like a barricade. A few of them lay where the mob had flung them aside to push through into the court. Their limp bodies made X shapes on the ground and their blood turned the dust into dark slime.

Jacques of Vaison was at the bottom of one of the heaps, which meant he must have fallen early on. No need to try to pull him out and help him. I only knew him by his striped tunic. Someone had beaten his head to pieces, spilling his brains into the dirt, blood and matter mixed with the petals of anemones. His handsome face no longer existed. I shuddered and ran through into the silent courtyard, calling out, 'Caterina!'

There was a dead woman just behind the men in a green dress and another by the wellhead in scarlet. I ran past them and called again, hoping against hope that she had found a place to hide herself. 'Caterina! *Gattina*, where are you?'

The woman at the well moaned. I turned and saw that she was a blonde. She was hanging from the well by her hands as if she was too weak to lift herself and drink. Then, even before I realised that it was her, my feet began to run.

The skirt of her dress was scarlet with her own blood. A thick spoor of it showed where she had crawled, trying to reach the water. I couldn't see the wound and I didn't dare to look. I knew what they had done to her.

I dropped my sword and flung myself down beside her, calling to her. Then I leapt up and hauled up the well bucket and cupped water in my hands. I turned her over gently and held her and put the water to her lips. Her beautiful lips, not beautiful now but drained, dry and grey as pumice, flaky as ashes. She drank and I stroked back her hair and trickled more water into her mouth.

'Caterina.' I could barely say her name. There were spots of blood on her tender lobes where her earrings had been wrenched away, and a line of sharp red around her neck. It would have been a bruise, but there wasn't enough blood left in her to bruise. I shut my eyes and struggled against sobs.

'Marcello,' she whispered. I opened my eyes and gave her more water. She moved faintly against my hands and moaned. Then she looked up at me and said quite clearly, 'Don't you dare say I told you so.'

Quick footsteps ran into the courtyard. I looked up, dangerous as a hit lion. A Sicilian roughneck swaggered towards me, sword in hand. He said, 'Isn't that a Frenchman's whore?'

My grief evaporated into white-hot anger. I laid Caterina's head gently against the well wall, grabbed my sword and lunged to my feet. I ran at him with a furious, incoherent shout. He cursed and lifted his sword to defend himself, but he might as well have tried to fend off the lightning of God's wrath. My sword buried itself in his belly. He gaped like a landed fish and I jerked the blade free, gasping with almost sexual pleasure. He fell and writhed at my feet. I ran back to Caterina and struck the sword into the ground and caught her into my arms. Her body was tense and arched with pain.

She opened her eyes again and moved a little. I whispered her name and put more water to her grey lips. She tried to smile and then lifted her hand towards my face. I caught hold of her wrist and guided it. Her fingers touched my cheek, grazed my ear, twined themselves into my hair. She whispered, 'Marcello.'

I stooped to kiss her. But before my lips touched hers her hand fell limply from my hair and her body softened and became heavy in my arms.

It wasn't her death that hurt me. I have seen many deaths, and hers could have been worse. It was the loss of her life that struck me like a spear. Of all the women I had ever known she had been the most intensely and absolutely alive, and now her blood had ceased to flow and she lay looking up at the sky, motionless, quietly and unprotestingly dead. I had shed my initial shock and grief in killing the Sicilian, and now I trembled with impotent rage and a bitter recognition of waste and loss.

I held her, hollow with helplessness. At last I closed her eyes and made the sign of the Cross on her forehead, then laid her gently back against the cold stone. My hands and clothes were stained with her darkening blood. I picked up my sword from the ground, struggling with my anger. I folded my hands around the bloody blade and knelt before the cross of the hilt to offer up a prayer for her unprotected soul.

A voice said, 'There he is.'

At once I was on my feet. There at the entry among the heaps of dead Frenchmen were Andrea, Blasio and Pietro. Pietro was flushed and the remnants of his wreath clung obscenely to his bloodstained hair, but the other two looked as though they had been taking a leisurely stroll. Andrea had spoken, and he was smiling. 'I thought we would find you here,' he said, 'looking for your French-loving whore.'

Blasio had a sword in his left hand and a spear in his right. He hefted them and came towards me with a snarl. I let him move two paces from Andrea, then without a word drew my dagger and flung it.

It would have struck Andrea, I'm sure of it, but Blasio moved faster than I could have expected for a man of such size. When he saw my hand go to the hilt he was already moving. By the time the dagger landed Andrea was sprawling on the ground and Blasio was where he had been, looking down incuriously at the blade protruding from his chest. A red stain began to spread out from it. I didn't wait, but dashed forward to hurdle over the dead Frenchmen and make my escape.

I would have killed Andrea on my way, but Blasio was still alive and still holding his spear and Pietro also shook himself and came for me. I dodged one blow, jumped another and scrambled over the heap of corpses. A sharp pain in my shoulder made me cry out and curse. Then I was over and running down the street.

For a while Pietro followed me, shouting imprecations, but I lost him quite soon.

I headed for the harbour, clutching my sword in one hand and my wounded shoulder in the other. My blood mingled with Caterina's on the silk of my tunic. I shivered with pain and shock, and the hot Sicilian wind was cold against my wet cheeks.

Time to go, Marcello. Nothing to stay for now.

TWENTY-FOUR

When a Venetian wants to go somewhere in a hurry, he goes by boat. However, if you should be thinking of undertaking a hundred-league solo sea journey, I wouldn't recommend it. Or if you have no choice, I would suggest that you do it when you are physically fit and that you make sure there is plenty of water on board.

For the first two nights the journey was undemanding in nautical terms. My wound gave me pain and I was weak from loss of blood and lack of water and sleep, but the weather was fair and I was so determined to reach Messina with my news that I think if I had died at the tiller my corpse would have continued to steer the little sandalo onwards, like something from one of the stories that galley crews tell to frighten new recruits.

The wind held up well until the second dawn, when it faded and then died altogether. I was within sight of the headland that shields Messina from the north and I cursed with fatigue and frustration to find myself becalmed. There were strange tides and currents around the headland, and on its far side was the extraordinary boiling-pot of water that the ancients called Scylla and Charybdis. I wasn't looking forward to negotiating them even with a good stiff breeze behind me, and now the sea was as calm as a fishpond. Besides, there was only a mouthful of water left in the little beaker under the steersman's bench, and that was after painfully careful rationing. I hadn't dared to put in to the coast in case the rebellion had spread along it.

The calm water was like a silk scarf, dark blue patched with pink and silver and dotted here and there with the tiny dark shapes of fishing-boats. The moon had set, and the last stars faded softly from the translucent sky. I said some charms to summon a wind, but without effect. The sail hung as slackly as the rags over a beggar's belly. It was still and cold. I shivered and put my face in my hands and drifted into an uncomfortable half sleep.

Dozing, you have no guard for your mind. Suddenly I found

myself thinking of the things I had left behind in Palermo. The gems I had bought as samples, the splendid tunic of Theban silk, valuable possessions. Their cost would come out of my own pocket. But I minded more about the amber wool tunic that Caterina had made for me. She had embroidered it as a remembrance, and I had lost it. An agent should not regret the loss of things, but I did regret it, most piercingly.

Thinking of it was like losing her all over again. I remembered her trailing one of her embroidery threads over our dusty floor for the kitten to chase, laughing with pleasure as the thread twitched and the kitten pounced and tumbled. I remembered her stitching that golden dress, her lower lip caught in her teeth as she concentrated, her face gilded with reflected light. I remembered her in my arms, her lips quivering and her face tense, her wide open eyes fixed on mine as the pleasure grew and we concentrated on the approaching moment. My grief bubbled up like a salt spring and my tears fell into the bilges.

The sun rose, and with it a steady north-easterly wind. It dried my wet cheeks and roused me from my lethargy. Mourning Caterina had purged me. I felt white and empty, but able to go on. I caught hold of the sail-rope and the little patched lateen sail tautened. The water began to hiss down the sides of the boat as it picked up speed.

Around the headland I entered the main shipping lane. It was busy with craft of all sizes, and I had my work cut out to guide the little boat through the myriad ships without getting run down by some great carrack or fouling a fishing-net. As tired as I was, it's a miracle that I didn't cause an accident.

At last, as the sun rose towards noon, I found myself outside Messina harbour. If it had been crowded before, now it was packed with ships as tight as stuffing in a sausage. Dozens, scores, hundreds of transports, low in the water with the weight of their stores, ready to receive their complement of men, and flanking them the long lean vicious galleys, like soldier ants protecting the workers. All the ships looked ready for action, clean-swept and taut, ready to take Byzantium. Above the harbour Mategriffon castle rose up glowing in the bright sunshine. It was flying the Angevin flag and another, presumably its commander's personal emblem.

Now I needed attention from the French, and quickly. I hoped that with so valuable a fleet in harbour the garrison would be wary, and they were. As I passed the mole a guard on it saw me and sounded a horn and the signal ran around the harbour edge. I steered the boat towards the fishing fleet and as I hesitated, trying to find a place to berth, a French sergeant yelled in Sicilian from the harbour wall, 'Name and business?'

When I tried to yell back I had no voice. My lips were cracked and dry with thirst and fever. The sergeant didn't find this amusing. By the time I had found a place to tie up he had three sturdy fellows with him ready to grab me the moment I set foot on land. I was philosophical about it. At least I wouldn't have to walk far to find them.

The sergeant wasn't one of the world's brightest, but one of his men knew which end was up. After a one-sided and fruitless conversation this lad said, 'Sir, I think he's thirsty,' and without waiting to be asked offered me the flask at his hip. I pray that when he dies serried ranks of cherubim lift him singing to the arms of the Virgin.

I drank the lot. Then I said to the sergeant, in French, 'Where is Herbert of Orleans? I need to speak to him.'

The sergeant scowled at me. I was talking about the Vicar of Messina, the most powerful man in Sicily. 'What's the joke?' he growled. 'Who are you, anyway, in the Devil's name, coming here in a fishing boat and a silk robe?'

Not so stupid, if he could tell that my robe was silk despite the stains of blood and ashes and seawater. 'My name is Marcello D'Estari,' I told him. 'I'm a Venetian citizen. I want to speak to the lord Herbert at once. It won't wait.'

I repeated the words over and over again, all the way through the ranks from sergeant to lieutenant of the guard, from lieutenant of the guard to captain of the guard, through the gatehouse of the massive castle of Mategriffon and on into its depths. Along the way they disarmed me, which made me uncomfortable.

After a while I started to have to explain why I was there. I did so succinctly. 'Rebellion in Palermo' seemed to do the trick. My news caused shock and consternation, but it didn't improve my treatment. I began to have a bad feeling about the direction in which I was being taken. We weren't heading towards the castle keep, where the Vicar had his headquarters, but towards more subterranean, ominous regions. At last I found myself in a little cell, quite bare except for a small image of some French saint on a pillar in the corner and some unpleasant-looking stains on the floorboards and walls. They told me to wait and shut the door.

Despite the evidence of old blood the floor looked immensely appealing. I sat down and propped myself against a wall and was instantly asleep.

Someone threw a bucket of water over me. I came up spluttering and then cursed and caught at my wounded shoulder. 'Is this the way you treat your allies?'

There were several Frenchmen in the room, a handful of ordinary sergeants and a young officer. None of them was Herbert of Orleans. They deferred to a middle-aged man in a rich robe whose pouched, heavy face was cold and intelligent. He was not Herbert of Orleans either, and he did not look welcoming. I wished that I had stayed asleep.

'What is your name?' the man asked me in the sharp, practised tone of a professional interrogator.

I wiped the water from my face and said for the hundredth time, 'Marcello D'Estari, a citizen of Venice. I have news of the gravest importance for his excellency the Vicar.'

'Tell me this news.'

'Who are you?'

He frowned at my imperious tone. 'I am Reynauld of Lisieux, deputy to the Vicar. He is a busy man, he will not deal with every lunatic who comes to the castle. You have been trying to undermine our garrison morale with tales of disaster.'

I snapped, 'The truth is not a tale, monsieur. I have come from Palermo. The garrison there has fallen and is destroyed. The men of Palermo will be fomenting rebellion in every other town in Sicily.'

The men looked at each other. They did not want to believe me. Reynauld in particular did not want to believe me. He laughed, then said coldly, 'You are an *agent provocateur* sent by Aragon to distract us from the expedition!'

'I am a Venetian agent,' I repeated through my teeth. 'I have no connection with Aragon. The Vicar knows of my mission, he has been informed of it by the Venetian ambassador signor Vallerio Dolfin. Speak with him, if you don't believe me.'

'You arrive in a small boat with tales of disaster and say you have come from Palermo. Why should anyone believe you? Did you wound yourself to give the story credence? The Aragonese sent you, or the Greek Emperor. They know that the King's expedition is almost ready to sail. You are a spy.'

'I am a Venetian citizen. Give my name to the Vicar, he will know it. Or summon the Venetian ambassador to vouch for me.'

His anger was unshaken. 'I will not concern his Excellency or the Venetian ambassador with such subversive scaremongering,' he snarled. 'It will be easier to screw the truth out of you.'

I was so tired that even the threat of torture couldn't excite me. I rolled my eyes to heaven and let out an exasperated sigh. The Frenchman's mouth thinned with rage, and I think in a few seconds he would have ordered his men to take me away and extract the truth from me by force. But then the young officer said very diffidently, 'My lord.'

'What?' De Lisieux swung on him angrily.

'My lord, the ambassador's son-in-law Aliusio Contarini is a friend of mine. He mentioned a Venetian agent at work on the island, and I think the name was Marcello, as this man said. Aliusio said he was incompetent, but –'

Aliusio said *I* was incompetent? I was incensed. Apart from anything else, Aliusio should not have mentioned my existence to anyone, let alone casually, over a cup of wine, no doubt, the toping fool. But then again it was just as well he had, since it had probably saved me from a painful trip to the castle's dungeons.

Reynauld scowled at the officer. 'You're certain of this, Jean-Marie?'

'Yes, my lord. Before Easter Aliusio went away on what he said was a secret mission. He returned wounded. He said this man was responsible.' The young man had a pleasant face, open and a little anxious under a shock of mousy hair. He looked short-sighted, more like a clerk than a soldier, and he moved as if his mail coat and long sword were too heavy for him. I thought he seemed an unlikely crony for Aliusio, but there's no accounting for taste. 'My lord, I think it would be well advised if we were to let his Excellency know of this.'

There was a little pause. Then Reynauld said, 'I will discuss it with my lord myself. Bring the prisoner up to the keep.' He looked at me and wrinkled his nose. I suppose I looked a fairly unsavoury specimen. 'Clean him up,' he ordered tersely.

When he had gone I muttered beneath my breath, 'The *prisoner!*' The young officer's face showed that he had overheard. I added for his benefit, 'I came here to try to do you all a favour. I wish I had sailed home to Venice.'

The young man was quite white. He said, 'You'd better come with me,' and jerked his head at a couple of the soldiers to follow him, though in my exhausted state I could hardly have posed a threat to a day-old chick. I nodded wearily and went with him out of the little cell and up flight after flight of stairs.

After a while he said to me, 'Is it true? Is what you say true? About Palermo?'

I nodded. He crossed himself and blinked rapidly. Then he said to me, as if I wanted an explanation, 'My brother is serving there.'

Was, I thought. But I said nothing.

Herbert of Orleans was possibly the most unattractive soldier I have ever seen. His teeth were blackened stumps, his face was crowded with pustules and scabs, and the body odour that seeped from his furred cloth-of-gold robe was enough to fell a horse at ten paces. However, nobody comments on the personal hygiene of a king's deputy. If his entourage stood a fair distance from him, it was surely only a sign of their exaggerated respect for his rank and position.

I didn't have the opportunity to keep my distance. He stood right in front of me and breathed into my face. It was as bad as you might expect. He told me to explain what had happened in Palermo.

My French was failing me. I hadn't slept for three days, I was weak from my wound and definitely falling into a fever. I swayed on my feet. In the corner of the room Vallerio Dolfin frowned and snapped, 'What's the matter with you?'

For answer I fell over. The floor felt as soft as a feather bed, but they hauled me off it and dumped me on the only chair in the room. It was his Excellency's chair of office, tall and heavy, with lion's feet and a red velvet cushion. I squirmed in it, vaguely afraid that his horrible skin diseases might transfer themselves to me.

'Pull yourself together,' said Dolfin. The young officer, Jean-Marie, sidled over to me and held a flask of honeyed wine to my lips. Then he withdrew, looking shifty. I said to Dolfin in Venetian, 'I hope you're ready for this.'

I spared them nothing. It had taken me a long time to make my way down to the Palermo harbour, since the Palermitans had suspected any man on his own of being a Frenchman. The practice of testing men by forcing them to pronounce *ciciri* had spread like wildfire, and I must have proved myself that way a dozen times in a journey of no more than a mile. In that time I had heard and seen enough to be brutally convincing.

I told them that by the time I sailed from Palermo the old royal palace had fallen into rebel hands and what remained of its garrison was massacred. I told them of the dead Frenchmen carpeting the streets, and of the others I had seen failing the pronunciation test and murdered in various ways, increasingly inventive as the blood-crazed Palermitans tired of simple slaughter. I described the poor wretches from the harbour-guard and customs office, some of them hung from the customs posts, some flung into the sea to drown with their weights tied around their necks, some dipped in naphtha and set alight to see if they burned as brightly as the harbour beacon.

When I paused for breath Herbert of Orleans said, 'What became of the commander of the garrison?'

'I don't know. I didn't hear that they had killed him. Maybe he got away. They said some of the garrison had fled to Vicari castle, away from the city.'

Orleans's poxy face tautened. 'Vicari is tiny. It couldn't hold against a determined siege.'

He turned away from me and signalled one of his men for a consultation. I gasped in fresh air while I could. After a short silence he said, 'I shall consider our best course of action. And I must send to the King.'

'Messire,' I said, trying to summon up enough energy to convince him, 'believe me when I say that this will not be isolated. There are potential rebels in every city, even in Messina. Double your guard. The Palermitans will encourage them to rise against you.'

He looked at me with hatred. Nobody likes the bringer of ill tidings, and besides, Dolfin had tried to warn him of this dozens of times. He had ignored the warnings and now he must be feeling stupid, and commanders don't like to feel stupid. 'As for you,' he said in a thin voice, 'I thought that your job was to discover who these agents of insurrection were. I will have further questions for you, you incompetent. Stay where you can be found.'

'I will undertake it, your Excellency,' said Dolfin quickly. 'He will stay at the Venetian residency.'

In accordance with his undertaking Dolfin took me back with him to the big commandeered house by the church. He had several of his entourage with him and they half led, half carried me through the hot noisy streets. All the way Dolfin cursed me as if I were personally responsible for what had happened in Palermo.

'You were supposed to inform me before the rising,' he hissed. 'There were five days to go!'

No use telling him that even the resistance hadn't expected what happened at Santo Spirito. I was exhausted, and as I staggered along I shivered more violently than could be explained by simple fatigue. My head ached furiously and my eyes were clouded with dark red swooping blotches like a film of blood.

'You'd better stay here until the fleet sails,' Dolfin went on, snarling. 'Do what you can to remedy this mess. Go on with your work in trying to uncover the Messina insurgents, in any case. I shall go home to Venice and report to the Security Committee. They will be severely displeased, I assure you. If I were you I should make sure that you make the utmost effort. Their eyes will be on you, Marcello.'

Off to Venice, eh? Obviously Signor Dolfin did not like the way the wind was blowing. It displeased me obscurely to know that Fiammetta's father was a bully and a coward. I said in a voice slurred with weariness, 'Will they not think your leaving a little premature, my lord?'

'Not when my so-called expert proved totally incapable.'

I sighed, too tired and sick to take offence. 'Signor,' I said, 'before you leave for Venice, allow me to explain to you what happened at St Margaret's Bay.'

'Aliusio has already explained! In detail!'

That was what I was afraid of.

TWENTY-FIVE

I slept on and off for what felt like minutes and turned out to
have been days. My blood burned and sang with fever. I had
nightmares, and worse than the nightmares, dreams in which
the past seemed not to have happened, so that I emerged from
sleep into freshly-turned grief.

At last a voice said in Venetian, 'Wake up, you fraud.' The
words 'son of a whore' were unspoken, but none the less audible
for that.

In an eventful life I have been accused of many things, but
malingering was novel enough to sting. I forced my eyes open
and made myself sit up. My shoulder hurt, but with the dull,
mnemonic ache of a wound that has started to heal.

It was Aliusio, of course, looking at me with his lip curled in
a manner that was presumably intended to be offensive. Did he
mean to take revenge? If he wanted to kill me there wouldn't be
very much I could do about it, since I was as weak as a newborn
pup. I didn't really know what to say to him. I hadn't ever before
come face to face with a man that I had intended to kill and failed
to.

He looked well, apart from the mark of my sword on his face.
It was really rather impressive, right up the left cheek from his
jawline to his hairline. It hadn't been stitched, which I could
understand. A simple scar is one thing, looking like a badly made
sail is another. I suppose I would have been well advised to
apologise to him, but I couldn't bear the thought. Instead I
cleared my furry throat and said, 'That should get you plenty of
attention in the Piazzetta. It's so decorative you might have had
it done to order.'

Aliusio's sneer became a snarl. 'Very funny,' he said. 'The
moment you're on your feet again I shall be requiring an
explanation of you.'

He thought that I was playing sick to avoid a reckoning with
him. That really annoyed me, but I was not idiot enough to fall

on his sword just to prove how weak I was. I said, 'You can have an explanation whenever you want. Have one now. I had to do something that looked convincing, Aliusio, or they'd have killed us both and my cover would have been broken. I let you get away, didn't I?'

That was too complicated for Aliusio. He frowned as if he didn't have an immediate answer. I drank the water that some thoughtful soul had left beside the bed and went on before he recovered what passed for his wits. 'Listen, what did you think you were doing? You ignored every instruction I gave you. It was a disaster! What in the name of Saint Mark did you tell Signor Dolfin?'

'He agreed with my suggestion that we ought to concentrate on the sea attack,' Aliusio said offhandedly. 'It would have worked, too, if it hadn't been for the ballista in that Genoese galley. The Devil take their souls!'

There was obviously no point in arguing with him. The pity of it was that the Committee would get his version of the tale too, at least until I could report to them in person. It was enough of a débâcle to threaten my future as an agent. I liked being an agent, or at least I had until this mission. I was seriously concerned.

'What day is it?' I asked, not wanting to initiate further discussion.

'April the ninth,' said Aliusio.

I had been sick for six days. Not usual for me, but then the circumstances were not usual either. 'What's the news?'

I didn't need to say what of. Aliusio made a face. 'You were right about Palermo,' he said. 'What was left of the garrison fled to Vicari castle, but the rebels took it a few days ago and killed everyone there. Including the Governor. Women and children, too. His Excellency Signor Herbert is furious, but there's no use shutting the stable door after the horse has bolted.'

'And the rest of the island?'

'The west and north has revolted, we think. There's been a few what d'you call thems, refugees, coming in from some places. And apparently one or two places have let the garrison go, but the rebels have won all the same.'

'The Byzantine expedition?' I didn't hold my breath. No king could throw himself into a war of foreign conquest with a massive rebellion in his own dominions.

'The French still mean to go. They say they'll be at the

rendezvous with our fleet on time. After all, the rebels are just a bunch of peasants.' Aliusio sounded as though he hadn't even convinced himself.

Something was puzzling me. Finally I asked it. 'Anyway, what are you doing here? I thought you'd have gone back to Venice with Signor Dolfin.'

He bridled. 'What? Absolutely not. If you can stay and fight so can I.'

I let out my breath like a snorting horse. I needed a mettlesome rival the way I needed a broken sword-blade. 'All right, companion in arms,' I said wearily, since I had no choice. 'What's the plan?'

The plan was this. In a few days a crack naval force would be sailing to besiege and recapture Palermo, and Aliusio had his name down as a volunteer. The force was commanded by the Messinese nobleman Richard Riso, which was fine. Nobody doubted Riso loyalties. They were one of the few Sicilian clans to have done very well indeed out of the French. Their loyalty was as sound as the family purse. I had reservations about the fact that the majority of the ships and crew were Messinese rather than French, but then there weren't that many French soldiers left to spare.

So Aliusio was going off for a bit of glory retrieving Palermo from the filthy hands of the rebel Commune. I, on the other hand, was to remain in Messina. The French government was expecting my advice and cooperation on a number of issues connected with repressing potential rebellion in the city. I wasn't looking forward to it.

One way or another Aliusio seemed to have decided that I hadn't wounded him maliciously. He left me in peace to convalesce, and I was allowed to sit around the Residency, sunning myself in the elegant colonnaded Arab courtyard, listening to the gentle splashing of the marble fountain and reflecting on my own failure. Vallerio Dolfin had left behind a handful of his men to serve Aliusio, but none of them talked to me. I had taken the whole of the blame for the disaster at Saint Margaret's Bay, and that meant that I was responsible for the souls of the men who had died on the beach and in the stricken boat. One or two of the survivors made the evil eye sign at me behind my back. Well, they could hardly think worse of me than I did of myself.

It wasn't just Caterina's death. I had abandoned Antonio, too, and Andrea was still alive. There was no chance that I would be able to return to Palermo to free one and kill the other, either now or in the future. Whatever happened, I was going to make very certain that when I left Sicily this time it was for good.

Bulletins came in daily, some confused, others unpleasantly clear. The whole of the west of the island from Palermo to Trapani was in rebel hands. Palermo had declared itself a Commune and a number of other cities had followed suit. I thought of Andrea victorious, leading the citizens of Palermo in their example to others, and shuddered with rage. It was easier to hate him than to continue blaming myself.

After a few days I was fully recovered, at least physically. The wound on my shoulder was healing well, with no pus or seepage. Two days' soaking with cold sea water wouldn't have been my treatment of choice for a sword cut, but it was undoubtedly efficacious. As for my mental state, it's hard to describe it. Sufficient to say that there was a serving-girl in the Residency with a delicious similarity to a ripe peach. She made it abundantly clear that if I was interested, she was. Unfortunately I wasn't. This didn't suit me, but it was a physical fact. We tried it one night, and she might as well have gone to bed with a small sausage for all the good I did her. She tried not to show that she was offended, but who wouldn't be?

There wasn't any point in continuing to mope at the Residency, so the following morning I dressed in some of the pathetic selection of castoffs that Aliusio had provided for me and went off to look around the city.

I hadn't shaved. Something told me that I would be well advised to preserve my incognito while I could. So I wandered about doing a secret agent's job, that is looking thoroughly disreputable and fading into shadows so that I could overhear conversations in the taverns and wine shops.

There was a lot of ostentatiously loyal talk delivered in loud voices in the area between the castle and the harbour. And why not? The place was thronged with French soldiers, all extremely jumpy. None of them swaggered about cheerfully in ones and twos the way they had done the last time I was in Messina. They moved in packs, eight or ten or twelve together, armed to the teeth, and they looked both apprehensive and dangerous.

On the face of it it wasn't easy to see why Messina should rebel. Compared to the rest of the island it had done well out of the Angevin government. But when you moved away from the areas where the French patrolled regularly the feeling was different. There, it showed that the Messinese hated the French just as much as the other Sicilians. The massacre of the Vespers was still vivid as yesterday in my mind, and I was sensitised to rebellion. In the poorer areas of the city in particular the atmosphere was enough to stand up the hairs on the back of my neck. If I'm honest, it scared me to death. The last thing I wanted to do was try to live through another Palermo.

I returned to the Residency, shivering inside my battered cloak, and found that I was expected. A party of French soldiers was lounging outside in the street, and within, in the courtyard, the young officer called Jean-Marie was waiting, tapping his booted toe nervously against the rim of the fountain. He was wearing a black surcoat over his mail and his face was white and strained. I supposed he was in mourning for his brother, who must have died with the Palermo garrison. Aliusio was standing beside him, looking aggravated. When I came in the Frenchman narrowed his short-sighted eyes, recognised me with an effort, and said, 'Monsieur D'Estari, His Excellency requires your presence at Mategriffon.'

I raised my brows, pleased to be treated with courtesy. 'At once,' I said, stooping to sluice my dusty face and hands in the pool.

Aliusio tagged along, of course. I wondered if Jean-Marie had invited him, but apparently not. He just hated to think that there was anything I could do that he couldn't. This meant that he was destined for a life of continuous disillusion.

It wasn't far to the castle. As we went Jean-Marie explained to me why I had been summoned. 'The lord Richard Riso came to see His Excellency today,' he said. 'You know that he is a loyal supporter of the King. He had a copy of a letter which he says is being circulated in the city, inciting the people to rebellion. This is the first written evidence of subversion we have found, and His Excellency thinks it is important.'

He talked like a clerk too, in precise, long-winded French which I found rather hard to follow. I tend to come by languages from the bottom up. However, he seemed quite intelligent, which surprised me in someone who described Aliusio as a friend. 'Was the letter from Palermo?' I asked.

'Oh yes. Signed by a number of the leaders of the rebellion, including a couple of great noblemen.'

'One of whom was Guglielmo Resetto?' I hazarded, raising one eyebrow.

He looked startled and uncomfortable. 'Yes. How did you know?'

'It's my job to know.'

'Yes,' he said uncertainly. 'Resetto, yes. I saw the letter. It offered the Messinese all sorts of assistance, if they would rise against their –' he hesitated, searching his memory. ' "Their cruel and oppressive Angevin masters," or something like that.' He stopped in the street and looked at me and I saw that he was afraid, so afraid that he could hardly conceal it. His white lips were trembling. In an undertone he said, 'You were in Palermo. Do you – do you think it could happen here? We've got so many men, the fleet, everything. Could it, could it happen here?'

I shook my head, not in reassurance but refusing to commit myself. Outwardly I looked composed. Inwardly I was wondering how I could get away from Messina before the inevitable happened, and whether it might be feasible to lose Aliusio in the process.

TWENTY-SIX

Herbert of Orleans listened carefully while I expressed, in my very best French, the opinion that revolt in Messina was a distinct possibility. If I were the Vicar, I said, I would not allow any of the forces available to me to dissipate. I would keep all French forces within the Messina walls and concentrate on the security of the fleet. He nodded sagely and inclined his head politely, then promptly gave orders that totally contradicted everything I had said.

Within a couple of days two separate missions left Messina. One was the naval expedition against Palermo, under the command of Richard Riso. As planned the forces were mostly Messinese, with only a couple of French ships. Another expedition was sent southwards under a knight called William Chirioto. Apparently the town of Taormina was threatened by a horde of rebels approaching from the west. Insurrection was coming uncomfortably close to Messina.

Aliusio went as planned with the naval expedition. He made a great business of going to Palermo to undo some of the damage I had done. To my astonishment, when he was gone, I actually missed him. Having someone to despise is a great boost to anyone's self-confidence.

I was thrown instead for company on Jean-Marie, who had been assigned to me as a sort of minder. He was only a junior officer but as well as his ordinary duties he had the main responsibility for intelligence at Mategriffon, which shows how warped the Vicar's sense of priorities was. With rebellion all around him Herbert of Orleans was still more than half concerned with the arming and provisioning of the fleet. It sat in the harbour and its men sat on shore or aboard their ships, eating their supplies and costing King Charles money.

Apparently when the Palermo massacre was reported to the King he said that as far as he was concerned it was a flea-bite. Are all kings fools? If that was a flea, I hoped he never had the misfortune to be bitten by a horsefly.

In fact Jean-Marie was rather good company. I saw him every evening to report on what I had heard in the city that day, and then we would often eat together and drink and pass the time. He liked to distract himself from his ever-increasing anxiety and his grief for his lost brother by playing games. I tried to persuade him to get us a pack of playing-cards, but he insisted that he couldn't afford one: toys of the wealthy, he called them. A Venetian sees these things differently. We manufacture playing-cards in the city, and though they are very dear they are not entirely out of reach. It would have been nice to have a pack. I could have played *solitario* to pass the time.

In any case, Jean-Marie and I stuck to chess and backgammon. He could destroy me utterly at chess, but when we played backgammon we gambled and the idea of having money riding on the outcome always seemed to throw him. In a week I had extracted most of his year's pay from him, which suited me. I'd come from Palermo with almost nothing, and none of the Residency's funds had come my way. Jean-Marie was a philo-sophical loser. He was well read, too, and could quote verse and learned men at length. I listened to poems in the Langue D'Oc and the Langue D'Oil and half a dozen treatises by the ill-fated Peter Abelard which he had from memory. I hadn't received so much concentrated culture since my mother died.

As well as playing board games with Jean-Marie, I did my job by circulating in the city and keeping my ear to the ground. What I found was the same sorry story all over again. I didn't have the time or the cover to go underground and try to track down the ringleaders, and to be honest I didn't really have the heart for it either. I didn't need to. I could report to Jean-Marie with more certainty each day that Messina was like a pot that is on the point of boiling over.

At least he believed me, and with his intervention the French started to take some sensible actions. Every man of the garrison who could be crammed within the walls of Mategriffon castle left his lodgings and moved up there. They grumbled, but they went. The castle was old and fairly squalid and conditions within its walls must have been uncomfortable at best, but at least it was secure. Patrols went out around the city every day, heavily armed and sharp-eyed, and they concentrated always on the areas where I had detected the most discontent on my expeditions. It seemed to work. The noble Messinese, led by the Riso family, continued to protest their loyalty, and the poorer sort seemed cowed by the show of strength on the part of the garrison. Perhaps, after all, the French might be able to keep Messina under control. That meant that in time they would be able to launch a strike against the insurgents in the rest of the island. With the full force of the Angevins behind it, a power that had cowed Byzantium, how could the rebels resist?

I didn't like to think about the punishment that might be meted out to the Sicilians if the French recovered the island. Jean-Marie was a quiet, intellectual young man, but when he mentioned Palermo his eyes glowed red and he almost frothed at the mouth. He talked about the old Roman punishment of *decimatio* as if the French would really line up the entire population of a city and kill one in ten, death by sheer bloody numbers. Perhaps they would. They were angry enough.

I was amazed when Aliusio returned, unannounced. So was Jean-Marie. We were sitting in the courtyard enjoying the cool of the evening and a glass of really quite decent rosé Sicilian wine, and then the door opened and Aliusio swept in, wearing his black 'secret business' cloak and looking dramatic. I just stared. Why question him? He would spill it all out anyway. I never knew a man worse at keeping a secret.

'So much for the attack on Palermo,' he said theatrically.

I was going to sit tight and let him stew, but Jean-Marie fell for it. 'What do you mean?' he asked, jumping to his feet with anxiety. 'What's happened?'

'Give me a drink,' Aliusio gasped, sitting down with a plump on the edge of the fountain and splashing the cool water over his face. Jean-Marie promptly gave him his own glass. He could have whistled for mine.

'What's happened?' Jean-Marie repeated. He was really scared. For a moment I felt scathing. Then I remembered how much the French had at stake and how much I had at stake and decided not to make such harsh judgements.

Aliusio drained the glass and held it out to be refilled. Jean-Marie served him. He got the last of what was in the flask, and I watched regretfully as it went instantly down his gullet. At last Aliusio shrugged off his capacious cloak and said, 'Well, we were supposed to attack Palermo, yes?'

Jean-Marie nodded desperately, eyes fixed on Aliusio's face.

You could see that this was just what Aliusio wanted. He bathed in his own importance for a moment, then went on. 'When we got there, guess what? The Palermitans didn't show any fight, didn't even chuck Greek fire at us, though they've got all the garrison's war-engines. They just hung poxy banners over the walls.'

'They did what?' Jean-Marie sounded as if he thought he hadn't understood the rapid Italian that Aliusio was speaking. I had, and I already believed it, but Aliusio explained anyway. 'Lots of the sailors in Messina came from Palermo originally. And the Palermitans just hung their banner and the Messinese banner side by side over the walls and yelled out, "Brothers, our brothers!" And when Riso gave the order to move in it was nearly bloody mutiny. The ships wouldn't do anything he said.'

'*Sainte Vierge*,' whispered Jean-Marie, which was strong for him. He rarely blasphemed. 'What happened to the ships?'

'Still there,' said Aliusio dismissively. He burped. 'Some sort of a blockade, I don't think. All they're doing is waving to the men on the walls every time they pass by. I got my lads in a launch and headed back for Messina as soon as I could.' He looked meaningfully at me. 'An easy passage,' he added cuttingly.

Jean-Marie jumped to his feet. 'Were there any Frenchmen with you?' he asked earnestly. When Aliusio shook his head he said at once, 'I must get back to the castle. Marcello, I'm sorry, but you understand –'

'If there's anything I can do,' I said. Jean-Marie was a very worthy young man, and it was impossible not to like him, particularly when he had lost so much money to me and with such good grace.

'I'll let you know,' he said. 'I'll send tomorrow.' He hurried for the door, calling for his guard. On the way out he stubbed his toe on a loose paving stone and nearly fell. Like many intellectuals, he was entirely incapable of holding his wine.

I was left looking at Aliusio. He looked at me. Then he raised his voice to call for another flask. 'Complete waste of time,' he said, when another glass had gone down. 'And of ships. Why send them at all if they weren't going to fight?'

'I said as much to the Vicar, if you remember,' I jibed gently.

'Hmph.' That was something he didn't want to remember. He drank another glass of wine so quickly it can hardly have touched the sides as it went down. Then he hiccuped and said, 'So what's going on here?'

'Not much.' I outlined the situation. 'But once this news gets around, I expect that the Messinese will be even more likely to rebel. The Palermitans are their brothers, are they? That sounds like bad news to me.'

He drank again. This time I drank one, to keep him company and because I found the news he had brought extremely depressing. For a while we sat in silence. Presently the flask was gone, and he called for another. When the servant brought it he brought a couple of tapers so that we could see to drink it, because the short Sicilian twilight was almost gone.

If you'd told me four months ago that I would be sitting in a fountain court drinking cool wine with Aliusio Contarini I should not have believed you. But here I was, gradually getting drunker and watching Aliusio becoming paralytic. If I really wanted to kill him all I needed to do now was push him into the fountain. He would have ornamental fish up both nostrils before his wine-soaked brain could react. The trouble was that I actually didn't want to kill him any more. He was such a pathetic specimen that it made me feel better just having him alive, so I could continue to be superior to him. At least as long as I was drunk.

He had reached the maudlin stage. 'Marcello,' he slurred, leaning over to clap me on the knee, 'let me tell you, you're my friend. You know what's what, eh? You know how much polenta fills the pot. You saved me at the beach.' I raised my eyebrows, surprised at his change of tack. He ploughed on. 'I'll tell you something. All this danger, all this, this, ah, risk, it puts a different compl– comp– face on things. Do you know what I'm going to do when I get back to Venice?'

Buy another section of exotic marble for the front of St Mark's? Found a church? Set up a hospital for orphans and bastards? I shook my head.

'I'm going to go to bed with my wife,' Aliusio announced.

I sat very still, swaying slightly. The darkness seemed to creep into my eyes. After a long moment I said very crisply, 'What?'

'Well,' he explained, ' 's like this, you see. I don't have an heir. Bastards all over the city, oh yes, but no heir. And on that beach, I nearly got it, didn't I? Nearly an ex-Aliusio. *Addio*, farewell, gone but not forgotten. Then what? My younger brother gets the lot, that's what. Makes a man think.'

My blood ran cold. I had saved his life at the beach and then missed my opportunity of ending it. What had I let Fiammetta in for? But I was intrigued. More than intrigued, fascinated. Also I was drunk. I leant forward and enquired in a heavily discreet undertone, 'D'you mean you don't sleep with her now?'

'Are you acquainted with my wife?' He drew himself up and spoke in the most upper-class of accents, the sort my mother used to affect to impress shopkeepers. 'Did you ever see her?'

'I have seen her, yes,' I said, finding it surprisingly easy to suppress the grin. 'Signor Dolfin introduced us when I came to his house. I would say she is probably the most beautiful noblewoman I have ever seen.' No lies there.

'Good looker,' muttered Aliusio. 'Sure enough, she is. Shame it's only skin deep.'

I stared at him, speechless and swaying slightly.

'Going to bed with her,' said Aliusio very precisely, 'is like sticking your prick into a bowl of warm tripe.'

My mouth dropped open. A 'But –' emerged and was swiftly strangled.

'Oh yes.' He was warming to his theme. 'I tell you, Marcello, she's as cold as a Lenten herring. Are you surprised I keep a few other girls around the city? I'm not wanted in my marriage bed, that's for sure. If you ask me, the woman's a misbegotten nun.' He rolled his eyes. 'Pity me, my friend.'

I pitied Fiammetta, not him. But a little demon of delight jumped free of all restraint and began to dance around behind my ear, buzzing into it like a red hot fly. 'He's not up to your mark, Marcello,' hissed the gleeful little voice. 'Remember that. You can do what he can't.'

I'm stubborn.

There is a new moon now. Darkness on her balcony, darkness in my heart, but still I come back and back and back, waiting, pretending that I still hope.

But not after tonight. This is the last. Tomorrow is her wedding day. I rest my head gently against the shutters that keep her from me and whistle our signal, faint as a breath. The last night of her maidenhood, and the last night of my life.

Then, unbelievably, a sound from behind the shutters. I recoil and hide myself behind one of the great plant pots, gasping. My eyes widen as the shutters part and a small slender figure appears, clad in white. A ghost? A spirit?

'Marcello,' the figure whispers. My heart beats so hard that I can't swallow. I get to my feet and come forward. It is so dark that I can barely

see the gleam of her open eyes. I stand in front of her and look down into her face. I have prepared two score of gallant speeches, and every one deserts me on the instant.

'Marcello, please.' Her voice is trembling. 'Please, don't hate me.'

I make a sound like a sob and snatch her into my arms. She is warm and real and she clings to me, small, pale, fragrant, delicate, like a jasmine flower. 'Hate you?' My fingers bury themselves in the gossamer mass of her silken hair. 'Hate you? Fiammetta, my darling, my little flame.'

I ask her for no explanations. It's enough that she is there, with me, touching me. After a moment I say, 'Come with me now, sweetheart. Come with me, mia bella.'

She tenses and pulls away. 'I can't. I can't.'

'Why? Fiammetta, why?'

'I'm afraid. I'm afraid.' Her voice is choked. She moves to me again, reaching out for me with fingers as fine as ivory. Where they touch me my skin burns. 'Marcello, my love. Marcello, forgive me.'

'I love you. I love you, Fiammetta, queen of my heart.' Nothing was ever so true. What is there to forgive? 'I'll always love you.'

'Promise. Promise you won't forget me.'

'My faith on it. My salvation on it. Madonna, rosa nel mondo, bellissima.'

She kisses me. She whispers my name. I fold my arms around her and we sink to our knees, face to face, mouth to mouth, enfolded. Again and again we kiss and our breath begins to come faster and faster. Her taut young breasts heave beneath my exploring hands. We sink sideways, as if we are very heavy, and the stone flags of the balcony are softer than goosedown. Virgin she may be, but she knows how a man is made. Her little hand lingers on my belly, creeps downwards. I am hard as a thigh bone and quivering with eagerness. Her tender fingers delicately explore my length and I groan deep in my throat. My hands, suddenly rough, catch up the hem of her shift and dive beneath it. She is slippery and hot and when I touch her she makes a strange little sound.

I lie her on her back and part her thighs. There is no one to see, not even the moon. I kiss her and she clutches me. A moment, only a moment –

'Fiammetta, cara.' A man's voice within the room. We freeze. Then swift as a snake she thrusts me away and jumps to her feet and calls out, 'Here, Papa.'

I fling myself across the balcony and hide again behind the plant pots. Vallerio Dolfin comes out with a single candle and speaks to her affectionately, a little fatherly chat on his daughter's wedding eve. She lies *to him and the darkness of the night hides her blushes, if she blushes indeed.*

Then her father takes her away. I should howl for frustration, but in fact I crouch behind the climbing roses smiling like a soul in bliss.

She came out to me. She wanted me. She heard my vows.

She loves me.

And now I sat hugging my knees on the rim of the fountain and grinning at Aliusio like an idiot. For ten years I had tormented myself with the thought of Fiammetta sighing in his arms. I knew they were not friends, but who can say what happens behind the chamber door? Whenever I was in the city I had watched her in secret, loving her, desiring her and not daring to offer myself to her. For ten years I had been unmanned by the thought of what I had lost. Even when I had the chance to speak to her all I had managed to ask was whether she was happy – and she hadn't replied. But now, now I knew that in all this time she had never given herself to her husband the way she had to me.

'You're a knowledgeable sort of fellow,' Aliusio was saying. 'Got any tricks I can try to warm her up? Any suggestions?'

'What?' I could hardly believe that he had asked.

'Most women like me,' Aliusio pouted. 'In fact, all the others like me.' They like your purse, you fool, I thought to myself. Your wife's the only one that that doesn't matter to. She's married to it, poor girl. 'Come on,' he said, breathing wine into my face as he clutched my arm. 'Ideas, ideas. Let's make Aliusio an heir.'

I shook my head, standing drunkenly on my dignity. 'I wouldn't dream of speculating on a noblewoman's likes and dislikes,' I said haughtily.

'Likes and dislikes.' He reeled away from me and slipped off the fountain rim to the tiles. His head rested against my knee. 'To the Arsenal with her likes and dislikes. Roger her, stuff her, give her the old sausage.'

I could have told him that women respond to passion, to earnestness and eager desire, not to the size of one's sausage. I could have told him to touch her, as I had, to kiss her, to want her so much that the spark of that wanting leapt from one body to the other as flames will leap canals when the houses are afire. By keeping silent I was condemning Fiammetta to a cold marriage-bed, to the absence of pleasure. But I shook my head and said, 'Stuff away, my friend. That's the only recipe I know.'

Aliusio grunted, then began to snore. I amused myself by trickling drops of water into his nostrils and open mouth, laughing as he sneezed and spluttered and waved his hand in the air. He opened his eyes once and looked up at the glowing stars and muttered, 'Rain?'

Fiammetta's marriage-bed might be cold, but there are other beds. Now I knew that she took no joy in her husband I might be emboldened to offer myself as a palatable alternative. She could not have forgotten the scalding heat of our kisses. And after all, Aliusio had a stable of mistresses, and what's sauce for the gander is sauce for the goose.

Suddenly returning to Venice seemed like returning to Paradise. The sooner the better. I would happily consign Sicily to the flames of Hell, if it would bring me more swiftly to Fiammetta's arms.

TWENTY-SEVEN

Things didn't improve. The next problem was serious enough for Jean-Marie to ask me to come to Mategriffon to back him up. Sensible lad. The commander of the garrison was the Vicar's deputy, the pouched, chilly individual who had threatened me with torture when I came to Messina with my news, and Jean-Marie was a nice sensitive boy.

'Messire.' My backbone was straight as a spear and I was watching my accent. Unfortunately I still looked disreputable, and the commander was the sort of soldier who values a man more if his chain-mail gleams. 'I am here because –'

'Because I chose to ignore what this young soft-arse has been telling me?' demanded Reynauld of Lisieux. Jean-Marie told me that Lisieux is a place in the north of France and that Reynauld was a Norman, a distant kinsman no doubt of the landless swordsmen who had taken Sicily for themselves ten generations back and given Venice several headaches in the process. Apparently Normans still fancied themselves as tough.

Tough often equals stupid. But this grim-faced mercenary was not stupid, just a firm believer in *force majeure* and the superiority of French-speakers over Italian-speakers. I set my teeth and said with diligent courtesy, 'Messire, in the absence of the Venetian Ambassador I –'

'Absence! You mean the white-livered dog has scurried back to Venice with his tail between his legs.'

'Because he took what I told him seriously, messire.'

Reynauld lifted his lip. 'Go on, then. Say your piece.'

'Messire, it is not much to ask that you tell your patrols to keep a light hand. I have noticed a real deterioration in the feelings of the Messinese in the last few days and I strongly recommend that you avoid giving offence whenever possible. I am not suggesting that you stop patrols –'

'I should think not. My men are the only thing that keeps this city quiet.'

'No, messire, you are wrong. The Riso are working their hardest to see that all the people of the city remain loyal to you.'

'The Riso? They've got their eyes on the main chance. If this city stays loyal, it's because there are enough soldiers here to kill every man twice over.'

'There were two thousand soldiers in Palermo,' I said. 'How many do you have?' He scowled at me, but he still didn't look convinced. 'Messire, your Vicar has retained me as your advisor. I am certain that an insurrection is being planned –'

'By whom? The Vicar retained you as a spy. Do your job, spy, and find out who is responsible so that I can take some real action!'

'– and I advise you in the strongest possible terms, messire, that you order your men to avoid –'

I hunted for the French words, soundlessly cursing the interruption to my eloquence. Jean-Marie timidly supplied them. 'Unnecessary provocation.'

'You want them to *ask* people if they have swords up their skirts?' The rough French voice was heavy with scorn. 'Apologise as they search them? I am so very sorry, O dutiful subject, but it is the Vicar's orders. If perchance you might be concealing any weapons about your person –'

'They don't have to be rough,' I insisted. 'Or rude. Or take the opportunity to feel up the women while they do it.'

'They've got their jobs to do. And the women in the South are all whores anyway. Another hand up their holes won't make any difference to them.'

'Listen!' I was fighting my temper. 'I was in Palermo. I saw what happened there. It wasn't planned. It was the fault of some sergeant with the brains of a cowpat groping a peasant girl. He started it! If he'd left her alone nothing would have happened. Not then, unexpectedly.'

'Covering up your own incompetence,' sneered Reynauld. 'I expect you didn't find out who was behind it there, either.'

I was nettled out of what diplomacy I had left. 'You want this place to go up in smoke as well? Are you mad, or just stupid?'

Jean-Marie drew in a quick hissing breath and flinched. He was right to. Reynauld lunged towards me and swiped his hand at my face. I caught his wrist before the blow connected and twisted his arm aside. We stood nose to nose, snarling and bristling. His men moved to grab me, then hesitated in the absence of an order.

Reynauld looked down at my hand. 'Let go of me,' he said icily.

I hung on. He was a big man, stronger than me, but there are grips a dirty fighter learns that are hard to break. 'I'm not one of your men,' I said. 'I'm an advisor to the Vicar and a Venetian citizen. Keep your hands off me.'

He said contemptuously, 'You're a spy,' but he knew I was right. His face writhed into reluctant agreement. I let go of his wrist and stepped back. He rubbed at the place where I had held him. I might have won that fall, but he was even more determined now that I should not win the fight. 'Monsieur, I have heard your advice. It is not practicable. My men are bound to keep the peace in Messina and will use as much force as they think necessary. I will not tie their hands by insisting that they are *courteous* to a pack of potential rebels.' His eyes narrowed. 'I suggest, monsieur, that in future you restrict yourself to providing us with information about likely nests of insurgents, and allow us to deal with them as we think fit.' His lip curled. For him, spies were sneaking cowardly peddlers of information, and soldiers were the heroes.

Certainly I didn't feel like a hero. Two days ago I had passed on details of a tavern where I had heard talk that was overtly rebellious, and yesterday the French had descended on it and burnt it to the ground. Not everyone got out, either. But what could I expect the French to do? Around the island they had lost more than four thousand men to the fury of the Sicilians. No wonder they weren't prepared to give anyone in Messina the benefit of the doubt. Was I asking too much?

I bowed to Reynauld. 'Messire.' Then I turned on my heel and left the room. Anything else would have been flogging a dead horse. Jean-Marie was going to follow me, but Reynauld called him back. I stood outside the closed door and listened to him receiving the verbal equivalent of the flogging of a live man.

When he emerged he was white and shaking. I didn't know whether he was more afraid of Reynauld or the Messinese.

'Sorry,' I said.

He gave a very Gallic shrug. 'We had to try. I still think you're right, Marcello.' He had followed me through the streets a couple of times, watching French patrols from the shadows. He had seen the barely suppressed savagery with which his people treated every Sicilian they encountered.

'I shouldn't have lost my temper.'

He accompanied me through the fetid passageways of the castle to the gatehouse. Every corner, no matter how chill, damp or squalid, was occupied by some man's kit or the man himself, wrapped in a dirty cloak and snoring. The courtyard was packed with horses and hummed with flies. There were men on the wallwalks, going to and fro with crossbows. The portcullis was down and the gates were barred and bolted. You might have believed that the rebellion had already happened.

The gatekeeper let me out through the wicket. Jean-Marie came through with me and we stood before the gates in an uncomfortable silence.

At last he said, 'You think they will rebel.'

'There's a good chance. I'm not certain, but it feels more likely every day. Someone is in charge. Everything feels – purposeful.'

His dim eyes widened. The pupils were black in the bright sunshine. He shook his head and muttered, almost to himself, 'What shall I do?'

'Stay in the castle,' I said.

I wondered as I walked just how long I had to stay to follow Dolfin's orders and redeem myself to the Committee. Until the fleet sailed? Until the French launched a counter-offensive against the rebels? Until the garrison fell to the Messinese? One day was too long, with Fiammetta in Venice, ignorant of my plans for her happiness.

Fiammetta. I thought again of her lifting her face to kiss me, all those years ago. I wasn't mistaken, she had begun it. Otherwise I wouldn't have touched her.

I had better act quickly when I got back to Venice. I wanted to be sure that I undercut anything that Aliusio might do to try to insinuate himself back into his wife's favours. I thought she had better taste, but –

Suddenly my dreams of the most beautiful woman in Venice vanished. I was still and staring, every muscle tense. Ahead of me in the busy street, walking unhurriedly away from me, was Andrea.

My heart pounded. I was dizzy with surprise. Andrea, here! The second thought that I formulated was that this proved everything I had said to Reynauld about organised rebellion. The first was, Praise God! Now I can kill him.

I took two quick deep breaths to calm myself and then plunged after him. I was unarmed, because to wear a weapon would be like painting 'Angevin agent' on my forehead, or possibly the Angevin flag, since so many of the Messinese couldn't read. But never mind that. There are plenty of ways to kill a man with bare hands. If I could only get him alone –

It was him, for certain. He turned a corner about a hundred paces in front of me and I saw his face clearly among the crowds of people. He was wearing a cloak and heavy hood despite the increasing heat, but I would have known him anywhere. He seemed to be without any form of human shadow; no guide or bodyguard. Had I killed Blasio, then, instead of him? Not what I had intended, but acceptable now I had a second chance at Andrea.

I hastened around the corner and found myself in a little street market, dozens of barrows and little ramshackle stalls with tawdry canopies erected against the hot sun and half a hundred individual peasants sitting with their surplus produce at their feet, a scrawny chicken or a handful of early peas or a pair of rabbits or a bunch of greens gathered from the meadows. It was like Babel, noisy with half a dozen tongues and stinking of wilting vegetables, hot bodies and meat that the flies had tested. I dived into the heave of people and was instantly assailed on all sides. Hands grabbed at my arm, at my tunic. 'Signor, a fine pair of quails!' 'Linen for a shirt, signor!' 'Sweet violets!'

The Prince of Darkness could not have found his servant Andrea in that crowd. I cursed and flung off the vendors who were trying to attract my attention. I struggled on for a while, until I reached the next cross street, but it was hopeless.

Now what? I could return to the castle, explain Andrea's significance as an inciter of rebellion and agent of Aragon, give them the best description I could and leave them to it. Or I could look for him myself. I agonised. If the French were hunting him they would make it obvious. He would probably go to ground, and possibly leave Messina altogether. I would lose my vengeance. But if I didn't tell them about him and it came out later, then I would look like a traitor, or at best an incompetent idiot.

The answer is usually a compromise. I went back to the castle and sought out Jean-Marie. The poor youth was struggling in a crowded corner of a busy room with a mass of correspondence from the fleet's victuallers, ably hindered by three punctilious secretaries and a quartermaster. He was one of the more literate of the French garrison and so a lot of tedious administration came his way. No wonder he was pleased to help me with the intelligence work. His face lit up when I appeared.

His expression changed when I got him into a quiet corridor

and told him why I was there. '*Nom de Dieu*,' he whispered. Knowing me seemed to be increasing his tendency to blaspheme, Our Lord knows why. 'Is this man dangerous?'

'Not physically. But personally he is, very dangerous. He's a rabble-rouser, and he can think. If something is being planned, he'll be behind it.'

Jean-Marie's white face contracted in a spasm of reluctance. 'Marcello, *mon ami*, I'm sorry, but I'm going to have to tell old Eyebags about this. I know you don't want me to, but I really don't have any choice. I mean, do I?'

'At least,' I suggested, 'tell him I only thought I saw the man. Tell him I'm working on it.'

'I'll tell him. But he doesn't trust you, you know. He'll probably want you to give a description so we can take direct action.' Jean-Marie shook his head, then looked up at me. 'I tell you what, Marcello. I'm going to take your advice. I'm staying in the castle.'

'Good idea.' I looked about at the dark strength of the stone. 'How long can this place hold out?'

'Long enough for help to come from Naples.'

'Let's hope so.'

'Marcello.' His voice sounded odd and I frowned at him. 'Marcello, why don't you and Aliusio come up here? Move into the castle? It's safer, you know it. You could bring your men.'

I prevaricated, feeling like a worm. I didn't want to tell Jean-Marie that if – when? – the Messinese rebelled I intended to get out of the city and on to a boat back to Venice as soon as humanly possible. I came up with some specious excuse that seemed to satisfy him. In a lot of ways he was still charmingly innocent.

I bet he's still a virgin, I thought to myself as I returned to the Residency. I had recently discovered Jean-Marie's age, twenty-two, and it seemed quite likely to me that such a bookish boy would have managed to avoid the company of women so far. If everything turned out well and we avoided disaster in Messina, perhaps I would find the time to take him under my wing before Venice beckoned. There were a couple of handsome brothels in the lower city that would do his business. I could afford to subsidise him, since I had most of his pay in my purse.

With this sort of thought in my mind it's not surprising that when I entered the Residency courtyard and saw Agnesina kneeling over the fountain I reacted as I did. It was a typical warm day for late April in Sicily, almost as hot as Venice ever gets and with such an accursed humid wind that even on a mountain top a man would sweat. Agnesina had been sweeping the brick-laid courtyard, her twig broom was propped against a wall, and now she was stooping down to splash the cold water over her throat. Her cheap gown was open to let the coolness run down to her breasts and her peach-like arse was sticking up in the air. A big, ripe, juicy peach. Any red-blooded man would have done what I did, which was to run my hand appreciatively over her luxurious curves and pinch her so that she squealed.

She rocked upright, fist raised for a punishing blow. I never met a less aptly named girl. She was more like a lean, feisty she-pig than a little woolly lamb. When she saw me she held her hand, but her face became scornful. 'Oh, it's you. Promising what you can't deliver again?'

My thoughts of Fiammetta and the brothel and the feel of Agnesina's ample, yielding backside had concentrated my attention. 'Try me.'

I'm so persuasive I surprise myself. She did try me, and this time I didn't disappoint her. Having her was like eating a meal with plenty of garlic and a red wine that scalds the roof of your mouth. It was her succulent backside that interested me, not her rather ordinary face, and I made her kneel on all fours like a beast, but she didn't complain, the little trollop. For once I didn't take any precautions either. I knew for a fact that Aliusio had had her and I believed that one or two of the others had as well. Even if she kindled, I couldn't be held responsible. The sense of relief as I spilled myself inside her was immeasurable.

Afterwards I watched her adjusting her grubby petticoats and fussing with her haystack of black hair. She hadn't asked me for any money yet, but she would. I don't know why, but I thought suddenly of the old woman I had met outside the Residency with teeth like spinach and how she had spat when she talked about Venetians.

'Agnesina,' I said, 'what do the Messinese think of us? Of Venice?'

She laughed. 'They think you're nearly as bad as the French.'

For a moment I was quiet as she hoiked her little round tits back into her gown and started on the laces. Then I said, 'Do we pay you well?'

'Why d'you think I'm here?'

'How much?'

She told me. It was criminally small, but she thought it was generous, so why pay more? Venice didn't become the greatest Republic in the world through charity to trollops. I multiplied the rate by fifty and reached for my purse. 'Look,' I said, holding out the gold and silver coins on the palm of my hand. 'See this?'

Her eyes stretched wide, wide open and her face slackened with simple greed. 'What would you do for this?' I asked her.

Expressions fleeted over her face. Confusion, disbelief, suspicion, surmise, revulsion, and at last reluctant willingness. She ran her tongue around her lips as if she were thirsty. 'It depends,' she said at last. 'What d'you want?'

I extended my palm further. Her eyes fixed on the glint of gold. 'Simple. I want you to leave this house tonight. Tell your friends that Venetians are all cocksucking bastards and you wouldn't go near one again if he was the last man in the world.'

'What?'

'Repeat after me. Venetians – are – all –'

She learnt the lesson fast. I am sure she thought I was quite, quite mad, or perverted in a way previously unknown to her. But she left happy, and after she had gone I laid down my head and slept at once, and for the first time since I fled Palermo I had no dreams at all.

TWENTY-EIGHT

I had almost forgotten what it felt like to wake up relaxed and comfortable, both in body and mind. I felt proud of what I had done for Agnesina. No slavering Messinese mob would call her a Venetian's whore and kill her as Caterina had been killed.

It was a still, clear dawn, pale and shimmering with the promise of more heat. I went unhurriedly down to the courtyard and told one of the men to bring me a couple of melons and watered wine. Then I sat on the edge of the marble fountain and enjoyed the delicacy of the light falling through the spray. The bells of the church along the street were ringing for Matins, and the sound hung in the air as if it clung to the sparkling drops of water.

Presently my breakfast appeared. Shortly afterwards so did Aliusio, frowsty and scowling. He had pulled on a linen shirt and nothing else and he stood yawning on the cold tiles, dozily scratching his bare bum.

'A hard night?' I asked him.

'Go to the Devil,' he said sullenly. 'What's this about Agnesina? I wanted her last night. Couldn't get to sleep.'

'She left,' I told him blandly. 'I think something I said upset her.'

'Upset her? One of the lads heard her out in the street shouting at the door that all Venetians were —'

I mouthed, 'Cocksucking bastards,' as he spoke. He didn't seem to think it was funny. 'What the Devil are you about?' he demanded. 'She had the nicest arse on her I've seen in years.'

'Calm down.' I poured another cup of weak, cool wine. 'Have a melon.'

He snarled at me. The scar on his cheek writhed as if it had a life of its own. Then he gave in and sat down on the fountain rim. The melon juice dripped onto his shirt. 'I could get to like this place,' he said, as he spat out the seeds.

'Don't. The chances are we'll have to leave it in a hurry.'

'You're such a pessimistic hound. It's nearly four weeks since Palermo rebelled. Don't you think the Messinese would have done it already if they meant to?'

I had no intention of telling him about Andrea. Instead, to distract myself, I carved into another melon with my dagger. I cut a face on it, with rolling eyes and jagged teeth, the way children do. I showed it to Aliusio and he laughed. Sometimes he was almost bearable.

We were still lingering over breakfast an hour later. I knew I should get up and go and look for Andrea, but it was getting hotter and hotter and the longer I waited the more reluctant I became. Aliusio fell asleep again, sprawled on the tiles with his head propped against the rim of the fountain. His face was in full sun. I considerately laid a melon rind over it to stop him from burning.

He woke up when someone hammered on the Residency door. He clutched at the melon rind and cursed when he realised what it was. 'Do you think that's funny?'

'Frankly, yes.' His face was sticky with melon juice. He was trying to stand on his dignity as well, which made it worse. Saint Jerome would have laughed at him.

He jumped at me with the intention of pushing me into the fountain. His technique, such as it was, was negligible. I ducked lazily and turned my shoulder to him and he flew over my head and landed in a shower of spray and small fish. 'You dog –'

Things were just getting interesting when one of the men showed Jean-Marie into the courtyard. 'Morning!' I saluted him. 'Aliusio fancied a dip. How about you? You look hot. What's brought you out of the castle?'

He did look hot, flushed and anxious. 'No time,' he stammered. 'Marcello, I was right. Reynauld wants to talk to you. He wants a description of this, this Andrea person. Right away.'

'Andrea?' Aliusio clambered out of the fountain and squelched on the tiles. He stripped off his dripping shirt and used it as a flannel. He had a much better body than he deserved, but I was relieved to see that his luxurious life was beginning to evidence itself in a certain slackness around his midriff. 'I remember that name,' he commented acutely.

'I was going to try to find him myself this morning,' I said, feeling guilty. 'Jean-Marie, can't you give me some time?'

He shook his head. 'I've already got into plenty of trouble over you, Marcello. You'd better come with me straight away. My orders were to drag you if you wouldn't come by yourself.'

'This I have to see,' said Aliusio. 'Jean-Marie, *mon ami*, don't stir a step without me.' He dashed off towards his room.

'Let's go,' I said urgently. But Jean-Marie's orders had apparently included Aliusio as well, so we had to wait for him.

I did look more than a little like a prisoner as we set off for Mategriffon. Jean-Marie had cautiously brought more than a dozen soldiers with him, fully armed in long coats of mail and kettle helmets and carrying eight-foot spears with wicked leaf-shaped blades. Aliusio, who wasn't remotely concerned about appearing connected with the French, was wearing a bright yellow silk tunic, a matching hat, his sword and, of course, his red boots. I looked rough and more than a little shady, unshaven and clad in someone's castoffs, and because I intended to go through Messina afterwards incognito I wore no sword. The soldiers surrounded the three of us, and Jean-Marie was preoccupied and said nothing.

The streets seemed oddly quiet. A few curtains twitched in the doorways we passed and skinny cats ran away from under our feet, but the normal tumble of children and babies and women with washing was absent. I doubt that Aliusio even noticed the quiet, and it didn't seem to bother the French, but it bothered me. If men have ordered their womenfolk to keep within doors there's usually a reason. There weren't even any old people sitting in the doorways to enjoy the sun. Normally the sunny side of the street is thickly populated with them, one in every doorway, dressed in black and as motionless as Egyptian corpses put out to dry.

We were more than halfway to the castle when my eyes lighted on a group of men standing in a shady alley mouth a little ahead of us. The street was narrow and we would be passing close by them. At first what caught my attention was that although it was rapidly becoming hot they all wore cloaks wound tightly around them. I thought they were Sicilians, but the cloaks made it hard to tell. Then I saw that they were first looking at me, then muttering together, then running their eyes over the French soldiers with rapid, deliberate appraisal.

We came closer. One of them seemed to reach a decision. He shook his head, and the party left their alley, walked down the street ahead of us a little way, and then turned a corner out of our path.

Street corners in hilly seaside towns are often breezy. This one was. As they went away from us a quick hot wind whipped past them, pulling their cloaks into swirls of darkness and briefly revealing what lay beneath before they caught them back and tugged them down.

I walked on, but turned my head to watch them. They were standing on the side street, looking at the French soldiers passing them.

You could not mistake the hatred in their faces. And I knew I could not mistake what I had seen.

It could mean only one thing. I caught at Jean-Marie's arm and he stared at me, startled out of his anxious abstraction. 'Those men,' I said urgently, 'the ones who went down the street back there. Jean-Marie, they were armed. Not daggers, even. Swords.'

'What?' Jean-Marie stopped dead. Aliusio cannoned into him and cursed. The soldiers walked on a pace or two, realised their young officer was not with them and hurried back to form a cordon round him. The elderly sergeant who led them shook his head at Jean-Marie with condescending tolerance. 'What's the matter, sir?'

Jean-Marie's stare was fixed on my face. He seemed to be finding it hard to speak. 'Swords?' he said at last. His big eyes begged me to say that I had been joking.

'Swords. It looked as if they thought I was a prisoner. They were wondering about freeing me, but they decided against it.'

'Sir —' said the sergeant with exaggerated patience.

'It's today, isn't it,' Jean-Marie whispered. His lips were whiter than the dust of the street and he gave a convulsive shiver. 'Or why would they have thought that they might attack us? It's now. *Jesu me protége*, what shall I do? Should we run after them?'

I shook my head. I could imagine it. There had only been half a dozen in that group, so we outnumbered them more than two to one. But every bystander, every man in the street was their ally. No one was ours. Potentially we were fifteen men against the whole of Messina.

This was worse than Palermo. At least in Palermo I had appeared to be on the right side.

'Look,' I said. 'Jean-Marie, get back up to Mategriffon. Go as fast as you can. If you know of any Frenchmen outside the castle, get them in. Are there any?'

'Yes.' He looked as though he were about to burst into tears. 'There's the patrols — and some of the men moved back out again because it was so hellfire hot in the castle —'

'Get them in. Tell the commander, tell the Vicar.' He didn't move. He just stared at me like a baby rabbit before a weasel. '*Tu comprends?*'

I'd never called him *tu* before. He started as if I had slapped him, then pulled himself together. 'Yes. I understand. What about you?'

I caught hold of Aliusio's arm. 'They won't be looking for us. We –' My brain whirled. 'We have to get our men. We'll join you later.' As an afterthought I added, 'I'd appreciate a sword, if one of your men can spare one.'

He nodded quickly and snapped an order. One of the spearmen reluctantly unbuckled his swordbelt and passed it to me. I said, 'Thank you.'

'All right,' Jean-Marie said. He hesitated, but all he said was, 'Take care.' Then he said to the sergeant, 'Come on, to the castle, run!' and vanished away up the street with his men. I wished I had shaken his hand, or at least wished him luck. It seemed very unlikely that I would see him again.

'What in the name of the Devil is going on?' demanded Aliusio, five paces behind as usual.

'Aliusio, listen to me.' I buckled the swordbelt around me, then took hold of his arms and looked most earnestly into his face. 'Those men were armed. That means the rebellion is going to start.'

'What, now?' He looked almost affronted, as if they should have asked his permission first.

It wasn't funny. I concentrated on preventing my hands from shaking. If I trembled Aliusio would notice, and I would have hated him to think that I was afraid. I was almost envious of his stupidity because of the way it cocooned him from fear. 'We're going,' I said.

'Going where?'

'Back to Venice. We're leaving Sicily.'

'But the French –'

'Will you listen?' I shook him, hard. 'The French are in the castle. They'll stay there until King Charles sends a relief or the Messinese burn it around their ears. Do you want to rot in there with them? We've done what we can and now we're going home!'

He folded his lips and glared at me, but he didn't say anything else. 'Get back to the Residency,' I told him. 'Get the men together. Then –'

'I don't have to take your orders,' he burst out. 'Who put you in command? *I'm* in charge! I say we should go up to the castle and help the French. They –'

'If you don't swear to do as I say,' I said furiously, 'I'll drag you back to the Residency.'

'Just try it!'

He reached for his sword. I caught his hand on the hilt and twisted his wrist till he let go, then wrenched his arm up behind his back. It was shockingly easy. He staggered in front of me, astonished to find himself helpless. 'Swear,' I gritted, 'or I'll drag you back there and let the men laugh at you.'

'All right!' He tried to pull away and I jerked his arm up higher, making him curse with pain. 'All right, I swear. By the bones of Saint Mark.'

That's an oath no Venetian would break. I let him go and he stared furiously at me. I ignored his expression. 'Get the men together,' I told him. 'Go to the harbour. Get a boat. *Buy* a boat. Get the men into it and wait for me.'

'Wait for you? Where are you going?'

'There may be something I can do.'

Then we both stood still, suddenly tense. Distantly, faintly, on the slight hot breeze, we heard men shouting, screams, the clash of weapons.

Aliusio gaped, then whispered, 'It's happening.' His eyes were wide. Till that minute I don't think he'd believed me. All his reluctance to obey me vanished instantly.

'Get to the Residency fast,' I said. 'If anyone asks you who you are, say you're Genoese, Greek, Aragonese, anything except Venetian. Wait for me at the harbour.'

'How long shall I wait?'

I hesitated. 'Till Vespers.' That would have to be time enough.

He nodded and plunged away down the hill. I stood for a moment, shivering uncontrollably. Every instinct in my body told me to run away from the sound of carnage. But where rebellion was, Andrea would be.

I checked the sword at my hip. It was a southern-type falchion, slightly curved with a one-edged blade. It was a trifle heavier than I was used to, but it would do. I closed my eyes briefly, then began to run towards the centre of the town.

The rebellion had started in the central piazza. That looked like planning to me. I stood breathing hard, looking at what the Messinese had left of the French patrol that had had the ill fortune to be in the piazza at the time. It was horribly familiar – the bloody dust, the pile of wantonly mangled corpses. It was like the worst sort of dream, where the thing you dread happens over and over again and you know that it's coming and can do nothing to stop it.

A trail of debris, including a few scattered bodies and bits of bodies, led from the piazza towards the castle. Some of the Frenchmen I passed were still breathing, but stopping to help them would have been a death warrant. I ran on, following the scarlet footprints of the mob.

Soon I could see the stragglers not far ahead of me. I turned and pelted through side streets, avoiding the crowds, making good time. The sounds of the progress of the rebels reached me over the rooftops. At one point they must have come upon some more Frenchmen, because the air was split with yells of pain and fury so piercing that they briefly stopped me in my tracks. I shut my eyes, breathing fast. Then I grabbed the eaves of one of the smaller houses and leapt, swinging myself up onto the flat roof.

That was the way to see into the crowd. I ran along the roofs, dropping to a crouch when anyone glanced my way, leaping the narrow streets between one house and the next.

It was not exactly like the Palermo revolt. There were no women in this crowd, only men, and they moved in a quiet, purposeful way that was both more and less frightening than the turbulent viciousness of the Vespers. There were fewer of them, too, perhaps no more than a thousand men packed into the hot streets. But they were all armed, swords and spears, even some shields. They meant business.

My head went back with a jerk as I saw Andrea. He was in the second or third rank, just behind a man whose servant was carrying the Messinese flag. The leader of the revolt, obviously. I put on a burst of speed and overtook them sufficiently to see the man's face.

I knew his name. Bartolomeo Maniscalco, a minor nobleman, one who had often in recent days backed up the Riso with pleas of loyalty to Charles of Anjou. A traitorous dog, but who expects anything else? And he had had Andrea to help him.

How in the Devil's name would I get Andrea out from among that crowd? I ran along parallel to them for several hundred yards, cursing.

Then I saw my chance. The rebels began to pick up speed, yelling and howling. They had spotted another French patrol ahead of them, this time trying to shepherd a clutch of off-duty soldiers and their women and children up to the safety of Mategriffon. With their quarry in sight rebel discipline began to evaporate. Men pressed from behind past Bartolomeo and their standard, waving their weapons in the air, as eager as hounds within sight of the kill.

A little square was opening up before them. The French were running, screaming, men and women. If the Sicilians caught them they didn't stand a chance. I couldn't make them my concern. My eyes were fixed on the sleek grey head of Andrea, surrounded now by whirling figures as men dashed past him. He was too far away for me to be certain of him with my knife, and in any case such a remote death would be insufficiently personal for vengeance. At the next cross street I marked where he was, then hung by my hands and dropped.

I forced my way through the mob. My head whirled with memories, but they didn't hold me back. I knew what I would do. When I saw the back of Andrea's head before me I lifted my dagger and caught him a glancing blow behind the ear with the pommel, not hard enough to stun but hard enough to topple him. He gasped and staggered. Nobody had seen me hit him, and now I plunged forward and caught him under the arms and tugged him against the tide of bloodthirsty men to one of the side streets. A curious face loomed before me. 'He fell,' I said in Sicilian, and the face withdrew.

With the lure of Frenchmen to kill nobody paid any attention. I dragged Andrea into the side street. It was a dead end, full of heaps of garbage, hot with sun and noisy with flies. Only one window opened onto it, and underneath it was a fetid little heap where a chamberpot was emptied every morning. It was very suitable.

As Andrea began to recover and struggle I flung him away from me. He hit a wall, hard, and slid a little way down it. Then his black lizard's eyes opened.

At once he yelled for help. But as he opened his mouth, just at the moment when he cried out, the Sicilians came upon the Frenchmen in the piazza.

It sounded like the harrowing of Hell. Men cried and cursed and women shrieked and above all the noise the terrified wailing of children and infants cut through the air. Nobody could hear Andrea if he burst his lungs.

I expected him to run and let me skewer him like a quail. But to my surprise he dragged himself to his feet and pulled out his sword. It was like seeing a shrew turn on the pouncing cat and spit. I laughed. 'Come on, then,' I challenged him. 'Come on, you cocksucking, boy-buggering bastard. No Blasio now.'

Like a cat, I played with him. The sound of the massacre beat in my brain and filmed my eyes with red. I dodged his frantic slashes, not even bothering to lift my sword, just letting him struggle and tire. At last he screeched and rushed at me and as I stepped aside he skidded on something and crashed to the ground, half stunned and smeared with shit and filth.

He reached out for his fallen sword and I stamped on his wrist. He twisted his head to look up at me. Even now, with his face white and sweating and his whole body shaking, even now those black eyes showed no emotion at all.

'This is for Caterina,' I said, and brought the heavy falchion down on his neck.

The sun burned brighter as I ran through the maze of streets, down and down towards the harbour. I felt as if my feet trod the air. We would be gone soon, away from this God-cursed island, back to Venice and safety and the promise of a happiness so great that I hardly dared even think of it. I don't think I even remembered to hope that Jean-Marie reached the castle safely. When I thought coherently at all it was just to wish that Aliusio had had the sense for once to do what he had been told.

The street I ran down curved and suddenly opened up to give a view of the harbour, not far away now. I stopped as if I had run into an invisible wall.

The vessels of the Angevin fleet filled the harbour and extended away into the Strait as far as the eye could see. It was like a forest of masts. And like a forest after late summer lightning, it was burning.

From the ships tied up at the harbour wall rose dark columns of smoke. Beneath the smoke were flames, licking upwards like bright snakes coiling around the masts and yards. There were men on the harbour wall running to and fro in panic and men jumping from the ships into the sea. Every vessel still had a skeleton crew on board. I stared, panting. As I watched half a dozen little fast boats skidded away from the fishing fleet, almost leaping from the water with the strength of their rowers. In each one stood two or three men, balancing effortlessly against the bucketing motion, holding torches in their hands, hurrying to spread destruction.

'Lord have mercy,' I whispered, then began to run again. My exhilaration had gone and exhaustion was taking its place. With the fleet afire how would we get away? Would Aliusio be there when I got to the sea, or would he have done what any sensible man would do and fled when the first ship burst into flame?

The breeze was blowing onto the shore. Before I reached the harbour front I was half choked with smoke, thick white woodsmoke contaminated with brief puffs of burning pitch. My eyelashes filled with ash. I flung up my arm to shield my face and staggered on.

I could hardly believe it when as soon as I appeared on the harbour front one of Aliusio's men ran up to me. 'Over here,' he called, 'over here, fast! Come on!'

I was almost past running. He caught my arm and steered me towards the fishing fleet, away from the fire. The men of war in the harbourside berths were burning like torches now. As I lurched across the cobbles a mainmast toppled, dragging down smouldering ropes. It fell across the harbourway and onto the roof of a tavern opposite and flames licked out across the tiles. People ran out of the building yelling for water, for blankets to put out the fire. They might as well have tried to fight the Apocalypse. A burning sail lifted from the next ship under its own hideous volition and flew upwards, twisting and crackling in agony before dropping back in a smudge of smoke. It landed on the harbour front, blocking all movement. A hideous shriek revealed that someone was underneath it.

'Quick.' I was handed down the harbour steps. There were a couple of dead Sicilians there. Aliusio's men reached out for me. Their bloodied swords were laid beside them and some of them were wounded. They had got a good boat, a sleek fast cutter with four pairs of oars as well as her big lateen sail, easily big enough for nine men and their baggage. Someone had even thought to raise a Messinese flag from its bows. Aliusio was at the tiller, pale and filthy and looking more competent than I'd ever seen him.

'Shove off,' he said tersely. Someone obeyed him and we were under way.

I wanted to collapse into the bottom of the boat and forget everything, but I had work to do. The sail filled, but the wind was contrary and wildly distorted by the massive gouts of flame streaking up from the Angevin ships. It was easy to imagine that we would be sucked towards them, caught up in that inferno and roasted like damned souls. Aliusio snapped, 'Oars,' and we scrambled to obey him.

One to an oar, we bent our backs. Someone gave the stroke, and all Venetians know how to row. The boat shuddered and answered, pulling away from the fishing boats and out towards the harbour. Not open water, but serried ranks of ships from which hideous palls of smoke were now starting to rise. I raised my head and saw disbelief and horror in Aliusio's face. He was the steersman, only he could see where we were bound. I had to trust him. I felt sick.

Now wherever there were no ships the water was crammed with burning floating wreckage and the bobbing heads of the ships' crews, where they had escaped the fire and could swim. The Sicilian fire-boats were out beyond the mole, carrying devastation to the vessels berthed in the outer anchorages. Ships aflame burned through their anchor-ropes and floated free, cannoning into their neighbours, spreading fire fast and fatal as the plague.

It was the death of the whole fleet. I love ships, and I was glad that I was at an oar and did not have to watch as one by one the Angevin navy charred and sank. We heard the galleys burn, the stacked oars crackling like kindling and the benches snapping into ash.

And there was worse to come. As we passed a munitions ship one of the panic-stricken French wretches we beat away from our gunwales to drown wailed, 'Greek fire, Greek fire!' and we dropped on our oars and covered our heads with our hands in mindless terror as a massive tongue of flame shrieked upwards into the smoke-blackened sky, enveloping three ships and flooding the sea with floating, liquid fire that burned even more furiously when it touched the water. A blanket of it slithered towards us, smothering the screaming Frenchman and extending blazing fingers towards our boat. 'Row!' Aliusio yelled, his voice hoarse with smoke and fear. 'Row or burn!'

We rowed, but not fast enough. The fire was overhauling us. The wind was still uncertain, but it was our last chance. 'Aliusio!' I shouted. 'The sail!'

Aliusio crossed himself and shook out the sail. The same wind that propelled the sheet of flame towards us filled it and pulled us onwards, out of range of the fire and into the open sea.

We rested on our oars then, staring back at the ruin of Angevin power. It was a kingdom that was burning, every penny that the French had screwed from the island of Sicily since King Charles took it. Everything Charles possessed was staked in that fleet, and all of it was ascending to heaven now on a plume of thick smoke, a sacrifice, an immolation of his vast pride.

'Hubris,' I said. I had a classical education. Aliusio and his men stared at me as if I was mad, and for their benefit I translated. 'Pride demands punishment.'

A great galley slipped below the sea, leaving nothing but charred smoking spars. Aliusio watched it vanish, then said very softly, 'Amen.'

TWENTY-NINE

We changed ship in Brindisi, and as a result we had a night to spend there. I could spend it with Aliusio and the rest of the Venetians, or I could find some other amusement. There was no contest, especially where the other amusement was Maria.

Maria was a Venetian lady of patrician family, married by some whim of her father's to one of King Charles's vassals, Nicoletto di Spada, a noble of Brindisi. Nicoletto was a real aristocrat of the old Southern school, interested in hunting and hawking and the life of a courtier. He wasn't particularly interested in his wife, whom he considered tainted by the mercantile nature of her family. He spent a lot of time with King Charles at the court in Naples, leaving Maria in Brindisi. I don't know if he expected her to take his negligence lying down, if that's not an unfortunate phrase. If he did, he underestimated Venetian ingenuity – Maria's, and mine.

Looking at the list of my amours it would be easy to conclude that I prefer maidservants, market girls and tavern servers to ladies. I don't, but I can see how I might give that impression. There is a reason for this, beyond the fact that working girls are abundant. I like to stay alive. Noblemen everywhere are quick to avenge an affront, and for most of them an insult to their marital honour demands murderous retribution. Add to that the fact that most noble ladies are surrounded by servants, half of whom are spies of their husbands, and you'll understand why I rarely find my way into the big soft feather beds of the aristocracy.

When I first met Maria my native caution would have kept me from her bed too, but she lied to me on our first encounter. She told me she was a widow. By the time I found out the truth it was too late, and what's done can't be undone.

Now I was anxious to see her again, if it was possible. I would enjoy it: and it would be excellent practice for my return to

234

Venice, where I intended to present myself to Fiammetta, in secret, as soon as I could.

Brindisi is a bustling port with a rather military reputation. Lots of Crusaders have set off for Palestine from there, including King Charles's predecessor the Emperor Frederick. The main port on this side of the Italian peninsula used to be Bari, but Bari foolishly rebelled against the Norman kings. They destroyed the port and town, realised that they no longer had a working harbour, and turned to Brindisi instead.

It was coming on towards evening, and my long shadow streamed away behind me as I walked briskly westwards through the cobbled streets towards Nicoletto's mansion. It was a little way from the centre of the town, on a fine square with a fountain in the middle which the townspeople swear was erected by Tancred on his way to the first Crusade. I've always felt that a land-grabbing lout of a soldier like Tancred was unlikely to have gone around erecting fountains, but it doesn't do to say so in Brindisi.

I walked straight past the mansion's tall gateway, whistling shrilly. The whistle was important. It was a gondoliers' chanty, a song of the Lagoon. She had first noticed me because of that tune. Beneath the window of the women's quarters that opened onto the square I stopped as if there was a stone in my shoe and leant against the wall to extract it, still whistling. When the long-drawn-out operation was finished I drew my dagger and made a business of paring my nails, like any wastrel looking for an excuse to enjoy the evening sunlight.

Before I had finished my left thumbnail something fell from the round-arched windows above me to the dusty ground by my feet. It was a piece of folded paper. I ignored it until I had completed my toilet, then caught it against the side of my foot and tossed it up to my waiting hand.

No need for code. The message was written in Venetian dialect. It said, 'Wait in the usual place after dusk. I'll drop you a rope. Be careful, Nicoletto is here.'

There was no signature, but I knew who it was from. Few women can write, noble or otherwise. In this respect, as in many others, Venetian women are rarities.

I smiled and crumpled the note, then strolled off. There was time for me to visit the baths before I presented myself again.

★　★　★

As the last light left the sky I walked through the square and down the little street at the left hand side of the mansion. This side of the building was a continuation of the women's quarters, and the third window along served the little cubby-hole, really no more than the corner of a corridor, occupied by Maria's maidservants.

I took up position in a doorway opposite the window and waited as the dark grew denser. I didn't count the time, though to an eager lover three heartbeats is infinity. Venus hung glittering in the dense blue sky.

Before the brilliant planet had set there was movement at the window and a glimmer of light. I darted forward as a rope flopped down the side of the building, grabbed it and jerked it hard to test it. It held. I began to climb, hands on the rope and feet on the wall, as quick and quiet as a monkey. At the top I caught hold of the window sill in both hands and hung a moment, breathing fast. It wasn't from the climb. At this stage I couldn't help wondering whether it would be Maria's maid waiting for me, or Nicoletto's men, swords drawn.

I took a deep breath and heaved myself up, my knee on the sill. All was well. The light was a candle, shielded behind the hand of a middle-aged woman in a dark dress with a white scarf over her hair. I knew her face, it was Maria's Venetian maid, her confidante. 'Salve,' I whispered with a grin, the gondoliers' ancient greeting.

She scowled at me and put her finger to her lips, then turned and led me out of the little enclosure. In noble houses the rooms open one into another. We walked straight into the anteroom to Maria's private chamber. Against one wall of the room was a tall linen press for the lady's clothes. The maid pulled the door open and jerked her head. I knew the drill, and I scrambled quickly in.

The door closed on me. I heard the maid's voice, talking the local dialect now. 'You girls, are you finished in there? My lady has a headache. Leave her. I'll put her to bed.'

Female voices passed me, Maria's other servants, heading off to their rest in the cubby-hole. I stayed very still. It was these girls, the local girls, who would be her husband's spies.

When they had gone there were a few moments' stillness. Then the door opened softly and the maid stood there, smiling now. She extended her hand to the door of Maria's chamber. Golden light flooded through it. I returned her smile, offered her a deep, ceremonial bow and a small handful of purely token silver, went through the door and closed it behind me.

The big room was lit by a fire and the glow of a dozen beeswax candles. The air was heavy with the scent of the wax and another, richer smell. The walls were hung with fine tapestries, and on a low dais in the centre of the room was the great bed, eight feet long, six feet wide, heaped with pillows for comfort and dark smooth furs to warm its lady's white body. The bed was empty, but before the fire there was a stool and a tall stand for embroidery, and there Maria sat, her back to me, industriously stitching. She did not turn to look at me as I came in.

I walked slowly towards her, feasting my senses, savouring every moment. The beautiful room, the heat of the fire, the distant sound of music filtering up from her husband's hall; and Maria herself, dressed for her leisure in a gown of ivory-coloured silk over her white shift, her long dark tresses plaited and bound with gold and scarlet bands, one thick shining cable of hair reaching down her back to her waist.

The dressing of her hair revealed her pretty ears, hung with heavy Byzantine earrings of gold and emerald and pearl, and the nape of her white neck. I stood behind her and breathed in luxuriously. She had her perfumes sent from Venice, and she exuded a fragrance of tuberoses and cinnabar, sharpened with tones of citrus. Slowly I stooped forward, brushed aside one dangling earring and placed my lips just behind her ear.

She stood up, turning into my arms. She was not smiling, she was concentrating on her pleasure. I tilted up her face to mine and kissed her mouth.

The music below us grew louder. Maria arched one plucked eyebrow. 'The message about my headache,' she said ironically. 'My husband takes such care of me.'

There was a wry twist to her mouth. She was past youth, and the expression showed it. I replied, 'All the safer for us,' and her face softened into a smile. I kissed her again, then moved my lips down her white throat.

She gave a long sigh as I unfastened the ties of her heavy silk robe. It rustled into a heap at her feet. Around her neck was a necklace matching the earrings, a complex web of gold chains and pendants, heavy enough to press the linen of her shift into tight folds over her bosom. I was tempted to strip her and have her there, on the sheepskins before the fire, but the temptation of the bed was greater. I caught her hand and drew her after me across the room and threw back the covers.

The sheets were Egyptian linen, decorated with drawn-thread

work and scented with lavender. I unfastened the neck of Maria's shift, which was embroidered with sprays of violets and roses, then stooped to lift the hem. As her body was revealed I kissed it.

When she was naked I guided her into the bed. She lay with her hands behind her head, flaunting her breasts at me, and said softly, 'Take off your clothes. Let me see you.'

I didn't hurry. Anticipation enhances satisfaction. As I undressed she began to breathe quickly, and when I at last untied the waist of my braies and let them fall she set her teeth. Her hands clenched among the silk-covered pillows. 'Before God,' she whispered, 'I could eat you!'

Smiling, I joined her on the bed. The feather mattresses were softer than wisps of cloud, and the sheets were as smooth and cool as polished alabaster. 'Why not? It'll keep you quiet.'

Her red tongue flickered out like a snake's, moistening her already wet lips. Then she reached out for me and began to kiss and lick her way down my body. I reciprocated. We must have looked like some fabulous creature from the land of Prester John, with legs at both ends.

When our first eagerness was slaked we lay together beneath the midnight softness of her otterskin bedspread. Maria pillowed her head on her arm and toyed with a curl of my hair. 'Well, Marcello, I have not seen you for so long, I thought you had forgotten me. Where have you been?'

I wondered whether to tell her. Why not? 'Recently, Sicily.'

'Sicily!' She had eyes the colour of hazelnuts and bristly, dark lashes. 'But there's been a rebellion there. Against Charles of Anjou!' You could tell she was a Venetian. Anyone else in Brindisi would have said 'the King' and crossed themselves.

'That's right,' I said.

'That news flew to Venice faster than a falcon,' she said, tugging at the curl she held and running her eyes hungrily over me. 'I heard from my father only a couple of days ago. They're all at loggerheads in the Council, trying to decide what to do about the expedition against the Emperor Michael. My father says it won't happen at all. Venice can't attack Byzantium without King Charles, and he'll have his hands tied for months. Where is he going to get another fleet from?'

My guts wrenched with apprehension. I knew that Maria's father was right, but I'd been trying not to think about it. Where were Venice's Aegean possessions now? The Chairman had told me that Charles's fleet must sail, and I had watched it burn.

Worse than that, I had laid out a great deal of the Republic's gold in a lost cause. The Chairman might forgive me, but the accountants never would. If I wanted to preserve my career as an agent, I was going to have a good deal of fast talking to do on my return to Venice.

Maria didn't seem to notice my abstraction. Her interest in politics paled next to her interest in pleasure, and she had other, more pressing questions in mind. She ran her hand down my body, looking up into my face. 'Tell me about the Sicilian women, Marcello.'

Maria was insatiably curious about my other women. Not jealous, just curious, and often I indulged her. Where was the harm in it? But I didn't want to tell her about Caterina. It would have seemed like a betrayal. Those memories were locked in my private place, quiet and secure, a fountain sealed.

'There was a girl at the Venetian ambassador's house,' I said. 'A little slut, but a bottom like a peach. Guess what I did to her.'

Maria sat up in the bed, flinging back the coverlet to show its scarlet lining. She linked her hands above her head, stretched languorously and smiled at me. 'No,' she said, arching her back. 'Show me what you did to her.'

In the dusk of the dawn I scrambled back down Maria's rope and staggered yawning towards the harbour. I felt fit to sleep all the way back to Venice.

But my route took me past the Duomo, and as I approached it I heard the brothers inside singing Matins. Something made me stop and listen. The music rose and fell, a dark, powerful stream of sound, and I remembered Maria's question of the previous night and my answer, and I thought of Caterina.

I slipped inside, into the gloomy, cavernous, impressive space, and stood a little while not far from the door, shivering slightly with my arms wrapped around myself. When the service was over one or two tonsured clerics came from the choir into the pillared nave. One of them was quite young, with an eager intelligent face. I stopped him and spoke to him for a while. I spoke in Latin, so he did not know where I was from, and he responded fluently. He was well educated. As we talked I also formed the impression that he was trustworthy, though that's by no means something you can say of every cleric.

I lifted my purse from my belt and hefted it. There was a fair amount left of the money I had won from Jean-Marie, but I was on my way home to Venice now and I wouldn't need it all. I poured most of it into my hand and held it out to him. 'I want you to say masses for a departed soul.'

He looked rather surprised, but he took the money. 'Of course, my son. For whom shall I say them?'

'For Caterina.'

'Caterina of Brindisi?' he asked diligently.

I shook my head. 'Call her Caterina *La Gattina*. Our Lord will know her.'

'Caterina *La Gattina*. The kitten?' The words had come out in Sicilian, and he wasn't sure that he had understood.

'That's right.' I swallowed hard.

He nodded. 'I shall remember and pray steadfastly for her.' He hesitated, then his eyes met mine. 'And for you, my son? When I say the masses, shall I pray also for you?'

I considered my present condition. An unshriven assassin, come straight from a bed of adulterous luxury, and currently premeditating further adultery with the wife of Aliusio Contarini. 'Yes,' was all I said.

Aliusio had been negotiating our onward passage. It was always easy to talk him into doing that sort of thing, since he was convinced he could do it better than anyone else. I found him with his men waiting on the harbour front. I was rumpled and smelling sweeter than I should have done after a visit to a town harlot, and they scowled at me with ill-concealed suspicion.

We were a pretty vagabond lot after our hurried exit from Messina. Even Aliusio's boots scarcely looked red any more, his cloak was tattered and his hair hadn't seen the attentions of a barber for some time. It hung limply around his cheeks, straight as reeds.

'You'll never believe it,' Aliusio fumed. 'A Genoese ship just came in! A galley, just like that one that –'

He pointed and I looked. He was right, it was Daniele's ship the *Basilisk*. I nodded in a noncommittal sort of way. Aliusio began to burble about getting our own back, capturing it, setting light to it, as if we were a company of marines and not just a handful of exhausted Venetians all eager to go home. I didn't even have to try to argue him out of it. One look at the faces of his men told him that he would never get the idea launched.

There was a little time before our ship sailed for Venice. Aliusio and the others were heading off for another visit to one of the local brothels. I excused myself, having no need for such entertainment, and went to find myself some breakfast. When I felt a little more human I began to wander around the harbour-side taverns, peering beneath each awning and vine and moving on.

In the eighth tavern I saw Daniele, sitting at a long table with several other Genoese. I walked in and stood looking at him, waiting for him to see me. He looked up. His eyes rested on me and widened. He stared. Then he looked away, discomfited. Agents are like cats, they hate to seem surprised or thrown.

I sat at another table and ordered a jug of wine. In a few minutes, as I had known he would, he came over and stood looking down at me. I raised my eyebrows at him.

At last he said, 'How in the name of God did you get out of Palermo? The place exploded. We were nearly in trouble ourselves.'

'Skill,' I said smugly.

There was a silence. Then Daniele picked up the jug of wine, uninvited, and drank some. 'I gave you the best chance I could,' he said. 'I waited till you were near the window.'

'Why did you do that?' I asked. I really was curious. 'And you didn't kill me at the bay, either.'

'You owe me ten florins,' said Daniele simply. 'I need the money. You have to be alive to pay up.'

'Forget the ten florins,' I told him angrily. 'The bet's off. You must have known about the resistance in Palermo before we ever met in Naxos.'

'I gave you my word. Are you calling me a liar?'

We argued it to and fro for a little while. He was adamant that at Christmas he had had no idea at all that he might get involved with the Sicilian resistance. But the job came up, and who turns down profitable work?

'Besides which,' he said, 'you owe me your miserable life. The least you can do is pay up ten poxy florins.'

'Right now I don't have ten pence. Come to Venice to collect your winnings.'

He laughed. 'I think not. There are quite a few men in Venice who would pay more than ten florins to have my head on a spike.'

'Well, you'll have to hope that I have the money the next time I meet you.' I grinned at him. We both knew that the bet was uncollectable, even though honour demanded that it should be paid. 'I tell you what,' I said brightly. 'Next time I have you down, I'll let you go. Then we can call it quits.'

'You keep on saying "next time". That means there has to be a next time. I don't get mixed up with Venetians when I can avoid it.'

The ship for Venice began to ring its bell. Time to go, or they would leave without me. I couldn't risk Aliusio getting back to Venice before I did. I wanted the chance to explain my side of the story to the Security Committee; and then, of course, there was Fiammetta. I got to my feet and drained the rest of the wine.

'Daniele,' I said, 'I don't think you need to worry. As I said on Naxos, it's a small sea. We'll run into each other.' And as I said it, I suddenly got the feeling that I wasn't just spinning him a yarn. Call it a hunch, but I was sure I would see him again soon. I held out my hand to him and finished with a grin, 'In fact, I'm so certain that I'll offer you another wager. Double if I don't see you within the year, quits if I do.'

He hesitated, frowning. Then his pock-marked face broke into a grin. He struck the back of my hand lightly with the back of his, knocking it away. 'No bets,' he said. 'If I do have the bad luck to see you again, Marcello, I want to collect.'

I hadn't really expected him to fall for it. I shrugged. 'Your loss, Daniele. See you round the Mediterranean.'

As I left the other Genoese looked at me curiously, and I wondered briefly what Daniele would tell them.

And then I forgot about him, because the sky was blue and there was a sharp fresh wind and the ship was waiting in the harbour to carry me to Venice and to Fiammetta's arms.

AUTHOR'S NOTE

The main events of this book are true.

On 3 July 1281 the Republic of Venice signed a treaty with Charles of Anjou, King of Sicily, and agreed to support him in his attack on the Byzantine Emperor Michael. A massive Angevin fleet began to assemble in Messina. The rendezvous with the Venetian navy at Corfu, planned for April 1282, would create one of the biggest invasion fleets ever seen. Byzantium faced an appalling threat. The Emperor retaliated by financing a conspiracy in Sicily intended to delay the departure of the Angevin fleet.

The Easter Monday riot at the church of Santo Spirito was provoked not by the Emperor, but by a French sergeant, one Drouet, who insulted a young Sicilian woman. The riot became a massacre and rebellion soon became general. The uprising culminated with the destruction of the Angevin fleet in Messina harbour, days before it was due to depart for Corfu.

King Charles never realised his ambitions of an attack on Byzantium. The war begun by the Sicilian Vespers occupied him in Italy for the rest of his life. Venice was left isolated, at war with Byzantium and without Mediterranean allies. Deprived of trade with Constantinople, she turned her attentions elsewhere.

The Admiral's Church and Bridge and the Church of Santo Spirito (now known as the Church of the Vespers) still stand in Palermo, much as Marcello knew them.

Jane Heritage
February 1997

ACKNOWLEDGEMENTS

Many people have helped me as I wrote this book. In particular I would like to thank Terésa Baraclough for her vigour and wit, and Anne Frances and Ali Temperley for their enthusiasm and affection for Marcello, as well as for me.

My colleagues in M&CD have been unfailingly warm and supportive. At times I must have been a sad trial to them, and I am very grateful for their forbearance.

I would also like to thank my editor, Peter Darvill-Evans, for being prepared to take a punt, and my parents, who never fail me.

And, of course and always, Jonathan, my husband. In loving him I learned to love the past.